AS SHE BACKE[illegible] STOPPED THE [illegible] WITH A MUSCL[illegible]

'Kate, we have t[illegible] lose you, I can't. Your . . . condition, it's not as important as us.'

This was the moment she had dreamt of, she told herself dumbly as she felt him take her into his arms, pulling her against him almost savagely. She ought to fall against him now, promise him anything, cry, tell him she loved him but . . . something was holding her back. He was murmuring persuasively against her hair, seemingly unaware of the stiffness of her body, as he told her they couldn't let anything, *anything*, spoil their plans for the future . . .

ABOUT THE AUTHOR

Helen Brooks was born and educated in Northampton, England, where she met her husband at the age of sixteen. Their three beautiful children and two dogs keep the house buzzing with activity, and being a committed Christian and fervent animal lover there is never a dull moment! Since writing her first book at the age of forty, a romantic novel which was published in 1992, she indulges her love of writing and reading, calling it work! She has had twenty-one books published since 1992, but still finds moments for long walks in the country with her dogs, trips to the theatre and cosy evenings at home with her husband.

Her previous romance, *A Twisted Cord*, is also published in Signet.

HELEN BROOKS

For a Mother's Love

The strongest bond of all is between
a mother and child

A SIGNET BOOK

SIGNET

Published by the Penguin Group
Penguin Books Ltd, 27 Wrights Lane, London W8 5TZ, England
Penguin Books USA Inc., 375 Hudson Street, New York, New York 10014, USA
Penguin Books Australia Ltd, Ringwood, Victoria, Australia
Penguin Books Canada Ltd, 10 Alcorn Avenue, Toronto, Ontario, Canada M4V 3B2
Penguin Books (NZ) Ltd, 182–190 Wairau Road, Auckland 10, New Zealand

Penguin Books Ltd, Registered Offices: Harmondsworth, Middlesex, England

Published in Signet 1996
1 3 5 7 9 10 8 6 4 2

Set in 9½/11½pt Monophoto Plantin
Typeset by Datix International Limited, Bungay, Suffolk
Printed in England by Clays Ltd, St Ives plc

For all mothers, would-be mothers, mothers whose children are possible only in their hearts and those who have decided that motherhood is not for them

Part One

A Time to be Born

CHAPTER ONE

Kate stared at the phial in her hand, at the indisputable evidence that her world was going to come crashing down about her shoulders. *One night.* One devastating, humiliating night. How could one night reach out and smash everything that was good in her life? But it would . . . 'Oh, God, don't let it. Please, God.' She heard the whimpering note in her voice with a burst of self-contempt, but at the same moment her stomach rose up in her throat and if it wasn't for the fact that the door to the laboratory opened with an imperious whoosh, she wouldn't have been able to fight the waves of nausea.

'Dr Henderson? I've been looking everywhere for you.' The prim female voice with its pseudo upper-class accent scratched at Kate's overwrought nerves like barbed wire. 'Mr Riley needs your assistance.'

'What?' The tone registered but the actual words escaped her as she fought the sickness.

'Mr Riley. There's an emergency in Casualty and he wants you there, Doctor.' Sister Brown's eyes were small and hard, like the rest of her, and as they fastened on the slim, young woman in front of her they were narrowed with dislike. She didn't care for any of the young upstarts fresh out of medical school, she thought tightly, but this one was in a realm all of her own. Been here five minutes and thought she was the cat's whiskers, with her blonde hair and holier-than-thou manner. And then there was that wealthy American boyfriend of hers, big mouth and big wallet to match, she'd be bound. Still, she'd never seen the Doctor looking like she was looking now, as though someone had punched her hard in the stomach. The gimlet eyes flickered with curiosity. 'Is there anything wrong, Dr Henderson? Anything I can help with –'

'Nothing, thank you.' Kate's voice was abrupt, her tone dismissive, but the moment the door had closed with a loud, offended click her eyes went back to the small bottle in her hand. She had known. She had known all along, hadn't she? Even before her body had lent weight to the gnawing anxiety by the non-appearance of her monthly cycle she had known. She'd felt different. From the first morning after that disastrous party she had felt different. Nothing she could put her finger on, just . . . different. Her stomach lurched and tightened, and she clutched on to the side of the work-top as the room began to spin and weave. Hank, oh, Hank . . .

Pull yourself together, you can't pass out now. She took a few deep gulps of air and sat down on one of the high-legged stools scattered about the room. She had to think. Had to work something out, fast. She glanced round the large laboratory desperately as her mind raced. But not now, she'd have to wait until she got home, the day staff would be here soon and Mr Riley was still waiting for her in Casualty . . . Damn, damn, damn! She made a sound in her throat like a little moan as the sick panic clawed at her vitals again, twisting her guts until her legs shook. What was she going to do? What on earth was she going to do?

Her hand went to the little bleeper in the top pocket of her white coat and, as she expected, the short, high-pitched call sounded the minute it was switched on. She'd have to go, but first . . . She walked over to the two porcelain sinks at the far end of the laboratory and tipped the contents of the phial into one of them as she turned on the hot tap, watching the liquid disappear with a rapid beating of her heart. No one must find out, no one. Imagine how they'd all love this juicy bit of gossip. Sister Brown and her cronies would have a field day. She put a hand to her mouth and bit hard on her fist, a whimper escaping her throat. Oh, how could she have been so stupid, so gullible? But there were ways and means, all was not lost. She nodded to herself, making a deep, obsequious movement to the voice in her head. All was not lost.

This thought carried Kate through the mayhem in casualty, the result of a multi-car pile-up, through the subsequent shop talk in the staff room when her shift had ended, and through the short car journey home to her flat, when she drove with controlled, military precision, her mind in automatic.

'Mornin'.' The sound of old Albert's voice, the elderly and cantankerous janitor who grudgingly cared for the flats, brought her head sharply upwards as she walked through the front door of the terraced, four-storied house in a less than salubrious part of Glasgow's inner city. Or houses, plural, would be a better description, owing to the fact that Cairn House was really three houses knocked into one, all of which were owned by Albert's entrepreneur nephew, whom the old man hated with a vengeance, at the same time as making full use of the free lodging and small wage he received in return for his services. 'What's up with you then?'

'Me?' Kate forced a bright smile as she met the intent, black-button eyes. 'Nothing is the matter with me, Albert.'

'Huh!' The loud sniff that followed the snort of disbelief spoke volumes. 'You always walk about as though you'd lost sixpence an' found tuppence then? I ain't blind you know.'

'I'm quite aware of that.'

'An' you needn't put on that hoity-toity voice with me neither, it won't wash,' the old man growled irascibly. 'If you don't want to tell me nothin', just say for me to mind me own business.'

'Mind your own business, Albert . . .' But she softened the words with a strained smile as she spoke, knowing full well the gruff, crusty exterior hid a heart of pure gold, with the folk he liked, that was. With the others, and they numbered quite a few according to Albert, he could be the very devil. But he liked her, and she could never work out why.

The two of them were the very antithesis in everything that mattered. 'But thanks for asking,' she added quietly as she put out a hand and touched the none-too-clean sleeve of his ancient jacket. 'I appreciate it.'

'Do you now?' He stared at her as he shook his wispy grey head, his lined face mournful. 'Well, just remember, lass, I've seen it all and then some. There ain't nothin' that surprises me no more, so any time you want a chat you know where I am.'

The kindness was too much and she blinked at him before walking quickly to the stairs that led to her first-floor home. She just wanted to get inside the front door and shut the world out while she thought. She had to *think* . . . She turned the key in the lock with the feeling of relief a small hunted animal feels when it reaches the safety of its burrow, and as she entered the clean, four-roomed flat the grey morning light filtering through the square window of the sitting room from the overcast March day outside revealed her well-furnished, comfortable little home.

She lit the gas fire, made herself a cup of tea in the tiny kitchen, and then walked back through to the sitting room, where she sat down in an easy chair in front of the fire, staring into the faintly hissing, flickering red glow, one hand cupped under her chin.

She was twenty-five years of age, one of Crompton General's very junior doctors, single . . . and pregnant. The word stuck in her throat and caused a solid lump even the hot tea couldn't dispel. And if it had been Hank's baby it wouldn't have been a problem, not really. Her gaze slid to the third finger of her left hand that looked too slender for the pretty, star-shaped diamond and ruby ring weighing it down. But it wasn't Hank's baby . . . She crossed her forearms tight round her waist and rocked herself backwards and forwards, her eyes burningly dry. No, it wasn't his. This live being that was growing inside her was the result of one stupid, brutal night of . . . Of what? she asked herself dumbly. Of passion? Hardly. She could have lived with herself better if it was.

No. She had to face it. She had had her drinks spiked at a New Year's Eve party and allowed a virtual stranger to penetrate both her reserve and her body. 'Oh . . .' She moaned out loud into the silent room. It had all been over in a few minutes. A sordid little episode in one of the bedrooms of the big house where the party was being held that no one would have known anything about but for . . . for her body's betrayal.

And there was no way she could pass off the baby as Hank's. Her eyes opened wider at the knowledge that if it had been possible, she would have done so. Yes, she would, she screamed fiercely at the accusing little voice in her conscience. Because she had seen what abortions were like, witnessed them at first hand, the mutilations that sometimes occurred when the foetus couldn't be removed in one piece. The memory of the last act of carnage brought her jerking upwards from the chair with her hand to her mouth as she hurried into the bathroom, leaning over the small round basin for long minutes as she heaved and retched the hospital breakfast into oblivion, before sinking down on to the cold linoleum, her legs shaking and her face white. If only there was someone to talk to, someone she could trust . . .

When, a short time later, she found herself in the basement knocking on Albert's flaking front door, she wasn't quite sure how she'd got there, but it was as if something outside herself had drawn her to the contrary old man.

'Aye?' The door opened almost immediately but Albert's surly tone changed on seeing her standing, pale-faced and shaking, in front of him. 'What's up, lass? You bad or somethin'?' he asked gently.

'I . . . Can I come in for a minute, Albert? Talk to you?'

'You don't need to ask that, lass, not you.' He took her arm and urged her into the small flat that smelt of cats and cabbage and old furniture, leading her over to a well-stuffed, shabby armchair close to the fire, in front of which two plump, contented tabby cats were lying. 'Well, what's it all about?' he asked quietly. 'You got problems then?'

She lowered her head, the odd feeling coming over her again that she had experienced in the hall when his kindness and concern had reached out to her. It touched something deep inside her, something she hadn't been aware of in the normal run of life, and even as she told herself she was being ridiculous, that she never cried, that she hadn't shed a tear in years, the storm erupted from her eyes and nose and mouth in a deluge she couldn't have stopped if she'd tried.

Albert, with the wisdom of age, made no attempt to stem the flood, holding one hand as she pressed the other over her face and saying nothing beyond making the odd soothing sound in his throat like the patient clucking of an old hen.

It was a good five minutes before she raised her head again, taking the surprisingly clean handkerchief he offered with a little nod of thanks. 'I'm sorry –' The words caught in her throat and came out as a hiccuping sob. 'I didn't mean to do that.'

'No?' He eyed her levelly. 'Seems to me it ain't afore time, you're a sight too capable for your own good. An' you needn't look like that, I'm not having a go, lass. I'm just concerned for you, that's all. All me life I've managed without help from no one an' look at me now, seventy-eight an' still managing, 'cos the more you do, the more they let you. It's the way of the world, lass, aye, it is that. But you, you should be able to rely on someone, let go of the reins now and agin. You know what I'm sayin'?'

She didn't give him an answer straight away, staring into the lined, old face for a full minute before she spoke. 'I've never been able to do that, Albert,' she said slowly, 'never.'

When the tears began to ooze from her eyes again Albert stood up from his crouched position in front of her, before moving creakily to the battered sideboard in the far corner of the room and reaching for the bottle of brandy standing on top of it. He poured two generous measures into two tumblers and brought them over to where she sat, handing her one with a little bounce of his head. 'Drink it down, lass, all of it. It'll steady the old innards.'

'I don't –'

'Drink it, Kate.' It was rare that he called her by name and it emphasized his concern for her, and after staring at him for one more moment she took a big gulp of the amber liquid before choking helplessly as it hit the back of her throat like fire.

'Good grief, Albert, what on earth have you got in there?' she asked croakily a few moments later when her streaming eyes had cleared.

'Well now, I can't be affordin' the kind of stuff that tickles your throat like silk,' the old man said imperturbably. 'Not with the bit I have comin' in. But this does for me.'

'It'll do for you all right,' Kate said with a trace of her old manner coming through. 'I hate to think of the state of your liver.'

'Always the doctor.' He shook his head at her but his smile faded as she turned quickly away, her hand to her mouth. 'Now come on, lass, no more of that. What is it? You can tell me.'

'I'm . . . I'm expecting a baby.'

'Well, there's been some afore you an' no doubt there'll be some after,' the old man stated philosophically. 'An' your fella loves you, don't he –'

'It isn't Hank's child.'

Oh no, not that. Albert felt something twist in his stomach that pained him. She was a nice lass this one, a good girl. He'd been around enough in his time to know the difference, and he would have bet his life on the certainty that she wouldn't have done the dirty on this big American of hers. 'You sure about that?' he asked softly.

'I'm sure.' Kate raised swimming eyes to his. 'It can't be

his, because we haven't . . . I've never –' She stopped abruptly. 'Oh, Albert, it's so unfair, so *unfair*. I know lots of girls, women, who have one man after another, they do really, one after another. Some of the nurses at the hospital . . . And there's me, I do it once and what happens? I get pregnant. And it wasn't even my fault.'

With anyone else he would have made the caustic comment that sprang immediately into his mind but he bit it back, speaking one word. 'No?'

'No.' Her gaze had dropped from him as they had spoken but now she looked straight at him, her blue eyes steady. 'I went to a party on New Year's Eve at one of the senior doctor's houses and there was someone there . . . I thought I was drinking a relatively harmless fruit punch but he'd been adding vodka all night. I was feeling miserable because Hank wasn't around – you remember he'd had to fly to the States because his mother was ill?'

He remembered all right, Albert thought as he nodded silently. That woman had a lot to answer for in his opinion. From what he could make out she was forever callin' that son of hers back to the maternal bosom if he was away longer than a day or two, and since Hank had got engaged to Kate his mother had been even more demanding. Kate'd have trouble there if she didn't put her foot down from the start . . . What was he thinkin'? She'd got trouble now hadn't she?

'And this friend of Dr Maddenson, he was so nice to me,' Kate continued quietly. 'Attentive, you know? He said he'd run me home when I started to feel groggy, sick, and I went upstairs to get my coat –'

'An' he followed you up there, eh?' Like a lamb to the slaughter. By, he'd like to get his hands on that bloke, he would. He never had been able to stand any truck with blokes who kept their brains atween their legs.

'Yes.' Her voice was small now, lost, and it made his anger increase.

'Have you told Hank?'

'No!' The reply was swift and high and for a full minute neither of them spoke until the sound of icy chips of sleet and snow hitting the window brought Kate out of her reverie. 'I shouldn't have bothered you with all this, Albert, it's not your problem. I'm sorry.'

'Don't be daft, woman.' He dug his thumb into his scrawny chest, his voice rough. 'It's me you're talkin' to, not some fly-by-night, toffee-nosed quack at the hospital.'

'I know.' She sipped at the brandy and, raw though the spirit was, it helped the trembling inside she had been experiencing ever since the test had proved positive. 'What am I going to do, Albert?'

'What do you want to do?' He stared at her hard. 'What do you *really* want to do? Because it seems to me whatever way you choose it won't be an easy ride, lass. Are you thinkin' –' He stopped and ran a hand over his face. 'Are you thinkin' of gettin' rid of it?'

'I don't know what I'm thinking,' she said slowly. 'I've been trying to pretend I was imagining things for the last few weeks, but deep down I think I knew straight away. If I . . . If I had an abortion, I could go away to a clinic somewhere, that wouldn't be too difficult with the people I know. Of course it might get out, these things are supposed to be confidential but people talk . . . But it isn't that that worries me,' she added suddenly, turning to him and taking his arm. 'It's the thought of what they actually do. I know it's silly,' she shook her head at herself as she closed her eyes tight, 'but I can't see it as a nothing, an embryo. It might only be an inch big but it's fully formed, Albert, it's a baby, and it's mine. The father –' She shook her head as she opened her eyes. 'He doesn't count, I don't even know if I'd recognize him again. But the baby is mine.'

'Aw, lass, lass . . .' He patted her hand now. 'It ain't goin' to help you, thinkin' like that.'

'I've never had anyone who was really mine, do you know that, Albert?' she said flatly as they continued to sit in front of the glowing fire, the two cats drowsing at their feet. 'My father ran off with another woman just after I was born and I think my mother always blamed my arrival for him going. She married again when I was two and my sister, Rosie, was born a week after my third birthday. I really think I ceased to exist for my mother from that moment on. I used to try at first to get her attention. I can remember doing all sorts of outrageous things until I was about eight, getting in trouble and even running away once, and then . . .'

'Then?'

'Then something happened that made me sort of give up, I guess. Rosie and I got measles, really badly in Rosie's case, and one night I got up for a drink of water –' She paused for a moment. 'And my mother was praying, kneeling by the side of her bed with my stepfather lying watching her, I saw them through the crack in the door, and she said . . . She said, "take Kate. Take Kate but leave us Rosie, please leave us Rosie."'

As Albert's head jerked upwards she saw his eyes were wide with shock and something else, something that made the tears want to flow again. 'An' you've been carrying that all these years?' He shook his head sadly. 'The things we do to our bairns.'

'But I'd got a brain, a good brain, Albert, so I started to use it. I passed for the grammar school and came top in all my classes there and my teachers persuaded my parents that university was a must, so I went. Not with their blessing, but I went. And Rosie stayed home and married the local vicar.'

'Where are they all now?' Albert asked carefully as he scrutinized her white face through narrowed eyes.

She gulped in her throat before she answered and then her voice was flat and low. 'My mother and stepfather are dead. He was killed in an accident at his works three years ago and my mother got cancer the following year. Rosie is still in the little village in Devon where we were born with her vicar.'

'Do you see her?'

'Occasionally.'

'Do you love each other?'

'I don't know.' There was a note of surprise in her voice as though she hadn't thought about it before. 'I like her. I do like her in spite of everything, because nothing that happened when we were younger was her fault, but I never got to know her when we were little, mainly due to my mother's attitude. I understand she's had troubles of her own since she got married five years ago, though. William is a good deal older than her, and they haven't been able to have children –' She stopped abruptly. 'Ironic, isn't it, when you think about it?' Her head drooped as she spoke. 'The very thing that would send her mad with joy is likely to send me just mad. Life can be so perverse. Do you think some people can have a jinx on them from when they're born, Albert? Like a curse –'

'Don't talk such rubbish, woman, an' put them ideas right out of your head. I credited you with more sense, you being a doctor an' all.'

'I don't feel like a doctor, Albert. I just feel . . . scared.' She was back on that landing again, her feet chilled but her head burning hot, as she listened to her mother wish her life away. She had known then that she was unlovable, unacceptable, some sort of freak – she had to be for her own mother to want her dead. And in spite of her understanding of the contrariness of human nature which maturity had brought in later years, the feeling of rejection and aloneness, the terrible sense of isolation that had been borne that night, had never left her. She loved Hank, of course she did, she had never met anyone else she could contemplate spending her life with, but even with him there were times when she felt so detached, desolate, that it was like being in a great vacuum. But it would be better when they were married . . . Oh, what was she thinking? She couldn't marry him now.

'Well it seems to me you've made up your mind you don't want to get rid of it.' Albert's voice was magnificently matter-of-fact. 'Whether you realize it or not. An' that bein' the case, I reckon you've got to tell that bloke of yours what's what.'

'I can't, Albert, I can't.' She stared at him, her eyes tragic. 'He . . . he's got me on a sort of pedestal, I can't explain it. He's never pushed me to . . . to sleep with him.' Her face was flaming now. 'Normally, after one or two dates, most men make it quite clear where they want things to lead but he's been so good . . .'

'The worst he can do is chuck you, lass.' Albert downed the last of his brandy in one gulp and got up to refill his glass. By, for this to happen to her. To her of all people. 'An' the best is to say he'll look after you and the bairn. Now you've got to sort out in your own head whether, if the worst comes about, you can stand that better than how you'll feel if you get rid of it.'

'You make it sound so simple.'

'No, it ain't simple, lass, I know that. But I've seen a few in me time who've took what they thought was the easy road and it's near broke 'em, that's all I'm sayin'. When you seein' him again?'

'In a couple of weeks.' She spoke the words like a death sentence. 'James Ross, the Scottish cousin I told you about, well he wants to know by then if Hank is going to accept the partnership he's offered him. I think Hank's keen, it's just . . .'

'His mother.' Albert nodded grimly. 'Aye, it would be. I suppose she's got your future all mapped out in America, eh?'

'Something like that.' She bobbed her head at him. 'But with his older brothers already in the family firm I think Hank feels he'd rather branch out on his own with James. His father is all for it, I understand, he's even offered to meet some of the finance.'

'I bet that went down a treat with the old lady,' Albert said drily. 'You want another one?' He indicated her empty glass with a jerk of his head.

'No thank you, alcohol isn't good for –' She stopped abruptly, and then continued sheepishly, 'for the baby.'

'An' you're sayin' you can't tell him?' Albert shook his head slowly. 'You ain't got no choice, lass, 'cos it's as plain as the nose on me face that your mind's made up, even if you don't want to admit it to yourself yet.'

'I haven't said I'm going to have it –'

'You don't have to.' He stretched his face at her as he walked back to his lumpy armchair, settling himself down with a deep sigh. 'You'd made up your mind afore you came here today, if the truth be known, now face it and get on with it, lass. It's all done bar the shoutin'.'

'And there'll be plenty of that.' She pictured Hank's broad, square face in her mind even as she questioned her words. Would he shout and rave? She really didn't know. She had met him when he had brought an injured child into casualty on 5 November of the previous year. His cousin, James, had been holding a Guy Fawkes party at his house for his children and one of their friends had got too close to a burning log. The big American had quite literally swept her off her feet and there had followed a crazy, exhilarating seven days at the end of which, when he had to go back to the States, she had got engaged to him without a moment's hesitation. Daily phone calls had followed until she saw him again at Christmas, but his visit had been cut short two days before the New Year when he had received a call that his mother was ill and asking for him. She had seen him once more since then but again the week had been cut short by maternal pressure and he had flown home early, although, weighed down by guilt as she had been, she hadn't objected. She loved him, she definitely loved him, she told herself firmly, but she didn't really know him, she hadn't had time.

'You could write him, lass?' Albert stared at her over the rim of his glass. 'Or phone him maybe?'

'No.' The tone was definite. 'He deserves a proper explanation face to face, he was going to marry me after all.'

'Was?' he asked quietly as one of the cats stirred and stretched at their feet, its eyes half opening and closing again.

Her voice was equally low as she answered. 'Albert, you know as well as I do what will happen when I tell him his fiancée is expecting another man's child. He isn't going to countenance that, is he?'

'He might surprise you, lass.'

'No.' There was a tinge of bitterness in her voice now. 'I don't think so.'

'Then perhaps he wasn't the right one for you after all. You can tell him it wasn't your fault, that you were taken for a ride, with nothin' atween you and your conscience but clean air. Now that bein' the case the rest will be up to him.'

'Albert?'

'Aye?'

'I can't believe this has happened to me. And it's funny, before this I would have sworn on oath I'd got lots of good friends, people I could go to in time of trouble, but when I knew for sure . . .' She looked at him out of pained eyes. 'There was only you I could really trust. That's terrible, isn't it?'

'It ain't so bad, lass.' The old eyes were suspiciously rheumy. 'There's many a body in this here city who couldn't say they've got even that. But I appreciate the thought.'

'I'd better get back, Albert.' They had been sitting for some minutes in a silence that was beginning to feel uncomfortable and now, as Kate rose to leave, Albert rose with her.

'You goin' to be all right?' he asked gruffly.

'I think so.' She nodded slowly. 'Talking to you has solidified a number of things in my mind. I'd been lying to myself, Albert, telling myself that, if the worst came to the worst and I was pregnant, I could always have an abortion, thousands do after all. The changes in the abortion law in the sixties, the pill and everything that went with it, I've been brought up with all that. I don't think I ever considered what the word actually meant until I was in medical school and even then it was just part of a whole. But since I've been working at the hospital . . .' She paused for a full thirty seconds before going on. 'I just couldn't do it. Some of those women have no choice, but I do, and I couldn't do it. Where I go from here I'm not sure though,' she added flatly.

'There's a pile of trite sayin's I could come out with, lass, but I ain't goin' to.' Albert looked her full in the face now. 'But I will tell you somethin' I ain't never told another livin' soul. Not even our Molly, me own sister, when she was alive, an' her bein' the closest to me bar none. If me own mother had done different to what you're doin' now I wouldn't be here an' that's a fact. An' in them days it was a disgrace, a real disgrace, not like now. When me mam found out she'd copped a load, her own folks tried to get her to see to it an' when she wouldn't, she was out on the street on her own.

She had a hell of a time of it afore she made her way to Glasgow when I was a bairn an' found work as a housekeeper in the house of the man who later married her an' brought me up as his own. He was no angel, mind, drank like a fish an' swore like a trooper, but he was good to me mam an' she was grateful for it. An' neither of 'em breathed a word about me beginnin's, I only found out about it when me mam was dyin'. So I'm with you, lass. If you get any stick from any quarter, it won't be here. An' you'll have it a darn sight easier than she did, if that helps at all. Folk are more broad-minded now, there ain't the stigma there once was.'

'Did she tell you who your father was?' Kate asked gently, more touched than she could express that the brusque, surly old Glaswegian had confided his secret to her.

'No, an' I didn't want to know neither,' Albert said

flatly. 'Mike McNab had given me his name an' brought me up as his own an' that was enough for me. This other bloke who'd put me mam in the family way an' scarpered, he was nothin' to me. Likely he'd scattered his seed round half of Glasgow afore he took off, with some men it don't mean a thing, does it?'

'No, you're right there, Albert.' She thought of Richard Wellington again, of the cold-blooded manoeuvring he'd employed that night and just how little it had meant to him, and her earlier resolution to resist the temptation to try and trace him and tell him what he had done strengthened ten-fold. Most likely he would refuse to acknowledge the child as his, but even if he didn't, did she really want a man like that to have any place in her life? She would rather manage on her own. Quite how she didn't know yet, but manage she would. But first she had to tell Hank. Her stomach turned over and the trembling deep inside started again.

Now that she had made her decision, faced the personal demons that had been on her back for the last few weeks, so to speak, she had to tell him. But all this had brought home to her how little she really knew him and that fact alone was frightening. Quite how they had ended up getting engaged so quickly she really wasn't sure when she thought about it, but Hank had been so persistent, so sure they were doing the right thing. And it had been wonderful to have someone love her so much, to need her, tell her she was beautiful, everything he had ever wanted in a woman. No one had ever made her feel like Hank did, wanted and adored.

But . . . she couldn't terminate the pregnancy. It might be the logical, the sane thing to do, but she couldn't do it and live with herself afterwards. So – she would tell Hank. As soon as she saw him again she would tell him, but oh, what was he going to say? she thought, as her stomach turned over for the hundredth time that day.

Chapter Two

Hank said nothing at all for the first few stunned moments after she finished speaking, his broad face blank and disbelieving and his eyes narrowed on hers.

Kate had been in a fever of unrest for the past two weeks, her moods fluctuating from the painful conviction that Hank would walk out of her life for good the minute she told him about the baby, through all kinds of hopeless variations on a theme leading to the final scenario, more impossible and crazy than anything else, that he would take her as his wife and bring up the baby as his own.

He had arrived earlier than she had expected on the Friday night but she had known the loud hammering at her front door was him – no one else ever knocked that way. She took a deep, shuddering breath as she opened the front door, her face unsmiling, but he swept her up in his arms before she could say a word, swinging her round and round as he carried her through to the sitting room. 'Oh boy, you sure smell good, sweetheart.' He kissed her lightly on the lips as he sat down on the sofa, still with her in his arms. 'A mixture of perfume and baby powder, very . . . British.'

'Hank? –'

'And after the time I've had the last week in the States, Scotland sure is looking good. You wouldn't believe how some of those bozos think a business should be run. That partnership is the answer, Kate –'

'Hank, please –'

'As long as you don't mind seeing more of me, that is?' He grinned at her, his smile dying as her face remained straight. 'Hey, what's this? Problems?' His arms tightened as she made to move off his lap. 'What's wrong, sugar? Nothing I can't fix –'

'Hank, please stop. There's something . . . something I've got to tell you.'

'Other than that you love me?' But it was said with a forced jocularity and he made no effort to stop her now as she rose slowly from his lap, to stand looking down into his large, broad face with its crew-cut of spiky dark brown hair.

'I –' She shook her head despairingly. 'I don't know where to begin.'

'That sounds ominous.' There was a deep look of strain about her face, he noticed now, and her mouth was a white line in the pale skin that surrounded it, the flesh pulled tight as though it was being stretched over a skull that was too large for it. 'Perhaps the beginning would be the best place?'

'The beginning . . . was at the New Year's Eve party you didn't attend. You remember? You had to leave here early to get back to America –'

'I remember.' She'd met someone else? He sat absolutely still as his mind raced. But he would have known, sensed something?

'Well, I went by myself like I told you but . . . but there's much more I didn't tell you.' She tried very hard, as she continued to speak, to put herself in some detached state of mind where she could say what had to be said without faltering or pleading her cause. Albert had said she had to relate the facts and then let them speak for themselves, for good or ill, however they were received, but it was hard, very hard, with those dark brown eyes fixed unblinkingly on her face. And now she had finished, and still he hadn't moved or spoken. 'Hank?' Her voice was small, tentative.

'You're telling me . . .' He shook his head as though clearing it from a blow. 'You're telling me you're pregnant, Kate? Is that what I've just heard?' There was a dark incredulity in his voice and manner now that frightened her but she didn't retreat as he stood slowly to face her, merely nodding her head in a sharp, abrupt movement as she kept her eyes fixed on his. 'And you expect me to believe that story you've just told? That it happened once? *Once?* That he forced himself on you?'

'He did.'

'Do I look like a fool? Do I?' he barked angrily, dark colour surging into his face. 'Because I can assure you I'm not. You're a doctor, damn it, you of all people should know the odds of getting pregnant like you've just described. A schoolgirl could've made up a better tale than that –'

'I'm not making it up.'

'The hell you aren't! This is 1978, not 1878, damn it, and you mean to tell me you fell for the oldest trick in the book? You knew what you were doing all right, why haven't you got the guts to admit it? You wanted a bit of fun and I wasn't around, that's it, isn't it? How many others have there been –'

'Shut up! You just shut up!' Kate's face was aflame as she hit him full across one hard, tanned cheek with all the force she could muster, the impact causing him to stagger slightly before he righted himself. 'It *was* like I told you and I don't care whether you believe me or not. Here . . .' She tried to wrench the engagement ring off her finger as she spoke but the tears raining down her face blurred her vision, although she was aware of the bulk of him as he grabbed her arms, shaking her like a dog with a bone.

'It should be me hitting you! You know that don't you? What you've done –'

'*I* haven't done anything! Whatever happened was done to me, *me*! And you're right, I am a doctor. So why, if what you're saying is true, didn't I do something about it before now? It would have been easy, wouldn't it, if I was the hard-bitten tart you're painting –'

'I didn't say you were a tart, Kate.'

'Not in so many words, no. Here . . .' She finally managed to twist the ring off her finger, thrusting it at him so savagely the outline of the star punched into his sheepskin jacket, leaving a small round indentation. 'Take it. That's your responsibility over with, you can walk out of here without a second thought, can't you?'

'I came here tonight –'

'I'm not interested why you came here tonight, Hank.' Her voice was low now, and deep, the words evenly spaced and carrying a weight that brought his head jerking upwards. 'I could have understood you calling me a fool, I've done nothing else for the last three months after all. I could even have understood it if you had been disgusted with my naïvety and what it had led to, and I certainly didn't expect you to condone what's happened or offer to stand by me. Why should you anyway? It's nothing to do with you.' She was breathing hard as she leant slightly towards him in her intensity, her eyes narrowed and startlingly blue with the rage that consumed her features. 'But what happened to me was filthy and horrible, an act of lust by an experienced man who had got a woman drunk with one purpose in mind. I'm not proud of it, I'll never forget it or forgive myself till the day I die, but one thing I *do* know and that is I was completely innocent of everything you've accused me of tonight. Now get out.'

'You don't mean that, Kate.' He was staring at her as though he had never seen her before, her fury so raw and tangible that it seemed to have evaporated his own emotion. 'We have to talk this through, decide what to do –'

'I've decided what to do, Hank.'

'You don't have to have it. Damn it, you know that better than me! With the people you know –'

'You're talking about an abortion,' she stated flatly.

'Well, yes. Isn't that the normal thing in a situation like this? If what you've said is true, it's tantamount to rape –'

'What I've said *is* true and yes, you could classify what happened to me as rape. Goodbye, Hank.' She walked quietly over to the door with a dignity that wasn't lost on the big man watching her so closely, turning as she opened it and gesturing with her hand at the corridor outside. 'You've made it plain how you feel.'

'Kate –'

'Please leave, Hank.' *Go, go now.* She could feel the trembling that was shaking her insides was going to become visible any moment and that final humiliation would be too much. What had she expected after all? That he would declare his love was strong enough to overcome all obstacles? That he couldn't bear to let her go whatever had happened? *Fool!* The word was hot and fierce in her head, spiking into her brain. But she hadn't expected that, not really, but she had hoped for . . . What? she asked herself tightly as he held her glance for one more moment before striding across the room. She had known he would be angry, disappointed, he had every right after all and she had been stupid, *stupid.* But she hadn't considered, in all her imaginings, that he wouldn't *believe* her. And she had hoped for a civilized goodbye, that was all. She would have been grateful for that.

Hank paused in the doorway, biting his lip before he spoke.

'If there'd been no repercussions, would you have told me you'd slept with him?' he asked flatly.

She looked up at him, swallowing deeply. 'I don't know,' she said truthfully. 'I would like to think so, but I don't know. And "sleeping" is the wrong term for what happened, it suggests an intimacy that wasn't there.'

'But you're pregnant.' He looked at her for one long moment before walking out. She shut the door quietly behind him, leaning against its solid bulk for a second as her heart thumped so hard the room went into shadow. So that was it. It had ended, just like that. Was this how her mother had felt when her father had walked out? Her tears were hot and acidic, born out of bitter pain and gut-wrenching fear of the future, but overall it was the sense of unfairness that had her wanting to scream and shout and drum her legs and arms like a child in a tantrum. She hadn't looked for an affair, she hadn't flirted or given Richard Wellington any sort of come-on that night, so how was it she was the one who was going to lose everything?

Perhaps she was being punished for not taking the matter further. Because Hank had been right when he had described Richard's violation of her body as something akin to rape. When she had stumbled into the bedroom that night to find her coat, the only thought on her mind had been how soon she could get home and rest her swimming head. She dimly remembered falling on to the side of the bed as the room had begun to sway and dip, and at first the warm hands and hot lips had barely registered on her befuddled senses. When they had, her struggles had been ineffectual against the hard male body pinning her to the bed as he had removed her pants and tights from her almost casually, before pounding her into the mattress until his noisy, shuddering climax. He had collapsed on top of her for a few seconds before rolling over and standing up as he adjusted his clothes.

'Don't pretend you didn't want it as much as I did.' She still could picture the satisfied sneer on his face as he took in her sprawled, shaking limbs. 'You nurses are all the same.'

'I'm a doctor . . .' Ridiculous, but she had been so shocked, so traumatized by what had happened to her that it was all she could say as he stared down at her.

'Same thing.' And then he had smiled at her, his eyes contemptuous, before leaving.

She should have been brave enough to do something about it then, or the next morning at least, but she had been frightened and so, so bitterly ashamed.

As the small wooden clock on the mantelpiece chimed the hour Kate glanced across at the window. She must pull the curtains, she thought wearily without moving. It was snowing again and it would soon be dark. She had to get herself together, eat something, a sandwich maybe, before she went downstairs to tell Albert the outcome of the confrontation with Hank. She had promised the old man she would. And then an early night, she was due at the hospital at seven in the morning and it would be a long day . . .

The thoughts ebbed and flowed, but still she didn't move as she sat in the small, swiftly darkening room as dusk fell, the glow of the fire comforting as it cocooned her against the winter chill outside the window, her mind and body exhausted and spent.

When the knock came at the door she thought it was Albert, grown impatient with waiting for news. The old man would doubtless have been keeping an eagle-eye out for Hank, she thought as she rose stiffly to her feet. She should have gone down before, she knew he was worried about her, but the effort it would have taken to move had been beyond her. Her eyes felt swollen and tight as she crossed the room and she didn't switch on the light, preferring the dim semi-glow from the fire with the state her face was in.

'Kate? Don't shut the door.' The involuntary movement she made as she saw Hank standing outside was instinctive self-protection, and now, as she backed slowly from him, he stopped the door from closing with a muscled arm as he thrust his foot across the threshold. 'I have to talk to you, please, Kate? Don't . . . don't look at me like that, I'm not going to hurt you.'

She stared at him, her eyes wary, as he carefully closed the door behind him and followed her into the sitting room. He had been out in the cold, the melting snowflakes on his hair and sodden jacket bore evidence to that and his shoes and trousers looked soaked through. 'Have you got wet feet?' she asked numbly.

'What?' He gazed at her for a moment before glancing down abstractedly at his shoes. 'Yeah, probably. Kate, I'm sorry. It was the shock . . . Hell, I know you wouldn't lie to me, I didn't know what I was saying.'

'Your feet –'

'Damn my feet!' He crossed the short expanse separating them in one movement, his face distraught. 'Kate, we have to work this through. I can't lose you, I can't. Your . . . condition, it's not as important as us.'

This was the moment she had dreamt of, she told herself dumbly as she felt him take her into his arms, pulling her against him almost savagely. She ought to fall against him now, promise him anything, cry, tell him she loved him but . . . something was holding her back. He was murmering persuasively against her hair, seemingly unaware of the stiffness of her body, as he told her they couldn't let anything, *anything*, spoil their plans for the future. 'We'll fix it, I promise you we'll fix it and no one will know,' he whispered softly. 'Do you hear me, Kate? Everything will be just as it was before.'

'It can't be, Hank. You must know it can't.' What was she doing? she asked herself faintly. She ought to be agreeing with him, not creating obstacles, but it *couldn't* be the same, whichever way you looked at it.

'But it didn't mean anything.' He moved her from him slightly to look down into her face.

'Hank . . .' She didn't know how to say this but then maybe there was no easy way. 'I told you what happened. I was stupid, naïve, and I paid the price in the worst possible way. It was humiliating and horrible and if you're asking me if I feel anything for the person who tricked me like that the answer is that I loathe him, hate him –' She stopped abruptly as her throat constricted, but when he would have taken her in his arms she held out both her hands, palms towards him, as though to push him away. 'No, let me finish, Hank. I know you want me to have an abortion and I can understand that, believe me, but . . . I can't. I just can't, Hank.'

'Why? Why the hell can't you?'

'I – I've seen too much I suppose, from the other side. It would haunt me, Hank. I wouldn't be able to handle it.'

'You're looking at this all wrong.' He hunched his shoulders for a moment in a characteristic gesture she had come to know meant impatience. 'I'm not saying I expect you to find it easy. Hell, Kate, it won't be easy for me coming to terms with the fact that some guy has –' He broke off abruptly as she put her fist to her mouth, and again the big shoulders hunched as he moved his head from side to side. 'I didn't mean it like that, I know it wasn't your fault,' he said, placatingly now. 'But you have to see we both need to make allowances, to compromise –'

'But it's a live being –'

'*No it is not!* It's not, sugar,' he repeated more softly, 'and you won't do yourself any good thinking in those terms.' He pushed her gently into the seat she had vacated a few minutes earlier as he spoke, kneeling before her as he held both her hands in his. 'Have . . . have you seen this guy since it happened?'

'No.' She moved her head slightly as she kept her eyes fixed on his.

'Do you want to?'

'No, no I don't want anything to do with him.'

'Then surely an abortion is the obvious solution?' he asked quietly, 'so we can put the whole thing behind us.'

'Could you? Put it behind you, I mean? I know how you must feel –'

'It wasn't your fault, none of it was your fault.' He was speaking almost as though he had drilled himself into thinking what he was expressing. 'And nothing has changed between us, not really. You love me. You love me and we're gonna get married. I won't let this jerk spoil anything I've planned, *we've* planned.'

She stared at him without speaking, a sick agitation adding itself to the turmoil she was in. For a moment it had sounded as though the success of the programme he had set in motion for their future, the blueprint for their life together, was more important than she was. Oh, how could she think like that? she asked herself in immediate and deep contrition. He had come back, hadn't he? That must prove the depth of his love for her. She was awful, wicked, to think like that. What was the matter with her?

'Kate?' His voice was soft, wheedling. 'You do see, don't you? It makes sense, doesn't it? You know it does.'

'Yes but, Hank . . .' She shook her head slowly as she put out a tentative hand and touched his cheek. 'I feel . . . I feel as though I know it, in a strange sort of way.' As his face straightened she spoke quickly, her words tumbling over themselves as she tried to make him understand. 'It's not that I want it, not really, I don't. A baby now . . . it's all wrong, terribly wrong, I know that. And I love you, I do, so much –'

'Well then?' He pushed his lips together and jerked his chin as he rose abruptly to his feet. 'You'll see to it?'

In the silence that followed she could hear the sound of the record-player in the flat above as it ground out the latest Sex Pistols number for the gratification of the resident punk, a tall, slim redhead with a safety pin through her nose and a different boy for every night of the week. But Candy was smart, Kate thought dully. She wasn't the one expecting a baby.

'I'll . . . see what can be done.'

'But discreetly, Kate.' He reached out a hand and drew her upwards and into his arms. 'There's no need for anyone to know about this, is there? Look, you have an early night, you must be tired. We'll talk tomorrow.'

'Hank?' He was about to shut the door after lifting his hand in farewell as he stepped into the corridor, when her voice arrested the movement.

'Yeah?' He made no attempt to step back into the flat, merely lifting his eyebrows as he spoke.

'Do you understand? I mean about the way I feel?'

'Of course I understand, Kate.'

He didn't, she knew he didn't, but perhaps that was

expecting too much of any man, she asked herself silently. 'If I can't arrange anything? What then?'

'You will.' He spoke, not in a threatening way, but with a quiet, calm assurance that in itself was intimidating. 'This whole thing wasn't your fault, I accept that, and once it's fixed, that's that, OK? You can see to . . . what's necessary and then we can forget about it all. It'll be as if it never happened.'

'As though it never happened?' She stared at him, unable to believe he'd actually said what she thought she had heard.

'You'll see.' He nodded, closing the door before she could say any more.

She stood for several minutes exactly where she was, her hand tightly across her mouth. 'As though it never happened'. The words were burning into her mind. Was he mad? Completely mad? Or was it her? Perhaps this whole thing had turned her brain. Did he really think she could forget that night, the humiliation, the degradation of it? Was that squalid, dirty little episode what she had kept herself for all these years?

She walked slowly to the sofa and sat down on the very edge of it, her knees and ankles tightly together and her hands clasped in her lap as though she was at church. The years at university and medical school had been full of work, not fun . . . She lowered her head until her chin was resting in her neck and shut her eyes tightly. Work, work, work. Oh, she'd been called a cold fish, she knew that, especially by more persistent males who couldn't understand why she didn't fall into their arms, but the knowledge that her mother was expecting her to fail, wanting it even, had driven her more effectively than any natural desire for a career, and she had done well. More than well. Her results had been a tribute to her dedication, the professors had said. Her upper lip curled in bitter self-mockery as she thought of it. And her mother had never once visited, or called, not even for her graduation . . .

Kate brought her chin up sharply, rising from the sofa in one abrupt movement as she refuted the wave of misery that had swept over her. No, she wouldn't think of that. It was behind her now. In the past.

She walked through to the kitchen, forcing herself to prepare and cook an omelette that she ate on a tray in front of the fire as she watched a silly quiz programme on television. The room was dark now, partly illuminated by the flickering television screen and the light from the street lamp just outside her window.

After taking the tray through to the kitchen she stood for a long time at the window, looking out into the dark street beyond, made attractive by the thick snow and Christmas-card prettiness of fat white flakes still falling from a laden sky. It wasn't like that normally . . . She thought of the rows and rows of identical grey terraced houses and high-rise blocks in the mean streets and shuddered, suddenly aching for the thick woodlands and small, quiet communities of stone and brick cottages of her youth. And yet at the time she had longed to get away, choosing a city university as part of her rebellion against a loveless home and everything her mother stood for, the total change of her way of life a necessary schism from all that had gone before.

Well, she had her change of life all right. She ran her hand across her still flat stomach as she continued to stare out of the window. And it had all been going so well until that awful night, nearly three months ago. She had met Hank, found someone she could love and who loved her . . . 'Why? Why, why, *why?*' Her own voice startled her as she spoke out loud. This was the sort of thing that happened to other people, people you knew vaguely but who were on the perimeter of your life.

'Oh . . .' She leant forward, crossing her arms over her middle and gripping the sides of her waist as she rested her head against the icy cold glass, her stomach churning. Could she do what Hank wanted? Cold-bloodedly book the date, enter one of those impersonal, sterile little rooms and don the hospital gown with the slit down the back and wait to be wheeled down to theatre after her pre-med? Could she? She rubbed her forehead up and down the window as the whimpering started deep within. *What was she going to do?*

CHAPTER THREE

'What you aimin' to do then, lass?'

Albert had sat and listened as she had recounted the events of the evening, and now he mirrored her own thoughts as he leant slightly towards her in his battered old chair, a cat snoozing on his lap, and the old grandfather clock in a corner of the cluttered room chiming midnight.

'I can't do what Hank wants,' Kate said flatly.

'No, I didn't think you could.'

'So, I'm back where I started.'

'Not necessarily so, lass, not necessarily so.' Albert paused for a moment before continuing. What was he a doin' on, stickin' his nose in like this when he'd spent a lifetime avoidin' messy tangles like this one? But this lass was different. Aye, she was that. A rose on a dung-heap. 'Now, your young man? It seems to me he ain't so bothered about the situation now you've told him your side of things, as the fact it might become public knowledge. Am I right?'

Kate stared at the lined old face in front of her. Albert had put his finger on the very thing that had been bothering her since Hank had left, the knowledge she had been skirting round all evening. She was grateful, very very grateful that Hank hadn't walked out on her when he had heard what she'd had to say. Many a man would have, oh yes, she knew that. But somehow . . . somehow there was something almost abnormal in the way he had been when he came back to the flat the second time. She could have understood him better if he had continued to rant and rave at her, shout, call her names. Or if he had insisted on learning Richard's name and finding out where he was to exact retribution. Or – oh, a hundred other possibilities. But . . . the pretending it hadn't happened? . . .

'So, that bein' the case, an' you feelin' so strongly about the other side of it, what about lettin' things run their course for a few months an' then givin' the bairn up for adoption?'

'Adoption?' Kate shook her head bewilderedly. 'But then everyone would know surely? Hank would never agree –'

'Hold your horses, lass, hold your horses.' Albert put up a gnarled hand to halt her protest. 'There's more ways than one to skin a rabbit as I see's it. You're a tall lass and it bein' your first it's likely nothin' will show for a good couple of months yet, if then. Some appropriate clothes an' the most folk'll think is you're puttin' on a bit of weight, you're too thin by half as it is. You could go away for a couple of months at the end, family trouble, somethin' like that, an' have it some place else an' come back when everythin's sorted. It happens, lass, it happens. More often than you'd think.'

'But surely people would see I was pregnant –'

'A good boned corset'd take care of that, an' you might not even need one at that. We've had one or two round these parts that've dropped 'em without a soul knowin' they was on their way. Next thing is the bairns are out in their prams, bold as brass. Why, Mrs Rivers, her that lives at number twenty-two, she didn't even know she was expectin'. Been tryin' their luck for years they had, he was fair worn out with it all, an' then she has what she thought was a jippy belly an' the next thing there's a seven-pound nipper on the bathroom floor. Straight up, lass, I'm tellin' you. It was the talk of the street for weeks. Even had a reporter round from the *Glasgow Chronicle* in the end, nosy blighter he was . . .'

'Albert, I know you're trying to help, and I would do it if I could, but I just can't see Hank agreeing,' Kate said quietly. 'He . . . he seems adamant about an abortion. But I think you're right, about the adoption idea that is. If I have it I shall be on my own, Hank's made that clear, and even if I wanted to keep it, a child needs a mother *and* a father, doesn't it?'

'So they say, lass.' Albert looked into the glow of the fire before turning to her again. 'But I'd mention it to him. The way I see it you ain't got nothin' to lose, an' he didn't follow the path you'd got set out for him the first road did he?'

'No, you're right there, he didn't.' Her voice was flat and the old man's gaze was keen as she rose slowly to her feet, her movements heavy as though her pregnancy was already telling. 'Thanks for being here, Albert.' She touched his hand before moving towards the door and he followed her, blinking quickly, his lips pursed against his emotion.

'Night then, lass.'

She nodded at him, turning for the stairs. 'Goodnight.'

'I don't like it, Kate. I don't like it at all, but then you knew I would say that, didn't you, hence the ultimatum.'

'Oh, Hank, that's unfair, it's not an ultimatum . . . or at least I didn't mean it to be.'

'No?' They had been sitting almost in a repeat of the night before, Kate perched on the edge of a chair and Hank kneeling in front of her, her hands clasped in his, but now he rose slowly to his feet to stand looking down at her.

'No.' She too rose, but her voice was soft. 'Really. It's just that I can't bear the thought of the other thing, and I wanted to make it clear to you that I don't expect you to understand or condone what I'm going to do. You've been marvellous, but if you feel you want to finish it –'

'How can you say that? How can you stand there, as cool as a cucumber, and come out with something like that?' he hissed angrily. 'Don't I matter at all?'

'Of course you do.'

'There's no "of course" about it as far as I can see. A virtual stranger got you pregnant and you're putting that before us. I don't understand you.' A tense silence ensued, one she found herself unable to break, because in the cold light of logic she didn't understand herself. She just knew, with an absolute certainty, that she could never live with herself if she went through with what Hank wanted. 'And you really think you could pull it off?' Hank asked disbelievingly. 'Keep it quiet from everyone?'

She nodded slowly. 'That wouldn't be difficult, I'm a doctor after all. I could do all the medical checks and so on –'

'And what about afterwards, when you've had it? Are you sure you could give it away? If you feel like this now, how are you going to feel then?'

'I don't know.' She stared at him anxiously. 'But the reason I want to have it is not because I want the baby itself. I mean it. That night was horrible, *horrible*, and I'd always think of that –' She stopped abruptly and took a long deep breath. 'But this is not its fault is it, and to kill it –'

He swore once, a harsh, explicit profanity that had her shrinking from him, and his voice was a low growl when he said, 'Stop talking like that, will you. You've made it into a person already and it isn't, can't you see that? It's just a mass of cells and tissue, it hasn't drawn breath yet, it hasn't *lived*.'

'No, I can't see that.' She stared at him. 'I just can't.'

Their eyes held for some moments before Hank turned away with a savage movement that spoke of furiously suppressed rage and frustration, but his voice was controlled when he spoke, his back still to her. 'I'll wait for you, Kate, but that's all I'll do, you understand me? If you insist on going through with this, I want no part in it. It could all be settled so easily.'

But the easy road would break me. Albert's words flashed into her mind with such sharpness that she thought for a moment she had spoken them out loud. 'I'm sorry, Hank.' She let out a long, slow breath as she fought the inclination to go to him, to promise anything to take the stiffness out of his body. He had been so good to her, what was she doing, repaying him like this? 'If there was any way I could do what you wanted, I would. I don't expect you to believe that, but it's the truth. I love you, I think you're the only person I've ever loved in the whole of my life –'

'Oh, Kate . . .' He turned swiftly, pulling her to him before she had finished speaking, and now they stood entwined together as he stroked her hair while she sobbed against the rough cloth of his sports jacket, her arms round his waist. 'Come on, don't cry. We're not going to speak of this again. Look . . . James wants to meet you, they all do. Why don't you come for Sunday lunch and meet the English side of the family? The American issue will have to wait for a bit, but mother has already expressed a wish to see you soon, perhaps when you can arrange some holiday?' He put her from him slightly to look down into her face. 'You'd like that, wouldn't you, and the break would do you good. You've been working far too hard recently.'

She heard what he was saying, saw his lips move, but the feeling of unease she had experienced the night before had returned a hundred-fold, preventing speech. How could he switch from discussing something that had the potential to ruin any chance they had together to meeting his family in the same breath? That couldn't be normal. It wasn't . . . Was it? But then this wasn't exactly a *normal* situation, and if he was handling it the only way he could . . . 'I – I'd love to meet James,' she said shakily. 'And I've got this Sunday off.'

'Good. That's settled then.' His face expressed nothing beyond mild satisfaction that his suggestion had worked out. 'I'll pick you up about eleven, if that's okay? I'm going to be tied up with James all day tomorrow discussing the whys and wherefores of the business, but we could go out for a meal tonight, if you like.'

'You're going to take the partnership?' She had thought his mother would get her own way, she acknowledged somewhat guiltily.

'I think so.' Hank let go of her, walking over to the fire and standing with his back to it as he nodded slowly. 'Yeah, I think so. Of course James's concern is chicken-feed compared to ours but with Dean and Edward already on board my bite of the apple is pretty small. This way I can build the business up slowly – Dad's already agreed to put a good deal of work our way – and do what I want to do without Dean and Edward on my back all the time.'

'And you think you'll like working with James?'

He shrugged off-handedly. 'Textiles are textiles whether here or in the States, there won't be any surprises, and James is all right. A bit set in his ways but I'll soon shake him up.'

'Perhaps he won't let you,' she suggested with a smile to let him know she was joking.

'He won't have any choice.' He looked at her for a moment and she saw something in his face she didn't like, although she couldn't quite pin down what it was. 'Dad's putting a hefty amount of cash in with me and James needs it, badly. He didn't offer me in because he likes the colour of my eyes, you know.' He smiled, but there was no humour in his face. 'He'll toe the line or else.'

'Hank? –'

'But we get along fine so there'll be no problems, honey.' He moved to her side before she could ask him exactly what he meant and now his eyes were warm as he put out a hand and touched her cheek gently, his mouth smiling. 'You'll like that won't you, being able to stay in Scotland after we're married?' he asked softly. 'That's the main reason I'm going along with this whole idea, you know. I want us to be rich, Kate, rich and successful. I'll be a good provider and with the plans I've got –'

'I don't care about being rich as long as we're happy, Hank. That's more important, isn't it?'

'Money may not buy happiness, sugar, but it sure oils the wheels. I want to know you'll always be with me, buy you everything you want.'

She stared at him for a moment before she forced herself to smile and speak lightly as she lowered her eyelids. 'Always is a long time, I hope you're aware of that, Mr Ross. You might get tired of me –'

'Never.' He drew her tightly against him now, his voice urgent. 'I need you, Kate. I want to get married.' She could feel the comforting solidness of him as he kissed her and the smell of his after-shave was familiar and reassuring. The embrace was no different to many others they had shared but the vague presentiment that there was something momentous she was missing, something it was important for her to understand, made her response automatic. This whole thing was bizarre, she told herself silently, surreal. It wasn't that she wanted recriminations, she didn't, but he was acting as though nothing had changed, as though nothing was going to change. She had let him down badly, but if it wasn't for the fact that the calendar told her differently, she could almost think the last twenty-four hours had been a dream and that she hadn't told him . . .

CHAPTER FOUR

She was still thinking along the same lines on Sunday morning when Hank called for her at eleven o'clock, although after speaking with Albert the day before her apprehension had lessened a little.

'There's such a thing as lookin' a gift horse in the mouth, me girl,' Albert had said stolidly after she had confided her concern to him. 'Seems to me the bloke is bein' more than reasonable an' if he wants to get on with life as normal, that bodes well, don't it? No point in weepin' an' wailin' now the deed's done an' all the talkin' in the world won't alter it.'

'No, I know that, Albert.' She gazed at the old man helplessly. 'I can't explain it, it just feels . . . odd.'

'Look, lass, he's told you he won't stand in the way of you havin' it but he wants no truck with it all. All things bein' equal, what more can the poor bloke do? You ought to be thankin' your lucky stars he's took it the way he has.'

'I am.'

'Well then.'

'Not long now.' She came out of her reverie to find Hank smiling at her, the sunlight turning his brown hair dark red. It had snowed again during the night but she had woken to a pale wintery sunshine and now, as the car reached the outskirts of Glasgow where James and his family lived, the sky was blue and clear.

Hank had driven carefully through the grimy, greasy streets of the inner city but since reaching the outskirts he had allowed the powerful car, a Rover, to pick up speed. They were passing a large park now on Kate's left, the mature, stately trees bare and stark against the skyline, and she noticed a group of children playing on the frozen surface of a small lake, slipping and sliding in an energetic game of tag.

'They're enjoying themselves.' She indicated the youngsters with a wave of her hand. 'And they certainly look better dressed than the children who play in the street where I live. Nothing but tenement blocks and pubs for miles and then they wonder why the crime rate is escalating. It doesn't seem fair such a relatively short distance can make such a difference.'

'There'll always be the haves and the have-nots, Kate.' Hank glanced at her for a second before returning his gaze to the windscreen. 'It's what makes the world go round.'

'It's not fair, though.'

'Depends on how you look at fair. My great grandfather and his brother were born on the wrong side of the tracks on a small cotton plantation in Alabama in 1855. When they were in their twenties they upped and moved to Birmingham, Alabama, and by deals that aren't discussed too much within the family made a mint of money. By 1895 they had settled in Sacramento, California, and were both prosperous businessmen with large, thriving families. Their brothers and sisters who'd stayed in Alabama were still scraping out a living hand to mouth, but I don't consider that unfair. They could have left too but they just didn't have what it takes. It pays to be single-minded in this world.'

Her eyes were wide, her face stretched slightly. She was seeing yet another facet of his personality and she wasn't sure if she liked it or not.

'I'm single-minded about you, Kate.' His voice was soft now, and low. 'You know that, don't you? Look, over there . . .' His voice changed, became bright. 'That's James's family seat. He was lucky, he picked the place up for a song at the beginning of the sixties when he and Liz got married.'

The road along which they had been travelling bordered the park on one side and a small housing estate of select detached dwellings on the other, and now Hank pulled into the slip road and drew up outside the first house surrounded by a high privet hedge that shielded it from its identical neighbour, nosing the car carefully through two open iron gates and on to the paved area, beyond which Kate assumed had once been the front garden. The house was large, the front door of studded oak with two thin rectangular windows of stained glass on either side of it, which gave a welcoming airy feel to the porch, and this was flanked on either side by two wide windows on the ground and first floor beneath a roof of bright red tiles. The single garage was separate, joined to the house only by a thin, wrought-iron gate, beyond which a path led to the back of the house. The whole effect was imposing, grand even, but a homely touch was added by a child's tricycle leaning haphazardly against the garage door complete with resident teddy bear, and a much battered and ancient Morris Minor parked on the far side of the square of paved slabs.

As Hank helped her from the car he glanced across at the old vehicle with a frown, and his voice was flat and slow as he said, 'I didn't know John would be home.'

'John?'

'James's oldest son. He . . . He's at university, doing Law.'

'How old is he?'

'Twenty-one.' His voice was abrupt now, dismissive.

'Don't you like him?' Kate asked quietly.

'Like him? What makes you say that?' The coolness of his voice surprised her. 'He's all right, I suppose. James would have liked him to come into the business but John would have none of it. He wants to be a lawyer and that's that.'

'That single-mindedness you were talking about?' she asked with a smile to diffuse what suddenly felt like a difficult conversation.

'Probably.' He gave her a perfunctory nod but there was

no answering smile in his face or voice. 'Or selfishness, one of the two.'

He didn't like John, she thought silently as he took her arm and led her to the front door. Whatever he said to the contrary, there was definite antagonism there.

Hank's knock was answered immediately and, as the door swung open, a small, slim girl of about nine or ten years of age flung herself into his arms. 'Hank! I've been waiting for you all morning since Daddy said you were coming.'

'Hi, sugar.' Hank gave the child a hug and then turned to Kate who was standing just behind him. 'This is Kate, Susan. Say hallo nicely to the other lady in my life.'

A pair of very blue and very direct eyes looked up at her and then the child smiled widely, holding out her hand politely. 'How do you do?'

'Hello, Susan.' Kate smiled back as another child, an angelic-faced little boy who looked to be three or four, toddled into view, his hand held in that of a well-built man.

'Hank, come in, come in. And this must be Kate? Don't stand there on the doorstep. Liz and John are in the sitting room, go on through.' Hank had told her that James and his family had lived in Glasgow all their lives, but there was none of the broad dialect characteristic of the area present in either the father's or the daughter's voice. In fact their speech was accentless, their diction slightly upper-class.

As the young girl led the way across the large, carpeted hall to a door on the right, James smiled at Kate as she passed him, his voice hearty as he said, 'That's right, that's right. Go on through, my dear. You are most welcome, most welcome.'

Hank had taken her elbow as they had entered the house and now he ushered her through the door in front of them, and into a very large and comfortably furnished sitting room, in which two people were sitting with their faces turned towards the door. The young man stood immediately, inclining his head in their direction, but the slim, fair-haired woman sitting on the Chesterfield settee merely smiled and patted the empty space beside her as she spoke directly to Kate. 'Don't let my brood overwhelm you, Kate. Come and sit down by me while you adjust to the bedlam. John? Would you see to the drinks, darling?'

'Thank you.' As Kate sat in one corner of the sofa she saw Hank nod at the young man, who nodded back, but neither of them smiled, and her earlier feeling intensified. The two men didn't like each other for whatever reason. She had always been susceptible to tension in the atmosphere, her childhood had made her particularly sensitive in that area, and now her keen discernment told her all was not well between the two. Still, it was none of her business, and after answering John's query as to what she would like to drink, she concentrated on talking to Liz Ross, who she was aware had set out to make her feel relaxed and welcome.

'So you're a doctor?' Liz smiled at her after John had handed her her sherry. 'How marvellous. I've always wished I had the brains to do something worthwhile like that.'

'Don't be silly.' James was standing at the foot of the sofa with his back to the coal fire burning brightly in the open grate, and his gaze was soft on his wife's face as he spoke. 'You could have done anything you set your mind to, you know that. As it was you chose to cast your lot with an old duffer like me and I'll never know why.'

'I think you do.' There was a certain inflexion in Liz Ross's voice as she gazed up at him that caused a little dart of envy in Kate's chest, and also a feeling of something akin to discomfort. They loved each other, really loved each other, and they didn't care who knew it. It made her feel . . . odd.

'How did you find medical school?' As John Ross entered the conversation, Kate turned to him gratefully. Somehow the rapport between James and his wife had emphasized the knowledge she was here under false pretences, that she wasn't at all what this nice family thought she was. What would they say if they knew she was, at this moment, carrying a child and its father wasn't Hank?

'Hard work.' She smiled, but it was a few seconds before an answering smile appeared on the face looking at her so intently. It was a good-looking face, exceptionally so, but serious, very serious. Although quite tall, he had the slender, finely-boned build of his mother rather than James.

'Yes, I suppose it would be. I can't say I'm looking forward to Law college once I get my degree.'

'Don't go then.' Hank wagged his head as he spoke, his face merry as though he was speaking in fun. 'We can always find a place for you in Ross Textiles, eh James?'

'The boy knows that.' James spoke quickly, the way someone does when they need to cover an inadvertent gaffe, but as Kate looked up at Hank she knew he had made the remark deliberately, and she knew John Ross knew it too.

'It might be hard work but it will be worth it in the end.' She spoke directly to John but it was a good ten seconds before he drew his gaze away from Hank's face and on to hers. 'I made up my mind I wanted to be a doctor when I was knee-high and nothing else would have done.'

'And you don't regret it?'

'No, no of course not.'

'How could she?' Hank entered the conversation again, his voice jolly. 'She wouldn't have met me otherwise.' He glanced across at her and his smile was intimate, too intimate. It made her feel embarrassed with everyone's eyes on them.

Liz must have sensed something of what she felt, because the older woman spoke swiftly into what had become an awkward pause, and when in the next minute little Adam spilt his lemonade over his mother's skirt the resulting hubbub provided the necessary diversion.

Sunday lunch was served in a dining room that was almost as big as the sitting room, the table large and beautiful in dark, gleaming wood and the deep red carpet and red velvet curtains at the French windows giving the room a warm, homely feel despite the grandeur. The roast beef and Yorkshire pudding were cooked to perfection, as were the accompanying vegetables, and Kate was touched to see that James did his part in serving the food and taking the dirty dishes through to the kitchen, pushing his wife into her seat with an admonition to sit still and relax when she would have risen. 'You've done your part, the rest is up to us,' he said softly when she protested, turning to Kate with a wry smile as Liz sank back in her seat. 'I'm afraid the actual cooking of the food is beyond me.' He grinned boyishly. 'I can never get everything to finish at the same time. Either the potatoes are as hard as iron or the beef is cremated. It's an art, a definite art.'

'I made the apple and blackberry pie.' Susan glanced round the table as she waited for her applause. 'It's Hank's favourite, isn't it, Hank? I used to make it for him all the time when he came to visit but he always stays in a hotel now, don't you?'

'Usually,' Hank agreed easily. 'I've been looking for a place of my own round about these parts, Susan, and I often get back really late from viewing properties. It's better I don't disturb you all with my comings and goings.'

'No, it's not.' Susan pouted, ignoring a warning glance from her mother on what was clearly a delicate matter for some reason. 'I liked it when you stayed with us.'

'So did I.' Hank smiled at the young girl. 'And perhaps I will again some time soon, little buddy.'

'I'm sure Hank will do what is best, Susan.' John's voice was loud and he lowered it before continuing. 'He's very busy, you know. I'm sure he would count himself lucky if all he had to do when he left work was the amount of homework you have.'

'I have masses, John, you know I do.' The topic was

clearly a sore point with Susan. 'Daddy said he didn't have half as much as me when he was at school.'

'Oh well, if we're talking about the Dark Ages . . .'

James's laughing protest to John's witticism turned the talk to an exchange of good-natured insults, and Kate would have thought no more about the conversation but for a glance she caught between John and Hank. It only lasted a split-second but the animosity shocked her. What on earth had happened to make the cousins dislike each other so intensely, she thought curiously, smiling her thanks to Susan as the child handed her a portion of pie, liberally covered with thick custard. And the strange thing was, the others didn't seem to be aware of any discord between the two, and it wasn't a feigned ignorance. No, she was sure of that. It was odd. But then families *were* odd, she thought with a touch of bitterness, she of all people should know that.

'Do you like it?' Susan was leaning across the table as she spoke. 'The pie?'

'It's absolutely delicious.'

'I was going to do a soufflé Mrs Brown taught us in domestic science last week but Daddy and Hank love pie.'

'Soufflé!' James snorted disparagingly. 'A big puff of nothing! I might be old-fashioned but I prefer food that sticks to the ribs, not these new-fangled ideas that look wonderful and that's all. It's like the new high-speed trains they introduced a couple of years ago – they'll bring nothing but grief. Dashing about here, there and everywhere, it really isn't on, you know.'

'Don't forget Concorde, Daddy.' Susan grinned wickedly as Liz groaned at her daughter's prompting.

'Exactly, exactly. Do you know how much that thing cost? Supersonic! Just an exercise in Anglo-French relations, if you ask me, with some very influential pockets being lined. The Boeing 747 is everything the aircraft industry needs and they know it at heart. The Wright Brothers must be turning in their graves.'

'I'm sure they are, dear.' Liz Ross smiled at her husband indulgently. 'But I think it's a little early to introduce Kate to your particular hobby horse on her first visit.'

'My father takes some time to be convinced of new innovations, Kate.' John was speaking to her but the glance he bestowed on his father held the same indulgent warmth his mother had displayed. 'But I can guarantee within twenty years he'll be all for them.'

'Do you see the way I'm maligned by my own family?' James asked solemnly, his eyes twinkling. 'Shocking, don't you think?'

'Oh, Daddy, you know we all love you.' As Susan left her chair to give her father a brief hug, Kate felt that strange feeling she had experienced earlier intensify. They were so happy, such a lovely family. Story-book people, like those Enid Blyton novels she had devoured all through her youth as she had searched for something that always eluded her. So why did she want to cry, why this overwhelming feeling of sadness? It could be her condition . . . The sudden lurch her heart gave as the ever-present shadow came starkly to the front of her mind made her feel sick. What was she doing, sitting here pretending everything was all right? She shouldn't have come, oh, she shouldn't. Everything was upside-down and round-about, she'd go mad before this was finished.

'Are you feeling quite well, Kate? You look a little pale.' As Liz's quiet, pleasant voice cut into her thoughts she realized Hank had said something a moment before and that everyone was looking at her.

'I . . . It's nothing, a headache. I'm sorry, Hank, were you speaking to me?'

'We were thinking of a walk in the park after lunch,' Hank said pleasantly enough, although his eyes had narrowed on her face. 'I asked you if you'd like to come. If you've got a headache, it would help to blow the cobwebs away, perhaps?'

'Yes, that would be lovely, I'd like that.' She stared at

him as she spoke, willing something, something she couldn't put a name to and didn't understand. It was strange but she had never, ever, not even through her childhood, felt as alone as she did right at this moment and the feeling was unbearable. And frightening, so, so frightening.

'I'll just go and see if Adam is awake.' As Liz rose from her chair she touched Kate lightly on the shoulder. 'Would you like to come with me, dear, and we'll find some aspirin for that headache of yours.'

'Thank you.'

As Kate left the room she was aware of Hank's eyes following her, but instead of the warm sensation his attentiveness always created, there arose in her a great sense of unease. She followed Liz Ross into the hall and over to the wide, curving staircase carpeted in rich autumn colours, where the older woman waited for her on the bottom step.

'It's lovely to meet you, Kate.' Liz smiled at her as they walked up the staircase. 'And I can see now why Hank fell so hard so quickly. He's a very lucky boy.'

'Thank you, but I think I'm the lucky one.'

'Ah, but that's love, my dear.' As they reached the top stair the wide landing split into two after a few feet, curving either side of the staircase with a number of doors leading off. The run of carpet had been continued from the stairs and that, along with one or two small upholstered chairs in pale green and a tiny occasional table to one side of the staircase holding a large arrangement of fresh flowers, gave an air of graciousness to the house that was impressive.

'You have a lovely home.' Kate's voice reflected her expression as she smiled at James's wife.

'Thank you.' Liz smiled, glancing about her as though seeing it all for the first time. 'I do love it here, although I can see there will come a time, once the children have left, when it will be too large for just James and me. Of course, with a large number of James's relations living in America we aren't short of guests.' She looked straight at Kate now as she added, 'Hank has been staying with us, on and off, since he was in his teens.'

'Has he?' Kate felt the words implied more than their surface content but was at a loss as to what to say next.

'Kate? . . .' Liz hesitated and then rushed on, 'has he mentioned to you why he started staying elsewhere? I mean, it could be for the reasons he indicated, but I would hate to think we had upset him in any way. If you knew . . .' She lowered her head for a moment as she pressed her hand against her throat. 'But I'm being most unfair.'

'No, no you aren't, of course you aren't.' She touched the other woman's arm tentatively. 'Hank hasn't said a word to me other than what he said downstairs, and I'm sure if anything was wrong he would have mentioned it. He's very fond of you all, I do know that. Perhaps he just wanted to be more independent, especially as he is going to join James in the company. Put things on a more business-like level?'

'Yes, you could be right.' There was a note of relief in Liz's low voice. 'Do you know, I hadn't looked at it quite like that before, but perhaps that is the answer. Working together and then sharing the same home might cause a little friction. Yes, I can see that.' She surprised Kate by putting out her hand and touching the younger woman's face for a moment. 'Thank you, my dear. I'm sure the patients under your care consider themselves most fortunate.'

'I don't know about that.' Kate grimaced wryly. 'I'm afraid quite a few of them endure a hospital stay under sufferance, and I've found Glaswegians aren't shy about putting you in the picture if they aren't pleased about something.'

'Oh dear. Do you ever think about moving back south?'

'Not really.' Kate was unaware of the stiffness that came over her face, but the older woman looked at her closely as she went on. 'My . . . parents are dead and I only have a sister there and we were never close as such. Most of my friends are in these parts, and of course, there's Hank.'

'Hank . . . Yes.' Liz paused for a moment. 'Have you met any of his family yet, besides us?'

'No, there hasn't really been time.'

'I see. But he's told you a little of his family history, I suppose? Dean and Edward are a good deal older than Hank. In fact, Dean is the same age as James, forty-three. There is a fifteen-year age-gap between Edward and Hank too, so he is very much the baby of the family, which can be irritating for a full-grown man, and as all the brothers still live at home, I think there were times when Hank felt . . . smothered.'

Kate nodded. 'I knew his brothers weren't married but I didn't realize they still lived with Hank's parents.'

'I'm afraid so.' Liz clearly didn't approve of the situation. 'Miriam, Hank's mother, is a very . . . strong individual, assertive, you understand? She tends –' She stopped abruptly. 'Oh, I really shouldn't be talking like this. I have no wish to prejudice your opinion of Miriam when you meet her and James would be most cross if he knew I was gossiping.'

'But you aren't.' Kate smiled gently. She liked James's wife, she liked her very much. There was something about the older woman that was very endearing. 'And I would appreciate any background about the family to be honest. I really know nothing at all about them. This engagement seems to have come about so quickly we haven't had much time to talk about anything but us on the few occasions we've been alone together.'

Looking at her straight-faced now, Liz said, 'Well, let me just say I think it is very wise you're making your home in Scotland, Kate. And . . . and don't be put off that, not by anyone. Now, I think I can hear Adam stirring after his nap. Let me get you an aspirin for that headache and then we'll go and get *my* late arrival.'

By the time they joined the others downstairs Adam

was claiming all of Kate's attention. The child had obviously taken to her and she, in turn, found the small boy a charming miniature combination of both James and Liz, with an intelligence that was remarkable in one so young. He continued to remain glued to her side until they were outside, but once in the park frolicked and rolled in the snow like a small puppy, his cheeks glowing and his eyes bright.

'You've made a hit there.' John was smiling as his glance moved from Adam, who had insisted Kate watch him roll over and over in the snow until a sharp admonishment from his mother had brought an end to that particular means of showing off, to Kate's laughing face. 'You obviously like children.'

'I haven't really come into contact with many but I'm finding I do, yes. In the children's wards at the hospital it seems . . . well, to put it bluntly, they are much braver and often much nicer than most of the adults I have to deal with.'

'You sound disillusioned.'

'Do I?' She slanted her eyes at him now, wishing that Hank was with her. John made her feel a little uneasy, although she had to admit he had given her no cause to feel that way, but Hank was some hundred yards in front, deep in conversation with James, Susan hanging on to his arm as the two men talked. 'I hope I'm not. I would say realistic is a more apt word.'

'That's what you would say, is it?' He turned and looked ahead now and, although his face was calm, his voice airy, she had the impression he wasn't feeling like that inside. His gaze moved to Liz and Adam, who were throwing snowballs at each other some distance away, and then back to her before he spoke again. 'Do you love Hank, Kate, really love him, or are there other reasons for this engagement?'

'What?' She was so surprised she stopped dead, and he actually walked on a couple of paces before he realized and turned, his face straightening at the expression on hers.

'I'm sorry.' As she made to march past him he took her arm and drew her round to face him, his blue eyes gentle. 'No, really. I'm very sorry, Kate, that was unforgivable. I had no right to ask you such a personal question.'

'It just surprises me you felt you had to ask it,' she answered honestly, her cheeks flaming. 'Why on earth would I be engaged to be married to him if I didn't love him?'

'I . . .' He hesitated, and then his head jerked upwards as though he was biting back what he had been about to say. 'You're right, of course,' he shook his head slowly, 'of course you are.'

'John?' She didn't move as he let go of her arm. 'What is it? Is there something wrong? Something I should know about?'

'Kate . . .' He drew himself up straighter, his face closing against her at the same time as she was aware of Hank calling her name.

'Is there?' she persisted.

'No.'

'No?'

'Hank's calling you.' He leant towards her and now there was something hard in his eyes. 'Hadn't you better respond?'

'If there's something wrong, I'd rather know.'

'Everything is fine, Kate. Wonderful.' He inclined his head towards her but there was still something dark in his face. 'Go on, you'd better catch him up or he won't like it.' They looked at each other for a long moment and then she turned from him, raising her hand to Hank as she hurried forward. She was aware that John wasn't matching his footsteps to her pace, that he was sauntering behind and making his way over to his mother and Adam, who were still engrossed in their snowball fight to her right, and once she neared Hank she thought his smile was forced, his voice a little too hearty as he spoke.

'Sorry, Kate, I didn't mean to neglect you. I thought you were with Liz and Adam.' He put his arm round her, looking down into her face.

'I'm not dressed for a snowball fight.' She indicated her expensive, hoodless coat and soft leather gloves that were more fashionable than practical, with a wry smile. 'And from what I've seen, Adam packs quite a punch.'

'He's a dirty fighter,' his father agreed. 'Takes after his mother I'm afraid.'

'Oh, Daddy . . .' Susan pushed herself into her father's side with a little laugh, and then the four of them continued walking slowly forwards, Susan between the two men and Kate still within the circle of Hank's arm.

Tea was a merry affair but strangely Kate found herself looking forward to the moment when they could leave. The nausea of the last few mornings was gradually making itself felt at other times, and she found she was tiring more easily. The symptoms themselves didn't bother her, she had been expecting something of the kind, but here in this warm, family atmosphere with the children playing on the floor in front of the fire and the adults sipping coffee and chatting about this and that, her secret felt so heavy as to be intolerable, and her present exhaustion an acrid reminder that she was living a lie. But lie or not, she had to go on with it. It was just that tonight, sitting in the peaceful comfort of this home, she didn't know how.

'I want Kate to put me to bed.'

'Now, Adam –'

'I do, I want Kate.' Adam was over-tired and it was telling. Instead of kissing each of them goodnight, as his mother had asked when he came downstairs fresh from his bath in blue Womble pyjamas and with a disreputable teddy bear tucked under one arm, the same one that had been parked on the tricycle earlier, the small child was standing in the middle of the room frowning and close to tears.

'I don't mind.' Kate looked at Liz and spoke quietly. 'Really, I would love to put him to bed.'

'He'll want a story,' James said warningly, 'no doubt a long story.'

'Oh, I'm sure Adam will forgo that tonight, won't you, dear?' his mother asked brightly.

'No.' The little face was uncompromising.

'I think I might be able to manage a story, Adam.' Kate smiled at the small, militant figure in front of them. 'But only one, okay? And then straight to sleep like a good boy.'

'Okay.' He nodded happily, all charm again, holding out his hand for her to take. As they walked upstairs to the large nursery next to his parents' room, which Kate had seen earlier that afternoon held more toys than the average toy shop, she was very aware of the small plump hand placed so trustingly in hers, so aware it brought a lump to her throat and a mistiness to her eyes. This was the end result of the process of intercourse. First an embryo, undeveloped and unseen, then in due course a baby with all the attendant paraphernalia, and then . . . Then a small, individual being like this one, with its own mind, its own thoughts, a breathing, *living* part of the people who had created it. Oh . . . She gripped the small hand more tightly now. She had to stop thinking like this, it wasn't going to do any good when the time came. Because she had to give it away, she knew she had to. And everything she did from now on had to prepare her for that.

It was a good half an hour later before she rejoined the others and Hank stood up immediately he saw her enter the room, his voice brisk. 'There you are. I thought we'd cut along now if that's all right? There's more snow forecast tonight and I'd prefer to miss it if we can.'

'Yes, of course.' Kate nodded her agreement and turned to Liz. 'Thank you for a wonderful day, I've thoroughly enjoyed it.'

'We've enjoyed having you, my dear,' Liz said warmly as she rose and walked to their side. 'I have been so looking forward to meeting you but it seemed as though each time we tried to make a date with Hank he had to fly back home unexpectedly. Still, we have met now and I hope you already count us as family?'

'I'd like that very much.'

'Good.' James answered for his wife as he rose, but Kate noticed John remained seated in his corner of the sofa, even after Susan joined the others as they walked to the door. 'And now you know where we live you are welcome any time, there's no need to wait until this cousin of mine fits in a visit.'

'You're very kind.' She smiled at them all as Hank helped her into her coat, and as her gaze flicked over John he rose to his feet, following them into the hall as they left the sitting room.

'You'll be at the office tomorrow, Hank?' James opened the front door as he spoke revealing an icy winter scene outside into which the first desultory snowflakes were beginning to fall.

'Bright-eyed and bushy-tailed.' Hank grinned at the older man, kissed Liz's cheek as he murmured his thanks and then bent down to tweak Susan's nose. 'Behave yourself, little buddy.' As he straightened, he took Kate's arm and nodded quietly to John who was standing just behind the others, his face concealed from Kate by James's bulk. 'Goodnight, John. Are you staying long?'

'Just a couple of days, there's an important lecture I have to get back for on Wednesday morning.'

'Then perhaps we could have lunch together before you go? It's been some time –'

'I don't think so.' John's voice was pleasant enough but there must have been something in his face that caused Hank to stiffen slightly at her side, and as she glanced up at him she felt he was keeping his smile in place with some effort. 'I've brought back a heap of work, as it happens,' John continued flatly as his mother turned round to him with a reproachful, 'Oh, John.'

'Don't encourage the lad to fritter away his time, Liz.' James was speaking to his wife but looking at Kate and went on, 'It's his last year, you see. Important time, every minute counts and all that. The finals begin in May.'

'It *is* an important time.' She inclined her head towards him. 'I remember we were all nervous wrecks at the end of our finals but it was noticeable in the results who had revised and who hadn't. Good luck anyway, John.' She moved a pace and peered round James. 'I'm sure you'll do fine.'

'Of course he will.' Hank was grinning widely now, taking her arm again and turning her round so that John's reply was lost as they walked down the steps into the bitingly cold air, but the impression that his geniality was for the sake of the others and not at all what he was feeling inside was strong. This seemed to be borne out a few moments later once they had waved goodbye and were on the road again, when Hank twisted irritably in his seat as he said, his tone abrupt, 'What were you and John talking about so cosily?'

'Cosily?' She stared at him in surprise. 'What do you mean, cosily?'

'Don't play the dumb broad, Kate.'

'I beg your pardon?' Her voice was tight and so was her face, and although Hank hadn't glanced at her, he must have taken warning from the tone of her voice, because his was more moderate when he next spoke.

'Look, sugar, I'm not getting at you, don't think that, but I know John. He's a good guy most of the time but he can be a real Charlie Roach at others, you know?'

'I haven't the faintest idea what you are talking about, and who is Charlie Roach?'

'Old Charlie? Haven't I told you about him? Well, Charlie Roach was a friend of my grandfather's, a real regular guy with a family and a good job, big house and so on, and my grandfather thought the world of him – he was best man at his wedding I understand. The two families lived in each other's pockets, kids went to the same school, all the normal stuff, and then one day the bombshell dropped. There was some sort of investigation at the firm where Charlie worked and it was found he'd been doing them down for years, and in a big way, I mean *really* big. And that was just the start. As the thing went on they found he had another wife and family in a different State, several false aliases and a string of creditors on his back and some very dubious business dealings with people who weren't too nice to know. Dad said it rocked my grandparents' foundations at the time, especially when, in the middle of it all, the wife killed herself and took the kids with her.'

'That's absolutely terrible, Hank.' She stared at him, horrified. 'I can't believe it.'

'They say truth is stranger than fiction, honey. Anyway, the name Charlie Roach became synonymous in the family with guys who had another side to them, split-personality types, you know? Couldn't quite be trusted –'

'And you're saying your cousin is like that? John?' Her voice was high but she couldn't help it, she couldn't believe he was accusing the nice young man she had met that afternoon of such a crime. 'I know you don't like him, Hank, but surely he isn't like that?'

'I don't dislike John, Kate.' His voice was low now and she watched him take a deep breath, his teeth biting at his lower lip, before he said, 'but he sure as hell doesn't like me. Oh, he's made it clear in that quiet, polite way of his on a number of occasions. Whether he feels I've usurped his place with his father or Susan prefers me to him, I don't know, but the guy's got another side to him, believe me. There's been times . . .'

'What?' She found herself scrutinizing his set face as he paused and shrugged without continuing. 'There's been times, what?'

'When he's tried to put me in a bad light, twist things. There's real hate there, Kate, and I'm not imagining it.'

'And you've no idea what it is all about?'

The hesitation was brief, just the merest second, but somehow she knew he was lying when he replied, 'No, I've told you, haven't I?'

She lowered her head for a moment. If he didn't want to tell her, he didn't, and she couldn't force a confidence after all. But there was something there, something . . . dark. She shivered and immediately one of his hands covered hers.

'Are you cold? I'll turn up the heating. Look, there's a car-rug on the back-seat, drape that round your legs.' She did as he suggested and it was a full minute later before he spoke again. 'So John didn't say anything about me then?'

'Not really.' She wanted to be home, home by herself, where she could digest all that had happened that day and find out what was troubling her. Because something was.

'Nothing?'

'He asked me if I loved you.'

'Did he?' She couldn't quite place the timbre of his voice but it didn't hold the indignation or affront she had expected. 'And what did you say?'

'That I did.'

His hand came out again and squeezed hers. 'That's all right then And there was nothing else?'

'No.' Her tone was definite now and he nodded slowly before taking his hand from hers.

They didn't speak again on the journey home. Hank seemed lost in thoughts of his own and Kate was too tired to try and engage him in conversation, besides which her head was spinning with impressions of the family they had just left. They seemed so happy, and kind . . . really kind. 'Salt of the earth', as Rosie's husband would say. Now why had she thought of William at this moment in time? Her brow wrinkled in a slight frown as she suddenly felt a longing to talk to her sister, a longing that the rational part of her mind told her was quite illogical. She could never confide in Rosie and William, they would be shocked beyond measure, she could just imagine William expounding the error of her ways in that dry, pedantic manner of his. No, she couldn't unburden herself to them but this urge to talk to the only other human being in the world she was linked to through blood was as strong as it was irrational.

And John . . . Surely Hank was wrong when he had maligned the young man's nature? John might not like Hank for some reason best known to himself, but that didn't make him the Jekyl and Hyde character Hank had painted, this Charlie Roach person, did it? Did it? . . . She sighed softly. What had John been going to say to her this afternoon before Hank had interrupted them? She would suddenly have given the world to know. Oh, this was doing no good, all this thinking. She had enough problems of her own, didn't she? More than enough. Every family had its secrets and this one's were no business of hers, not really. Hank was only James's cousin, after all, which made John his cousin once removed, it wasn't as though they were brothers or anything. She would probably hardly ever see him in the future, he wouldn't feature at all in their lives. Oh, she was tired, so, so tired. She wished this journey was over.

The flat was cold and dark when she opened the front door some time later, Hank having left her in the downstairs lobby with the explanation he wanted to get back to his lodgings before the snow started in earnest. She hadn't tried to dissuade him. She was probably being most ungrateful but she wanted nothing more than to be by herself.

She lit the fire before walking through to the bedroom and switching the electric blanket on to full, leaving the bedroom light on when she left the room. It might be wasteful but she needed light tonight. In the same way she turned the television set on as a background noise, although she had no intention of watching the programme. She just felt strange, odd . . .

She made herself a cup of tea, taking several chocolate biscuits from the tin on the work surface before walking back through to the sitting room. She would have to watch this, she thought wryly as she munched her way through the snack. She was eating like a horse at the moment, she would resemble a barrel before she was finished, although as yet there wasn't the faintest trace showing of what was happening deep inside. She shut her eyes and relaxed back into the chair, but the next moment the raised voice of James Callaghan, the Prime Minister, intruded into the room as a political debate on the television got heated.

She got up and switched off the set irritably. What did these politicians know about real life anyway, she asked herself bitterly. No doubt most of them lived protected lives in great big houses with no real problems save that of appealing to the general public at the next election. Oh, she was being unfair . . . She rubbed her face wearily. She was all out of sorts, in fact, she felt worse than before she'd gone today. Perhaps it was seeing the love and friendship within James's close-knit little family, highlighting, as it had done, all she had missed as a youngster.

'Enough self-pity!' She spoke the words out loud into the quiet room. 'And if you want to phone Rosie, phone her.' She nodded to herself as though an argument had just been settled. Rosie was her sister after all, she could phone her for a chat couldn't she?

There was one telephone for all the flats situated in the lobby and, for once, as she peered down past the last corner of the stairs, she saw it was not being used. She glanced at her watch. Quarter past ten. Not too late to phone surely? She knew William always took an evening service that lasted until eight o'clock but it was often half past nine before they got home, she doubted whether they would be in bed yet.

'The Vicarage, can I help you?' Rosie's voice came on the line and Kate leant back against the wall as that debilitating weakness swept over her again, but stronger this time. She had the urge to cry, to wail, at the sound of her sister's voice.

'It's me, Rosie. Kate.'

'Kate?' Rosie's voice was full of surprised delight. 'How lovely to hear from you. I was only thinking the other day it must be at least three weeks since we'd spoken last. We are a pair, aren't we.'

'I suppose we are.'

'How are you?'

'Fine, just fine.'

'And work's okay?'

'Not bad. Hectic, you know. How are you and William, anyway?'

'We're . . .' There was a pause. 'We're all right. I –' The pause was longer this time and Kate's eyes narrowed as she heard what sounded like a muffled sob from the other end.

'Rosie? Rosie, are you there?'

'I . . . I'm sorry, Kate. Hang on a moment.' A full minute ticked by before Rosie spoke again, and Kate was surprised at just how concerned she felt about this sister she barely knew. 'Are you there, Kate?'

'Of course I am. What's wrong?'

'I . . . I'm being stupid,' Rosie said weakly.

'I doubt that. You might have some faults but stupidity is not one of them. What's the matter?'

'I'm all right, Kate, really, or at least I was until I heard your voice and then it all sort of flooded over me again.'

Oh, Rosie. Rosie, Rosie, Rosie . . . You'll never know how much I needed that tonight, just to know you care. 'What flooded over you?' Kate asked gently.

'We've . . . we've had some bad news, William and I. You know I told you we were having some tests done? Over the baby thing?'

'I remember.'

'Well . . .' There was another pause and then Rosie spoke in a little rush, her voice thick. 'Oh, Kate, it's awful. I feel so sorry for William but I feel sorry for myself too, I can't help it, and I don't think I'm supporting him like I should. I never dreamt how much I wanted children.'

'Rosie, just tell me.'

'William's . . . William's sperm count is low, exceptionally low, and they don't think he'll ever . . . father a child.'

'Can't they do anything?' Kate asked softly.

'No.' The one word was bleak. 'But that's not all. We heard this morning from the adoption agency that they consider William too old at forty to be suitable for adopting a baby. They . . . they said an older child might be possible, or we could consider fostering, but I want a baby, Kate. It might be selfish and unreasonable and a million other things I've been telling myself for months just in case this happened, but I *do*. I want a baby.'

'Oh, Rosie.' Kate bit her lip as she felt a rush of hot guilt flood through her. 'Of course it isn't selfish or unreasonable, it's the most natural thing in the world. It's quite definite, with the adoption agency I mean? Couldn't you try another one?'

'It wouldn't alter William's age and it seems that's something they all don't like. The fact I'm so much younger than him is another problem. One of the women who interviewed us –' Rosie's voice had begun to rise and she stopped abruptly, obviously fighting for control. When she spoke again her voice was low and flat. 'One of the women asked me, actually asked me to my face, whether I had some sort of father fixation and whether I'd married William as a substitute of some kind. I could have hit her.'

'What did you say?'

'I smiled politely and said, no, of course not, I married him because I loved him in the way I presume all women love the man they want to spend the rest of their life with. I wish now I'd done what I really wanted to do, slapped her face and told her to stop the amateur psychology. Some of the questions they asked, Kate, you've no idea . . . It was so . . . so degrading.'

'Oh, Rosie.'

'And William, he just doesn't seem to feel the same way I do about it all. He wants children, there's no doubt about that, but his attitude is, if God doesn't want us to have our own, we can live just as fulfilled a life without them. The only thing we seem to agree on is that neither of us wants an older child, we both want a baby, although our reasons differ. William has got this thing about the child being ours, completely ours, and he feels if there was any chance we might come into contact with the natural mother, or any other relations for that matter, he couldn't cope with it, not when the child was young. That doesn't worry me though, I want a baby simply because I know I could feel it was really mine if I had it from being tiny. It's different when they're older, at least for me. I've got to be honest, haven't I, Kate?' The last words were in the form of a wail.

'Of course you have.' What could she say? What *could* she say?

'Oh, I've just heard William's car pull up and it'd perhaps be better if he didn't find me discussing things on the phone. He got delayed at church, we've got a leak in the roof. I'd better go, he'll want his supper. Kate?' Her sister's voice was soft now.

'Yes?'

'Do you know what really hurts the most? They've turned us down as adoptive parents when we could provide the most wonderful home for a child. The vicarage is huge and you know what the garden's like with all those trees and the orchard and the swing, it's the most idyllic spot for a child to grow up in, and William would make a good father, I know he would.'

'I do too, and you'd make a fantastic mother.'

'And we really love each other, Kate. How many couples can say that from the bottom of their hearts? It would be a stable, secure home . . . Oh! Stop it Rosie.' Her sister's voice took on a disgusted note. 'I'm whining now, aren't I.'

'No, you're not. You're telling your big sister how you

feel. I don't think either of us have done enough of that in the past.'

'Oh, Kate.' Rosie's voice was very quiet now. 'I've never said this before, although I wanted to. Mum was awful to you, wasn't she.'

'Awful, but that's in the past now and the future is what's important. Look, I can hear William calling you, we'll speak again soon. I'll give you a ring in the week, if that's all right?'

'Yes do, I'd like that. And, Kate?'

'Yes?'

'Thanks. I felt desperate tonight and it's helped talking to you.'

'Good. 'Bye, Rosie.'

She remained where she was for a long time before mounting the stairs. Life was one big rotten joke, wasn't it . . . A sick kind of merry-go-round where the strong and the powerful dominated the weak and nothing was fair. William had spent his life helping people, and when he had wanted something, something reasonable and right and worthwhile, he'd been kicked in the teeth. And Rosie was right, they would have made excellent parents, and they had a beautiful home . . . And here she was, pregnant and in her own way as desperate as Rosie, and why? Because again the strong had taken what they wanted with no thought for anything but their own need. And what could ordinary, decent people do? Nothing. The answer came back at her with something approaching fury. Nothing. *Absolutely nothing.*

CHAPTER FIVE

It was a full eight weeks later, and two weeks after Kate had felt the baby move for the first time and experienced such a wild, fierce burst of love that it had stopped her breath, that the crazy, impossible idea that had been hidden deep in her mind since that first night she had talked to Rosie on the phone brought her bolt upright in bed in the middle of the night, her heart pounding. She sat there without moving, one hand clutched to her throat and the other in a fist between her breasts, as she let herself absorb the enormity of it.

Could she do it? The May night wasn't warm, in fact there was a distinct chill in the air, but she found she was sweating profusely as her mind took grasp of the notion her subconscious had been carrying for weeks. *She was going to give Rosie her baby.* And not through any high ideals of love or compassion towards her sister, no, she would be honest with herself over this, although she did feel terribly sorry for Rosie and William. The main component of her decision *was* love but it was for the minute little being hidden away inside her, this tiny creature that was hers, wholly hers. Her baby.

She had read somewhere that women in her position often felt rage and resentment towards the unborn child, an anger that was directed as much at their circumstances as the unfortunate infant. But . . . she didn't feel like that. No, she didn't. She lifted her head now as if in wonder. She wanted this baby, oh, how she wanted it. It was the first thing that had ever needed her, its very life depended on her and the knowledge had caused all the latent love that had been hidden for years, waiting for a chance to express itself, to surface in an agony of deep and protective tenderness. She couldn't give it away and never see it again, she just couldn't. She hugged her middle tightly now as she swayed back and forth in the dark room. But she couldn't keep it either. A child needed a mother and a father, and it wouldn't even have a full-time mother if she held on to it. She would have to work to support them both and that meant long hours, long shifts. No . . . As Rosie had said, it would be brought up in a wonderful home in the heart of the country where it could grow tall and strong, free from the grime of the Glasgow streets, and most of all . . . Most of all she could see it.

Albert had said, all those weeks ago, about this neighbour of his, hadn't he? She cast her mind back. This woman hadn't known she was pregnant, that was what he had said. She'd ask him about it in the morning. She lay back down in the bed, her head spinning. She needed to talk this through with someone and Albert was the only person she could trust, the only one she could rely on. He would support her, help her, he would.

'You've lost your marbles, lass. What the 'ell are you a thinkin' on?'

'Albert, just listen.'

'Listen! Eeh. I can't believe what I'm hearin'. All this has turned your brain, that's what it is.'

'Albert, *please*,' she implored on a little sob.

'Now, now, don't start blubbin'.' His voice dropped as he moved uncomfortably. 'Go on then, have your say, but don't expect me to be for it. It's against the law, what you're proposin'. You know that don't you? You could be up before the beak.'

'I don't care. I don't care if it's illegal and anyway, if Rosie agreed and we actually did it, who would know? No one. No one except them and me and you.'

'An' what if there were problems, when the bairn's being born like? You're puttin' your life at risk, lass. An' didn't you tell me this sister of yours is married to a vicar? He ain't goin' to agree to anythin' that's criminal, is he?

By . . .' He stared at her now with a grudging respect in his eyes. 'I thought I'd met 'em all but you take the biscuit, lass, you do that. They say the quiet ones are the worst.'

'I don't know if William would agree.' It was the thought that had been haunting her all night. Rosie would, she knew Rosie would, but William? It would just depend on how badly he wanted a child, or perhaps on his understanding of his wife's need in that area. She didn't really know William, she had only met him on four separate occasions and one of them had been his wedding day. She had found him a somewhat dry, precise kind of individual. Kind, oh yes, she was sure he was kind, and certainly devoted to his parishioners, but on each occasion she had been left wondering why on earth her sister, her young, lively sister, had fallen in love with such a man. And she did love him. That much had been evident.

'An' you're sayin' you wouldn't tell 'em the bairn was yours?'

'I know William definitely wouldn't agree if I did. Rosie said he was adamant he didn't want any contact with the natural parents when they were talking about adopting, and it wouldn't be fair to tell Rosie and expect her not to tell her husband. Even if she agreed not to, it might slip out at some time in the future and anyway, I don't know if she would like the idea if she knew the child was mine. It might feel like the baby wasn't theirs.'

'Well, it won't be, will it. It'll be yours, an' how do you think you're goin' to like that when it's older an' got a tongue in its head, 'cos it won't be you that'll be Mammy. Have you thought about that side of things in this plan of yours?'

'Yes.' She nodded painfully. 'And I won't like it, of course I won't, but it will be better than not knowing where it is, if it's being looked after properly, cared for. My childhood was miserable and I just want to be sure . . .' She stopped as her throat tightened and swallowed deeply. 'I want to be sure it's loved, Albert.'

'Eeh, lass, lass.' He blinked his eyes at her, shaking his head slowly. 'I think a bit about you, you know that, an' it's 'cos of that I have to say I hope this don't come off. It'll be torture, lass, down through the years it'll be torture, mark my words. An' if you don't go away an' have it in a hospital someplace, where are you goin' to have it?'

'Here.' She brought her chin up with a jerk at his exclamation of disbelief. 'You said yourself that babies don't always show and I'll have to corset myself up, wear loose clothes. I'm already twenty weeks, Albert, nearly twenty-one, and there's hardly anything there. I'm carrying a bit in the back and a bit in the front which is perfect for what I want to do. At work I wear a baggy, loose white coat anyway, so that's no problem.'

'An' you're goin' to suggest to this sister of yours that she starts paddin' herself out a bit, like she's puttin' on a bit of weight? What if they don't play ball?'

'Then I'll have to think again.' She put down her cup as she rose and went to stand in front of the fire before turning and looking at him again. He was sitting in the same armchair he had sat in ten weeks ago when she had first told him, and even the cats were lying in the same spot in front of the fire. But she felt that the frightened young girl that had been in this room then – and she had been young in spite of her twenty-five years, she acknowledged silently – was dead and gone, never to return. Quite when the metamorphosis had taken place, she wasn't sure. Perhaps it had been a gradual process from the time she had first told Hank of her condition, but the change had been completed the moment she had felt the baby move inside her. She had known then she couldn't let it go, not completely. Whatever happened. It was hers, part of her. It would be until the day she died.

'What about this bloke of yours? You tellin' him?'

'Hank?' She shook her head, her mouth twisting in a bitter little smile. 'Oh, Albert, he's the last person to tell. He's made it clear that, as far as he's concerned, this child has never existed. I can't blame him, I suppose, he's being supportive in every other way, but he wouldn't countenance the baby being part of my life. No, I wouldn't tell him. He's moving over here in July, at which point the partnership with James begins, and he's already told me he will be busy for a few weeks after that sorting everything out. I think it was a tactful way of telling me he didn't want to see me until after the baby's born. So . . . for the next three or four months it looks like I'm on my own.'

'It's what you wanted, lass.'

'In a way I suppose, I just wish . . .' Kate paused as she tried to formulate her thoughts into words, 'I wish he'd wanted to be here now and again, but I suppose that's asking a bit much.'

'I reckon.' Albert nodded slowly. 'If he thinks anythin' of you, this can't be easy for him, an' if he don't see you, it's not shovin' it under his nose. Likely that's what he's thinkin', lass.'

She stared back at him but couldn't speak. She knew Albert was trying to be kind in his own blunt, northern way and perhaps she *was* asking too much . . . No, not 'perhaps', she *knew* she was, and yet she couldn't put this feeling she had about Hank into words, not even in her mind. But it was there all the time, even on the good days, niggling away at her . . .

'You aimin' to go and see this sister of yours?' Albert's heavy tone indicated exactly how he viewed such a trip.

'Yes.' Then, getting to her feet, she said, 'It will have to be soon, I need to know one way or the other to make plans now, and anyway, it would be better if I didn't see them the last two or three months and we communicated purely by phone, just to be safe.'

'How the 'ell are you goin' to say it, lass? You thought about that? An' what if you get the jitters, eh, what then? You ain't a natural liar, Kate, I've seen enough in me time to know that. I can't see 'em swallowin' it –'

'Albert, please.' Her voice was sharp and her hand went

to her mouth as she said, 'I'm sorry, I didn't mean to snap, but don't . . . don't be like that, Albert. I need your help, you're the only one I can talk to about this. And I have thought it out, all through the night I thought about nothing else. I shall say I know someone, a nurse at the hospital, who's got herself into a mess. She was going to have an abortion but couldn't go through with it, that much is true at least, but now she's panicking at the thought of anyone knowing and just wants out. I . . . I advised her to go to a clinic but she went hysterical at the thought and then I thought about Rosie and William. I mentioned to this girl that I knew a couple who couldn't adopt but were desperate for a child, I didn't give any names, and she said they could have the child as soon as it was born if they were prepared to say it was theirs, that the wife had given birth to it. And then . . . then I shall go on from there.'

'An' you think they'll buy it?'

'They might.'

'Aye, well . . .' He rose, walking across to the sideboard and pouring himself a good measure of brandy from the bottle half hidden amongst the clutter covering the surface, and then swallowing the contents of the glass in one gulp before facing her again. 'Kate, I've a nasty feelin' you're storin' up a whole heap of trouble for yourself, but ten to one I'll be gone afore I see it any road. If it's what you want, I'm with you, lass. I can't be anythin' else, can I?'

'Thank you, oh, thank you, Albert.'

'Don't thank me, lass. I ought to be gettin' a kick up the backside for not talkin' sense into you, but there it is, there it is. If your mind's made up . . .'

'It is.'

'Aye. Well far be it from me to try to alter a woman's mind, there's better men than me tried it an' come a cropper.'

'Will you ring the hospital for me tomorrow and say I'm

sick? Say I'll be back at work in a day or two, all being well.'

'You're goin' tomorrow?' he asked in surprise.

'Today, this morning.'

'Stone the crows, lass. If I'd have met you fifty years ago me life'd have been different. I dunno if it'd have been better, but it'd certainly have been different.'

She was thinking of Albert's words later that evening as she stared into the shocked faces of her sister and brother-in-law. It had been a long train journey and a tedious one, with several changes that had necessitated irksome waits on dreary platforms, and by the time the taxi had delivered her to Rosie's front door she had been feeling tired and slightly ill.

Nevertheless, after she had paid the taxi driver and he had disappeared, she stood for long minutes drinking in the sweet, moorland-scented air, her eyes lingering on the cobblestoned packhorse bridge some way down the village road, under which a group of children were playing on the stepping stones that forded the crystal-clear waters. The whitewashed pub, the cottages with their mullioned windows and well-proportioned gables and gardens glowing with fuchsias, roses and creepers, all took on a poignancy that made it seem as if she had never seen them clearly before. Glasgow, with its mean streets and dirty, crowded tenement blocks, into which human beings were sometimes packed as tightly as sardines, seemed a million miles away. A different lifetime . . . *This* is what she wanted for her child.

She took a long deep pull of air, her eyes misting. They had to agree, *had* to. She wasn't doing anything wrong, after all. How could it be wrong to want the best for her child, to want it to grow up loved and secure in a happy family home free from the grime and dirt of the big city where she had lived and worked for the last seven years?

*

'Kate, let me get this straight.' William pushed Rosie into a chair as he spoke and then straightened with his hand on his wife's shoulder, looking for all the world as though he was posing for a photograph that would have been taken at the turn of the century, the noble patriarch and ruler of his own domain. 'You are saying this friend of yours –'

'Not friend, acquaintance. I merely work with her, that's all.'

'This . . . acquaintance is proposing that we take her child, a new-born infant, and bring it up as our own?'

'William? –'

He checked his wife's voice with a movement of his hand as he continued to look straight into Kate's flushed face. 'Is that what you are saying, Kate?'

'Yes.'

'And you think we could even consider such a preposterous suggestion? Please,' his hand moved again as Rosie made a sound in her throat, 'don't misunderstand me. I'm sure your coming here was motivated by the very highest regard for your sister but you must see such an idea is quite impossible.'

'Why?' Kate longed to sit down but she felt that would put her at a worse disadvantage than she was now.

' "Why"?' William stared at her, his fine, almost classical features cold and his pale blue eyes clear and direct. 'You are an intelligent woman, Kate, I hardly think I have to explain why. There are laws against such things for a start. Laws made to protect innocent children from the potentially tragic consequences of such foolishness.'

'And in ninety-nine cases out of a hundred those laws are probably perfectly necessary and justified, but can you honestly tell me that this baby wouldn't have a better life with you and Rosie as its parents than being brought up in a Glasgow slum with a mother who is unmarried?'

'She could offer the child for adoption.'

'Exactly, and that is what she is doing now.'

'Legal adoption.'

'Yes, yes she could go through legal adoption, the same bureaucratic channels that refused you and Rosie for no other reason than that you didn't quite fit into the standard pattern of the ideal couple in their eyes. And the child could still be brought up in something approaching a Glasgow slum instead of here, in this beautiful house with all the advantages you have to offer. You live in an ideal part of the world; even the fact that Rosie apparently gives birth without realizing she was pregnant could be carried off due to your circumstances. The nearest hospital is miles away and most of the women round here give birth at home anyway, with old Amy attending. What could be simpler than getting hold of her once the child is here and asking her to notify the appropriate authorities? You and Rosie are deeply respected in the village, no one would have any cause to suspect that it hadn't happened just as you said.'

'What . . . what if she changes her mind when the baby is born?' Rosie leant forward in her seat as she spoke, her eyes intent on Kate's face. 'What then?'

'Then your hopes would have been raised for nothing, but I don't think she will. She doesn't want to keep the child, Rosie, it would be impossible for her.'

'And she doesn't know who we are? You wouldn't have to tell her?'

'No.' The strength it took to keep her eyes from wavering as she lied made her break out in a cold sweat. She was doing the right thing, she was doing the right thing . . . The words drummed through her head. This was best for everyone, it was, in this case the means justified the end. 'A chance like this will never happen again, I'm sure you realize that, and I think you ought to at least discuss it before you refuse.' She turned her head to William. 'I don't have to go back to Glasgow for a day or two.'

'I can tell you the answer now –'

'No! No, William.' Rosie twisted under his hand as she

turned to look up into her husband's face. 'I think we should talk about it.'

'Rosie –'

'I want a baby. We did everything the adoption agency asked of us and they said we weren't good enough. Oh,' she flapped her hand as she rose, 'they dressed it up a bit but that's what it boiled down to. Well, *I want a baby*, I do. I don't care if this isn't ethical or within the law or anything else, I mean it. We wouldn't be hurting anyone –' Tears were streaming down her face now, but as William moved to take her in his arms, she backed away, her hands restraining him. 'I'm young, William, I'm twenty-two years old. I don't want to go all through my life without a child, I . . . I can't stand the thought of it. Really, I can't stand the thought of it. I've been trying to come to terms with it but I can't and now I'm just resenting God, and my life, and . . . everything.'

'Me?' His face was stricken. 'You resent me?'

Oh, what had she started? What had she started? Kate didn't know whether to move or continue to stand there, but they seemed to be unaware of her presence.

'I love you, William, I do, but please, I want a baby. If we can't have one of our own then this is the next best thing, don't you see? Because we'll make it ours. We'll be the ones holding it, loving it, getting up in the middle of the night, cudd . . . cuddling it . . .' She was crying uncontrollably as she sank down on to the carpet and, as William knelt beside her, Kate took the opportunity to leave the room, shutting the door quietly behind her, her own face wet. She hadn't wanted to hurt them. She found she was ringing her hands as she paced the small bedroom where Rosie had shown her earlier when she had first arrived. She had wanted . . . 'Oh, God, help me . . .' What had she wanted? Really wanted? Suddenly she didn't know any more. Was this wrong? Wicked? Was it? 'Tell me, God . . .' She was muttering feverishly as she walked. 'Am I bad, wicked? But if I am, why don't I feel like I am? Oh, what am I going to do? What am I going to do? I don't want to lose Hank, and I will, I know I will if I keep it. And this isn't my fault, and it's not the baby's fault either. You know that, You're supposed to know everything so You know that.'

It was almost an hour later when she lay down on the bed and almost immediately fell asleep, still fully clothed. At some time in the night she was aware of stirring and the weight of a heavy quilted bedspread on her limbs, but the thick layers of sleep were too heavy to fight, and when she next opened her eyes it was to a room full of bright sunlight and Rosie bending over her, her voice urgent. 'William's agreed to think about it, Kate, consider it further.'

'What? . . .' She felt her face stretch slightly, the saltiness of her tears of the night before making the skin tight.

'Did you hear me? Oh, Kate, I can't tell you what it means –'

'But, William? Last night he was so adamant.'

'Last night was last night.'

'What did you say to him to make him change his mind?'

'All sorts of things, we sat talking until it was light. He's asleep now but I can't sleep, I'm too excited –' Rosie stopped abruptly. 'She won't change her mind, Kate? This girl?'

'No, she won't change her mind, but William hasn't agreed yet has he? He's just said he'll think some more about it.'

'If you knew William like I do, you'd know what that means. He'll agree. For me, he'll agree.'

'Rosie . . .' Kate hesitated. She could find no words with which to express what she was feeling for a moment. She didn't want to dissuade Rosie from coaxing William round, or disturb her in any way, but she had to express the fear that had suddenly sprung to mind. 'William wouldn't reject the baby, would he? I mean, if he doesn't really want it –'

'Oh, he does want it, Kate, he does.' Rosie clasped her fingers together in her fervency, interlinking them as though she was about to pray. 'That's not the problem at all, it's just . . .'

'Just?'

'The fact that we're lying, fabricating such a massive . . . Oh, you know.' She shook her head now, her eyes downcast. 'He's such an honest man. I mean, he doesn't even tell the ordinary sort of white lies everyone does to make life easier at times, and this . . . Well, it isn't an ordinary lie, is it.'

'No.' Kate's voice was flat and dull sounding.

'Oh, but we're grateful, Kate. Don't think for a minute we're not grateful, will you?' Rosie's eyelids blinked and she swallowed deep in her throat, her colour rising. 'I . . . We must seem awful to you, when you've come all this way just to try and help.'

'Don't be silly.' Kate sat up in bed as she spoke, brushing her hair out of her eyes and forcing a smile through the guilt that was lying like a dead weight on her chest. She should tell her, explain how things really were, but having seen William last night, she was more sure than ever that that would put the death knell on any possibility of Rosie taking the child. Rosie's next words seemed to confirm just that.

'And this girl would never know who we are? That's right, isn't it? Even if she wanted to trace us, you wouldn't say?'

'The situation wouldn't even arise, but if it did, no, I wouldn't say, Rosie. I don't expect to stay at the hospital much longer, anyway. Once I marry Hank things will change I guess, and my first year ends in the summer. I might stay on for another twelve months, but then again, I might not. We haven't really discussed it yet. Whatever happens, I can assure you that no one will want to take the baby away.'

'Oh, Kate.' Rosie sat down abruptly on the bed as though her legs had given way. 'I can't believe this is happening. You've no idea . . . When . . . when they said we wouldn't be able to have our own children it was awful, terrible, but at the back of my mind there was always adoption, it wasn't the end. And I'd never say this in front of William but the fact that it wasn't me who was at fault helped. I didn't feel . . . less of a woman, as though I'd failed, you know? I said all the right things to William, encouraged him along when he was feeling wretched, in fact, I was quite smug about how well I was coping. And then . . . then, when we heard from the adoption people,' she raised tragic eyes to Kate, 'I was filled with such rage against William. I was, Kate, and I know it's awful, wicked, but there were moments when I looked at him and really hated him. He . . . he coped so much better than me, partly, I think, because of all the reassurance I'd given him in the past, and also his faith helped, I know that.'

'Rosie –'

'I didn't want to lose him, Kate, don't think that, but . . . all the dreams and the hopes that had gone, I couldn't bear it. I just couldn't. I know people say they can't bear things and then they go on, but . . . I wouldn't have. I know that now. I would have left him.'

'*Rosie.*'

'So, thank you.' For the first time in her adult life Kate felt her sister's arms tight round her. 'I love you, Kate, and I'll never forget what you've done, never.' She was speaking into Kate's hair and then, as she hitched back a few inches, Rosie looked her full in the face, her eyes bright with unshed tears. 'Yesterday morning I was at the end of my tether, rock bottom. And today . . .' As the tears spilled over it was Kate who pulled Rosie close, stroking her sister's hair as Rosie sobbed against her shoulder.

'So you pulled it off then?'

'Yes. I pulled it off, Albert.'

'It's a dodgy road you've started down but then you know that, eh?'

'Yes, I know it.'

'Lass, lass . . .' Albert stared into the young face in front of him as he searched for words to break through the unnatural calm that had clothed Kate like a veil since she had walked through his door five minutes ago. He hadn't liked the bruised, stricken look deep in the blue eyes and the whiteness of her face then, and he liked it still less now. She was composed and quiet, oh aye, she was that, but it had the marks of shock, like the poor blighters he had seen come out of the trenches with their nerves shot to pieces. He just hoped this bloke of hers didn't let her down now, that'd put the tin lid on it as sure as eggs were eggs. 'I'm not gettin' at you, lass. Don't think that.'

'I wouldn't blame you if you were.' She didn't look at him as she spoke, her gaze directed into the grate where the dead ashes of last night's fire had spilled out onto the tiled hearth. The basement flat was damp and chilly and necessitated a fire even on the hottest summer's evening.

'I've told more lies in the last forty-eight hours than I have in the whole of my life, do you know that, Albert? And not only that, I've persuaded two more people, honest people, to start doing the same.'

'They wouldn't be doin' it if they didn't want to.'

'Oh yes, they would. At least, William would. Rosie . . . Well, apart from the fact that Rosie wants a baby so badly she'd do almost anything, she doesn't have William's conscience. He's a true academic, intellectual to a fault, you know? And aesthetic too. He has the highest principles about everything, *everything*. He resents what I've made him do, Albert, he bitterly resents it. Oh, he didn't say so, he's far too aware of Rosie's feelings to do that and anyway, he's very well-mannered, painfully so.'

'You don't like him?'

'I . . .' She raised her head now and stared at him for a moment before replying. 'I don't know. He . . . he gives me the shivers a bit, or at least he did this time, but that's probably because I sensed he was angry. I tried to talk to him about it, get him to say how he felt, but he was meticulously polite at the same time as keeping his distance.'

'Well that's better than a slangin' match, ain't it?'

'I suppose so.' She paused, nipping at her lower lip before looking away to the fireplace again. 'He reminds me of a poem, a silly poem I read when I was at school. It bothered me then and I didn't know why, I still don't really except it gives me the creeps, you know?'

Albert nodded. 'Go on then, say it.'

'I think it goes something like this, I can't remember exactly:

> Mr Max is a very good man
> A very good man is he,
> He works all day and prays all night
> And has orphans home for tea.
> He wears a suit of the finest cloth
> And his house is spick and span,
> But who are you really, Mr Max?
> What's there inside the man?'

'Well, as ditties go it ain't my cup of tea, lass, but I get your point. An' he's like that there Mr Max is he, Rosie's husband?'

'Oh, I don't know, Albert. Perhaps it's me being silly . . .' Was it really William she felt that ridiculous poem alluded to, she asked herself silently. It did, in a way, but somehow Hank was mixed up in there too, which confused her thinking still further. 'I thought I'd feel wonderful if Rosie agreed to have the baby, but . . .'

'You don't,' Albert said flatly.

'No, I don't, but it's too late to change my mind. If you'd seen Rosie . . . Anyway, there's no alternative, I know that.'

'Lass, it's up to you what you do with the bairn until the minute you hand it over, now then. Don't you be foolin' yourself on that score.'

'I wish I could believe that.' She shook her head, then on a whisper she said, 'I'm frightened, Albert, terrified, but I can't think about it. I dare not. If I do, I shan't get through.'

'Kate –'

'Look, I'll see you later. I haven't even taken my overnight case up yet.' Her voice was brisk now, with a brittle liveliness that indicated the agonizing was over, and as she rose to her feet Albert made no move to try and stop her.

'Damn it, damn it all . . .' He sat muttering to himself for some minutes after Kate had left, his head sunk down into his neck and his hands limp on the arms of the chair. He loved that little lass, oh, not in any carnal way . . . He flapped his hand at his need to justify his feelings, but in this day and age folks were always thinkin' mucky thoughts, now weren't they . . . He nodded agreement to the voice in his head. But she was the daughter he'd never had, the bairn that could have been his so alike they were in everythin' that mattered. Aye . . . She had more guts in that slender, fragile-lookin' body of hers than any of the big fellas he'd worked with in the breweries or fought alongside on the battlefields. Most of them were wind and water, and the women were worse . . . Minds like sewers and mouths to match. By, he'd met a few in his time, but Kate? Kate was different. Aye, she was different, and much good had it done her . . .

He jerked to the edge of the chair now, rising stiffly and walking over to the sideboard where he poured a measure of whisky and drank it down fast without stopping for breath. This was goin' to end bad, he knew it. He half-filled the small tumbler and took it back to his chair, sitting down with a deep sigh, his body tense. Aye, it was goin' to end bad and, damn it, hadn't he been the means of puttin' this daft idea in her head in the first place? Why couldn't he have kept his great trap shut? But who'd have thought she'd listen to his talk about Florrie Rivers and come up with such a crack-brained notion?

He cursed some more before tipping half the contents of the tumbler down his throat, but the neat alcohol couldn't dispel the chill deep inside that had started when she had first mentioned her trip to see her sister and had intensified in the last few minutes. He had had this feeling twice before. He finished the whisky as he cast his mind back to the other occasions. The first time had been that mornin' he'd woke to the sound of his best mate, Robbie Thomson, coughin' alongside him in the trench and he'd known then Robbie was goin' to buy it when they went over the top. An' he had. He flinched at the memory of how he had died, choking on his own blood, his legs blown away by a land mine. And Molly. He'd known long afore them fancy doctors had told her. Hadn't he been the one to make her see the quack even afore she felt bad? He'd known there was somethin' growin' in her, he'd been able to feel it, smell it . . .

He'd only cared about three people in his life, apart from his mam and Mike McNab: Robbie, Molly and now Kate . . . He paused in his thinking, his head tilting to one side. Was that why? Was it that which gave him this knowledge about them, love? He could damn well do without it if it was, especially this time. But perhaps he was wrong. No, he wasn't wrong. The knowledge was hard and solid in his gut. The best he could hope for was that he'd be long since gone when disaster struck 'cos he didn't think he could stand it a third time. Not with Kate. Not that bonny young lass.

CHAPTER SIX

'Albert!' It was the first week of September, she was thirty-six weeks pregnant and the baby wasn't due for another four, and she had been having contractions all night. But now Albert had appeared like magic at her front door after an endless night and Kate fell into his arms as she began to cry.

'Here, none of that, lass, none of that. Come on, now. Sit yourself down an' I'll make a cup of tea.'

'I think . . . I think I'm going to have it, Albert.'

'Aye, I think so an' all, but it's got to come out some time, lass, so it may as well be now.'

'But it's early, four weeks early. What if something's wrong –'

'You want me to take you down to the hospital?' he asked flatly.

She stared at him for a moment before shaking her head as she sank down into a chair, her hand to her mouth.

'Well then.' He had recognized the onset of hysteria and dealt with it in typical Albert fashion and now, as Kate watched the old man shuffle from the room, she felt a rush of emotion for him that brought more tears.

What would she have done without him, she asked herself as she heard him clattering about in the kitchen. It was a question that came to mind several times a day and had done over the last few weeks. She hadn't seen Hank since the beginning of July, although now he was living in Dumbarton, in a detached house on the outskirts of the town, she understood. He called her most evenings. But it was Albert who had insisted he prepare and cook her main meal each day when she returned home dog-tired from the hospital. Albert who did all her shopping, cleaned the flat and took care of her laundry when she was at work, despite her protests that she could cope. He was there when she wanted company, and didn't intrude when she needed to be alone. He was, in effect, the mother and father she had never had and she had grown to care deeply for the frail old man, and rely heavily on his friendship. And how she had needed his encouragement over the past weeks, she thought now, as he shuffled back into the small sitting room with two mugs of tea.

She wasn't sorry the baby was coming early, not really. Forcing herself each morning into the tight corset she had bought was little short of torture, and she had wondered more than once over the last few days how she could endure another four weeks or more of the same. But always, in the next breath, she reminded herself she would suffer a hundred times worse for this little being inside her. How could you love someone you had never seen? Someone who had been the result of the most humiliating and debasing incident of your life so far? But she did, oh, she did.

'Get that down you, lass.' He wished she'd spoken to one of them fancy doctor friends of hers, Albert thought grimly as he handed her the cup of tea. Or a nurse, a midwife, someone. It was all right her sayin' she was a doctor now but when them pains really started all that would go out of the window. An' what if things went wrong? Eeh, shut up, man. He felt a burst of irritation at himself as he sat down opposite Kate. Stop your whinin'. If the little lass can stand it, you damn well can.

'I've been having contractions most of the night.'

'Aye, I thought somethin' was wrong, somehow.'

'You think I ought to have this baby in hospital, don't you? You do, don't you, Albert?'

For a moment he didn't speak, then looking at her he sighed deeply. 'Lass, I'm worried about you, that's all.'

'It'll be all right, I promise.'

'Aye, aye course it will.' His voice was over loud and he lowered it a tone or two as he continued, 'Look, I'll go an' phone the hospital now, afore the day starts proper like. Tell 'em you've got a touch of that jippy belly that's about, eh? You get that tea down you an' I'll be back afore you can say Jack Robinson. You want anythin' to eat?'

'No, no thank you.' The pains were coming every five minutes now and the thought of food was nauseating.

'You just sit tight then.'

But she wasn't sitting tight when he hurried back into the flat a few minutes later, her voice filtering through from the bathroom. 'Albert? It's all right. I just had to go to the loo. I won't be a minute.'

After five minutes he was just contemplating knocking on the bathroom door when she emerged, flushed and breathless, her face frightened. 'The . . . the waters have broken, and the last contraction was very strong.'

'Right.' The effort it took to keep his voice cheerful and matter-of-fact was making him sweat. He had never felt so terrified in his life . . . He rubbed his hand across his face. He'd fought in two world wars, seen things that had put him off his fellow man for good, abominations, but he'd never known such gut-wrenching fear as he did at this moment. 'What . . . what do you want me to do, lass? Boil some water for a start?'

'Albert, you don't have to stay.' Kate crossed the room and touched his sleeve gently. 'I can manage, really. I'll be all right.'

'Don't talk such bloody rubbish.' He rarely swore in front of her and it settled the issue without another word being spoken.

By ten o'clock the contractions were every three minutes and Albert's hands were aching from rubbing Kate's back. Her stomach was as hard as a rock now and the contractions were long and fierce but bearable. 'This could go on for hours yet.' Kate had just walked through to the bedroom to lie on the bed feeling she needed a change from the sofa, and smiled at Albert who was standing in the doorway trying to look unconcerned. 'A first baby can take ages –' Another pain cut off her voice and she was panting hard when it ended, but had barely drawn breath before the next contraction hit.

'I don't want to argue, lass, seein' as you're the doctor, but I'm bringin' in the water and towels.'

She couldn't have argued anyway, the pain was excruciating now, taking over the whole of her, and there was no respite between contractions, just one long, unbearable pain that she was fighting, despite all she had read and seen on breathing exercises and procedure. And then she wanted to push. She *had* to push. Everything in her was burning to push. She tried to pant, aware it was happening too quickly and she needed to slow it down, but in the next instant she was pushing with all her might. This was all wrong, she wasn't controlling it . . . The thoughts were there but the force in her body, the overwhelming urge to expel what was tearing her apart, was too powerful.

As Albert reappeared he slid a thick bath towel beneath her, covering the immediate area with some more as she held on to the brass rail of the headboard behind her and pushed again as another contraction had her groaning. 'I can't stand it, it's killing me . . .'

'No, lass, no it ain't. You're doin' fine, just fine.'

Come on, come on. He was talking to it, willing it to be born as each contraction had her red in the face, her eyes bulging, and then, just fifteen minutes after she had started to push, Kate's daughter made her entrance into the world with a loud wah of a cry that brought her mother on to her elbows as she raised herself and stared at the tiny baby in between her legs. She was beautiful. Beautiful and perfect, with a mop of sticky, black hair and wide open eyes that stared straight into Kate's with what looked like astonishment.

'Oh, Albert, it's a girl isn't it? A little girl . . .'

'Aye.' He was crying unashamedly as he wrapped the infant in a towel and handed her to Kate, still attached to her mother by the umbilical cord.

'You're beautiful.' As Kate looked into the tiny, delicate face of her daughter, emotion constricted her throat and flooded her eyes with tears. Her baby. *Her baby.* 'So, so beautiful. And you're mine, I can't believe it.' The smoky blue eyes held hers for a moment longer, and then screwed up as the baby gave a huge yawn followed by a little whimper. For months she had felt this tiny person move inside her, they had shared a secret world that just the two of them had inhabited. Only she had known when her daughter was awake or asleep, she had felt each movement, talked to her, felt her get stronger . . . Oh, how could she give her up? . . . One minute hand was resting on top of the towel Albert had wrapped her in and Kate stared spellbound at the perfect little fingers with their diminutive nails. This was her daughter . . . Tears blinded her vision for a moment and she wiped them away with the back of her hand impatiently. She couldn't miss a second of being with her, not a second.

'She's a beauty, lass. I don't usually reckon much to babies, they all seem to look alike to me, but she's a beauty all right.'

'Albert, what am I going to do? . . .'

'Well, for starters I'll get them there instruments you've got soakin' in the kitchen, lass, so's we can do the necessary.'

'All right.'

When he returned to the bedroom the infant was at the breast, and the look on Kate's face made him swallow deeply before he could speak. 'Here we are then, an' I've put the kettle on for a cuppa –'

'I can't keep her, can I . . . What sort of a life would she have with a mother who has to work and no father?'

'Kate –'

'With Rosie, she's got everything, with me, nothing.'

'Now that ain't true –'

'To coin a phrase of yours, as near as damnit.' She made an attempt to smile through the tears coursing down her cheeks but it was beyond her. 'But I love her. I *love* her. How can I give her away?'

'It's to your sister, lass, don't forget that. You'll . . . you'll be her aunty. It ain't like mammy I know, but you'll be in her life, Kate.'

'Oh, Albert, I can't bear it . . .'

Kate phoned Rosie at ten that night to say she had heard the birth was imminent. She felt too weak physically and too emotionally drained to contemplate the journey to Cornwall that day, besides which, and she told herself it was ridiculous and childish, she wanted the birth date of her daughter to be just between the two of them, and Albert. Albert . . . She stared at him now as she put the phone down. He hadn't left her flat all day, insisting she stay in bed and fussing about her like an old hen, and he had all but carried her down the stairs to the telephone. 'Well, that's it. I'm committed.'

'I told you, you ain't committed, as you put it, till you give 'er to 'em,' he said quietly as he took her arm.

'I want the best for her.'

'I know you do, lass, I know you do.'

'If Hank would have agreed to let me keep her, to give her his name –'

'That's askin' an 'ell of a lot of any bloke –'

'Are you sticking up for him?' She shook off the hand at her elbow as they reached the landing and swung round to face him, her face hot. 'Are you? And don't fuss! I'm not ill. I could have walked up the stairs on my own.'

'All right, lass. All right.'

'Oh, I'm sorry, Albert.' As he opened her front door the tears spouted from her eyes, and but for his quick arm round her waist she would have sunk to the floor. As it was, he supported her sagging body into the sitting room and pushed her down in a chair, all the time murmuring words of comfort that he knew were no comfort at all. Eventually she stopped crying and he stopped talking and they sat in silence until a squeak from the carrycot in the bedroom brought Kate to her feet. 'I . . . I'd better change her.' The carrycot and blankets, a pack of terry nappies and three tiny babygro's were all Kate had allowed herself to buy, although her heart had ached to shop for more, and now, as she lifted the baby from her snug nest, a tiny mouth opened and yawned and a pair of very small hands clutched briefly at the air.

She was exquisite. Kate sat on the edge of the bed with her daughter in her arms and examined the sweet little face as a pair of small blue eyes, in turn, surveyed her. She really was. Most of the babies that were born at the hospital were red and blotchy, and seemed determined to stretch their faces in endless contortions at every opportunity, but she didn't seem like a new-born infant at all. 'I want you to be happy, darling,' Kate whispered, shifting along the bed and leaning back against the brass headboard as she rested the baby on her chest, her black, downy head nuzzled under Kate's chin and smelling of the baby shampoo she had washed her with earlier. 'With me you'll have an endless round of nurseries and babysitters while I work, you'll be brought up in this stinking city, you'll never breathe clean fresh air or be able to play in your own garden. There'll be no daddy to romp with, no pets, not here, just a tired mum always trying to make ends meet.' But she loved her. She loved her more than Rosie and William ever could. Didn't that sweep all the other considerations away? She wanted it to, oh, she did want it to, but . . . wanting didn't make it right.

'I'm makin' you a cup of cocoa, lass, an' then I'll leave you to settle down. I'll be back in the mornin'.' Albert's voice called from the sitting room and, a minute or two later, after a gentle knock, he shuffled in with a small tray holding a mug of cocoa and a plate of biscuits. 'Get to bed, lass. It's been a long day.'

'Thank you, Albert, thank you so much. I don't know what I'd have done without you.'

'Get along there, you'd have managed. You're a fighter, me girl, had to be to get this far, it seems to me. You'd have got by. Now, you get to sleep an' the little 'un'll let you know if she wants anythin'.'

Once Albert had gone she drank the cocoa and ate two biscuits, the baby asleep in her arms. Just as she finished the last mouthful she awoke, snuffling against Kate's breasts as her rosebud mouth drew in her cheeks in a sucking motion. Water and glucose. She had made the decision to give her water and glucose weeks ago to avoid forming any attachment and already she had fed her at the breast twice. But the colostrum was good for her, providing antibodies . . .

'Don't fool yourself.' She spoke out loud into the quiet room. 'You *want* to feed her, you want her to need you . . .' It was natural wasn't it? The inevitable outcome of nine months, or eight in her case, of nourishing and protecting her child. But she couldn't afford the luxury of any natural feelings . . . Nevertheless, she drew her blouse aside, lowered the lace cup beneath her breast and offered it to the searching mouth.

The baby slept most of the night and the next day but Kate felt too exhausted to make the drive down to Devon. She had decided months ago that to travel by train was too risky. In a village as small as the one she had been brought up in even the walls had eyes and ears and her arrival had to be unnoticed. She had approached a hire firm, arranged the future loan of a car, and intended to make the journey at night, but she hadn't allowed for just how tired she felt. Added to which every minute, every second, alone with her child was precious.

But on the morning of the second day, as she held the baby close after another restful night and felt an overwhelming sense of love and tenderness flood her soul, she knew she had to go. Another day, another half day, and she wouldn't be able to give her up. She made the call to the hire firm as soon as the office opened and, after leaving Albert in charge of the sleeping baby, collected the car and drove it to the house.

'I don't like this.' Albert followed her about the flat like an old woman as she gathered what she would need for the journey and an overnight stay. 'You ain't drove a car regular like since you passed your test, an' the roads'll be busy this time of day. Why can't you wait till evenin' if you insist on goin'?'

'I'll be all right.'

'Huh! If I had a shillin' for every time I've heard that in me life an' then someone's come a cropper I'd be rich by now.'

'Shillings went out in 1971 with decimalization.'

'An' you needn't try an' be clever, I don't like this, I'm tellin' you.'

'I'm not trying to be clever, Albert. I . . . I have to go, that's all.'

He opened his mouth, glanced at her face, and shut it again.

Kate had parked the car directly opposite the front door and, after she had made sure the coast was clear, Albert emerged like lightning with the carrycot and deposited it on the back seat, as Kate slid into the front of the vehicle. 'What'll I say to this fella of yours if he phones?' Albert asked a moment later as he poked his head into her open window. 'I can't say what I've said the last two nights, that you're sick.'

'Why not?' She stared at him, her eyes hard. 'He didn't exactly come running round to see what was wrong, did he?'

'Is that what you wanted him to do?' Albert asked shrewdly.

'No.' But she flushed scarlet and Albert's eyes narrowed. That's what she'd got in mind as sure as eggs were eggs. If he knew anythin' about this lass she'd hoped that big galoot of an American of hers would have high-tailed it round here and then she'd have presented him, all casual like, with the bairn. By, no wonder it was Eve that'd offered Adam the apple and not the other way round. Even the best of 'em had more sides than one of these new fifty pence pieces and Kate was the best. Aye, she was that. His face softened as she reached out a hand and touched one of his gently. 'I'll see you tomorrow, Albert. I shall just stay overnight with Rosie.'

'You ought to stay a day or two after what you've been through, all that an' then this drivin' –'

'I can't.' She raised limpid eyes to his. 'I can't see her with them, not for long.'

'No, course you can't, lass. I ain't thinkin' straight, am I. But it's a long old journey, you're goin' from one end of the country to the other. Now, you promise me, if you need to hole up somewhere overnight you'll do it. Don't push yourself beyond what you're able. There's the bairn to think about an' you need your wits about you on the roads these days.'

'I know, really. I won't take any chances.'

The baby slept for the first three hours and when she woke Kate stopped for something to eat, feeding and changing her at the same time. She took the opportunity to call Rosie – she had tried earlier before she left Glasgow but had been unable to get through. This time, however, her sister's voice answered immediately and they exchanged a few brief words, Kate giving her a rough indication of when she would reach the village before she made an excuse to finish the call. Rosie had been unable to hide her excitement and she had resented it, bitterly, at the same time as telling herself she was being wickedly unfair.

She reached Breadale long after dark but the September night was warm and balmy, and she stopped just before she reached the village to wind up the windows in the car. She couldn't risk the baby crying when she drew up outside Rosie's house, although she had slept like an angel all the way, only stirring and making her presence known when she had needed feeding and changing. Kate glanced across at the unused bottles of glucose and water she had brought with her. She had given her the breast each time but now that would have to stop, even as her body was telling her it was preparing itself to provide nourishment. Already her breasts were aching and full but that was her fault, she acknowledged silently. In giving the baby what she had needed she had stimulated the milk flow. But it was little enough when she was going to abandon her –

'*Stop it, Kate.*' She cut ruthlessly across her thoughts, her voice loud and harsh in the slumberous warmth inside the car. 'You're tired, and you're not thinking straight, and you'll get through the next twenty-four hours as best you can. *You will.* If you can't keep her then you'll give her the very best life you can. You owe her that at least.' And she was as innocent as the sleeping child in this thing that had befallen her . . . The thought lifted her eyes to the carrycot and her mouth was soft as the tears trickled from her eyes. Two innocents in a world that was anything but. If she could think like that, just keep on thinking like that, she might get through without hating herself more than she did at this moment.

Because at this moment, *at this moment*, she wanted to die.

PART TWO

A Time to be Silent

Chapter Seven

'Correct me if I'm wrong, lass, but I thought it was a weddin' I was attendin' this mornin' an' not a funeral?'

'Oh, Albert, what am I doing? What am I *doing*?' As Kate threw the front door of the flat wide open to allow Albert entry, her voice was a low wail. 'I don't want to get married to Hank, I don't want to get married to *anybody*. I want . . .' She bit tightly on her lower lip as a rush of emotion constricted her throat, preventing further speech.

'Now come on, lass, none of that.'

'I can't help it. I've tried . . . I *have* tried to be sensible and logical, but I keep thinking about her. All the time I think about her, Albert.'

'I know, lass. I know.'

'You *don't*. How could you? Oh, I'm not getting at you, Albert, really, but you don't know. No one could. I should never have parted with her, I know that now. It gets worse, not better. If it wasn't for the fact that it would break Rosie's heart and cause untold trouble all round, I'd go and snatch her back.' She stared at him fiercely. 'I would. I mean it.'

'I know you do, lass.' Albert swallowed deeply and wetted his lips. 'But it's early days yet, now then. You haven't given yourself a chance to let the dust settle, you need time –'

'I *need* my daughter.' They were standing in the middle of the sitting room now, and although the small gas fire was full on, the air was distinctly chilly from the raw November day outside.

'Look, this is weddin' nerves, pure and simple, an' I blame that fella of yours. He should never have rushed you the way he has. He knows you're goin' through a rough patch, he should have stood back a pace.' Aye, but he knew why Hank hadn't, Albert thought grimly, watching Kate press a hand hard across her mouth as she sank into a chair. The lass was all mixed up at the moment and hurtin' bad. Aye, she was that. And rightly or wrongly she felt her big American had let her down. Not that she'd said as much but the feelin' was there, he knew it. And so did Hank, he'd be bound. And that was why the big fella was anxious to get that ring on her finger, arrangin' things at the registry office and bulldozin' the lass along. But perhaps it was for the best. His thoughts wrinkled his creased brow still more but then, as Kate glanced up, he forced a quick smile to his face, speaking out his train of thought. 'Perhaps it's for the best, lass, you gettin' wed now. You need to put the past behind you an' look to the future, make a fresh start –'

'Albert . . .' Her tone of voice cut off his words like a knife and she drew in a deep breath before continuing, 'I know you mean well and I'm behaving badly, I'm sorry. It's just that . . . Oh, you know what it is and all the talking in the world won't change things now. I've made my bed and I've got to lie on it, isn't that how the saying goes?'

'Lass, lass.'

'And I can see her sometimes, can't I. At least I have that. Albert? –' She paused abruptly and looked him full in the face. 'Do you like Hank?'

He stared at her for a few seconds and then blinked rapidly. 'Like him? It don't much matter if I like him or not, now does it, lass? Any road, I don't know the fella. I've not spoken to him above once or twice.'

'You don't, do you?' His evasiveness was all the reply she needed. Albert had a definite opinion about everything from the price of butter to the Pope, and wasn't shy about making his feelings known. 'I know you don't.'

'Then you know more'n me.'

He wasn't going to be drawn and their eyes held for a few moments more before Kate rose to her feet, indicating the beautifully cut, calf-length dress and matching jacket she was wearing in pale lemon. 'You haven't said how I look,' she said with forced brightness.

'You look bonny, lass, right bonny,' he said softly. 'He's a lucky so-an'-so, an' no mistake.'

Kate smiled but said nothing as she walked across to the mirror on the far side of the room and smoothed her cap of honey-blonde hair into place. Bonny. Oh, she hoped she did look bonny. She was going to need every little bit of courage she possessed to get through this day. The feeling that she shouldn't be marrying Hank had intensified to such a point in the last twenty-four hours that it was making her physically sick, added to which she had to run the gauntlet of meeting his mother and the rest of his family from America for the first time.

She shut her eyes tight for a second and then opened them to stare back at her reflection. But the main thing that had her blood surging and ebbing in great waves and was making her legs weak was the thought of seeing Joy again. Joy, her daughter. She breathed deeply and swung round to face Albert. 'Shall we have a cup of coffee?' she asked quietly.

'Aye, lass, if you want.'

If she had suggested a cup of arsenic he would have agreed with her today, she thought fondly, as love for the irascible old man brought tears to the backs of her eyes. What would she have done without him over the last few months? She couldn't even begin to imagine how she would have got through.

'What time is your sister gettin' here?' Albert asked, following her into the tiny kitchen and watching her spoon coffee and sugar into two mugs before switching on the kettle.

'Any time now. They did most of the journey yesterday and stayed overnight in a hotel about an hour's drive away. Rosie was worried how the journey was going to affect Joy.' Joy. The name was a subtle mockery to her agony of mind.

'Joy Kate.' Rosie's face had been beaming when Kate had left the vicarage the morning after she had arrived. 'That's what we're going to call her, Joy Kate. Joy, because I know she's going to bring so much of that to us, and Kate after you.' She had been cuddling the sleeping baby close to her breast as she had spoken, and Kate had felt something akin to a sword pierce her heart as she had looked at them both. 'I do wish you'd stay for a day or two, Kate. You look tired, you've been working too hard.'

'Comes with the territory.' Kate had almost fallen down the steps outside in her haste to escape, and by the time she had started the car William had joined his wife on the threshold, standing with his arm round her shoulders as Rosie had cradled the baby close. The perfect family.

She never did know how she managed to get home without an accident. In between the bursts of frantic weeping, the painful ache in her swollen taut breasts was a constant reminder she had made the worst mistake of her life. And she had, she knew it. She should have done anything, sacrificed herself, her career, Hank, to keep her child with her. She couldn't bear it, she wanted to die, she would die . . .

She was sobbing desperately as she stumbled through the front door of the house later that night, and Albert was there in the hall like a shot. He took one look at her ravaged face before taking control, leading her into his flat and making her a drink of something that tasted disgusting, and standing over her until she finished every drop. 'It'll help you sleep.' The bitter tang on her tongue told her it was some kind of sleeping draught, but she didn't care, she would have welcomed something to help her sleep forever at that point.

He had helped her to her flat and remained there for the next three days, apart from going home to feed the cats while she slept, and at the end of that time, which forever remained a blur of hysterical weeping, wild dreams and the constant bitter taste in her mouth from Albert's concoctions, she had woken one morning knowing she had to face life again. Face the fact that she must learn to live with the knowledge that part of her was torn away, that she would never be truly happy again, that she would always have a sweet little face printed on her consciousness day and night . . .

'You all right, lass?' Albert's voice just behind her reminded her the kettle had boiled, and her back straightened as she nodded silently.

Rosie arrived just before eleven and Kate felt as though her heart was being squeezed in a vice as she watched William manipulate the carrycot through the flat's narrow front door. 'Oh, you look beautiful, Kate, doesn't she, William?' Rosie's gushing voice barely registered, all of Kate's being was centred on the squeaks and rustlings from within the carrycot's quilted depths, and it was only when Albert took her arm and pressed it in unspoken warning that she managed to speak.

'Thank you.' She smiled at her sister after tearing her eyes away from the carrycot, but as her gaze moved to encompass William she saw her brother-in-law's eyes were narrowed on her face, and something in his glance caused her to start gabbling nervously. 'Did you have a good journey? Where did you stay last night? How has the baby been? Is everything all right?'

'Kate, Kate . . .' Rosie was laughing as she gave her sister a hug. 'I know it's your big day but calm down, you won't be in a fit state to enjoy it if you get so worked up, will she, William?'

'Possibly not.' William continued to look at her for a few moments more. 'Where would you like the carrycot put, Kate?'

'Oh . . . here, in front of the fire on top of the coffee table would be best.' He suspected something. For some reason he suspected something, she knew it. But he didn't *know*, he couldn't know, so all she had to do was to keep calm and think before she spoke. But did she want to? The thought brought her spinning round and she walked quickly into the kitchen, calling over her shoulder as she went. 'Coffee? We've time before the cars come at half-past, and I'm sure you could do with one.'

'You shouldn't be doing that in your wedding clothes.' Rosie's voice was scandalized as she joined Kate in the kitchen. 'What if you spill something down the front of your jacket? Let me do it.'

'No, it's all right, really.' Kate managed a smile as she turned to face her sister, but panic was uppermost and she fought against letting it show. 'I've been ready since nine and I haven't dirtied my bib yet.'

'Oh, you . . .' Rosie giggled, pushing against Kate with her shoulder before catching her hand. 'Come and see Joy, Kate, she's beautiful and so good. She's been going through the night now for two weeks.'

'Has she?' Talk normally. Communicate. You can't do anything else now. Act the fond aunty . . . She followed Rosie out of the kitchen in obedience to the last command, and as her sister drew the tiny quilt and blankets aside and reached into the carrycot, Kate found she was holding her breath. And then she was looking into her daughter's face, that dear, dear little face . . .

'I won't suggest you hold her with all your finery on.'

'Oh don't be silly, that doesn't matter.' Kate held out her arms and, after a moment's hesitation and with a laughing, 'don't say I didn't warn you', Rosie placed the baby into them. She was so beautiful and so tiny, so tiny . . . Kate knew she was going to cry and there wasn't a thing she could do about it, in spite of William's eyes tight on her face. Joy smelt of baby powder and the warm, milky fragrance that was common to all babies, and as Kate stared down enraptured into the minute features, Joy opened her mouth and yawned before rubbing her tiny fists across her eyes. 'She's sleepy . . .'

'She's always sleepy. I told you, she's so good we can't believe our luck,' Rosie said softly, and then, 'Kate? You're not crying, are you?'

'Silly, isn't it, but I feel so emotional today.' Any questions, any questions at all, and she would blurt it all out, she thought frantically. It was there, hovering on her tongue . . .

'It's your weddin' day, lass, you're allowed a little emotion.' As Albert cut stolidly into the conversation he rose from the easy chair where he was sitting and moved to their side, looking down at the baby in Kate's arms with a little nod of his head. 'Aye, you're right, William.' He turned back for an instant and smiled at Rosie's husband. 'She's a beauty, a real grand little lass. You're goin' to be hard put not to spoil her.' He met Kate's eyes then and his voice changed, becoming almost flat. 'William here was just tellin' me he reckons the bairn'll knock 'em dead when she's a few years older.'

'Well, I didn't put it quite like that.' It was unusual for William to make any attempt at humour and as Albert chuckled, making a deprecatory comment against himself, Kate stared at the old man for a moment before lowering her eyes back to the child in her arms. He'd done that on purpose, defused a potentially explosive moment, because he had sensed how near she was to telling Rosie and William the truth. And she resented it, bitterly. Oh . . . She clenched her teeth together as she kept her gaze fixed on the baby, who appeared to be sleeping soundly now. What did that make her? What sort of monster did it make her? She was being selfish and unfair, she knew she was, but somehow the world seemed to have narrowed down to the child in her arms, nothing else mattered.

'It's nearly half-past, lass. I reckon you'd best forget about that coffee an' put the bairn back in her bed, the cars'll be here any time now.' Albert touched her arm gently and she obeyed automatically, her face stiff with the effort it was taking to remain in control.

The next half hour seemed interminable and yet, as the car drew up outside the town hall, it seemed to have gone like a flash. 'Albert?' She clutched frantically at his arm, her face distraught, as she noticed Hank in the distance surrounded by a group of strangers who were undoubtedly his family. 'I can't go through with this, it's all wrong.'

'If you mean that, really mean it, give me the nod an' I'll have the car turn round this minute, lass. But you'd better be sure, 'cos there'll be all 'ell let loose after.'

'I . . . I've got no choice, have I.'

'Aye, you've got a choice, lass, course you've got a choice.' He pursed his lips and jerked his chin upwards before continuing, 'But I can't help you make it, lass, no one can. All I can say, an' I don't know if it'll help or hinder, is that in my book it wouldn't be right to go back on what you decided as regards to the bairn. But you were right about one thing, lass, I ain't over-keen on your intended now I've seen a bit of him. Nothin' I can put me finger on, mind, an' he might be a good bloke for all I know, but . . . I ain't keen.'

'I thought you weren't.' They sat staring at each other for a moment but when, in the next instant, Rosie appeared from the car behind and opened the car door with an exaggerated flourish, Kate swung her legs onto the pavement and faced the approaching group, Albert's hand pressing reassuringly at her elbow a second or two later as he joined her.

'Kate, sweetheart . . .' Hank was smiling as he reached them but his eyes were strained. 'I'm sorry about the meal last night, but you understand Mother's plane was delayed?'

'Yes, of course, it's perfectly all right. I had plenty to do, so the time wasn't wasted.' In actual fact, the last-minute phone call from Hank the night before explaining that the flight from America had been two hours late that afternoon, and consequently his mother felt too exhausted to go out that night and, of course, Kate understood he *had* to stay with her, had greatly added to her panic and confusion. The whole tenor of the conversation had been strange, Kate had felt, with something dark bubbling just below the surface, and her fiancé hadn't sounded like himself at all. Hank had booked a table for six at the hotel in which his parents and two brothers were staying so that Kate could meet them all before the ceremony the next day, and it seemed ridiculous his mother couldn't make the journey from her suite to the dining room without undue stress.

However, she had bitten her tongue and kept her thoughts to herself in deference to Hank's feelings, merely expressing polite regret, but now, as she glanced over Hank's shoulder and met the hard, calculating eyes of the large, square-faced woman behind him, she wondered if it had been the right tack to take.

'This is Kate, everyone.' Hank took her other elbow as he turned to face his family, so Kate was standing between her fiancé's broad bulk and Albert's scrawny frame, with Rosie, and William who was holding Joy, to the other side of Albert, and just for a moment she felt it was like the confrontation of two opposing armies as she let her eyes sweep across the faces in front of her.

'Kate.' If the word had been a profanity it couldn't have carried less warmth. 'How do you do?'

'This is Mother, Kate,' Hank cut in before she had a chance to respond to his mother's cool greeting, his words tumbling over themselves. 'And Father, Dean, Edward . . .' The three big men who were standing just behind his mother nodded quietly, their faces wary but not unfriendly. 'And Uncle Brad, Aunt Caroline,' and so it continued for a few moments more.

When the introductions came to a halt, Kate's face felt stiff with smiling, but she murmured a general 'I'm very pleased to meet you', before gesturing at Albert, and Rosie and William, on either side of her. 'This is my sister and brother-in-law, and –'

'Yes, yes.' Miriam Ross cut across Kate's voice as she

inclined her head sharply. 'We won't go into all that now, it's too cold to stand socializing out here. Come into the building, everyone.'

As the American contingent turned, seemingly connected to each other by one controlling wire, Kate stood with her mouth half open in a state of absolute shock at the other woman's unmitigated rudeness. And then Hank sprang forward to take his mother's arm, turning after a few steps to signal for Kate to follow them.

'What a perfectly *dreadful* woman.' Rosie was shaking with outrage as they still all stood as one by the car. 'I don't believe she just did that, Kate. How dare she –'

'Rosie.' William's tone was one of quiet warning as he nodded at Kate's white face.

'But, William, how dare she think she can get away with that? I'd like to –'

'*Rosie.*' It was rare for William to raise his voice, and Rosie bit down on her lower lip as he continued, 'you aren't helping matters, so just leave it, my dear. Now, if we're all ready? . . .'

'You all right, lass?'

'No, Albert,' Kate replied truthfully as Rosie and William busied themselves getting the carrycot and wheels out of the hired car, Rosie's face a picture of indignation. 'Far from it, actually.'

'She's a tartar, lass, an' no mistake,' Albert said quietly, as they watched the party in front pause at the bottom of the town hall steps. 'You're goin' to have your work cut out with that one.'

'Then I might as well start as I mean to carry on.' She leant against the old man for a moment before straightening and taking a deep breath. 'This is my wedding day, *mine*, that's right, isn't it?'

'Aye, lass, dead right.'

'Come on, then.' She turned to Rosie and William now as they joined them, William pushing the carrycot. 'I'm sorry Hank's mother was so discourteous, Rosie –' she included William in her glance – 'I had no idea she would behave in that fashion.'

'It's not your fault, Kate.' Rosie was clearly dying to say more, but William's presence forbade it. Instead she contented herself with a long, narrow-eyed stare at the group on the steps, before lifting her chin in a haughty sweep as she turned away.

'There's someone tryin' to get your attention, lass.' Kate noticed James and Liz, with Susan and Adam just behind them, at the same moment Albert spoke, and the next second she was enfolded in Liz's perfumed embrace.

'You look beautiful, Kate, absolutely beautiful.' Liz hugged her close for a few moments before standing back and smiling up into Kate's face. 'We're a bit late, I'm sorry, James couldn't get a parking space. And you must be Rosie?' Liz's sweet smile did much to restore harmonious relations. 'It's lovely to meet you.'

And so it was that Kate entered the town hall encircled and enclosed by a laughing, merry throng, that opened to include Hank as he moved to join them, and closed immediately until the bridal pair were seated at the front of the room where the ceremony was to take place.

The service was short and to the point, and Kate couldn't believe she was a married woman at the end of it, Hank's brief peck on the cheek in response to 'You may kiss the bride' doing little to convince her that she wasn't dreaming it all. The small reception, for family and a handful of close friends, was booked at the same hotel where Hank's family was staying, and as they turned to face everyone with the registrar's 'I now pronounce you man and wife' ringing in her ears, Kate wished it was all over.

Once outside the building again the icy northern air made Kate gasp after the warm central heating, but the sky was clear and blue and a weak, watery sunshine gave the illusion of warmth, so when James, who had pronounced himself official photographer, began marshalling the wedding group together, everyone seemed happy to oblige.

'Liz, where's John?' It was only as James drew them into position that Kate realized John was missing, but even as she asked the question she felt Hank's hand tighten painfully on her arm and his muttered 'Leave it, will you?' brought her head swinging up to meet his gaze.

'Work pressure, I'm afraid, Kate.' She heard Liz's reply just behind her and acknowledged it with a bob of her head, but her eyes didn't leave Hank's face. There was a look on his face . . . She couldn't rightly explain it even to herself but it had the effect of making her want to put out a hand and smooth the lines at the side of his mouth, to comfort him in some way. Something was troubling him . . . But then his mother's voice, loud and authoritative, sliced into the moment.

'I really don't think there is any need to take any photographs here, James, it isn't exactly the most picturesque of settings, is it? Now, if it had been one of those pretty English churches . . . But there it is, what is done is done.' This was followed by a loud, disapproving sniff. 'I understand the hotel has a nice little garden area –'

'I would like several photographs here first before we leave.' As his mother had spoken, Kate had been incensed to feel Hank's hand slip from her arm as he prepared to move, and the knowledge that he had been about to obey his mother's command without question, and with no consideration of her wishes on the matter, made her voice sharp. 'Then we can take some more at the hotel, okay, Hank?'

'What? Oh, right. Well, if that is what you want . . .'

'It is.' Kate partly turned slipping her arm through Hank's, and her tone was pleasant as she spoke to the group clustered behind them. 'We'll take six or seven photographs here before moving to the hotel, all right, everyone? Now, you tell us how you want us, James.'

'Certainly.' There was a grin on Hank's cousin's face

that was clearly on the point of spreading into laughter, and his eyes were twinkling as they met hers. 'For the first one we'll keep everyone tiered on the three steps behind you, so don't move, anyone . . .'

'One all.' Albert moved to her side for the next photograph and his whisper was gleeful. 'Start as you mean to carry on, eh, lass?'

Miriam Ross maintained a grim silence for the rest of the photographs, her face set and rigid and her eyes lethal as she stared back into the camera for each shot. Kate was aware of Hank's anxious glances at his mother, and this fact alone kept her chin up and her back straight as she forced herself to smile, her thoughts racing behind the outwardly calm façade. What on earth had she let herself in for? Hank's mother was like some dreadful caricature of every mother-in-law joke she had ever heard, and *Hank* . . . Where was the man she had known for the last twelve months? He had metamorphosed into the kind of male she – her mind wouldn't let her say despised and substituted disliked.

And over and above everything, even while she was talking and smiling and acting the happy bride, she was vitally aware of every single movement the little pink bundle in William's arms made. The gnawing emptiness, the sheer horror at the finality of what she had done, it was there. Every minute. Every second. Joy . . . Oh, Joy . . .

'About time.' Miriam's acid tones were an immediate response to James's 'All done for now, thanks folks', and a few moments later Kate was sitting by Hank's side in the car, waving to the others through the window as it sped away towards the hotel.

She waited for him to reach for her, to say something, anything, to dispel the tension between them. His mother's behaviour wasn't his fault, she had to remember that, she told herself firmly. Besides which, and here she heaved a deep sigh of relief, with the Atlantic between them her visits to their home would be severely curtailed.

Miriam Ross was clearly an assertive, overbearing type of woman and a dominant mother, but she had heard American women were more forceful than their English counterparts, so perhaps it was just that. And Hank was the youngest son, the baby of the family; such late arrivals were often spoilt before they left the nest, but once he was away from Miriam he'd see he had to stand up to her. Of course he would . . .

She nipped at her lip as her thoughts whirled on. Who was she to expect perfection anyway, with a secret like she had? Things would work out, now they were together properly, man and wife. She jumped as she was pulled out of her thoughts by Hank touching her cheek gently. 'It went off well, don't you think?'

No, no it was awful. She wanted to tell him what she really felt but her musing had mellowed the initial hurt and anger and so now she smiled, her voice holding a determinedly bright note as she said, 'Yes, not too bad.'

'It was good of James to offer to pay for the reception.'

'He's very kind, they both are.' What were they doing sitting here talking about James and Liz when they had just got married, she asked herself helplessly. Shouldn't he kiss her, cuddle her, draw her against him at least? Display some kind of . . . oh, excitement, enthusiasm?

'Hank?' She stopped and then rushed on quickly before she lost her nerve. 'You *are* glad we're married, aren't you? You're not having second thoughts? Regretting it?'

She wanted to remind him that he had talked of nothing else but their wedding for the last two months since she had rung, a few days after arriving back in Glasgow after leaving Joy with Rosie, and told him she was free to see him again. He had arrived at the flat an hour after her phone call, his arms full of flowers and his face smiling, and hadn't left until she had agreed a date some weeks away, brushing aside all her murmurs that they should wait a while.

He hadn't asked about the baby, hadn't acknowledged

its existence in even the most obtuse way, it was as if the last few months had been completely erased from his memory. And when she had tried to talk about it, both that night and in the days that followed, he had parried every attempt until she was forced to admit defeat. She didn't understand him . . .

'Regretting it?' The expression on his face was one she hadn't seen before and couldn't quite place, even to herself, but it held a kind of defensive wariness among other things, and caused her hands to tighten in her lap. 'Don't be silly, sugar, why should I be doing that?'

'I don't know.' Her heart began to thump when he continued to look at her without saying any more. She didn't know what had made her ask the question in the first place, but now . . . Now she felt something was amiss. Had he met someone else in the time they hadn't been seeing each other? But no, that was ridiculous. If that was the case there had been no logic in his insistence of a quick wedding, none at all, and he *had* been insistent, doggedly so. Perhaps he was angry with her because she had dared to take a stand with his mother? Was that it? She drew in a long, steadying breath and then let it out slowly before saying, 'Are you vexed because of the photographs?'

'The photographs?' The surprise in his voice was genuine. 'Kate –' He stopped abruptly and paused for a moment before continuing, 'don't make problems where none exist, everything is fine, I've told you. Look, we're at the hotel and if I'm not mistaken that's James outside. The guy's a maniac, he must have driven like the devil to get here before us.'

She followed his glance to where James and Liz were standing, arm-in-arm and pressed close together on the pavement, and the sight of them hurt her. There arose in her a bewildering feeling of confusion and panic, similar to that which she had been experiencing over the last few days but stronger this time, and it took all the willpower she possessed to climb out of the car and meet their smiling faces.

The rest of the photographs were taken in a sheltered part of the hotel garden, and although Hank's mother made her presence felt in a number of ways during the short time it took to finish, Kate said nothing more. The whole day was taking on the semblance of a dream, and Kate found she was doubting herself more and more with every minute that passed, her instincts, her feelings, her common sense. Perhaps she was imagining Hank's . . . well, you couldn't call it coolness exactly, but more a strange kind of detachment, she thought wearily. She must be, no one else seemed to have noticed anything was amiss, not even Albert. It would be better when they were alone, when the day was over and they could relax, just the two of them. The thought brought the sense of panic into her chest again and she thrust it away before it could develop further. She wasn't looking forward to her wedding night. The brief, very brief, encounter with Richard Wellington that had produced Joy nine months later had been both painful and shocking, and although she had told herself it would be different with Hank, the man she loved, her *husband*, that other time was at the forefront of her mind and she was afraid.

Once the guests were assembled in the large, pleasantly furnished reception room where the informal buffet was to take place, Kate found herself beginning to relax a little. Her bouquet of white and yellow roses was placed next to the sculptured, three-tiered wedding cake, and she felt less on show now it was gone, and once the meal and the brief speeches by Hank and James, his best man, were over, everyone began to mingle. Hank, too, seemed to be more like his old self as they circulated, his arm round her waist and his manner jovial as they chatted to first one guest, then another.

Kate had tried several times, first as they were leaving the town hall and then as the photographs were being taken in the hotel garden, to strike up a conversation with

Hank's mother, but each time the older woman had avoided her. So now, as she saw the large, heavy-set American woman approaching, with the equally bulky male members of her family flanking her sides, she felt a moment's disquiet. Miriam Ross could be described as a handsome woman but not a feminine one, although that had less to do with her generous figure and height than the intimidating, almost menacing air of authority that exuded from her imposing frame. There was scarcely a touch of grey in the strong, virile brown hair that glowed with health, and the face below it was big-boned but attractive, the dark brown eyes penetrating and observant. All in all, she looked a good ten years younger than her sixty-two years, Kate thought, and her air of vigour would have sat well on a woman half her age.

'You understand, of course, that this whole affair was something of a surprise to Hank's family?'

Kate stared back at the formidable woman in front of her but couldn't speak. She was aware of Hank stiffening at her side, and Albert, on the perimeter of her vision, drawing closer, but the naked hostility in both Miriam's voice and manner had frozen her thought process.

'Well? What have you got to say for yourself?'

'Mother –'

'Be quiet, Hank.' As the hard brown eyes left her face for a moment to slice into that of her son's, Albert reached their side, and his presence gave her the courage she needed to reply.

'I'm sorry, Mrs Ross, but what exactly are you trying to say?' Kate's voice was cool and controlled and it surprised her, considering how she was feeling inside. It was evident that it surprised the elder Mrs Ross too, because her eyes narrowed for a moment and when she next spoke her voice was lower, deeper, but all the more ominous for its quietness.

'I'm asking you how you persuaded this son of mine to marry you so fast, is that plain enough for you?'

'We have been engaged for nearly a year, I would hardly term that fast.' She was aware that Hank, after his mother's admonition, was making no attempt to come to her aid, and although part of her was finding it difficult to believe the confrontation was taking place, another part of her was consumed with rage at the older woman's audacity and her husband's acquiescence.

'Then there is no . . . reason for this hasty marriage?' As she spoke, Miriam allowed her eyes to wander insolently across Kate's stomach, her meaning crystal-clear to everyone within earshot, and just for a moment, as her face flamed, Kate wondered if the older woman knew. But she couldn't know, of course she couldn't, her innuendo made that clear in itself. No, Miriam was insinuating she was pregnant with Hank's child and in that, at least, she was innocent.

'Mrs Ross, if you are asking me if your son and I have been intimate, then I think that is both impertinent and ill-mannered, don't you?' Kate replied levelly. 'Besides which, it is none of your business –'

'*None of my business*?' Miriam's voice was a low hiss now, her face flushed with heavy colour. 'He's my *son*, everything he does is my business.'

'He's twenty-five years old –'

'That has nothing to do with it.'

'Nothing to do with it?' Was Hank's mother crazy? Kate asked herself silently as she felt her grasp on reality begin to fade. 'He's a grown man, for goodness' sake. Look, I don't want to quarrel with you, but I really think you have misunderstood the situation.'

'Then that makes two of us, because if you think you are going to get a dime of my family's money by marrying Hank you are very much mistaken.' Miriam's voice had dropped to little more than a whisper now but it had the effect of a trickle of acid on bare skin to those listening, such was the depth of its ferocity.

Hank's 'Mother!', along with Albert's sharp intake of

breath, barely registered on Kate's senses as she stared back into the maddened eyes of the woman in front of her, and indeed, at that moment, Miriam Ross didn't look quite sane.

'Don't "Mother" me! I told you what I would do last night if you went through with this ridiculous whim.' Miriam's face was thrust close to her son's now, her eyes venomous as she glared into his white features, and it was a full ten seconds before Kate realized Hank wasn't going to say another word. 'She's a slut, they're all sluts, I've told you often enough, haven't I? Haven't I?'

'Aye, I don't doubt you've filled the lad's head with such poison.' Such was Kate's horror at the scene unfolding in front of her that she had completely forgotten Albert's presence at her side, but now, as the old man stepped forward a pace, she tried to pull him back, only to have her hand pushed roughly away. 'You're a queer 'un, an' no mistake. One of them that can't abide their sons leavin' the breast, eh? Well, I'll tell you this, you ought to be down on your knees thankin' the Almighty that your son has found himself a good lass, you know what I'm sayin'? So think on, missus, think on. An' while you're contemplatin', spare a thought for those poor devils at the side of you, 'cos you've castrated them as sure as if you'd cut off their –'

'*Albert.*' Kate's agonized whisper pulled the old man up short, but time hung suspended for long moments before anyone moved, and then it was Miriam Ross, her face scarlet with outrage, who swung round and left the room, her husband and two sons trailing in her wake, still without saying a word.

CHAPTER EIGHT

'I don't believe I'm hearing this.'

'No? How do you expect me to react then? Give that dirty old guy a cheer and thank him for insulting my mother the way he did?'

'And what about me? What about the way *she* insulted *me*? Albert was only sticking up for me, which was exactly what you should have been doing.'

'Don't be so dumb! The best way to defuse a situation like that is to say as little as possible. Mother was . . . upset, it's natural, isn't it? This has all been one hell of a surprise to her.'

'*Natural?*'

It was the evening of their wedding day, and as Kate faced Hank across the bed in their hotel room she was feeling almost numb. Once Hank's parents and brothers had left the reception, leaving a deathly hush behind them until the murmur of voices had politely tried to fill the tension-packed atmosphere, she had stitched a smile on her face and forced herself to act as though the fact that her mother-in-law of two hours had called her a slut and a gold-digger was the sort of thing that could happen at any wedding. Exactly how much the other guests had heard she wasn't sure – fortunately Rosie and William had been getting Joy off to sleep in an adjoining room at the time of the incident and by the time they returned it was all over – but from the covert glances and hushed conversation a certain amount of Miriam's poison had filtered through. But it was Hank's attitude that had upset her the most. He had barely talked to her for the rest of the afternoon and had ignored Albert totally, his whole manner one of suppressed rage, which had done little to lighten the general mood of strained embarrassment.

Suddenly, the humiliation she had endured for endless hours swept over Kate with renewed intensity, shattering the torpor her senses had taken refuge in, and she strained towards Hank across the bed, her hands flat on the counterpane as she hissed his word back at him. 'Natural, you say? I don't think there is anything natural about your mother, Hank, anything at all, and you expect me to have nothing more to do with Albert simply because he faced up to her?'

'That is not what I said.' Hank's face was a turkey-red and he had never looked less attractive. 'I just don't want you associating with someone whose mind is at sewer level, that's all.'

'And your mother? What about her mind?' Kate yelled, all restraint gone. 'Don't you care about the things she said, what she called me? How could you stand there and let her get away with it, anyway, what sort of man are you?'

'She's my mother!'

'And I'm your wife.' She slowly straightened, and now her words were slow and weighty and without heat. 'Don't you understand what we did today, Hank? We joined our lives together in the sight of God and to me that means for life. You are my husband, I'm your wife, we come first with each other from now on.'

'You don't have to tell me that.' His face was as stiff as hers and his voice a low growl as he spoke.

'I think I do if today is anything to go by. Your mother set out to deliberately ruin our wedding day, and you know it. She could have seen me last night and said all she wanted to say but no, she made an excuse that she was tired, that the journey had exhausted her. Her! She's built like an –' She stopped abruptly and shut her eyes tightly for a second as she drew in a steadying breath. She mustn't let her tongue run away with her, this was too important. She had to make him *see* . . . 'And today, there were several occasions when she could have spoken to me on my own, I even tried to bring about that very thing several times. But no, she bided her time, being as awkward as she could while she did so, and then attacked me –'

'Oh, come on. She didn't lay a finger on you.'

'I'm not talking about physical assault, Hank! What she did was worse, much worse than that. She tried to make me look a fool, to destroy my reputation in front of our families and friends. Can't you *see* how it is?' she asked urgently.

'No one could hear what was being said,' he muttered sullenly. 'And if that stupid old fool hadn't interfered, everything would have been all right.'

'I'll ignore that because I really can't believe you are so stupid.' His face darkened but she continued, 'Everyone in that room knew what was going on, even if they couldn't hear the actual words, and they were all aware that you were allowing it, too. If, as she said, you'd had all this out the night before, you knew what she was going to say and you just stood there and let her lay into me with just a couple of weak "Mothers" as protest. Albert loves me, and he stood up for me in the only way he knows how.'

'So you aren't going to do as I ask?'

'And not see him again? Of course I'm not, I can't believe you're really serious, and if you are, that makes everything that's happened today ten times worse in my book. You ought to be round there thanking him that at least someone in that room had the courage to put your mother in her place.'

'So that's how things are.'

'Hank . . .' She sank down on to a corner of the bed as the hardness in his face made her want to cry. His mother had won. She had deliberately set out to drive a wedge between them at the very start of their married life, and he was letting her win, without protest, without any sort of challenge. Instead of blaming his mother for what was inexcusable behaviour, all his censure, all his wrath, had fallen on Albert's innocent head. Like with the Israelites of old, a scapegoat was being sent outside the camp with all the sins of the world on its back or, in this case, his mother's sins. Well, she couldn't sacrifice the old man in such a way, *wouldn't*, however much she wanted things to be put right between them. And she did want things put right, she realized suddenly, she wanted it very much. 'Please, Hank, I don't want to fight with you, not today of all days . . .'

As she held out her hand to him, her lower lip quivering and her eyes great pools of liquid light, he stared at her for a good thirty seconds without moving and then walked round the side of the bed, passing her without a word, and left the room.

She sat, too stunned to move, exactly where he had left her, for several minutes before rising slowly and walking over to their suitcases at the side of the door where the porter had placed them earlier. She unpacked the clothes and toiletries mechanically, hers first and then Hank's, her ears tuned all the time for the sound of his footsteps in the corridor outside. He wasn't going to leave her alone on their wedding night, was he? She wanted, she *needed*, his presence at this time and suddenly his mother and, yes, even Albert too seemed terribly unimportant.

The whole world had narrowed down to a tall, well-built American who had told her he loved her, that he adored her, that she was the most important thing in his life . . .

It was well past midnight when Hank returned to the room, and Kate was lying in bed reading a book in which she had no interest when the sound of a key turning in the lock brought her eyes to the door.

'Hallo.' She smiled nervously as he stepped over the threshold.

'I'm going to have a shower.' He didn't look at her as he crossed the room to the en-suite, and she sank back down in the bed again blinking away the tears hovering at the back of her eyes with furious intent. She wasn't going to cry, not now. And she wasn't going to let his mother ruin their marriage before it had even started either. When he came to bed she would make the first move towards reconciliation, it didn't seem important any more who was right or wrong . . .

He was a long time in the bathroom, and Kate had placed the book on the bedside table and was lying in the semi-gloom of the two bedside lamps when he at last appeared, clad in pyjamas, and walked stiffly across to the bed. The odour of whisky was strong as he slid under the covers on the very far side of the bed, taking great care not to come into contact with her body, before switching off his lamp.

'Hank?' She reached for his hand as she spoke, but in the next instant he turned on his side, his back towards her and his voice cold.

'Goodnight, Kate.'

Oh, he couldn't be doing this to her, it was so unfair . . . She hadn't done anything, she hadn't. She lay rigid for some minutes before stretching out a hand and flicking off her own light, and as the room plunged into darkness she was vitally aware of the man at her side, every nerve, every sinew in her body tense and painful.

Her wedding night! Her wedding night . . . She lay without moving, her mind churning. And she had been worried about the physical side of things! She felt the throb of hysteria in her throat and quickly checked the paroxysm before she made any sound. She should never have gone through with the ceremony today, she had known, she had *known* for days it was all wrong. There had been a part of her mind that had niggled at her day and night that all was not as it should be, but how could she have known about his mother? And yet, really, Miriam Ross wasn't the problem . . . An irritation maybe, a difficulty, but if they had faced her together she wouldn't have been able to hurt them.

Oh, how she wanted Joy . . . The longing she attempted

to keep behind a closed door in that segment of her brain labelled 'no entry' escaped from its confines. Seeing her today, holding her, smelling her . . . Oh, the smell of her, the deliciously scented, warm, milky fragrance, she could smell it now. A wave of misery, black and deep, washed over her head and she wept silently, her face buried in the pillow, until at last she drifted into a dull sleep of exhaustion beside the taut, still figure of her husband.

When Kate awoke the next morning, Hank was already dressed and shaved and was sitting watching her at the end of the bed, and such was the look on his face in that first unguarded moment that it took some of the sting out of his rejection of the night before. He looked miserable, and she felt miserable, and his mother wasn't going to spoil everything . . . 'Hallo,' she said softly, flushing slightly at the knowledge that he had been able to observe her while she had slept, and grateful that the covers were in place up to her chin.

'Hi, sugar,' he answered just as softly, and then, 'some wedding day, eh? I'm sorry I sounded off like that, Kate, I shouldn't have let it get to me.'

Shouldn't have let it get to you, she repeated silently. Oh, but you should, Hank, there was nothing wrong in letting it get to you, merely in the way you handled it, that's all. But it would do no good to start the ball rolling again, so she smiled and held out her arms to him, her eyes warm.

He hesitated for a moment before standing and moving to lean over her, kissing the top of her head as he folded her tousled hair from cheeks that turned bright pink. 'Come on, Mrs Ross.' He straightened and smiled down at her. 'Breakfast is waiting.'

'Oh, right.' There was no reason to feel rebuffed, no reason at all, she told herself as she dressed quickly after a lick and a promise of a wash. She hadn't meant for her gesture to be anything other than a healing of the differences between them, but somehow . . . somehow she sensed he had thought she was inviting more, and had dealt with it accordingly with the call to breakfast.

Oh, for goodness' sake, she was imagining things now, she told herself crossly as she brushed her sleek hair in the bathroom mirror. It was the fiasco of the day before, upsetting her equilibrium, which had been fragile enough anyway over the last few weeks. And that's enough feeling sorry for yourself, too. She stared back into the clear blue eyes in the mirror before shaking her head slowly. This was her weakness, self-pity, born of the experiences of her childhood, but it did no good, no good at all. A sweet little face topped by a few wisps of downy hair suddenly sprang into her consciousness, and again she spoke sharply to herself. None of that, none of that. There's no going back so just get on with your life now, count your blessings.

And it actually wasn't difficult to do just that through the remainder of the day as Hank set out to be an amusing and entertaining companion, solicitous of her welfare as they toured Loch Lomond before a wintry storm drove them back to their hotel at Helensburgh for an early evening meal. They were leaving the next day having agreed some weeks before that a weekend away, followed by a more exotic holiday early the next year, would suit their respective work commitments better than a long honeymoon, and Kate wasn't sorry. As she sat in the hotel's small dining room watching the thick fat flakes of snow falling from a laden sky, the urge to be back at work, exhausting though the hospital routine often proved, was strong. But it was normal, tried and tested, she knew what she was doing there.

And here? She glanced at Hank and, although she knew he was aware of her eyes on him, he didn't acknowledge her, continuing to lean back in his chair as he sipped the brandy he had ordered with his coffee, his gaze remote. In the last half hour he seemed to have withdrawn from her again, the charming consort of the day a distant memory.

'Hank? Are you all right?' For a moment he didn't speak and then, as though it was an effort, he slowly looked at her. 'Do you feel unwell?' she asked anxiously, unable to explain the expression on his face to herself in any other way.

'Unwell?' It was as if his thoughts had been far away. 'I . . .' He paused, and then said, 'Yeah, I don't feel too good, Kate. I'm sorry.'

'Don't be sorry.' She could hear the relief in her voice and despised herself for the fact she was so grateful he wasn't angry with her for some reason. 'I've some aspirin in my bag, would they help?'

'Maybe. Yeah, maybe. Thanks, honey.'

He took the aspirin with the last of his coffee, and they sat for some minutes more before Kate turned her head to him again as she said, 'I think I'll go up now if we're leaving early in the morning. You haven't forgotten I've got to be at the hospital for mid-day?'

'No, I haven't forgotten.' He smiled at her but she sensed he was agitated in some way. 'Look, you go up and I'll follow shortly. I might go for a walk to see if it clears my head.'

'In this?' she asked in surprise, her voice high, as she indicated the swirling snowflakes that had already settled in a white blanket over the hotel grounds.

'Well, I'll perhaps have another drink then, give those aspirins a chance to work.' Just leave it, Kate, will you? Give me some space, damn it. That's all I'm asking.

Something of what he was thinking must have shown on his face because her voice was quiet and flat sounding when next she spoke. 'See you later, then.'

'Sure, sure, I won't be long.'

When Kate had left the dining room, Hank Ross sat for another minute at the empty table before rising slowly and walking through into the small bar adjacent to the lounge, where he ordered a double whisky on the rocks and downed it in one swallow.

'You're either cold or thirsty.' The pretty, blonde

barmaid smiled at him, her eyes flirtatious, and he smiled back. She had told him the night before her name was Noreen and that she was eighteen years old. *Eighteen years old* and she looked at him like that, as though she knew all there was to know, but then she had also told him she'd been brought up in the slums of Glasgow, so she probably did.

'Another double, and have one yourself.'

'Oh, ta, I will. I told me mam last night we'd got an American staying, I love your accent.'

'And what did your . . . mam say?'

'She told me to watch me step, that you Yanks are all the same.' The small nose wrinkled. 'She remembers the war, you see. I think she was a bit of a devil by all accounts, an' there's nothing worse than a reformed sinner, is there.' She smiled widely now and he couldn't help laughing. 'But I said to her, he's here with a lady friend. You are, aren't you?' At his raised eyebrows she giggled again as she admitted, 'I asked Sue on Reception.'

'The lady is my wife.'

'That's what they all say.'

'No, she really is my wife,' he said amusedly.

'Oh . . .' The knowledge didn't seem to dampen the girl's enthusiasm, in fact just the opposite. She clearly thought a wife was less competition than a girlfriend. 'Well, chin chin.' She raised her glass to him with a pert tilt to her head.

It was much later when Hank went upstairs and Kate was fast asleep, one arm flung above her head and the other nestling under her chin. She looked as though she had been crying. He sat, in much the same manner as he had that morning, looking at her while she slept as his guts writhed and twisted in hot panic. What was he going to do? What the hell was he going to do?

CHAPTER NINE

It was the following Sunday and the marriage had still not been consummated, and as Kate pulled on her coat, she stared at her reflection in the hall mirror as she asked herself why. She knew the fact that she wouldn't agree to cut Albert out of her life still rankled, but Hank refused to discuss the old man with her, neither would he speak about his mother. He was pleasant enough on a surface level, but . . . She shut her eyes for a moment and when she opened them again there was a faint flush of embarrassment on her cheeks, as though she had voiced her thoughts out loud. He hadn't made her his wife in the real sense of the word. And it was driving her mad. She stared blankly ahead, her hands falling slack by her sides. It was.

Sleeping in that bed each night next to him, his back turned against her, how much more of it could she take without screaming at him? He was punishing her, that much was for sure, and if all this was about trying to force her to do what he asked, then they'd still be in the same position years from now, because she wouldn't give in. Her eyes narrowed as she shook her head slowly. No, she wouldn't. She wouldn't be able to live with herself if she hurt Albert like that. And she wouldn't beg either, she wouldn't give him that satisfaction.

Perhaps this was judgement on her for letting Joy go. Perhaps that's what really bothered him.

'*Stop it.*' She ground the words out through clenched teeth and then jumped violently as Hank appeared behind her, buttoning his coat.

'What?'

'Nothing, I was talking to myself.'

'You can get pills for that.' He grinned at her, and then

walked through to the sitting room where he had left the car keys, whistling softly.

She didn't understand him, she really didn't. She gazed after him, her lips trembling in spite of all her efforts to control her emotions. You would have thought they were the happiest newly-weds in the world today from the way he was acting. From the moment he had opened his eyes that morning he had been all charm. Perhaps he was trying to get her in a good mood because they were going to James's for lunch and he was worried she might confide in Liz. Yes, that could be it. Well, he needn't worry, she thought bitterly as her mouth hardened. She wasn't about to tell anyone, even Liz, that she was so sexually unattractive that her own husband wouldn't make love to her.

'Ready?' As he reappeared in the hall she nodded in answer and then followed him to the front door, where he stood to one side to allow her to precede him from the house. Always the gentleman, she thought sourly, and then berated herself for the rancour.

The cold frosty air smelt of pine needles and Christmas, and she turned to survey the house for a moment as Hank locked the front door. She could be happy here, she knew that now, if only things were right between them. The comfortable detached house wasn't modern, having been built almost eighty years ago at the turn of the century, but the light-coloured walls and large bay windows made it seem so. Downstairs, the wide, square hall led off to the sitting room on the right, which had delightful French windows that opened on to a lawned garden surrounded by mature trees and shrubs. On the left of the hall, beyond a small cloakroom, the dining room led through to a beautifully fitted kitchen which had been extended by the previous owners into a large L shape and was both functional and attractive, with light wood cupboards and brass handles. The four bedrooms all had washbasins, the master bedroom enjoying its own en-suite, and the main bathroom was equipped with all the normal facilities plus a jumbo-size corner bath and bidet.

A perfect house for a family . . . As Hank joined her and they walked over to the car parked in the drive, Kate's thoughts mocked her. Definitely a house for children, but the way they were going they wouldn't have one baby, let alone several, unless it was by this test tube technique that had been announced in July. As Hank opened the passenger door and she slid into the car she felt the frustration increase. And now she was going to have to pretend everything was wonderful for Liz and James's benefit, she'd go mad before she finished . . .

'Hallo, Kate.' John didn't smile as he spoke, and such was the state of her mind that her pained recognition of his coolness enabled her to keep straight-faced herself as she nodded a reply. They had only met once again since that first time she had come to Sunday lunch, when she had been at James's house with Hank finalizing some details about the wedding, and on that occasion she had been left with the impression that John didn't care much for her. She had tried to be pleasant, engaging him in conversation that was little more than a succession of monosyllables on his part, but the incident had left her feeling distinctly uncomfortable, as though she had tried too hard, and she had determined not to make the same mistake again.

'John.' Hank put his arm round her shoulders as he spoke his cousin's name and she tried not to show the action surprised her. It was the first affectionate gesture he had made in days. 'How's Law college?'

'Fine.' The tone was dismissive and again that flash of indignation brought Kate's lips tightly together.

'Good, good.' Hank's voice was too hearty and she would have liked to tell him it was the wrong tack to take. 'Managing to fit a little work in between the parties, then? Your father tells me you're sharing a house with some other students at the college.'

‘That’s right.’ John opened the door to the sitting room as he spoke, but instead of going in, moved to one side to allow them to pass him as he said, ‘Kate and Hank are here.’

‘Kate.’ Liz had been sitting by the fire but rose immediately, her face wreathed in smiles. ‘Come and get warm, this weather is beastly, isn’t it. I was worried you wouldn’t be able to come.’

‘It would take more than a little ice and snow to stop us tasting one of your Sunday roasts, Liz,’ Hank said cheerfully. Kate was glad he had replied – for the moment the urge to cry was overwhelming. It was the sight of Liz’s warm friendly face that had done it, and it didn’t help to tell herself she was being silly.

‘Flatterer.’ Liz smiled at him before hugging Kate and leading her over to the chair she had just vacated. ‘Sit there and get warm, I’ve been on top of the fire all morning.’

‘I’ll tell Dad you’re here.’ John shut the door as he spoke, but the next instant it had burst open again as Adam entered on a trot.

‘Kate! Kate!’ The small child knocked her backwards in the chair with the impetus of his leap onto her lap, and as two plump arms entwined round Kate’s neck, Liz spoke apologetically.

‘He’s been waiting all morning for you to come. Now please, Adam dear, allow Kate some air. She will be staying all day so you’ve plenty of time to see her.’

‘Are you?’ Adam leant back to look up into her face. ‘Staying for a long, long time?’

‘I certainly am.’ Kate smiled into the little face looking at her so intently.

‘’Cos Grizzle has got a bad leg and he’s been crying and crying . . .’ The childish treble took on the tone of someone who had been extremely patient under trying circumstances. ‘I told him you would make it better but he didn’t believe me.’

'Grizzle didn't believe you?' Kate shook her head sadly. 'Oh, that bear. He really is the limit, isn't he.'

'Yep.' Adam settled himself more comfortably on her lap. 'He is the limit,' he agreed with great satisfaction.

Kate smiled at Liz over the small boy's head as she ruffled his silky hair, but as her gaze swung to include Hank, she noticed John standing in the open doorway, and the expression on his face as he watched her holding the child caused her own to stiffen. He had no right to look at her like that, as though he resented her presence in the house, she thought hotly, her cheeks turning pink. She hadn't done anything to him, had she? Offended him in some way? Her brow wrinkled as she considered their previous meetings. No, she hadn't, she was sure she hadn't, but if the opportunity presented itself, she'd ask him straight out, no beating about the bush. And Hank, she'd clear the air with him tonight when they were on their own, this ridiculous situation couldn't be allowed to continue any longer. She'd had enough and she was fed up with the male gender and their moods, they were children, the lot of them.

The opportunity did present itself, that very day, but in a way Kate couldn't have envisaged. She was ensconced with Liz in the sitting room in front of a roaring fire, flicking through the pages of an old photo album while the men tackled the mountain of dirty dishes in the kitchen, when a long-drawn-out howl of fright somewhere above their heads, followed by a thud, brought both women jumping to their feet.

'What on earth was that?' Liz had clutched her in her panic. 'It must be one of the children, there's only Susan and Adam upstairs.'

The three men emerged from the kitchen as Liz flung open the sitting room door, and they ran upstairs as a group to find Susan just leaving her room, her eyes wide with fright. 'Was that Adam, Mummy?'

'Adam . . .' Even as Liz breathed her son's name, James

had opened the nursery door, but the sight that met their eyes froze all movement for one split-second. One of the large, diamond-leaded windows overlooking the garden was swinging open, and there was no sight of the small boy.

'*Adam?*' James seemed to reach the window with one spring, and then, 'What in the name of . . . Stay still, Adam, don't move. Stay absolutely still, there's a good boy.'

'James?' Liz was still in the doorway, her face terror-stricken, and he gestured for her to remain where she was.

'He's all right, Liz, he's landed on the roof of the bay, but let me deal with it. Hank, would you take Liz and Susan downstairs please, and I'll go and get the ladder from the garage and bring it round.' James was talking in the steady monotone a doctor uses to reassure a disturbed and vulnerable patient, and as Kate met his eyes across the room he beckoned to her with his head. 'Perhaps you'd come and talk to him a moment, Kate? Keep him calm. You've had experience with this sort of thing.'

Experience? She forced a smile to her face as she peered down at the small form lying precariously close to the edge of the curved roof, which was only three foot at its widest point in the middle. It was one thing dealing with panic-stricken patients in the comfortable environment of the hospital, and quite another when the person in question was barely four years old and known to her.

'Adam, everything is going to be all right, I promise you.' He had landed on his side in the two or three inches of snow covering the flat roof, one small leg outstretched and the other bent at the knee. The same snow that had broken the small boy's fall was also the very thing that might send him over the edge of the roof on to the concrete patio below if he moved, the fresh layer that had fallen during the night having settled on an icy surface that was lethal. 'Have you hurt yourself?' She received a careful shake of the head in answer. 'Good. Now I want you to show me how still you can keep, like that game, "dead fishes". Have you played it before?'

'No.' The response was a whispered quiver.

'Well, it's quite hard but I'm sure you can do it, you're so clever. Grizzle is doing it already, he's lying absolutely still in the garden, I can see him, so you see if you can beat him, yes?'

'John, I think if we try and climb down to him he might slide off,' James said softly, his eyes still fixed on his younger son. 'If I go and get the ladder and lift him down that way, can you stay here? If you think he's going to go anyway, try and get him before . . . You'd probably climb out quicker than me.'

'I get the message, Dad, and he's not going to fall,' John said steadily. 'You go and get the ladder.'

'Right.'

As James left the room Adam spoke again. 'I was trying to show Grizzle the icicle, Kate.'

'The icicle?' Kate repeated quietly, and then, 'You're so good at this game, I can't believe it. You're the best little boy I've seen.'

'I am, aren't I,' he agreed matter-of-factly, his voice a little perkier now the initial shock had diminished. 'The icicle was on the bottom of my window and Grizzle wanted to touch it. I told him he shouldn't, I did, honest injun, but . . .' There followed an affected sigh. 'He's the limit, isn't he, Kate.'

She met John's eyes for a second as they both gave an involuntary smile in spite of the circumstances, and then they resumed their watch on the small figure some feet below them.

'I'm afraid he is, Adam, so don't let him win this game by you moving, will you?' The sight of the teddy bear on the ground some twelve feet below was chilling.

'No.' There followed a moment's silence and then Adam spoke again, his voice less confident. 'John, do you think Dad will smack me?' He raised his head slightly to look at his brother and the movement caused him to slide an inch or two towards the edge of the roof. 'Oh, I forgot,

Kate. Does that count?' he asked, tearfully now, as John swore quietly, his body tensing.

'No, you're allowed one practice in every game but this is it now, you've got to keep absolutely still,' Kate said quickly, her hands tightening on the window sill. 'Grizzle used up his practice before you.'

'Did he?' Adam said happily. 'So I'm still winning then?'

'Definitely.'

She felt faint with relief a second later when they heard James's voice from the garden below. 'I'm bringing it round.' Within moments the ladder was in place and James's head and most of his torso had just come into view, when he lurched violently as the ladder slipped on the icy ground below. There was the sound of metal scraping against brick, a loud crash, and then the sound of muffled cursing from the ground below.

'Dad? What's happened?' John leant as far out of the window as he dared just as Hank, Liz and Susan appeared in view, their voices mingling with his. 'Have you hurt yourself?'

'What do you think?' James's voice was terse in the extreme. 'Blasted ladder. Are you all right, Adam?'

'He's fine,' Kate called down reassuringly. The small boy had remained perfectly still through the pandemonium, although now she could see him shaking a little and guessed he was crying. 'Just keep still, Adam.'

The next rescue attempt was more successful. Hank gingerly climbed up to the roof as Liz and Susan held the ladder below, scooping Adam under one arm before descending slowly. But once everyone had congregated downstairs it became clear James had done himself some damage in the fall. Hank had had to virtually carry his cousin into the house and James's face was tinged with grey, his white lips clamped together in pain.

'I'm sorry, James, but I think you've broken it.' As Kate felt the ankle beneath her fingers it told its own story. 'You'll have to go to hospital.'

'Damn and blast it.' James rested back against the sofa for a moment as he shut his eyes. 'Are you sure, Kate? I don't want to go if it isn't necessary, with the hospital engineering supervisors on strike. The waiting lists are already up to 60,000, I don't want to add to an overloaded system.'

'James, you need treatment, and you know as well as I do that at the moment Crompton General is working as normal,' Kate said firmly. The October strike was a sore point with Hank's cousin, and one on which he waxed lyrical given half a chance. 'There's no problem with an emergency situation like this anyway, and I can feel a definite break.'

'Oh, James . . .' As Liz's lips began to quiver, Adam, who was sitting on his mother's lap, started to wail loudly, joined a moment later by Susan.

'Now, now, that's enough.' Her children's distress restored Liz's control immediately. 'It's nothing serious, the doctor's will make it better for Daddy. I want you and Adam to be very good, Susan. Would you mind staying with them, Kate?'

'Of course not –'

'No, no, Liz. There's no need for you to come with me, I'll be fine.'

'I'm coming with you.' The look that Liz gave her husband settled the matter. 'John, we'll use your car if that's all right, darling.'

'It wouldn't start this morning,' John stood up as he spoke, 'but I'll go and try it again.'

'No need,' Hank said quickly, 'I'll be glad to take him. Liz, you get your coat and a blanket or two, and perhaps you'd help me get him to the car, John?' Once Hank and John got James outside it became apparent that the drive to the hospital would be less painful with the patient lying on the back seat, his foot supported by two bulky cushions.

'It would be better if you stayed with Kate, Liz,' Hank

said quietly, once James was settled in position. 'There's only room for one more and –'

'I'm coming, Hank.'

'But we're going to have to carry him once we get there –'

'We can get a wheelchair.' Liz turned to John, resting her hand on his sleeve. 'You understand, don't you, darling? And look after Kate and the children.' She slid into the front seat of the car as she spoke, and there was nothing more Hank could do but join her, although his face was grim. 'Kate dear, I'll ring you once we know a little more . . .' Liz waved as she spoke and then Kate and John were left standing on the drive in the last of the afternoon's light, a few desultory snowflakes drifting down from the darkening sky.

'Well, never a dull moment . . .' John smiled as he turned to look at her, a real smile, that transformed his rather serious face completely. 'And I must say that idea of the game with Grizzle was a brainwave on your part. Grizzle . . .' He shook his head as he mentioned the teddy bear. 'It's amazing what that furry creature is responsible for, you wouldn't believe what he persuades Adam to get up to.'

'I would,' she said feelingly. The three or four minutes at the window had seemed like a lifetime.

'Still, I guess we were all the same when we were little.' John put out a hand and gently turned her round, and as they walked towards the front door he said, 'I had a toy rabbit named Bugs that was a real little monster. He got me to sneak down in the middle of the night and eat all the Easter eggs that had been put away for rationing out in one go. I was sick for days . . .'

'Were you?' She stared at him as they entered the warmth of the house. She couldn't imagine John, serious responsible John, doing such a thing, even as a little boy.

'Don't look so shocked, you must have had something you blamed for your misdemeanours.'

'No.' She spoke without thinking. 'There was only me,

my mother didn't allow any make-believe. Toys had to be educational.'

'I see.' His voice was soft now, and very deep, and somewhere in her toes a little shiver started. 'You must have been very lonely.'

'I . . .' She opened her mouth to make a throw-away remark, a light comment, but instead found herself saying quietly, 'Yes, I was, but I think all children are to some extent. Childhood and adolescence isn't all it's cracked up to be.'

'No, I guess not.'

They were standing outside the sitting room now but as John's hand reached for the door handle, Kate touched his arm for a moment. 'John? Can I ask you something before we go in?'

'Ask away.' But she had seen the flash of surprise in the sky-blue eyes, and swallowed deeply before she said, 'You may think I'm being impertinent, or imagining things, but I feel I might have done something to offend you.'

John didn't answer her right away and they remained staring at each other for a good ten seconds, as Kate willed her eyes not to fall before the steady blue gaze that seemed to be boring into her very brain. He would be a good lawyer. The thought came from nowhere and wasn't at all relevant to the present circumstances. 'You haven't offended me, Kate,' he said at last, his voice flat.

That was all? No explanation for his coolness, his offhand manner? She felt her temper rise but her voice was calm as she spoke. 'Then perhaps you just don't like me? Is that it? I know you and Hank don't get on –'

'No, we don't.' He had cut into her voice with razor sharpness and, as she blinked, her hand fluttering to her throat, he shook his head slowly before running a hand through his hair in a gesture that spoke of inward turmoil. 'Look, I'm sorry, Kate, but there are things you don't understand, can we just leave it at that? And I do like you, of course I do. I'm sorry if I gave you the impression . . .' He broke off, lowering his head for a moment before looking at her again, his eyes veiled. 'I'm sorry,' he said again. 'Shouldn't we see to Adam?' He thrust open the door as he spoke, and she knew the conversation had affected him more than he was revealing when his normally impeccable manners failed him and he moved ahead of her into the room. And as she followed, her hands joined tightly together and her face tense, she knew, with unswerving conviction, that there was far more to all this than met the eye.

'He'll be in plaster for at least six weeks I'm afraid. It's broken in two places.' It was ten o'clock that same night and the others had just returned home, James plastered from toe to knee, in the rapidly worsening weather. 'Still, I can drive him in to work –'

'Don't worry about that, Liz.' Hank inclined his head towards James who was stretched out on the sofa, eyes closed, clearly feeling the effects of the accident. 'Once he's feeling okay I can pick him up as I drive in, it's on my way. But there's no rush, let him have a few days convalescence.'

'Would you please stop talking about me as though I'm not here?' James said tersely, opening his eyes and glaring up at them all. 'And I shall be perfectly fit for the office tomorrow, Hank, if you wouldn't mind calling for me in the morning. I don't like Liz driving in all this snow and ice.'

'No sweat. Give me a buzz if you change your mind, though.'

Once the goodbyes had been said and they were on their way home, the windscreen wipers labouring under the thickly falling snow, the silence in the car became heavy. Kate had been aware, from the moment Hank had returned, that he was in the grip of some dark emotion. It was there in the forced heartiness of his voice and the narrowing of his eyes every time they had touched her face. He was angry, very angry, but for the life of her she couldn't work out why. Should she ask him? She glanced at the hard, square profile warily. She wanted to say, 'Right, enough of this, Hank Ross, I'm not standing for more of your moods. The last week has been a nightmare and you're being totally unfair, you know you are. I don't know what's upset you tonight and I don't care, but we're going to get things sorted once and for all.' That was what she *wanted* to say, but she felt too tense, too emotionally worn out, to cope with what she might hear.

The evening with John had been tense and full of lengthy, painful silences that had wound her up to the point where she felt like a huge coiled spring just waiting for release, and exhaustion was drumming away in her head in the form of a grinding headache at the back of her eyes. No, she wasn't in any fit state to start a war of words with Hank, it was best left until they had both slept and re-charged their batteries. But something would have to be done . . . Her teeth dragged at her lower lip for a moment. Something would certainly have to be done.

Not a word was spoken on the drive home and once they reached the house, she opened the car door before Hank could assist her and walked swiftly into the warmth of the hall.

She went straight upstairs and into the bedroom, and after a quick shower took two aspirins for the headache before climbing into bed. She had heard Hank come in after putting the car away in the garage but after that nothing, not even the sound of the television that he had taken to watching, the last few nights, until he thought she was asleep. Well, he could sit down there forever. She had had enough of all of them, Hank, John, yes even Liz and James, and she missed Joy so . . . What she would give to have her here now, just to see her smile, to hold her . . .

How long she lay awake she didn't know but she must have fallen asleep, because when the hands started to move over her skin, raising her nightie over the tops of her legs, it was some seconds before she could come fully alert. 'What? . . .' Hank's face was inches from hers and she could smell the whisky on his breath as, breathing heavily and noisily, he straddled her inert body. 'Hank? Hank, stop it, what are you doing?'

He didn't answer, he didn't say a word, merely pushing her legs apart and entering her in the same instant. The act itself was over quickly and apart from a tight, stretching sensation was not painful, but the suddenness of it all, the utter lack of any words of love, of tenderness, was shocking. Once he had climaxed he withdrew immediately and to Kate's stunned amazement rolled over and off the bed, going over to the en-suite and shutting the door behind him. The whole thing hadn't taken more than two, at the most three, minutes and had been conducted in absolute silence, and now, as she lay amongst the ruffled covers, she felt herself begin to shake. It had been no better than that other time, with Richard Wellington, no, worse if anything. At least Richard had *looked* at her, she thought hysterically, had known whom he was taking. Hank had kept his eyes shut from start to finish, she could have been a rubber doll for all the difference it would have made . . .

She sat up in the bed, pulling her nightie down over her knees and winding her arms round them to try and still the trembling that had taken her over. Were all men like this? Was this the way the average male made love? First Richard, and now Hank . . . But no, she knew that wasn't true, if all the books and films she had seen weren't enough, the talk in the staff room among some of the nurses would have convinced her that the act of love could be wonderful, marvellous, at the very least tender and loving. Then was it her? Was there something the matter with her? *What was she doing wrong?*

She had fallen asleep with her bedside lamp still on and now she stretched her hand and clicked it off, plunging the room into darkness with just a thin strip of light showing under the bathroom door. She wanted to wash . . . She swayed back and forth in the bed, the urge to scrub herself clean overpowering. She felt dirty, used, abused, as though she was a whore out on the streets of Glasgow rather than a married woman, a *wife*.

As the door opened to reveal Hank, now clothed in striped pyjamas, Kate became perfectly still. He switched off the bathroom light before shutting the door, and then his dark outline moved across the room. She remained sitting up in bed for some moments after he had climbed in his side, pulling the covers over him and turning into his usual position, his back to her. He wasn't going to say anything? To explain?

'What was that all about?' Her voice, when it came, was low and steady and the sound of it surprised her, considering how she was feeling inside.

There was a long pause, and then, 'What?'

'You heard me. I asked you what you thought you were doing a few minutes ago.'

The pause was even longer this time and then he said, his voice slurred, 'Go to sleep, Kate.'

He was drunk! The knowledge swept away all the trembling weakness his assault on her body had caused, and now anger took its place. How dared he! How dared he sit down there drinking himself into a stupor before coming up here to take her in an act of lust? An act that had carried less consideration than a dog mating with a bitch?

'No I won't go to sleep,' she said furiously, 'not until we've got this sorted out. How could you treat me like that?'

'Like what?' He still didn't move and the urge to beat her fists on his back, to shatter that infuriating impassivity was so strong it was a red mist in front of her eyes.

'How can you say "like what"?' she screamed as she tore back the covers, 'and look at me, damn you, look at me! I'm your wife, Hank. You're supposed to care about me, to consider my feelings –'

'Like you consider mine?' He sat up in bed now, switching on his bedside lamp to reveal her kneeling amongst the covers, her face aflame and her eyes blazing.

'What does that mean? I always consider you –'

'Don't give me that.' He glared at her, the whisky making his accent even more pronounced. 'That's garbage and you know it! You sure weren't thinking of me when you let that other guy in there, were you!' He made an obscene gesture at her lower stomach that had her shrinking back on the bed, her eyes enormous. 'And tonight, what sort of night do you think I had, trying to sort James out with Liz hanging on my coat-tails while you were nice and cosy back at home? You think I had fun, eh?'

'But that wasn't my fault.' She stared at him, anger still uppermost but a feeling of bewilderment gradually taking its place. He was trying to make excuses, to find some reason for his actions, to blame her . . . 'You know that wasn't my fault, it was just the way it all worked out. John was going to come to help you originally –'

'But John didn't come, did he.' The words were savage and spaced out.

'You're blaming me for that? For John not coming to the hospital?' Her stomach was turning over so much she felt nauseous. 'That was Liz's idea, and you know it. What do you think anyway, that I'm going to have an affair with him or something?' There was a dark flicker in the back of his eyes as she spoke and she stiffened, every muscle tensing. 'That's it, isn't it,' she said slowly, her voice high with disbelief. 'You're jealous, jealous of me spending the evening with another man, even your own cousin. You don't trust me. Is that why you've been punishing me, refusing to –' She stopped abruptly. She couldn't bring herself to voice the rejection of the last week. 'I don't believe it,' she said weakly. 'You know what happened that other time, how it was, and I haven't looked at another man since.'

'How do I know that?' he asked, turning away from her and sitting on the side of the bed with his back to her, his head in his hands.

'You said you understood, Hank, how it was. You *said.*' She took a deep breath, her voice shaking with reaction. 'You were the one who wanted us to stay together, who pushed for this marriage. I never, at any point, tried to force you to stay.'

'I know.'

'Then why . . . why are you doing this to me, to both of us? I love you, you know I do, and I want our marriage to work, I want it with all my heart.'

'Kate –' He swung round to face her as she finished speaking, and such was the depth of misery in his eyes that it stopped her breath. 'I have to explain . . .' He paused, looking at her for an endless moment, his gaze searching her white face.

'Explain what?' she asked gently.

'How things are,' he said at last. 'How things really are.'

'I know how things are.' She reached out to him now, taking his limp hands in her own as she hitched across the bed to his side. 'And we'll work it through together, if that's what you want.' She rested her head against his broad shoulder, her body slim and fair beside his bulk. 'Is it, Hank? What you want?'

'Yeah . . .' But as they sat there in the semi-darkness amongst the ruffled covers, the wind howling and moaning as it shook the window, his voice held a weary, hopeless kind of ring, and Kate had an eerie presentiment, quickly dismissed, that the storm outside was nothing to the one within.

Chapter Ten

'But I can't believe I am, Albert, not so soon.' It was two days before Christmas and Kate was sitting in Albert's flat, her hands clasped in those of the old man.

'With your track record once would be enough, lass. I reckon you're one of them fertile females, me own mam was the same. She always used to say me da, old Mike McNab, only had to look at her with a certain glint in his eye an' she'd be up the spout. Ten of us she bore, eight lads alongside of me, an' they all copped it in the war, leavin' just me and our Molly. Broke old Mike it did, he was never any good after that. Aye, once is enough all right, and I dare say you've had a bit of practice an' all.' He grinned at her but she couldn't smile back, neither could she bring herself to tell him Hank had only made love to her the once, if that brief animalistic act could be termed such. 'Now don't get yourself all worked up, lass, it might be somethin' or nothin'. You say you hadn't really got back to normal after the bairn?' She nodded wearily. 'Well then . . .'

'I don't know, Albert. I don't feel right, I feel different, like before.'

'An' you don't want it, if you are?'

'Oh no, I want it, of course I want it, it's just that it's so soon. There's my job . . .' But she knew, even as she spoke, that her career wasn't a consideration. If things had been right between her and Hank she would be over the moon, ecstatic. The aching void her daughter had left would only be filled by holding her own child close to her heart, she knew that now. She should never have parted with Joy. It was the biggest mistake she would ever make in her life, and the most far-reaching, and she would never forgive herself until the day she died . . .

'An' you haven't told him yet? Not even hinted at it, like?'

'No, I told you. Anyway, I can't be sure . . .'

'The job you can take up where you leave off when the time's right, lass, an' it's not as though you're strugglin', now, is it. You've a nice house, your own car, there's many that'd be glad to be in your shoes.'

She doubted it, she really did, but now was not the time to say so. Albert hadn't been well the last two or three weeks, and now he was feeling a little better she wanted him to enjoy his Christmas. She would have liked him to stay with her over the holiday period but she knew, without asking, that Hank wouldn't countenance it. Nevertheless, she had been on the verge of risking a confrontation and telling Hank she wouldn't see the old man left alone, when Albert had received an invitation to a war veteran reunion in Edinburgh on Christmas Day, with a note to say the twenty or so elderly troopers were going to make a celebration of it and stay at a hotel for Christmas Eve through to Boxing Day. Albert had been delighted, and her problems had been solved, or at least one of them. Following through on her train of thought she said now, 'I hope you are going to behave yourself with all your old cronies, no painting the town red.'

'Red, lass? It'll be all colours afore we've finished.' He grinned at her and she felt a surge of love for the irascible old man who had been so good to her.

'I don't doubt it. Anyway, I've brought your Christmas presents early, you'll see why when you open them.'

'Oh, aye?' He nodded at her curiously. 'You want me to open 'em now, then?'

'You'll have to. I might have to change them if they don't fit.'

She watched him as he unwrapped the parcels festooned in festive paper and bows, grumbling about the prices of such frippery, but when the smart warm overcoat, two new suits and three shirts were laid out on the table, he was unable to speak, his eyes wet with emotion.

'I knew you wouldn't bother to get anything new to go to the reunion in,' she said quickly to cover the charged silence, 'and as I'd been pondering for ages what to get you, this seemed ideal. Try them on before I go and then there's still time to get the right size if they don't fit.'

'Lass, lass. Aw, lass.'

'It's nothing, Albert, nothing in comparison to what you've done for me.' She leant forward now, kissing the parchment-thin cheek, her own eyes damp. 'You're the father I never had, and I couldn't love you more if I was really your daughter.'

'Aw, lass.' He blinked his eyelids and swallowed deeply before saying, 'You sayin' that, it means the world to me, 'cos I think of you as me own bairn, I do that. But look . . .' a touch of the old acerbity showed through, 'I can't accept all this, now then. It must have cost a small fortune.'

'And you're worth every penny so I don't want to hear another word about it.' She grinned at him, suddenly feeling happier than she had in days, weeks. 'Go and try it on, all of it, and show me how the suits look. We'll have a fashion parade.'

'Clothes modelled by Albert, eh?'

He was grumbling as he left the room but she knew he was pleased, and the warm glow his pleasure had induced remained with her during the drive home through icy, snow-packed streets, only to fade when she drew into the drive some time later to see Hank's bright red Ford Cortina parked in front of the house. For a moment the inclination to turn her little Morris Minor round and press her foot hard down on the accelerator pedal until she had left Dumbarton far behind her was strong. 'But that will solve nothing.' She spoke out loud as she cut the engine and then sat slumped in the seat, the moonlit evening and thick snow giving the house and garden a pretty, chocolate-box appearance.

This was her home, even though she had had nothing to do with its purchase, the furnishings, the colour schemes. Even the saucepans in the kitchen were Hank's choice, bought in the weeks before Joy's birth when they had seen nothing of each other and the only contact had been a ritual evening telephone call. Had he excluded her from everything that was going to make up their life together on purpose, or had it merely been a wish to provide a solid base for her, to get himself settled and organized in his new life in Scotland? 'I don't know.' She'd have to stop this talking to herself, people were committed for less. 'He's my husband but I don't know. I don't have a clue what makes him tick, what sort of man he is, what he thinks about . . . *I don't know him*. And now I'm going to have his baby.' His baby. But she didn't know for sure. She clutched on to the thought desperately. No, she didn't know for sure, she didn't, not really . . .

She could hear the television set blaring as she opened the front door, and took a deep breath before walking through to the sitting room. He switched it on the moment he was home and no doubt there would be a glass of whisky by his side. There was.

'It stinks . . .' Hank inclined his head towards the set after a brief nod in her direction. 'They're trying to hold the country to ransom. Callaghan's gotta be firm but he's handling this all wrong. Can't the guy see it?'

'I suppose not.' She knew he had intended no pun with his reference to the dustmen and sewerage workers strike that was being reported on the news at that moment, but nevertheless she couldn't resist pressing the point. 'You think it stinks, then?'

'Surely.' He didn't glance in her direction again. 'But Labour should have called a general election in the summer after the Liberals ended the Lib-Lab Pact, at least that way they could have gone out with a bit of class.'

They had been married for just over seven weeks and for most of that time he had either been glued in front of the television set, or drinking himself into a stupor, or both, she thought wearily, as she turned without a word and left the room. She didn't *care* that the government had restricted pay rises to five per cent, she didn't *care* about the rash of strikes that continued to disrupt daily life to an unprecedented degree, and she was sick of the election fever that had been high all year. And if that made her non-political and brain-dead and all those other things Hank had said the last time she had voiced her sentiments, then so be it. All she wanted – she leant against the cupboard door for a moment and shut her eyes tightly – all she wanted was a normal married life, a family, the things other people took for granted, was that so wrong?

She'd get Christmas and the New Year over, let everything settle back to normal, and then, with any luck, she'd have started her monthly cycle again properly and this niggling worry at the back of her mind would be dealt with. And then – she squared her shoulders, pushing herself away from the support of the door – then she and Hank would have to have a long talk. Because one thing was for sure, she couldn't carry on like this much longer and remain sane. The wild visions she'd had lately, of leaving this house and dashing to Joy's side and snatching her back, were becoming more and more real as everything else in her life became more unreal.

When, on Christmas morning, she awoke to find the bed empty and the smell of bacon pervading the house, she lay for several minutes in the downy warmth, her mind quiet and idle as she watched fat, feathery snowflakes drifting past the window. Christmas Day . . . She sat up suddenly, hugging her knees against her chest. A day synonymous with peace and happiness, laughter and fun, the joy of giving and receiving gifts . . .

How many times throughout the long years of childhood had she longed to be Rosie – hundreds, thousands? And never more so than on Christmas Day, when she used to watch her sister dive into her huge sack of presents, her pretty face alight as she ripped at the paper to reveal one expensive gift after another. But it wasn't the lack of presents that really bothered her, or her mother's time-worn phrase that she parroted year after year to explain her own empty sack, 'Father Christmas only comes to really good children, Kate.' No, she had known even then, with a knowledge far beyond her age, who bought the presents that filled Rosie's sack to overflowing and why she hadn't got any. And it was that knowledge that used to prompt the passionate bursts of rebellion before she was nine and got the measles and finally accepted her mother would never love her . . .

'Breakfast in bed?' She came out of her reverie to find Hank standing in the doorway, a loaded tray in his hands and a broad smile on his face. 'You were fast asleep when I got up – all those extended shifts at the hospital I guess, you're exhausted.'

'It's this flu bug, it's decimated the staff,' she said numbly, stunned with surprise, 'so the ones still on their feet have had to work twice as long.'

'Yeah, well you're on vacation now, and you haven't got to cook dinner so just enjoy the luxury of a lie-in for a while.'

'Are you eating with me?' she asked faintly as he placed the tray on her lap.

'Nope, I've had mine. I'm just going to ring Liz to confirm what time we'll be over. Twelve suit you?'

'Yes, yes that's fine.'

When she was alone again she looked down at the tray, her mind spinning. She hadn't seen him in such a good mood since – she raised her head to stare across the room – since that last time they had gone to James's for Sunday lunch, the day that had ended so badly, first for James and then for her. But surely visiting his cousin wouldn't make such a difference to him, would it? And if so, why? Her eyes narrowed as she continued to gaze blindly ahead. No, it couldn't be that, there was no logical explanation for it, she was imagining things.

She made an exclamation of impatience. Oh, what was the matter with her anyway? What did it matter *why* he was so happy today as long as he was? And last night, when they had exchanged their presents, he had been nice. Not loving . . . Her mind moved on swiftly when she recalled how she had made a move to kiss him for the gold bracelet and earrings he had given her, and the way he had moved his head so her lips just brushed his cheek. No, not loving, but quiet, gentle.

She ate everything on the tray to please him, although she never felt hungry first thing in the morning, and then hurried into the bathroom to wash and make up, brushing her hair until it hung either side of her face like liquid silk. One thing she did know about Hank was that he liked her to look good, he had made it clear on several occasions since their marriage that her appearance reflected on him, and more than once he had arrived home with some item of clothing for her that had caught his fancy. She stared at her reflection in the mirror. But she didn't much care for the Annie Hall look, inspired by Woody Allen's film the year before, that Hank favoured for her. It was too masculine for her taste, with its tweed jackets and high-collared shirts, and she suspected that the only reason Hank liked it was because it happened to be in fashion.

She frowned thoughtfully. But it didn't suit her. Nevertheless, she now dressed in a military-style shirt with matching baggy trousers that had been Hank's latest offering, wearing a twilled woollen jacket over the top of the outfit, the severe cut of which was softened by the honey-gold shade of the material. The resultant modern, somewhat aggressive young woman who stared back at her from the full-length mirror in the bedroom didn't *feel* like her, but she shrugged philosophically after a few moments' keen contemplation.

She would meet him half way, three-quarters even, if that's what it took to get this marriage on an even keel.

It was six hours later and Kate was full of turkey and plum pudding and trying hard to concentrate on a rambling story James was telling, Adam fast asleep on her lap and Hank and Liz either side of her on the comfortable sofa. 'He does adore you, you know.' Liz gestured at the sleeping infant with a warm smile. 'But then we all do, Kate. Hank's a very lucky man.'

'Oh yeah, and what about Kate?' Hank asked with a broad grin, but he couldn't hide the pleasure Liz's compliment had given him and Kate felt a warm glow at his obvious pride in her. If only they could always be like this, then everything that was wrong had a chance of becoming right.

Probably lots of married couples had difficulties in their sexual relationship at first, a settling-in period, it didn't have to mean anything. And when that side of things was sorted he would be more affectionate, warmer and loving, and not just because they had an audience. Her thoughts stopped abruptly and her eyes opened a fraction wider as she realized where they had headed. But it was true . . . She lowered her gaze to Adam as the talk ebbed and flowed around her. Hank was a different person when they were with people, whoever they were. At those times he was like the old Hank, the Hank of their courting days, the Hank she had thought would love her and protect her and want to be with her. Because that was what marriage was all about, wasn't it? Sharing, being there for each other, *wanting* to be there?

'John's going to build a snowman with me!' Susan skipped into the room, her face alight. 'Who else is coming?'

'Oh darling, it's so cold.' Liz looked at the eager young face in front of her, laughed, and shrugged her shoulders.

'Well not me, and certainly not your father. I don't want him breaking his other ankle.'

'I'll help.' Hank's voice was light, off-hand, as though he didn't really care one way or the other, but Kate had felt his body tighten at the side of her and wondered why.

'Oh brilliant! What about you, Kate? Will you come too?'

'Kate's got Adam, and anyway, she's like your mother, she doesn't like the cold.' Hank had answered before she could acquiesce to Susan's plea, and she bit back on the words of protest she was about to make as John came into the room. If Hank didn't want her there, and it was clear he didn't, she certainly had no intention of forcing herself on him.

'Hank's helping, John,' Susan said happily as Hank added, 'if that's all right by you?'

John hadn't exactly been smiling as he had entered but now his face straightened and his voice was flat as he replied, 'it's a free country.'

There it was again, that animosity. Kate blinked, her gaze moving between the two men. Their faces were still and expressionless but she knew she was right, even when Hank smiled and rose from the sofa saying in a laughing aside to Susan, 'he's worried my snowman will be better than his.'

'Are we making one each? Oh, bagsy me has the big spade then, you two are bigger than me.'

They left just after eight and, like before, Hank said little on the way home, lost in morose thoughts of his own. And when, later that night, Kate was awoken by the groping hands and whisky-laden breath she endured what had to be endured before turning over and staring at the dark expanse of wall at her side. There was something wrong with Hank, she had to face it, but having faced it she didn't know what to do. Her eyes were dry and burning hot as she heard him leave the bathroom and join her in bed. But whether it was disloyal or not she had to talk to someone, unburden herself and get advice, and the only person she knew who had the wisdom to understand what she didn't say as much as what she did was Albert. She needed the old warrior's common sense and blunt honesty, she should have spoken to him about all this before, and the day after tomorrow, once he was home, she'd go and see him.

Now the decision which she had been putting off for weeks was made she felt a sense of relief, which enabled her to lie still and quiet by Hank's side as she listened to the sound of his thick, soft snoring, her body aching slightly at the abrupt invasion which had lasted no longer than a minute or two.

Twenty-four hours, she could last twenty-four hours more and then she would discuss with Albert the resolution that had been growing steadily over the last few weeks, although she hadn't been able to admit it to herself, that of the prospect of leaving her husband of six weeks and living on her own again.

Chapter Eleven

She heard the miaowing of the cats first as she reached Albert's front door, and it was something in their plaintive cry that persuaded her to walk along the street and turn into the thin dirt alley bordering the back of the terraced gardens when her knocking brought no reply. She opened the narrow, rickety gate into the wasteland that was the garden of Cairn House, and, picking her way among the mass of rubbish interlaced with the odd clump of spiky grass, walked to the back of the house and down the two or three steps to look in the window of Albert's sitting room. She could just see the top of the old man's head as he sat in a chair in front of the dark fireplace in which no fire was burning. No fire? Albert always had a fire, summer and winter, it was something he was adamant about.

She tapped the glass now and the two cats who were restlessly pacing in front of the front door came leaping over to the window sill, winding their way amongst the clutter as they pressed against the window, miaowing loudly.

Albert? *Albert* . . . Fear constricted her throat, churning her stomach and turning her bowels to water. She had to see if he was all right, get in somehow – 'An' what might you be about then?' The shriek and start she gave sent the man behind her back a couple of paces, and his voice wasn't quite so steady when next he spoke. 'By, lass, I didn't know it was you, not with that hood up over your head.'

'Mr Pattison? Oh, Mr Pattison, I think there's something wrong with Albert.'

'Albert?' Albert's next-door neighbour peered at her in the evening twilight. 'He was all right last night when he got home from this old comrades do of his, lass. The missus said she had a natter with him afore he went in to see to his cats, an' he'd had a right old time.'

'Well I couldn't make him hear and I came round to the back and he's sitting in the chair –'

'All right, lass, all right, take it steady.' He pushed past her now and leant against the crumbling wall, inspecting the room through the grimy window, before straightening and turning to face her again. 'Aye, well, it don't look too good, does it, lass. I reckon we need to get in there and see what's what.'

'You don't think . . .' She couldn't go on, and there was a long pause when the middle-aged man just stared back at her before saying, 'like I said, it don't look too good, lass. Look, you come home with me a minute and we'll get the missus to give that fancy nephew of his a ring. We had the phone put in a few months back, an' I know she got the number then, for emergencies like.'

Albert, oh, Albert. Albert, Albert, Albert . . .

By the time Willie McGuire, Albert's nephew, had arrived at the house Kate had prepared herself for the worst, but still, as Willie turned the key in the lock, she found herself hoping desperately that it was all a mistake, that the old man had fallen into a deep sleep, anything . . .

They said, later, that he must have died almost immediately after entering the house the day before, and the fact that he was still sitting in his new suit and overcoat bore evidence to this. His face was smiling, peaceful, his hand still resting on the arm of the chair by the side of a half-full tumbler of whisky. They said his heart had just stopped beating, it wasn't a heart attack as such, he hadn't known anything about it, he had simply shut his eyes and gone to sleep.

She wanted to shout and cry and scream, to demand him back, to tell him he couldn't leave her, he couldn't just go without a word, but she did none of those things. She sat, quietly, while the police doctor did what was necessary, she answered a whole host of questions and listened to Mr Pattison and Willie doing the same, and then she left with Albert's cats secured in two baskets the kind young policewoman had thoughtfully provided, and drove away.

She had only gone a few miles when the shaking, which had begun as a sick trembling in her stomach and spread to every part of her, became so bad she knew she wasn't safe to drive. She pulled into a lay-by, in which two large lorries were parked, and sat for some minutes, the cats wailing loudly from their baskets perched on the back seat. She couldn't believe she wouldn't ever see him again, talk to him, and yet another part of her mind was screaming against the knowledge it had somehow absorbed the moment she had heard those cats mewing behind Albert's front door. He shouldn't have gone to that reunion, he hadn't been well for some weeks before Christmas, she should have stopped him, had him stay with her. This was her fault, *her fault*. Albert, oh, Albert.

The tears were raining down her face but she wasn't even aware of it. And yet he had wanted to go and see all his old comrades, he had, he'd been looking forward to it. She shook her head blindly from side to side as she leant forward in the seat, her arms crossed round her middle as the pain inside became too much to bear. Oh, Albert . . . His lined old face swam before her eyes and she would have given the world, and everything in it, to have him there with her, to be able to touch him, kiss the wrinkled, thin cheek, tell him she loved him. She hadn't realized just how much she loved him and now it was too late, too late to spend more time with him, to spoil him a little as he so richly deserved. She'd left it too late –

'Miss? Is anything wrong, miss?'

She was so sunk in misery that the tap on her window barely registered, and even when her door was opened and the big burly lorry driver knelt down by her side, it didn't occur to her to be frightened. 'I . . . It's . . .' But she couldn't speak as she gasped and shuddered and shook, and she leant forward again, resting her head against the steering wheel as her heart broke.

'You wait there, I'll be back in a minute, love.'

When, a moment or two later, a steaming mug of tea laced with alcohol was pushed under her nose she couldn't control the trembling enough to take it, and it was another full minute before she raised her head and looked through streaming eyes at her knight of the road. 'I'm sorry . . .' She gulped deep in her throat as another hiccuping sob cut off her words. 'I've had a shock.'

'I thought you might have had, love. Now look, don't you be scared of me, will you? I've got two girls of my own about your age, and my boy is going on eighteen, and I wouldn't want any of them to be in the state you are with no one around to help. My mate, Patrick, is in the other lorry in front of mine, you want him to go and ring someone for you?'

'No, no really, I'll be all right in a minute.' She reached for the mug and took a mouthful of hot tea to prove she meant what she said. 'It's just . . . I didn't expect it, you see.'

'Bit of bad news, eh?' He nodded understandingly. 'Well, you just sit quiet and drink that down, it's got a shot of brandy in it for the nerves, but not too much, we don't want you tiddly.'

'You're very kind.'

'We're only in this world the once, love, and if we can't help each other along the way it's a poor old do, isn't it. I don't hold with the "I'm all right, Jack" spirit that seems to be about these days. My old mother used to say that the good and bad we do comes home to roost in the end, and I'm damned if she's not right. Do unto others as you'd like to be done by, that was another of her little gems, but these days it's more like, do unto others before they do it to you, you know what I mean?'

She nodded, forcing the tears back that threatened to erupt again at his obvious concern for her. He was a huge giant of a man, six foot tall at least and nearly as broad, with muscles on him like a prize wrestler and a crew-cut that added to the intimidating whole, but his eyes were the kindest she'd seen in anyone, man, woman or child.

He continued to talk, more to give her time to compose herself than because he wanted any answers, she suspected, and by the time she had finished the mug of tea she was sufficiently recovered to thank him properly and assure him that yes, she really was all right now, and no, she didn't want him to follow her in his lorry to make sure she got home safely. 'But it's very good of you to offer,' she added hastily.

'No problem, love.' He inclined his head towards the back seat where the cats were still wailing their displeasure at being confined. 'Enough to make your eyeballs rattle! What you got in there anyway, cats is it?'

'Yes, two tabbies. My . . . friend's died suddenly, that's why I was upset, and so I'm looking after his cats. There wasn't really anyone else and I didn't want them to end up as strays or worse. He'd –' She paused and forced herself to continue. 'He'd have liked me to take care of them, I know that.'

'I'm sure he would, love.' The crescendo in the back reached new heights and he winced slightly. 'They've got a good pair of lungs on 'em, that's for sure, you got far to go?'

'Dumbarton, it's on the outskirts.'

'Yes, I know it. Well, drive carefully, love, especially in view of that racket.'

'I will.' She reached out her arm and touched the beefy hand resting on the door. 'And thank you again, you're a very nice man.'

'Tell that to the missus, love.' He grinned at her. 'And the kids when they're on the want. It don't make no difference if they're married or not, they still expect good old dad to fork out for this and that.'

'And I bet good old dad does?'

'Well, you know how it is . . .' No, she didn't, not really, but she didn't say so, merely smiling and nodding as he closed her door and waved before marching back to his lorry. There were nice people, good people, generous people in the world, she thought pensively, as she started the engine and guided the little Morris Minor on to the road. People like that lorry driver, and Liz and James, and Albert – her heart caught on the name – and they more than made up for the Richard Wellingtons and Sister Browns.

Hank was seated in front of the television set when she let herself into the house, and she deposited her noisy cargo in the hall before walking through to the sitting room. 'What the hell is making that din?' he asked as he rose from his chair, his eyes on the door. 'It sounds like something's being tortured.'

'It's Albert's cats.'

'*Albert's cats?*' He glanced at her for a moment before his gaze swung back to the doorway. 'Are you mad? Why are they out there? Where's Albert?'

'He's . . .' She couldn't go on.

'Kate? Where's Albert?' He turned to her then, and she stared back at him but couldn't speak, the tears pouring down her face. 'He's not? . . . Kate? Is that it? Oh, Kate . . .' He came across and put his arms around her, holding her gently against him as she sobbed her distress into the new cashmere sweater she had bought him for Christmas. She hadn't known what to expect, how he would react, and his quiet sympathy opened the floodgates again. They stood together in the centre of the room for some minutes before he put her from him slowly, taking her hand and leading her over to the sofa. 'Sit down there, sugar, and I'll fix us a drink,' he said softly, 'Then you can tell me all about it.'

'Oh, Hank . . .' She relaxed against the cushions, feeling utterly spent, brushing damp wisps of hair from her sticky cheeks with a shaking hand. 'I found him, it was awful . . .'

He handed her a glass of sherry before mixing himself a

whisky and soda, and then joined her on the sofa, putting his arm round her in a comforting gesture as she began to talk.

'And the police think it happened yesterday?' he asked when she finished speaking.

'That's what their doctor said.' She rubbed at her nose before taking a big gulp of the sherry. 'I shall be tipsy at this rate, that lorry driver put some brandy in the tea he gave me.' But the alcohol had relaxed her, allowing her to lean against him in a way she wouldn't do normally, not these days anyway.

'It won't hurt for once.'

'I can't believe it, Hank, not really. I just can't believe I'll never see him again.'

'Don't think about that now, give yourself time to take it in, and look, you're doing what he would have wanted, with the cats.'

'Do you mind? Having them here, I mean?'

'Of course not, if it makes you happy. We'll settle them down in a minute, find some old blankets and open a tin of sardines or something, they'll like that.'

He was being nice, so nice, she thought pensively, now, when it really mattered. 'Thank you, Hank.' She raised her head from his shoulder, turning slightly to look into his face as she touched his cheek gently with the tips of her fingers. As their eyes caught and held the moment stretched and lengthened, her hand still on his face and an unconscious pleading in her gaze that turned her eyes liquid. And just when she thought he was going to kiss her, to move her into him in an embrace that was more than merely a wish to comfort, he removed her hand from his face and stood up, his movements abrupt, jerky.

'Let's get the cats out of those baskets, they're driving me crazy with their yowling.'

'Hank?'

He hesitated as she spoke his name, for just one infinitesimal second, and then his back straightened and he continued in his march out of the room, leaving her sitting alone as she shrank down inside herself, until she was nothing, less than nothing, worthless and unloved.

By the end of January Kate knew she was expecting Hank's baby, but such was the depth of her grief over Albert's demise that her pregnancy, along with the worsening relationship with Hank, were pushed to the back of her mind. Ever after, when she looked back on the months leading up to her first summer as a married woman, they remained something of a blur, with just the odd occasion standing out in stark clarity to the shadowed whole. One such occasion was the day she told Hank he was going to be a father.

It was a dark overcast Sunday morning in the middle of February and she had been sick three mornings on the trot, and now, as she struggled back to bed and snuggled down gratefully in the warmth of the electric blanket and thick duvet, Hank appeared in the doorway, eating a slice of toast. 'You thrown up again?' he asked off-handedly. 'You wanna take a few days off and get this bug out of your system, else it'll hang on for ever.'

'Not this bug.' From the first morning they were married he had vacated the bed the moment he was awake, as though even that modicum of intimacy was unacceptable, and, although she would have rather died than admit it, it hurt.

'What does that mean?' he asked disinterestedly, already turning away.

'I'm pregnant.'

'What . . .' She watched him gulp audibly as he faced her, and his voice was no more than a strangled whisper when he said, 'what did you say?'

'I'm pregnant. With child, if you prefer the biblical terminology, and before you ask' – here she shut her eyes tightly as though he had already asked – 'it's yours.'

'Kate, I didn't think for a minute you'd . . . It's just . . .'

Her eyes opened to see the strangest expression stretching his face. Pride, sheer wonder, were warring with what looked suspiciously like panic, but of the stark, undiluted kind. 'When . . . I mean . . .'

'It must have happened that first time,' she said quietly, her voice softer now. 'It's due the middle of August, but of course it could be early, like before.' She didn't know what made her add that last bit, especially when he had taken the news so well, contrary to her expectations, but in this moment of truth she needed his acknowledgement of the existence of that first precious life desperately. Perhaps because of her own guilt, she thought bitterly. On the occasions she allowed herself to dwell on her condition she had been consumed by that emotion, eaten up by the feeling that she had betrayed Joy in the worst possible way.

He ignored the comment, as she had known he would, in the same way he ignored everything else he chose to block out of his mind, and she could almost have thought he hadn't heard her last two words but for the flicker at the back of his eyes as she had spoken. 'I'm pleased, Kate, don't think I'm not pleased, but it's just such a . . . surprise.'

'Shock, you mean?' She didn't smile. 'Because if you do, I understand perfectly. I was shocked, more than shocked, especially in view of the fact we have only been intimate twice. But, of course, it only takes once.' *Albert, oh, Albert* . . . She could hear his voice echoing down the long hours and days and weeks, and it was that alone that enabled her to go on as his face stiffened. 'Do you see our marriage continuing, Hank?'

'*What?*'

It was clear the confrontation had astounded him and in fact she had surprised herself, but the need to bring things out into the open, to talk, to *communicate*, was fierce. He had taken to coming home late, maybe once or occasionally twice a week, since Christmas, and when she had tackled him about it he pleaded pressure of work as the excuse. But she didn't believe him. She didn't know why, she just didn't, but neither could she bring herself to accept he was seeing another woman. That would mean he would have had to have known her before they were married, had been deceiving her for months, that their whole relationship was built on a lie. He wouldn't do that to her, not Hank, would he? . . . But if he was still upset over her insistence to have Joy, still unsure and jealous of her, punishing her by withholding his affection and trust, they had to *talk* about it, especially now.

'I said, do you see our marriage continuing?'

'What sort of question is that, for crying out loud? You've just told me we're having a baby, haven't you?'

She didn't give him an answer to this but stared at him, hard, and it was his eyes that dropped from hers.

'Of course I see our marriage continuing,' he said eventually when she maintained her silence. 'What the hell fire do you think I'm working for anyway? We've the house, the cars, a good standard of living . . .'

'That's not marriage.'

'The hell it isn't! You don't want for anything –'

'*Hank* . . .' Although her voice was low, its tone cut through his blustering like a hot knife through butter. 'I'm talking about us, us as a couple.'

'What do you want from me, Kate?' He closed his eyes and screwed up his face, his whole manner indicating she was being unreasonable, unjust. 'I told you before we were married I would provide for you, provide well, there's no need for you to work, you know that. And I've accepted you don't want anything to do with my family –'

'That's not fair! You know that's not fair! Your mother –'

'And now you'll have a baby, too, won't you? So I don't see, I really don't see, what you're getting at.'

'You don't see . . .' Her voice died away on a long shuddering breath. 'You want me to spell it out?'

'I don't want you to spell anything out, Kate, there's

nothing *to* spell out. Married life is a composite, you know that as well as I do, and on the whole I'd say you're getting a very fair deal.' She didn't believe it, she just didn't believe he was saying this, and her amazement was reflected in her wide-open eyes and mouth that had fallen into a silent gape. 'Now, I'll go and fix you some toast and coffee and later you can call Liz, tell her the good news.'

'I don't want to tell anyone yet –'

'Don't be silly, there's no need to be shy. It's the most natural thing in the world and you know Liz will be thrilled.' And he smiled at her, he actually smiled at her, his manner almost teasing as though he was completely unaware of the dark undercurrent in their conversation and the reason for it.

She continued to stare at the doorway for some moments after Hank had gone downstairs, her head spinning. Natural? Having a baby might be natural, she thought bitterly, but it was the only aspect of their marriage that *was*. And he had known what she was trying to say, he must have, and he could still smile at her like that? *Smile* at her?

But Hank wasn't smiling as he walked downstairs, neither was his expression defensive or angry as it had been at different times during the conversation with his wife. His face was bare and exposed and wretched, his eyes despairing, and once in the kitchen he leant with his arms outstretched and his hands resting palms down on the scrubbed table, his head bowed. What was he going to do? *What was he going to do?*

There was a feeling tearing through his body compounded of intense pain and searing guilt and a thousand other emotions besides, and although he told himself to get it in check, to put it into that closed room in his mind that he rarely, and never voluntarily, opened, he couldn't do it. She was pregnant. He'd made her pregnant . . . He lifted his head for a moment and his eyes reflected the same wonder Kate had recognized. But the other, he couldn't do without the other, the pliant willing bodies and frantic gut-wrenching excitement that always ended one way, damn it, in frustration and hurried, unsatisfying pleasure that made him sick to his soul. Why? Why did it have to be like this?

Unbidden, his mother's face swam on to the screen in his mind, and with it a hundred dark, screaming nightmares that caused his buttocks to clench in protest. A small child held up as a laughing stock among his peers at his own birthday party. A cruel public debasement at a Thanksgiving gathering because of a minor infringement of her rigid rules . . . But it was the humiliations that were committed in private that were buried deepest, the unmentionable abuse . . . He shook his head as though to clear it from a blow. But she loved him, in her own way his mother loved him, she loved them all. She had told him so every day of his life before he had married Kate, along with what she expected of him, the accomplishments he could attain with her guidance, her . . . guidance.

He ground his teeth, straightening abruptly as he pressed his hands either side of his head, as though to crush the memories that ravaged his mind. Don't think about it. Don't think about it. The hard-won technique, born in the fire of desolation, took over. He was in control. *He* was in control. Not his mother, not Kate, not . . . the others. And he could handle this, of course he could.

He walked across to the kitchen window and stood looking out into the garden where a host of birds were fluttering about the wooden bird-table he had filled with scraps, much to the disgust of the two cats, who were sitting on the window sill surveying the scene with gently waving tails and low growls.

'A baby would be good.' He spoke out loud, causing the larger of the cats, Murphy, to cease his murmuring and push up against Hank's arm, his body arching in welcome. There was no doubt the two animals had transferred their allegiance wholesale to him, Kate merely being tolerated as consort, and although he explained their affection away by telling himself they had always been used to male company, nevertheless their devotion gave him great pleasure. 'Yes, a baby would be good,' he said again as he idly stroked the brindled fur, 'it will satisfy Kate's maternal streak, keep her occupied.' But he knew, even as he spoke, that that wasn't the real reason for his easy acceptance of the situation, and that his motive, buried under layers of guilt and pain and desire, mustn't be voiced, even to himself.

That had been a nasty moment up there. His eyes narrowed on the wintry vista outside as his thoughts sped on. But he had handled it well, yes, he had. He could manage Kate, he'd always known that, hadn't he . . . She wasn't like some of these hard-boiled broads that were around these days, no, she was a lady. That had been the first thing he'd noticed about her, that air of refined modesty that sat on her like a decorous cloak. He'd looked at her and seen the perfect woman for his requirements, that's why he'd been so gutted the night she'd told him about that other guy . . . But it hadn't been her fault, he'd known that, although the sleaze-bag could have ruined everything.

He took a deep breath as the rage that had filled him that night began to boil up again, and deliberately forced his thoughts into safer channels. But that was all over, it couldn't touch him now, he was safe . . . A respectable married man whose young wife already had a baby on the way. He laughed quietly, much to the surprise of the cats, who glanced at him enquiringly, but the sound held no amusement whatsoever. Yes, all in all, a baby would be good.

CHAPTER TWELVE

She wished this was over. Oh, how she wished it was over. Kate glanced down at her huge stomach, stretched as tight as a drum under her maternity dress, and sighed wearily. And to think she had carried on working right up to the moment Joy was born. She shook her head in disbelief. She couldn't have done so this time, that much was for sure, she had been so relieved to leave at thirty weeks she could have cried. Perhaps it was twins after all? Her eyes narrowed as she considered the possibility that had seemed likely in the early days. But no, they were sure it was just one baby, one big baby and plenty of water.

She sighed again as she poured herself a glass of lemonade before waddling out to her deck-chair in the garden under the shade of a large Bramley-apple tree. The first week of July and she still had weeks to go. She glanced across to where Murphy and Tripe, so called because of his love of the stuff, Albert had once told her when she had first been introduced to Murphy's brother some years before, were basking in the full glare of the noon-day sun, but her eyes didn't really see the cats as she continued to look inwards.

The nursery was ready and Hank had done a wonderful job, she had to give him that. The bright, sunshine-yellow walls and pale green carpet and curtains were a perfect backdrop for the white wooden cot, small wardrobe and chest of drawers and comfortable nursing chair; and the army of colourful mobiles, cuddly toys and children's books that festooned the shelves and every available surface would have filled a toy shop. Every night he came home with something different . . . She lay back against the striped material as she pictured the latest acquisition, a big red ball in soft foam that Hank had bought the day before.

'To get him used to kicking a ball about from day one.' Hank had been grinning as he had spoken but she hadn't returned the smile, and her voice had been cool as she said, 'You're going to be terribly disappointed if it's a girl.'

'Not really, but I've told you, boys run in my family, it'll be a boy.' His voice had been reasonable, gentle, and it had made her want to scream. He always spoke to her like that these days, his manner verging on the patronizing at times, as though the swelling in her stomach had affected her brain.

A slight headache began to throb at the back of her eyes and she reached down for the pair of sunglasses lying to one side of the deck-chair.

He had used that tone a month ago, on the day she had finally left work and arrived home with her arms full of presents and cards, to explain why he was in the process of moving into the spare room. 'You know you toss and turn at night and can't get comfortable, you need more space,' he'd said softly. 'It's just until the baby's born, Kate, it'll be better for both of us, and once he's here things can get back to normal.'

Normal? She'd wanted to laugh and shout hysterically into his bland face and see the false, benign and kindly expression wiped clean to reveal what he was really thinking. What was normal? Certainly not their celibate lifestyle. He had seized upon the fact that she was pregnant as an excuse for his continuing lack of ardour, making it clear, when she had nerved herself to make an overture one day, that he couldn't countenance physical intimacy when she was carrying his child. She had thought, she had really thought at the time that the baby was going to make a difference to them, his whole manner had been so tender, so sympathetic towards her for days, but with that last rejection something in her had hardened, withdrawn, and it was that attitude that had enabled her merely to nod stiffly as he had passed her on the landing with his arms full of clothes, and turn and walk downstairs without protesting his departure from her bed.

As the afternoon progressed her headache got worse, and when Hank didn't return at his normal time of six o'clock, she left his dinner covered with foil in the oven on a low heat and went up to her room.

His 'late' nights had become fairly regular at one or two a week over the last few months, but she had ceased to worry about the reason for them. She was biding time, she recognized the fact without ever putting it into words in her head, biding time until the baby was born and she could work again once it reached the toddler stage and didn't need her so desperately.

And then? Then she would find a small flat, settle the child in a responsible nursery during the day, and begin to start some sort of life again. Because this wasn't living, this existence in a barren vacuum with a man who made her feel she was the plainest, most unprepossessing woman in the world. In the early days of her marriage she had caught herself looking at women, especially plain or downright ugly women, and wondering why they could hold a man with such seemingly little effort and she couldn't. What made her so repulsive that her own husband didn't want her? But she was past that now. She didn't want a man in her life, not ever again. The future was her child and her career, and if she could have added Joy to that future she would have been content with her lot.

When the headache seemed to transfer to her stomach she decided she must have caught a summer virus, and after showering and putting on a clean nightie she pulled the curtains and lay in the shaded room, trying to concentrate on something other than her physical condition. But she felt strange, odd, and when she felt the dampness between her legs she knew what had happened, her waters had broken. She was in labour.

Over five weeks early? She felt a moment's panic and then spoke to herself sternly. It's all right, don't panic, Kate. Joy was a month early and she was a good size, there's nothing to worry about. But where was Hank, when she needed him most?

She rose from the bed and walked through to the bathroom, showering again and then dressing slowly, a bulky pad in place to catch the seeping fluid as she timed the contractions. Every six minutes, but they were strong, powerful. *Where was Hank?* She lifted the telephone by the bed and dialled the work's number, letting it ring for some time before she replaced the receiver. Perhaps he was with James, discussing business? She would try there. James answered almost immediately, and her voice was shaking slightly as she said, 'James, it's Kate. Hank isn't with you, I suppose?'

'Hank? No, he's not here, I'd have thought he'd have been with you hours ago.'

'Oh don't worry, perhaps he stopped off somewhere, a drink or something.'

'Are you all right, Kate?' She heard him say something more but his voice was muffled and indistinct, as though he had his hand over the telephone, and then the next moment Liz's dulcet tones came down the line.

'Kate? What's wrong?'

'Nothing, well, not really. It's just that I've started and Hank isn't home yet.'

'The baby? You mean the baby's on the way?' Liz asked anxiously, before moderating her tone somewhat as she continued, 'Now don't worry, Kate. A first baby can take ages, I was all day and night with John. Are you sure you've started, dear?'

'Quite sure. The waters have broken and the contractions are coming . . .' She gasped as the pain continued to build, stronger this time, making speech impossible.

'Kate? *Kate?*'

'Wait . . . wait . . . Liz.'

When she could speak again there was a slight dew of perspiration on her brow and her heart was pounding. 'I think I need to get to hospital, Liz.'

'We'll come and get you –'

'No, thanks anyway, but a taxi would be quicker.'

'I don't like to think of you going by yourself in a taxi, dear. Let us come over, we could be with you quite soon and I'm sure there's no rush.'

And I'm sure there is, Kate thought grimly. Joy's birth hadn't been a slow one and this looked to be even quicker. 'No, really Liz, I'll get a taxi. Look, I must go.'

'I'll meet you there then, you must have someone to hold your hand, and James can try to locate Hank in the meantime. Now, darling, keep calm. I know you're a doctor and quite au fait about all this sort of thing, but it's different when it's actually happening to you, and although the pains seem agonizing, they really can last ages, so don't worry.'

Waiting for the taxi seemed like an eternity and Kate found herself longing for Hank with an intensity that surprised her, considering their present state of affairs. But he was her husband, this was his child, and she was frightened.

The taxi-driver was the sort of salt-of-the-earth type that was heaven-sent for just such a situation as he now found himself in. He carried her case to the car, holding her arm tightly and keeping up a steady stream of reassuring chatter as he did so, and settled her on the back seat as though she was the finest Meissen porcelain, before leaping round the car and into the driver's seat. 'We'll be there in no time, lass, don't you worry. They don't call me the fastest thing on four wheels for nothin'.'

Everyone was telling her not to worry, Kate thought weakly as she went through the breathing exercises the ante-natal classes had drummed into them, and she wasn't, not really, not now it was happening. It was too late for worry after all . . .

'Your husband away then?' The driver was watching her through his mirror and had obviously decided talk was the best therapy.

'He's just late.' The contraction was finishing and she could manage a smile.

'He is that, an' all. By, I bet you'll give him some stick when he puts his nose round the door, eh, if you're anythin' like my old lady? I was pacin' the waitin' room for all eight of ours, bar one, but that's the one she never lets me forget. I've only got to put a foot wrong an' our Florence is dragged up again, regular as clockwork. I was at a darts match you see, enjoyin' meself, that's what she can't forgive. How was I to know the little blighter'd decide to come a week early? She was the sixth an' all the others arrived bang on time. This your first, is it?'

She hesitated, but something in her couldn't deny Joy, and so she said, 'Not exactly, I was pregnant last year.'

'Oh, right then.' He was clearly embarrassed, assuming she had lost the baby, but she didn't correct him or elaborate on her statement, and there was silence in the taxi for some minutes before he cleared his throat and said, 'You'll be fine, lass, I'm sure of it.'

'Yes, so am I.' She smiled at the pair of eyes watching her in the mirror to let him know he hadn't upset her. 'And it's a nice time of the year for a baby to be born, isn't it.'

'Aye, you're right there. Our youngest two were born about now an' they're the healthiest of the lot.' His eyes narrowed as her face twisted and she began to pant frantically. 'Just hold on a bit longer, lass, we're nearly there. Cross your fingers an' whatever else it takes an' hold on.'

'Whatever else it takes'. Once the contraction had finished she found herself smiling at the back of the grizzled head. He reminded her of Albert, he had the same dry way of putting things as her old friend, a way that was entirely natural and all the more droll because of his unawareness of the fact he was being funny.

'That's it, lass. You keep smilin' an' I'll keep drivin' an' atween us we'll reach dry land.'

And reach dry land they did, and just half an hour later,

with Liz clutching her hand and urging her on, Kate's son made his appearance into the world.

'He's beautiful, he's absolutely beautiful, dear,' Liz cried ecstatically, as the midwife cut the umbilical cord and cleaned the tiny face of debris before weighing him and wrapping him up.

'Can I hold him?' Kate asked weakly.

'Just for a minute.' The midwife smiled at Kate as she placed the baby in her outstretched arms, but there was a touch of concern in her eyes. 'He's a good weight at 6 pounds, considering he's so early, but I think his breathing needs a little help for a few hours. He'll be fine in one of the incubators and I'm sure he'll be with you by morning.'

'There's nothing wrong?' Kate asked anxiously, staring down into the small, distinctly boyish face which was so different to that other tiny baby's forever in the forefront of her mind.

'Nothing, I promise. Now, wouldn't I tell you, Dr Ross, if there was?'

'I hope so.' Kate smiled at the midwife, whose reputation within the hospital was first-class. She had been at Crompton General since qualifying twenty years before and everyone, without exception, liked the cheerful and good-natured woman whose slightly phlegmatic nature meant she was unflappable in a crisis.

'You know so. Now, if you've finished getting acquainted? . . .'

Kate held her son close to her heart as she kissed the soft downy head, her throat full. A son. Hank had wanted a son. Would he make any difference to their shell of a marriage or was it too late for that? Strangely enough, now it was all over, she realized she was glad he hadn't been around at the birth. Neither of her children's fathers had seen their offspring in those first few vital seconds and neither of them had deserved to . . . She shut her eyes for a moment against the bitterness in the thought, not liking this side of herself. Nevertheless, it was true.

'Oh, Kate, this has been the most wonderful experience of my life.' Liz hugged her once they were back in the ward where most of the other occupants were already asleep.

'What about the births of your three?'

'They were different, marvellous, miraculous, but different. I had dreadfully long labours with each of them, anyway, and frankly I was too exhausted to get over-excited at the time,' Liz said ruefully. 'But you, you were so quick, I can't believe it's your first child.'

Kate glanced at her quickly but Liz's face was completely guileless. 'Working in a hospital I suppose you get blasé about it all,' Kate said quietly, as she shrugged her shoulders. 'I've seen plenty of women who were quicker and plenty who took their time, it's just the luck of the draw.'

'Well, believe me, your way is best,' Liz said with great feeling. 'I'll go now and let you get some rest, you've earned it. I'll see you tomorrow, and little Paul Albert too, of course. Who chose his names?'

'I did.' She had no idea what names Hank favoured, it was one thing, among many things, they had never discussed.

'They suit him, he really is a gorgeous baby with those great big blue eyes and blond hair. You must be feeling so proud.'

Kate smiled and nodded but said nothing, her heart too full for words. She *was* proud of her son, he was beautiful, but she was proud of her daughter too and had never longed for her more. She was a mother again, *again*, and the maelstrom of emotion that had her in such turmoil made her desperate to be alone. She had to think, get her thoughts in order, talk logic to herself before she said or did something she would regret.

'Goodbye, dear.' But Liz had no sooner left the ward than she was back, tiptoeing among the beds after an apologetic word with the sister. 'James is out there and he said to tell you he couldn't find Hank but he's left a note at your house, pinned on the front door. Is that all right?'

'Fine, thank him for me and now you go home and tell Adam he isn't the youngest Ross anymore. He's been longing for this moment.'

'I'll tell him tomorrow morning when he wakes up. He's being very tiresome about going to nursery school at the moment but this will be something to tell his friends about. And Kate? . . .' Liz paused as she tugged at her lower lip with her teeth. 'I'm sorry about Hank, it really is too bad of him and James will tell him so. He should let you know where he can be reached if he's delayed. Has he done this before?'

'No, no of course not.' She couldn't, she just couldn't, bare her heart to Liz at this precise moment of time. If Albert had been there it would have been a different matter, but he wasn't, and no amount of longing could bring the old man back. 'I expect he started discussing business with someone over a drink and one drink led to another.'

'Yes, I expect so.' Liz smiled uncertainly. 'Men are such children, aren't they.'

When she was alone again, Kate lay back against the iron bed-head sipping the cup of tea one of the nurses had brought her as she considered Liz's last remark. Children? Perhaps some men had an endearing, child-like quality about them – she had noticed that trait in James more than once – but Hank? . . . No, not Hank. There was nothing of the child about Hank. In fact, the very opposite was true.

She placed the cup and saucer on the bedside locker but didn't lie down, merely adjusting the pillows behind her back as she remained sitting, her hands clasped across her now flat stomach and her eyes closed. She was tired, so tired, but her head was full of Hank. It was true, what she had just thought, there was no natural gaiety in her husband. It was as though the normal exuberance one would expect in a young man of his age, the buoyant zest for life, the – her mind sought the description she was looking for and found it – the *joy* of living, had been crushed out of him.

She thought for a moment her cogitation had conjured him up when she opened her eyes at the sound of hushed voices to see Hank standing at the far end of the ward talking to the ward sister, his face wearing the gentle, patient expression he did so well. But it wasn't real. She stared at him now as he remained unaware of her glance. It was an act. Like the considerate, kind husband of the last few weeks, moving out of his bedroom to give his young wife the rest she needed. As he turned she had to drag her gaze from his face, shutting her eyes again as she heard his soft approach.

'Kate? Darling?'

'Dr Ross?'

She focused on the ward sister's face and saw immediately Hank had won her round, because the somewhat austere, plain-faced nurse was beaming. 'Your husband has begged for a few moments with you but then you must settle down to sleep, all right? I'll be back with a sleeping pill in a few minutes.'

'Thank you.' Kate's face was unsmiling, and when her gaze left the older woman and moved to her husband without changing she sensed the sister's bewilderment before she bustled away. 'Where were you, Hank?' she asked quietly, her voice flat.

'I had to work late.'

She just checked herself from saying, 'You damn liar,' and instead raised her eyebrows as she shook her head slowly. 'I think not, but if you want to play your little games, go ahead. I'm too tired tonight to care.'

He had leant towards her as though he was going to kiss her when the nurse left them but had straightened at her tone, and now she saw that flicker at the back of his eyes as he said, 'Little games? What does that mean?'

'Have you seen the baby?'

'What?'

'Your son. Have you seen him?'

'Just for a moment.' He ran his finger round the inside of his collar, his eyes on hers. 'He's beautiful.'

'Yes, he is.' She stared up at him and her voice trembled slightly as she added, 'Liz stayed with me, while he was being born.'

'Kate, I'm sorry –'

'I don't want to hear it.' She raised her hand so savagely he actually took a step backwards before he collected himself. 'I just don't want to hear it, Hank. You can't or won't tell me the truth, you weren't working, I phoned the factory and James had no idea where you were.'

'James doesn't know everything, it was a business contact I made recently, for crying out loud, it could be worth thousands if the deal comes off. We had a few drinks and got talking, it's not the sort of thing you walk away from until it's right. How was I to know you'd have the baby so early? You know I would have been there with you if I'd known.'

'And you didn't think to phone me?'

'I did phone, later, but there was no answer, you must have been in here.'

'And what about all the other times, all the other nights you've been late recently? Was that business too?'

'*Of course it was.*' His voice was a low hiss and now he crouched down by the side of her, his face on a level with hers. 'I swear it was. This particular deal has taken a great amount of setting up, involving lots of different contacts. These things don't happen all by themselves, Kate, they involve hard work and long hours. You know the mess James's business was in when I joined him, it was on its last legs. Now I've got to turn that round, recoup the losses and try to make some sort of a profit, and I won't do that sitting on my backside and singing Dixie. I thought you understood . . .' He saw the shadow of uncertainty move across her eyes, the softening of her mouth, and the adrenalin flooded through his system. He could convince her, he knew he could convince her. He'd been crazy, foolish, to take such chances but he'd be careful from now on, discreet.

'Come on, honey, don't be mad,' he said softly as he put his arms round her, feeling her body remain stiff for a moment before it relaxed against him as she gave a little sigh. 'I'm doing it for us, you know that, and our son. Everything is going to work out just fine.'

'Oh, Hank . . .'

He had her, *he had her*, and he'd have to play it close to his chest from now on, he had too much to lose. He hadn't realized how the sight of that tiny, screwed-up face, that perfect little being that had come from his loins, *his loins*, would affect him. He was so small, so helpless, and looking to him for protection among other things, protection and security. He would make sure his son had what he had never had – a childhood, a normal childhood, a chance to grow up into the sort of person he really was. He had been born and reared in darkness, his son would have light.

'Are you pleased?'

'What?' He had almost forgotten Kate's presence and now he blinked rapidly moving back a little to look into her face. 'Pleased? About the child?' She nodded, her eyes tight on his face. 'I can't find words to tell you, he's . . . he's all I ever imagined and more.'

There was no doubting the sincerity in his voice and she nodded again, satisfied, a small smile touching her mouth as the ward sister joined them, her eyes darting from one to the other. 'Time for that sleeping pill, Mr Ross, I'm sorry . . .'

'Don't be, and thank you, ma'am.' As Hank smiled at the nurse he straightened to his full height before bending and kissing the top of Kate's head. 'I'll see you tomorrow, sugar.'

'All right.' She would have preferred a kiss on the lips, a reiteration that all was well, but as she watched him walk away she felt happier than she had in weeks, months, and she smiled at the sister as she reached out for the glass of water and plastic receptacle holding the sleeping pill. 'Thank you for letting him pop in,' she said quietly, after she had swallowed the tablet. 'I know it can be annoying when people come out of visiting hours.'

'Not to worry, I'm just glad everything is all right. I wondered for a minute there if I'd done the right thing.'

'He missed the birth.' Kate shrugged her shoulders. 'And I was annoyed.'

'I don't blame you, but you were a few weeks early, weren't you? I suppose it caught him on the hop. He was terribly upset when he first came, so apologetic, and so thrilled about the baby. He's obviously a first-time dad?' Kate nodded. 'Well, he'll make sure he's there for the second one, no doubt, and when they're as dishy as him you have to forgive them in the end, don't you. He looks a bit like Rock Hudson, doesn't he, being so big and American and all . . .'

'Yes, I suppose he does.'

'Anyway, I musn't talk any more, you settle down for the night now. Baby is fine, I've just checked with the nurse in charge, and we'll bring him along first thing in the morning. No doubt you'll be inundated with visitors once word gets out you're here. I understand Mr Riley offered you a private room if you wanted one.'

'Yes, he did, but I'd rather be on the ward like everyone else,' Kate said quietly. 'If there had been complications, that would have been different.'

The sister nodded approvingly. 'Well, if you want anything during the night, don't hesitate to call, Dr Ross.'

Hank was the first visitor in and the last one to leave during her five-day stay in the hospital, and on the morning he arrived to fetch her home she felt more positive about the success of their marriage than in all the preceding months. The optimistic mood lasted through all the farewells from staff and the other patients, most of whom had been thrilled to find out she was a doctor, and right up to the moment Hank turned to her in the car, with Paul secured in the carrycot on the back seat, and told her his mother was in residence.

'You're joking.' He wasn't, and she knew it. '*Hank!*'

'It's not my fault, Kate, listen to me. She arrived last night with Dad, they were literally standing on the doorstep, no phonecall, no nothing. What could I do? . . .'

'Send them to a hotel, anything.'

'How could I? Now think a minute, be reasonable. She's my mother, Kate, not some distant relation you can give the brush-off to. They've come all the way from the States just to see their grandchild, I couldn't tell them to take a cab and clear off to a hotel when we've got four bedrooms –'

'Three of which are occupied.'

'And one of which is not.' So he hadn't moved his things back into the master bedroom, she thought as her heart began to pound. She hadn't plucked up courage over the last few days actually to voice the question that had been haunting her days and nights, and now she acknowledged it was because she had feared the very thing he had just admitted. That he wasn't planning on sharing her bed.

'How long are they staying for?' she asked flatly.

'A few days, no more. They won't like leaving Edward and Dean at the helm too long.'

This was all she needed. His mother, *his mother*, of all people. 'I see.'

'Don't be like this, you must see I couldn't do anything about it, and besides, perhaps it will be a chance for you to make things right.'

'*What?*' Her mouth was slightly agape as she stared at him, unable to believe her ears. 'What did you say?' The shrill tone of her voice caused Paul, who had been fast asleep when they had placed him in his cocoon, to stir and whimper.

'You're upsetting him.' Hank started the car as he spoke, giving her one hard long look before putting it in gear and driving out of the hospital car-park.

'Hank, let's get this straight once and for all. I haven't done anything, *anything*, to your mother that needs to be put right, the boot is totally on the other foot and you know it.'

'Well perhaps she wants to extend the olive branch.'

'Does she?' He didn't answer and she asked him again, her voice low now, 'Does she? Is that what you really believe?'

'How do I know? She's here, isn't she?'

'Oh yes, she's certainly here, Hank.' On the very day I come out of hospital, when I'm at my lowest physically and mentally, Kate thought bitterly. Miriam couldn't have planned it better. She wanted to put her arms round her waist and hug herself, to sway back and forth and whimper her distress out loud, like Paul, but she did none of those things. She sat straight as a ramrod on the journey home, during which they exchanged not a word, her head high and her chin up. If Miriam Ross *was* offering to make amends, she would accept the gesture wholeheartedly, but having seen the venom and coal-black hatred in the other woman's eyes that November day eight months ago, she doubted it. But she was prepared now, she had that, at least, in her favour.

'Home sweet home.' She had looked forward to coming home with their child, so much, but now as Hank cut the engine and turned to her with a tight smile she felt nothing but a sick foreboding in the pit of her stomach. And when, in the next instant, the front door was flung wide and that large aggressive figure she had been picturing all the way home appeared on the doorstep, she knew her fears had been well founded. There wasn't a shred of conciliation in Miriam Ross's handsome features, not a shred, and as she moved down the steps, followed by her husband, her face was disdainful and cold.

'There you are.' She spoke as though Hank had popped round the corner shop for a loaf of bread, and her haughty gaze didn't acknowledge Kate by so much as the flicker of an eyelid.

'Yes, here we are, Mother.' Hank had left his seat and walked round the bonnet of the car to open Kate's door, and, although his face was obscured by the vehicle, she sensed from the placatory tone of his voice that he was smiling. 'And your grandson is fast asleep on the back seat.'

'Well bring him in then, bring him in. I'm sure he's been bumped and banged around enough for one day.'

'Hallo, Miriam . . . Michael.' It took some effort but her voice was pleasant as she swung her legs out of the car. 'I trust you've recovered from your flight yesterday?'

'Just about, just about.' There had been a brief pause before Hank's father had answered her and she knew instinctively he wasn't used to speaking first in his wife's presence. 'And what about you? How are you feeling?'

'She's had a baby, Michael, not an illness.' Miriam's voice was as sharp as a knife, and the animosity evident in every word hit Kate like a physical blow, and yet she sensed, somehow, that it wasn't her as an individual Hank's mother found so hard to take, it would have been anyone, any female, her son got involved with.

'I'm fine, thank you.' She answered Michael directly, inclining her head with a warm smile, and she saw the older man give a shadow of a smile in return before his wife dug him hard in the ribs, making him wince.

'Don't stand there smirking, do something useful and fetch the baby carriage in from the car,' and with a swiftness that belied her bulk Miriam turned and stalked back into the house before any of them moved.

'Come on in, Kate, Hank can see to the baby.' Michael's voice was quiet, expressing something that could be taken as regret for his wife's rudeness, and from the narrowed stare Hank gave his father she assumed, rightly, that it wasn't often Miriam's orders were countermanded. She allowed Michael to take her arm as they walked into the house and forced herself to respond to his embarrassed conversation, but all the time her temper was at boiling point. That woman! That awful, awful woman, who did she think she was? If she hadn't known better she would have thought this was Miriam's house and she was the guest, and an unwelcome one at that. And this feeling was intensified when, once she had divested herself of her coat and walked through to the sitting room, she found Miriam sitting in a chair at the side of the brightly burning fire, the small table in front of her set for morning coffee.

'Do sit down, Kate.' Hank's mother inclined a gracious head towards the sofa as she added, 'Coffee? White or black?'

'Miriam –' Miriam cut off her husband's voice with one long penetrating glance in his direction, her eyes narrowed, before Hank came hurrying into the room with the carrycot.

'Where shall I put him, Kate?'

'Here, on the sofa beside me. I'll have a cup of coffee and then I should imagine he'll be awake, he's due for a feed soon. Once you've all had a hold I'll take him upstairs to the nursery.' Nice and easy, Kate, nice and easy . . . The little voice in her head was cautioning her even as she spoke. You know the woman is trying to get to you, don't give her the satisfaction. Just play it cool, she won't be here forever, and she is Hank's mother after all . . .

Coffee was a strained affair for everyone except the perpetrator of the unease, who sat in regal indifference to the others as she sipped at her coffee with tight lips. The heavy atmosphere lifted slightly once Paul awoke and Hank picked him up and placed him in Miriam's arms. 'Your first grandchild, mother.' The faintly obsequious note in his voice caused Kate to wince inwardly but she didn't allow herself to show it, sitting quietly on the sofa as she watched Hank's mother survey her grandchild with what only could be described as a censorious air.

'He's very small.' Miriam's voice wasn't so much concerned as disapproving.

'He's actually a very good weight for nearly thirty-six weeks,' Kate said calmly, 'and he's already regained his birth weight.'

'Hmm . . .' Kate would have loved to be able to smack the doubtful expression from those handsome features. 'Well, my babies were all nine-pounders, big strapping boys from day one. I never had a moment's worry that they wouldn't do well.'

'Hank and I aren't worried about Paul.'

'No?' The sceptical note was meant to be heard. 'But then this is all new to you, isn't it.'

'I think I'll go and feed him now.' Kate smiled as she reached for her son, and it was the best piece of acting she had ever done. She was burning with indignation as she marched up the stairs with Paul a few moments later, her cheeks hot and her eyes fierce. She wasn't going to be able to stand much more of this, she knew she wasn't. She sank down into the small armless chair in the nursery and, having established Paul on the breast, shut her eyes tightly.

Her son, her beautiful, healthy son. How dare Hank's mother be so disparaging, so . . . insulting? Normal grandmothers weren't like this, just the opposite, in fact, but then – she opened her eyes wide as she shook her head wearily – the woman wasn't a normal grandmother, or mother, or wife . . . Oh, the next few days were going to seem like weeks, months. How could Hank have asked her to stay at the house, how could he? He knew how tired she was, what a vulnerable position he had placed her in . . .

Tears of self-pity stung her eyes but she blinked them away, sniffing determinedly. She wasn't going to cry or get annoyed or do anything else that might affect her milk supply and upset Paul. He was the only thing that mattered at the moment, the one solid certainty in a world that was anything but. She didn't know how things were between her and Hank from one day to the next, the last few hours had told her that, but she would get through, she must, for Paul's sake. She mustn't react now, not when she was feeling like this. She had to give things a chance to settle down.

She had just finished feeding and changing Paul, putting him down for a nap before washing her hands in the small wash-basin, when Hank poked his head round the door of the nursery. 'Everything okay, sugar?'

No, everything is not okay, everything is far from okay, you stupid fool, she shouted in her mind as she kept her head bent over the basin. But she said nothing, knowing if she spoke at that precise moment the whole tirade that was tearing through her head would explode in hot angry words.

'Only I wondered if you'd like your lunch up here in your room where you can rest quietly? It's just cold chicken and salad, quite light.' She raised her head now and turned to face him but he didn't meet her eyes, pretending an interest in a mobile that was moving slowly in the slight breeze from the open window. 'Then you can have a nap when you've eaten and I'll see to Paul if he wakes up before his next feed.'

'Haven't you got to go to work this afternoon?' she asked quietly, her voice flat and slow as she struggled to keep all trace of how she was feeling inside from showing.

'No.' He still didn't look at her. 'I've told James I'm taking a few days off to look after you and the baby, give you a chance to get into the swing of things gradually.'

She ought to be grateful, there were plenty of women who would give their eye teeth for their husbands to do such a thing, so why didn't she feel anything beyond this suspicion that he was more concerned how things looked to James and Liz and the rest of the world, than worried about her? She felt the thudding of her heart that always accompanied such thoughts. But look how he had been yesterday afternoon, when John had popped into the hospital with a card and present for the baby. All over her, that was the only way she could describe the sudden excess of attention he had exhibited. And she knew John had been embarrassed, uncomfortable, she'd seen it in the glazing over of those sky-blue eyes and the way his mouth had thinned. And now this apparent concern for her physical state, it couldn't have anything to do with keeping his mother and her apart as much as possible, could it? Well, even if that was the motive, she wasn't going to refuse, she had no wish to spend the afternoon socializing with Miriam and Michael and she *was* tired, painfully so.

After Hank had taken away her empty lunch-tray she slept soundly for most of the afternoon, awaking just after four when the biological clock most mothers develop rang loudly, announcing it was time for Paul's feed. He was just beginning to stir as she walked into the nursery and she stood looking at him for a few moments as he squirmed about the cot, at the way his head of soft, downy hair met in a wispy curl in his neck, the tiny hands and perfect eyelashes.

He was gorgeous, the nurses at the hospital had described him as a textbook baby and she ought to be very grateful, and she was, she was, oh, she was. She offered up a quick prayer of thankfulness, the same one she had said so often in the last few days, that he was healthy and normal with all his fingers and toes.

Nevertheless, since her son's birth the longing for her daughter had intensified, not diminished. It might be illogical, counter-productive, unreasonable, and the hundred and one other things she had told herself over and over again, but she wanted her just as much as she wanted Paul. She knew Joy was doing fine with Rosie and William, she had a detailed progress report every time she spoke to her sister on the telephone, and she ought to be satisfied that Joy was happy and loved with two parents who adored her. She knew it, but it was head knowledge, not heart . . .

She leant against the cot, her hands clasping the rounded wood of the top bar, as a shaft of pain shot through her at the thought of that other tiny face. She was glad Joy was safe, protected, of course she was, it was just that she wanted her so fiercely at times all the logical reasoning in the world didn't seem to make an iota of difference to the severity of her need. It was there every moment, whether she was awake or asleep, hovering on the perimeter of her mind like a dark, accusing shadow with finger pointed condemningly.

Paul gave a hungry little grunt and she lifted him out of the cot, settling him on her lap as she began to feed him and gaining some comfort from the knowledge she was giving her son the best start she could. Yes, she had a lot to be thankful for, she told herself again, and that was what she had to home in on, although it was so much easier to think it than do it.

When she had fed and changed the baby she decided to take him downstairs for a few minutes before she put him back in the cot. His grandparents would no doubt be pleased to see him and conversation would be easier with Paul as mediator.

She heard the murmur of voices as she reached the quiet sunlit hall, and walked through into the sitting room and out through the French doors that were wide open to the scented warmth of the late afternoon.

'Kate . . .' Hank rose immediately at her approach, offering his chair as he took Paul from her, nuzzling the baby's head as he positioned him in his arms.

'Isn't it lovely?' She smiled at Hank's parents who were sitting in deck-chairs at the side of hers, shaded by the thick, leafy branches of a magnificent copper beech. 'I do so love the summer months, and this is a wonderful garden with all the trees and flowering bushes.'

'I've told Hank he'll need to get a tree surgeon in in the fall,' his mother said loudly, ignoring the portent of her words. 'It's all very well admiring the look of things but you need to know a bit about them, and some of these trees are out of control. Look at that flowering cherry, for example, and that row of conifers. Michael would have had those trimmed the first week we moved in, wouldn't you, Michael?'

She didn't wait for a reply before continuing, 'and I hope you're going to get rid of those now.'

'What?' Kate shaded her eyes as she glanced in the direction Miriam was pointing but all she could see were the two cats basking in their favourite spot.

'Those . . . animals. They're not healthy, not with children, they carry all sorts of diseases.'

'The cats?' Kate sat up straight.

'Yes, of course the cats,' Miriam said irritably. 'You should never have brought them home in the first place. I've never allowed any animal of any description to set foot in my home, it's just asking for trouble. They were that old man's weren't they? Alfred's?' She almost spat the last word out of her mouth.

'Albert, his name was Albert,' Kate said quietly with no expression in her voice at all. 'And the cats are ours now, they are part of the family.'

'Huh! You'll have them trying to take over next.' It was so paradoxical all Kate could do was stare, and then she caught Michael's eye, the wry twist to his mouth telling her quite clearly he was aware of what she was thinking. A few months, perhaps even a few weeks ago she would have blushed fiercely but now she stared straight back at him, her gaze steady, before he turned away. Was she getting hard? The sudden thought bothered her. She hoped not, she really did, but she was changing, that much was for sure, and she didn't know if it was for the better, she just knew it made life easier to bear.

*

The explosion that had been fermenting all day finally occurred just after dinner that evening, and when Kate looked back on it later she realized it had been inevitable from the moment she had stepped out of the car, because Miriam Ross wanted it that way. The detonator happened to be Paul, but if not him, Hank's mother would have found another means of blasting what should have been a special day sky-high.

They were sitting at the dining-room table over coffee when Paul's 'wah' of a cry drifted down from the nursery upstairs. 'He's hungry.' Kate drank the last of her coffee in one gulp preparatory to leaving the room, but just as she made to rise Hank's mother fixed her with one of the icy stares she did so well.

'You don't have to jump when they demand attention. You should be in charge, not a little scrap of nothing.'

'I'm hardly jumping, I've finished dinner and now Paul is telling me he'd like his.' She tried a smile but it met with frosty indifference. 'He is a few weeks early, after all, he's doing extremely well not to be more demanding.'

'A few weeks early . . .' Miriam let her voice trail insolently over the words. 'Really, Kate, you aren't going to try and keep that up are you? People aren't fools, whatever you may think.'

'I beg your pardon?' She hadn't intended to speak, she had wanted, needed, Hank to take charge, but when the seconds had ticked on and it had finally dawned on her he didn't intend to say anything, her temper which had been at simmering point for most of the day boiled over.

'Honey –'

Now Hank did make a move to join the fray but she swung round on him so violently as she shouted, 'Shut up!' that he subsided in his seat immediately.

'Repeat what you just said to me.' She rose as she spoke, leaning across the table towards Miriam Ross who stared back at her unblinkingly, a satisfied sneer about her mouth.

'Really, Kate, there is no need for such hysterics, the truth may be a little unpleasant at times but you'll find it is best, none the less. It might be somewhat embarrassing that you've been . . . caught out, especially as I did ask you if that was the case before, you remember, but in this modern day and age it is not uncommon.'

'My son was born five weeks early,' Kate ground out through clenched teeth. 'Now whether you believe that or not, I really couldn't care less, but I will not have you sit at *my* table in *my* house and suggest otherwise, is that clear?'

'Honey –'

'And one more "Honey" from you, Hank, and I'll hit you, I mean it. Now tell her, tell her I wasn't pregnant on my wedding day.'

'Does it matter?' he asked sullenly.

'Yes, to me, because I'm fed up with her snide cracks, that's why.' She swung back to Miriam, who was sitting quite still, her eyes darting between her son and daughter-in-law. 'Your thoughts are your own affair but just keep them to yourself please.'

'Oh, come on . . .' Miriam's voice was a low hiss. 'You're talking to me now, not that dopey, soft son of mine. I knew what your plan was the moment I saw you, don't you understand that? *I knew*. You wanted a rich man, a life of luxury, and you went about it in the way all you young girls do.'

'You're mad.' Kate had gone lint-white as she stared into the twisted face in front of her. 'I didn't have to persuade Hank to marry me, ask him if you don't believe me. And as for wanting a rich man, that's ridiculous! I've trained for years to be a doctor –'

'A doctor?' Miriam's scornful face and flick of her hand dismissed the years of study and back-breaking hours with unconcealed contempt. 'What can you earn, a mere pittance a year compared to what Hank was used to in the States. You tricked him, you tricked him into marrying you, what other reason would he have had for leaving home? He was always happy with me, Dean and Edward are happy with me, but you've spoilt it. He wouldn't have dared to have done this before he met you, you put him up to it –'

'To what?' Kate was genuinely horrified. 'He's just got married, that's all.'

'But he's mine, they're all mine. They do what I say, they've always done what I say. And at times I've had to correct them, set them on the right track again, but it was for their own good. They had to understand, you see, to obey me, love me. Spare the rod and spoil the child, that's what I used to say, because Mother always knows best, always.'

'Miriam, stop this –' But it was doubtful if Miriam Ross even heard her husband's voice.

'You remember, Hank, Mother knows best? You remember?' Miriam's voice was quiet now, with an unnatural softness that set the hairs on the back of Kate's neck pricking as they rose. 'Girls, they're dirty, their bodies are dirty, contaminated. How many times did I tell you, how many, but did you listen? And I thought you were a good boy, such a good boy.'

'I was.' Hank could have been six instead of twenty-six as he faced the woman who had given birth to him. 'I am.'

'No, not now, you've let her spoil it, drag you down to her level. You aren't the boy I thought you were, Hank, I'm disappointed in you, very disappointed.' There was such an intensity of spirit in Miriam's face and body, such presence, such power, that even Kate felt herself grow smaller and smaller as she looked into the other woman's eyes. This wasn't love, Kate thought with a sickening lurch to her stomach that threatened to expel her dinner. Whatever stared out of those dark eyes wasn't love, she didn't dare even to begin to put a name to it.

'Stop this!' Kate hit the table with her clenched fist with such force that the cups and saucers rose in the air, coffee spilling on to the white linen table cloth as the crockery went flying. 'You just stop it! There's nothing wrong with me, I can tell you that, but you! You talk about being dirty, contaminated, but what are you? *Sick*, sick at the very least to say such things and I don't want you within a hundred yards of my son. You're not going to poison him like you've tried to poison Hank and the others. If anyone is dirty in this room it certainly isn't me.'

'Are you going to sit there and let her talk to me like that?' Miriam had glanced first at her husband, whose averted head was sunk down on his shoulder, his eyes shut, and then to Hank. 'Are you? Because I won't stand for it, I tell you, Hank –'

'You won't stand for it?' Kate bent even further across the table, her head thrust as close as it could reach towards Hank's mother and her words low and guttural, dragged up from the depths of her stomach. 'You've got it wrong, it's what *I* won't stand. I've had enough of you and your evil, twisted mind and if you are what Hank wants, he can have you, I don't care, but I tell you, Hank' – she now fixed her eyes on her husband, who was sitting seemingly paralysed in his seat – 'if you go, there's no coming back. And I'll have Paul, I'll fight you to the death and beyond to keep him.'

'This is crazy, let's all calm down.'

'Yes, it's crazy, *she's* crazy!' Kate flung her hand wildly at Miriam, whose narrowed eyes and jutting jaw made her face even more malevolent. 'But don't you see it is her that is making you choose? She won't let you have both her and Paul and me, she never was going to, and I mean what I say, that woman isn't coming within a hundred yards of my son. There's something wrong with her –'

'I've had enough of this.' Miriam rose to her feet like a dark avenging angel, her face terrible. 'Go and get our things, Michael, we're leaving.'

'Mother –'

'You've made your choice, I can see that, and as far as

I'm concerned I only have two sons now, the third is dead. Remember that, Hank, the third is dead.'

'Miriam, I think you've said more than enough.' As Michael took his wife's arm she jerked him aside so savagely that he stumbled and almost fell, clutching hold of the full-length velvet curtains to save himself and bringing the whole curtain track, pelmet and several large pieces of plaster down about his head. Miriam swept out of the room without a glance in her husband's direction and Hank still sat in a stunned silence at the table, so it was left to Kate to approach her father-in-law and help him untangle himself from the debris.

'I'm sorry, Kate.' He stood looking at her for a moment as she stopped brushing plaster dust off his jacket and stared into his face. 'I can't figure her out sometimes, she's . . . she's a strong-willed woman.'

Strong-willed woman? Kate opened her mouth to speak and then shut it again. It wasn't just a strong will that had glared out at her from Miriam's eyes, that she could have handled. Was Michael really unaware of the portentous content of the scene they had endured, could he be that naïve? Or had he purposely chosen to look the other way and allow his wife's unbalanced and dangerous maternal instinct to have free rein? Either way, from what had been said it was clear there were deep and dark undercurrents flowing from Miriam's obsession with her sons, undercurrents that must have been in force for a long, long time.

Suddenly she felt weak and faint, and, turning from Michael, stumbled across to the table and sank down on one of the vacant chairs, shutting her eyes as she took several long, deep breaths. She must go and see to Paul, the baby's cries were more demanding now, but even after she heard Michael leave the room with a muttered farewell she couldn't force herself to move, her legs and arms feeling as though they were weighted with lead.

'I can't let her go like this.'

'What?' She opened her eyes to see Hank's face rent

with a mixture of fear and panic, although the fear was uppermost.

'You don't know what she's like, Kate, what she's capable of. She –' He stopped abruptly and literally glanced over his shoulder, his eyes terror-stricken. 'I must talk to her –'

'Hank, after what she said –'

'You shouldn't have argued with her, that's what started all this, everything was fine before that –'

'It was terrible! *She* was terrible, you know she was. She was looking for a fight from the moment I stepped out of the car, and you can't say I haven't fallen over backwards to avoid a row.'

As they heard heavy footsteps treading down the stairs Hank leapt up as though propelled by a spring, dashing past her and into the hall and now Kate did move, following just a few steps behind him. Miriam Ross and her husband were standing by the front door, their suitcases at their feet as Michael helped his wife on with her coat.

'You're not going?' Hank's voice sounded like that of a little boy.

'Of course I'm going, you don't think I'm staying here to be insulted by that common little whore you've taken for your wife? Your wife!' Miriam spat the words into Hank's face. 'You'll regret this, my boy, mark my words you'll regret it. I've given my life to you and what thanks do I get?'

'Miriam, that's enough.'

'Get the cases.' She didn't waste further words on her husband, silencing his protest with a scathing glare as she kicked out at the suitcases by their feet before opening the front door herself.

'Mother, if you insist on going I'll drive you –'

'I've ordered a cab and we'll wait at the end of the drive, I don't want to spend another minute in this house, and I've told you' – she turned to face Hank now, and such was the look on her face it made Kate's blood run cold –

'I've terminated the right for you to call me mother. From this day on I only have two sons, Dean and Edward. Remember that.'

'You don't mean it, you can't. *Mother* . . .'

Miriam didn't even bother to reply, her gaze cutting him in two before she swung round and marched out of the house, her back straight and her head up.

'I'll talk to her, son.' Michael rested his hand on Hank's shoulder for a moment, but when he got no response, he patted him awkwardly before following his wife down the drive without a word to Kate, who had leant back against the wall for support, her face ashen.

'Look what you've done.' As Hank spun round to face her Kate thought for a moment he was going to strike out but she didn't flinch, her body stiffening as she levered herself fully upright.

'Don't you blame this night's happenings on me, Hank. I didn't ask for your parents to come here but I was prepared to try and make it work.'

'Try and make it work?' he ground out bitterly. 'You think calling my mother every name under the sun is trying to make it work?'

'I didn't and you know it, the boot was completely on the other foot, and while we're about it, I want an apology from her before she stays here again.'

'You think she'll ever want to stay here again?'

'I don't know and I don't care. She's mad, she's got to be mad the things she said . . .' She gulped, deep in her throat, fighting to control the tears that were threatening to overwhelm her and then thrust herself past him, slamming the door shut with a bang that jolted the house. 'I'm going to see to Paul.'

'Not before we sort this out.' He grabbed her arm as she made to pass him for the stairs, jerking her back with more force than was necessary so that her neck muscles snapped painfully. 'You had no right to say those things.'

'No right?' She moved her hand up to where his fingers

were gripping her other arm and, with a strength that was born purely of rage, tore them off her. 'You talk to me about right? You let her say all those wicked things, call me dirty and worse, and *you* talk to *me* about right? I hate you, Hank, I really hate you, I won't ever forgive you or her for doing this to me today. She's a monster, and you're the spawn of a monster –' As he raised his hand she actually took a step forward so that she was right up against him, her eyes blazing. 'You dare, you just dare hit me and that will be it. I'll be out of here so quick it'll make your head spin and I'll take Paul with me. You hear me? And don't think I can't do it, you know Albert left me some money and I can easily use that until Paul is a bit older and I can go back to work. I'm not joking, Hank. I wanted us to be a normal family, that was all I ever wanted, and Paul deserves to have a father around for his growing years, but if the price I have to pay for that is to be abused by you and your mother –'

'I've never abused you.'

'That's a matter of opinion.' She glared at him, her face fiery. 'It's quite funny when you think about it, isn't it, your mother accusing us of sleeping together before we were married. You can't even manage it after, let alone before. Why didn't you tell her, Hank? Why didn't you give her the satisfaction of telling her that her little boy still prefers Mummy to his wife?' The shock of her words reverberated in the air and there was total silence for what seemed like forever to Kate's screaming senses, and then, as Paul's wailing called her, she pushed past him without looking into his face, walking with careful, measured steps to the bottom of the stairs and ascending them without once looking back.

CHAPTER THIRTEEN

'I thought someone told me you got married some months back?' The young face, framed by its halo of dark blond hair, smiled consideringly at Hank. 'An' you've got a bairn, haven't you? A little lad, born round July sometime?'

'The grapevine doesn't miss much, does it.'

'Well, you know how it is.' Long-lashed eyes flickered to Hank's mouth and then back to meet his gaze. 'Word gets around.'

'So it would seem.' Hank glanced nervously over his shoulder as footsteps came towards the shop doorway and then, as a giggling courting couple passed, their arms wrapped round each other, he tensed until all was quiet again. 'So you're saying you don't want to?'

'Don't be daft.' The small rosebud mouth pouted and then smiled again. 'I don't mind if you don't, come on.'

The alley at the side of the shop was grimy and sordid and the act that followed more so. Why did he do it? Hank found himself asking the question even as his loins tightened to penetrate the nubile body in front of him, but as always desire drove him on until it was finished.

And then, once he was walking home in the raw December night, he found himself listing the reasons for his continued absence from his wife's bed. Kate had ruined his relationship with his family, she was totally wrapped up in the child, she didn't understand him, didn't try to communicate any more, didn't even seem to care if he was there or not except to pay the bills . . . He had become an expert, in the five months since Paul's birth, at finding excuses.

Kate was putting Paul to bed when he let himself into the house, calling down to him as she heard him enter the hall. 'If you want to see him before he goes to sleep you'd better come up now.'

'I got delayed, a business client . . .' He didn't look at Kate as he walked into the nursery and she didn't raise her head from the task of folding a pile of freshly laundered terry-towelling nappies away into a drawer. She didn't believe him. She didn't know where he had been but she suspected a woman, maybe the same one from before they were married, because she was sure in her own mind this . . . affair, liaison, had been going on that long. She didn't understand why he had felt it necessary to marry her, or why he continued to go through the ritual of pretending everything was wonderful for the outside world, but slowly, day by day and week by week, she had begun to understand and accept that nothing was going to change however much she tried.

And she had tried . . . She bit her lower lip hard, her eyes narrowing at the memories that were humiliating and embarrassing. And with each effort had come further rejection, cold, painful rejection, that had caused something deep inside to wither and die, shadowing even the precious moments with Paul. She had to leave Hank and soon. Her heart thudded at the thought, at the fact that both of her children would grow up without their natural fathers. But if she was ever to look into the mirror again without flinching in self-disgust she had to do it.

'Rosie telephoned earlier.' She continued folding the nappies as she spoke. 'She suggested it might be nice to get together for Christmas.' She kept her voice casual, light, as though the thought of being with both her children over Christmas hadn't blown her mind. 'I thought, considering Liz and James had us last year, Rosie and William could come up here and stay with us and we can have a party on Christmas Day for everyone. What do you think?'

Hank didn't raise his head from the cot where he was gently stroking his son's face. 'Swell, whatever you want, you think you can manage?' There was no real interest in the enquiry and her voice was in the same mode as she answered, 'Yes, of course. Rosie and Liz will help.'

Both of them! To have both of them with her for Christmas! The excited churning in her stomach brought a flush to her cheeks, and as she continued packing the nappies away she shut her eyes tightly for a second before opening them wide.

'Won't William need to be around his flock?' Hank asked a moment later, tucking the quilt more securely round Paul's small form as Kate shut the drawer and moved towards the door, dimming the light as she reached the doorway. 'I'd have thought Christmas was his busiest time?'

'I told you, he's moving to a new diocese in the New Year,' Kate said quietly as he joined her on the landing after shutting the nursery door carefully. 'The new vicar has already been appointed for Breadale and he wants to start in time for Christmas, so it means William is free for the first, and probably only, time in his life.'

'You didn't tell me.'

'I did.'

There was no animosity in either voice and as they walked down the stairs, Hank following a few steps behind her, Kate had the thought that a fly on the wall would have had every reason to think they had been married fifty years instead of twelve months, such was their lack of interest in each other. And yet that didn't really bear up under the light of scrutiny, did it, because she knew couples who were vitally aware of each other after many years of marriage, Liz and James for instance. And at the other end of the spectrum there was John and his new girlfriend, she was head over heels in love with him and didn't care who knew it. The thought brought an ache to her heart and she dismissed it quickly without asking herself why. And they had only known each other a few weeks . . . Oh, stop it, Kate. The voice in her head was sharp. What do you care about love, that sort of love, anyway? You've enough on your plate without thinking along those lines.

'So you've no objection if I call Rosie and tell her they are welcome to stay?' she asked Hank now as they walked into the sitting room.

'No, you're going to be the one doing most of the work.'

It was William who picked up the phone a few moments later and Kate felt her heart thud as she heard his calm, measured tones speaking the Breadale number. She hadn't seen her brother-in-law since her wedding day, although Rosie had travelled up to spend a few days with her in August when the country had still been reeling from the shock of the IRA's murder of the Queen's cousin, Lord Mountbatten, and their time together had been bitter sweet.

Joy had already been toddling about, having taken her first steps at the early age of ten months, and with her blonde curls and big blue eyes was an enchanting child. William had telephoned each night to speak with his wife, and on the couple of occasions that Kate had picked up the phone he had been polite enough but there had been something . . . something that had made her uneasy, apprehensive. She had told herself she was imagining it, that her guilty conscience was making her ultra-sensitive where her brother-in-law was concerned, but the conviction that he suspected the truth wouldn't go away. And it returned in full force now as he said, 'Kate? How are you? I understand Rosie spoke with you earlier.'

'Yes, about Christmas.' Kate took a deep breath and forced herself to breathe out slowly to calm her racing heartbeat. 'We would love you to come and spend the holiday up here, if you'd like to.'

'That would be very nice.' There was a brief pause, and then, 'It will be pleasant for . . . everyone to see the two children together, won't it.'

He did know. She closed her eyes tightly but kept her

voice light as she replied, 'Yes, won't it, being at opposite ends of the country I don't suppose they'll have much contact as a rule.'

'Just so.' Had she imagined the note of warning which stated that was exactly the way he wanted it? 'Well I'm afraid Rosie is at the Women's Institute meeting at the moment,' he continued after a brief, but she felt significant, pause, 'but I'll certainly get her to confirm details with you tomorrow. My regards to Hank.'

She stood for a full minute staring at the telephone after she had replaced the receiver, her lower lip caught between her teeth and her stomach churning, and then she shook her head at her own panic. He might suspect Joy was her daughter but he didn't *know*, he couldn't, only Albert had been in her confidence and he was dead. But she would be on her guard from now on, on the rare occasions their paths crossed, circumspect in all she did and said, and perhaps that was no bad thing.

'Everything okay?' Hank asked as he walked back into the sitting room carrying a tray on which reposed two rounds of ham sandwiches and a glass of beer. She had stopped cooking dinner in the evening a month or so before Paul was born, finding she was throwing Hank's away more often than he was eating it when he arrived home late. She now fixed herself a light lunch mid-day, which suited her far better, and Hank bought his meal at a small café round the corner from the factory. It meant they rarely ate together, which had bothered her at first, but since Miriam's visit their relationship had deteriorated to the point where it no longer concerned her.

'Yes, I think so. Rosie wasn't in but William thinks it will be fine.'

'Good.' He sat down in a chair facing the sofa on which she was sitting and took a big bite of sandwich before he spoke again. 'I guess you're expecting John and this new broad of his to come at Christmas? You know she's angling to move in with him?'

'Is she?' She glanced up at him then, there was something in his voice she didn't like, but the hard masculine face staring back at her was quite blank. 'No, I didn't know, and don't call her a broad, she's his girlfriend.'

'Same thing.' He shrugged indolently. 'According to James it's the real thing, on her side at least. He isn't so sure about John.'

'He's discussed it with you?' She couldn't quite imagine James discussing John's private business with anyone other than Liz, he wasn't that sort of a man.

'More or less, we share the same office you know.'

'You mean you've been listening to his personal phone calls?'

'What am I supposed to do? Take a hike every time the phone rings?'

She stared at him for a moment but said nothing more, there was no point.

'So, do you intend them to come?'

'Yes, of course, if we invite James and the family. Why? Don't you want them to come?'

'No skin off my nose either way.' He took another large bite of sandwich and stood up with the tray. 'I'm gonna have a shower, I'll finish this upstairs.'

'All right.'

She gazed after him as he walked out of the room, her mind trying to anatomize the content of his words and the way he had spoken them, but all she was left with was the vague impression of contention and dislike she always had when he spoke of his cousin, and yet . . . There was something she was missing, she was sure of it.

It was snowing heavily the day before Christmas Eve when William and Rosie were travelling up to Dumbarton, and when the light began to fail towards late afternoon Kate started to worry, but it wasn't until she had put Paul to bed, at just after seven, that the butterflies of apprehension became a gnawing anxiety that had her pacing to and fro.

Where were they, she asked herself fretfully, moving the lace curtain aside which covered the small narrow hall window and peering out on to the snow-covered drive illuminated by a brass carriage lamp fixed to the house wall which Hank had installed in the summer. She knew they had broken the journey in two by travelling to Wigan the day before and staying overnight with William's sister who had recently moved to that area, but Rosie had told her, when she had telephoned the previous evening, that they planned to leave early the next morning in view of the forecast of imminent snow and blizzard conditions.

They still hadn't arrived when Hank returned home at eight o'clock and by now Kate was convinced something was wrong. 'They would have phoned, Hank, if they had broken down,' she argued when he tried to reassure her the weather conditions could have delayed them, 'now wouldn't they?'

'Not if they are stuck in a drift somewhere.'

'But they've got the baby with them.' She stared at him appalled. 'She'll freeze to death.'

'Of course she won't, get a hold of yourself, Kate.' He never used the old endearments of 'honey' and 'sugar' now unless he had an audience, but for once it didn't irritate or rankle, she was too worried about Joy for that. 'William is one of the most solid, down-to-earth guys I know, you don't think he'll leave home without kitting the car up with everything they might need in an emergency? Now, do you have William's sister's address?'

She shook her head silently.

'Then we wait, it's as simple as that, and if we haven't heard anything by eleven we'll think again.'

It was logical, sensible, but she could have hit him for his lack of urgency. Joy could be out there with nothing but a frame of metal to protect her from the elements, or – and here her heart missed a beat – involved in something much worse than a mere breakdown, and all Hank could suggest was that they sat and waited? 'Hank, I can't –'

The shrill tone of the telephone cut off her voice and when Hank reached it first and lifted the receiver she knew immediately, even before his, 'Yes, I am,' and 'I see,' that something was dreadfully wrong.

'Certainly, yeah I can do that. I think it is better if my wife stays at home, we have a young baby ourselves. No, I understand. Thank you for calling.'

'What is it, what's happened?' She faced him, her hand clutching at her throat.

'Kate, come and sit down –'

'I don't want to sit down, Hank, I want you to tell me what's wrong.'

'There's been an accident.'

'I knew it! Joy?'

'Joy's fine, so I understand, but they need to keep her in for observation.'

'And Rosie and William?'

'Rosie is in surgery now, her legs were pretty badly mangled and they suspect some internal injuries but she's going to be all right.'

'Oh, Hank . . .' She wanted him to reach out to her, to draw her into his arms even though she knew it wouldn't mean a thing to him, but he gazed at her for a long moment and then turned away from the appeal in her eyes, walking across to the drinks cabinet in the corner of the room and pouring a large brandy which he handed to her silently, before guiding the hand holding the glass to her lips.

'Drink it, all of it, it'll help.'

It did help, and she needed the strength it gave her when he went on to tell her that William had died at the scene of the accident. 'Oh no, no . . .' She felt the room begin to swim and sat down abruptly. 'What happened? Does William's sister know?'

'I don't know. I'm going to the hospital where they've taken Rosie to find out more, the police are sending a car –'

'I'm coming.'

'You can't, it'll mean waking Paul and taking him with us and it's not fair. You won't be able to do anything, Kate, or see them –'

'I could see Joy.'

'No, you couldn't, they said she's asleep now and they expect her to sleep till morning. Let me find out what's what and we'll go from there.'

'I'm not leaving Joy in there tonight.'

'Now, Kate!'

'*I'm not.*'

'You damn well are. Now then, stop being so hysterical and pull yourself together.' When she burst into tears in the next moment he hesitated for a second before walking across and sitting down beside her, patting her shoulder as she covered her face with her hands. 'Look, the car will be here in a moment, I have to go. I'll ring you from the hospital and tell you what's happening, but you must see Joy is in the best place tonight. They need to keep an eye on her, make sure she's okay.'

'I'll go, you stay here.' She lowered her hands as she spoke, her eyes streaming.

'It would be better for me to go, they want . . . They want someone to identify William.'

'Oh . . . Oh, Hank.'

'And Paul might need you.'

As though on cue the very next moment there was a wail from the direction of the nursery, and Hank patted her shoulder again as the sound of a car outside brought him to his feet. 'Your place is with your own son, Kate, he needs you. I'll go to the hospital.'

But my daughter needs me more. She thought for a moment she had spoken the words out loud, so violent were they in her head, but when Hank nodded a goodbye, his face sombre, she knew her secret was still her own. 'Hank –'

'I'll ring you.'

The young police officer was grim-faced as they exchanged perfunctory goodbyes as Hank got into the car, and she couldn't bring herself to ask him any details about the accident, merely nodding in acknowledgement of his courteous farewell before he slid into the driver's seat. Joy, Joy, Joy . . . And Rosie, and poor William . . . William, oh, William . . . As the tail-lights of the police car disappeared she stood for some minutes at the front door looking out into the drive. It had stopped snowing . . .

They fetched Joy home on the afternoon of Christmas Eve, but Rosie was still in intensive care, unaware that her husband had been killed by a drunk driver, who had been so intoxicated after the office Christmas party that he wasn't able to stand by himself when the police had hauled him out of his car. He escaped without a scratch and had sung all the way to the police station, but they had had to stop the car twice to allow the young policewoman, who had been with what remained of William in his last moments on earth, to be sick.

Liz and James had brought over Adam's old cot and all his baby equipment they had stored in their roof on the morning of Christmas Eve, Joy's travelling cot, which had been in the car, having been smashed beyond repair, and Kate had left Hank turning the spare room into a second nursery and driven into Glasgow to buy clothes, toys and bedding for her daughter.

She was hardly aware of the Christmas shoppers or the bright festive displays as she moved round the stores in a state of automatism, her face set and her mind still stunned from the enormity of the tragedy that had taken them all unawares. It was only when Hank drove her to the hospital in the afternoon, and she walked into the children's ward and saw Joy sitting in her cot, thumb in mouth and small hand twiddling a lock of hair, that the shock receded enough for sheer agony to take its place. William dead, Rosie badly injured, and Joy without the two people who represented security and love in her life. How was her daughter going to cope?

She coped just fine. From the moment her bright blue eyes fixed on Kate's face it seemed as though Joy's world was back in order again, and she snuggled up to her mother as though Kate was all she had known as they went through the inevitable red tape and hospital procedures.

Kate couldn't have described her feelings to anyone as Hank drove them home, the red glow of the late afternoon sun setting the snow on fire and turning the sky into a river of scarlet and orange and gold. She was desperately concerned for her sister, the internal injuries had been far worse than the doctors had expected and Rosie's tenuous hold on life was sustained only by the tubes and wires connecting her to the machines scattered about her bed.

And William . . . He had been such a kind man, a good man, it just didn't seem fair. When Albert had died she had comforted herself with the thought that he had lived out his life span, that he had died peacefully, comfortably, in a way in which he would have wanted. But William – She forced her mind from the horror of the facts she had learnt about the crash, the facts that would have to be kept from Rosie if her sister was to remain sane. And yet . . . there was another part of her, a part she was painfully ashamed of, disgusted by, that acknowledged a thread of relief in her grief that the threat to herself and her daughter was no more. But she hadn't wanted anything to happen to William, she told herself wretchedly, she hadn't.

'He's been as good as gold.' Liz was waiting with Paul in the hall as Hank opened the front door and Kate carried Joy in, who was fast asleep in her arms. 'It's as if he knows he's got to be a good boy, isn't it, darling.' She nuzzled the top of Paul's head as she spoke, her eyes filling with tears as she looked at Joy. 'How is she?'

'Remarkably well adjusted at the moment but whether that will last, I don't know. This is a strange house, a strange environment after all, and no one knows how much she saw or took in. The front of the car was crushed out of recognition but she was strapped in the back seat, which remained relatively unscathed, although the boot was concertinaed, so the police say.'

'She's a lucky little girl.' And then Liz realized what she had said and turned away, shaking her head as her lips trembled. 'Oh, I'm sorry, Kate, I didn't mean . . .'

'I know what you meant, Liz, and she *is* lucky in that way. If she had been on Rosie's lap . . .' She hugged the child to her as the thought made her nauseous. 'There ought to be a law against children riding in a car without being adequately restrained.'

'It will come,' Liz said quietly. 'The roads are getting busier all the time. How . . . How's Rosie?'

'No change at present, but that could alter in the blink of an eye.'

'Come and sit down,' Liz's gaze encompassed Hank as she spoke, 'and I'll make a cup of tea.'

'No need.' Hank reached across for Paul, taking him into his arms and smoothing a silky curl from his brow as the baby gurgled in recognition. 'I'll get the tea while you talk to Kate, I'll give Paul a rusk in his high-chair so you can have some peace.'

Kate walked through to the sitting room, placing Joy on the sofa with the car rug still wrapped round her before sitting beside her small daughter. 'I can't believe it, Liz, not even now,' she said softly as she gazed at the sleeping child, the cats winding round her legs as they pushed against her in greeting. 'I just can't take it in.'

'How long do you think you'll have her?' Liz asked quietly.

'I've no idea, weeks at least but it could be months. Oh, Liz . . .' The look on Kate's face made Liz kneel down in front of her and stroke her hand gently as Kate said, 'Rosie looks awful, awful. All those tubes, and her poor face is bruised and cut. I've seen it a million times in my job but it's so different when it's someone close to you. And when she does come round she'll have to be told about William, I don't know how she'll take that.'

'If she's anything like her big sister she'll be very brave,' Liz said softly.

'But Rosie . . .' Kate's voice trailed away as she searched for the right words to explain her apprehension. 'She's never had to deal with the unpleasant side of life, Liz, not even when she was a child. My parents spoilt her, she really was my mother's pride and joy, and she met William so young, he was her first boyfriend and he just took over from where Mum left off. She's always been used to being petted and adored, looked after, she just doesn't know anything else.'

Liz stared at her but could find nothing to say, nothing that was acceptable in the present situation anyway. She had found it hard to believe that Rosie was Kate's sister when she had first met her at the wedding, and even after James had explained the circumstances of their births and their different fathers, she could see little resemblance to Kate in the girlish, slightly petulant woman who was her sister. She hadn't exactly *disliked* her but – she paused in her thinking as a wave of guilt washed over her – she hadn't liked her either.

'She'll be all right, you'll see, and it will be a great comfort to her knowing Joy is safe with you. It's not as if Rosie's on her own, is it, she's got her daughter to live for.'

'Yes, yes she has, hasn't she.' Kate tried to smile. 'I just hope that's enough.'

'It will be, and she's got you and Hank too. Some people are left with nothing and no one. She'll rally round.'

'Yes, I'm sure you're right.' But Kate's voice was doubtful.

'Cross your bridges, or help Rosie to cross hers, when you come to them,' Liz said practically. 'You're going to have enough to do without worrying about things that might never happen. Talking of which' – she paused as Hank entered the room with a tea tray and included him in her next words – 'we obviously aren't expecting to come tomorrow as planned, but I'm available if you need me to look after the children while you visit the hospital.'

'Of course you must come.' Hank placed the tray on the coffee table before bending and kissing the top of Kate's head, resting his hand on her shoulder as he straightened. 'Mustn't they, sugar? Everything is ready and we can all do our bit, it'll take Kate's mind off things, having everyone here.'

'Hank, really –'

'I'd like you to come, Liz.' Kate interrupted the other woman's embarrassed protest with a weak smile even as she berated herself for the surge of self-pity and hurt that caused hot tears to prick the backs of her eyes. He hadn't needed to rush in like that, she had been going to insist Liz and the others came as planned, but she knew there was no consideration for her feelings in Hank's mind. He had wanted this party even more than she did, she had realized that over the last few days, although she didn't quite understand why. 'I really would. Please.'

'Well, if you're sure,' Liz concurred doubtfully.

'I am.'

She was less sure about the wisdom of her decision by evening of the next day. A broken night's sleep – although not with Joy, it was Paul, who was teething, who had awoken at hourly intervals – added to the gnawing anxiety about her sister, and the sheer chaos a family party can cause had her feeling light-headed with exhaustion by teatime, and the strain of trying to prevent her grief from spoiling the day for the children gave her a white-faced, hollow-eyed look which caused John to sit her firmly on a kitchen stool when she made to pass him with a tray of sandwiches. 'John, I've got to take these –'

'You've got to take nothing,' he said firmly, his blue eyes

intent. 'You haven't stopped all day, if I didn't know better, I'd think you had a big key in the small of your back that someone was winding constantly.'

Several people actually. She lowered her head quickly as though he could read her mind. Apart from Hank who was acting strangely, and John himself who had been uncommunicative all day, it was Louise, his girlfriend, who was troubling her the most. From the moment the well-dressed, elegant brunette had entered the house on John's arm, her body pressed against his in a manner that could only be called embarrassing, Kate had felt the other girl didn't like her. Louise's manners had nevertheless been impeccable and her naturally cultured accent spoke of breeding and class, but there was a stiffness in her attitude to Kate, a restraint, that was quite absent with the rest of the assembled company. She had felt the other girl's eyes burning into her flesh all day even when her back was turned, and although she told herself she was being ridiculous, that Rosie's condition along with the shock of William's death was making her over-sensitive and touchy, the feeling persisted.

'Please, John . . .' As she made to rise his hand came out to check her, pressing her back on the stool. 'I've things to see to.'

'You didn't eat more than a mouthful at lunchtime and to my knowledge you have eaten nothing since. This whole thing is dreadful, quite dreadful, but you'll only make yourself ill if you continue like this.' The unexpected warmth of his voice, the understanding, when Hank had barely spoken a word to her all day, unless one of the others was present, when he metamorphosed into the considerate and caring husband, was almost too much and she gulped audibly before shaking her head slowly, her head still downcast.

'I'm . . . I'm all right, really.'

'No, you are not.' She was conscious that he moved irritably as he spoke, transferring his weight from one foot to the other as he raked back his hair with an impatient hand. 'Why the hell Hank permitted you to carry on with all this today is beyond me.'

'I wanted to.'

'I don't care if you wanted to or not.' The tone of his voice brought her eyes snapping to his face, but she recognized the anger darkening his features was not directed at her. 'Damn it all, Kate, your sister's in hospital, your brother-in-law is dead and you've suddenly added another child to your family –' He stopped abruptly as she gave a strangled sob and when, in the next moment, his arms went round her and she buried her face in the roughness of his jacket and cried as if her heart would break, she was aware of his voice, softer than she had ever imagined it could be, murmuring words of endearment and consolation above her head.

How long he held her close to his chest as she sat on the stool she had no idea but when Liz's voice came at her side asking softly, 'What's wrong?' she heard him reply just as softly, 'My big mouth,' and then John had gone and Liz was bathing her face in much the same way one did a distressed child.

'I'm sorry, Liz . . .' She could hear John's voice ordering Adam and Susan to find their shoes and coats, and the knowledge that she had, albeit inadvertently, brought an abrupt end to the day produced a further flood of tears. 'I don't want you to go, you haven't eaten.'

'Kate, everyone had enough dinner to keep them going for a week,' Liz said gently, as she patted Kate's face with a towel. 'You're absolutely exhausted and no wonder. Now let Hank help you to put Paul and Joy to bed, they're both ready to drop, and then the pair of you can curl up in front of the fire with a couple of very large brandies and have a few precious minutes together.'

Liz would never know how much the picture she had painted hurt, Kate thought silently as she looked deep into her friend's face. It was a picture of what marriage could be, *should be*, a reflection of James and Liz's partnership, perhaps even John and Louise's? The name prompted her to speak. 'Liz? Louise . . . Is there something wrong? Has someone upset her?'

'I . . . I really don't know what you mean, dear.' But Liz's eyes had shifted from her face and that, more than her own feelings, told Kate she was right.

'It's me, isn't it?' she asked flatly. 'What have I done?'

'You haven't done anything, really, so don't worry about Louise on top of everything else, for goodness' sake. It's like John just said, actually, his big mouth.' Liz's voice was rueful. 'They arrived at our place earlier with John up in arms about you – he thought it was too much for you, this party. I told him I'd tried to call it off and that Hank wouldn't have it, and he got a little . . . over-excited. It's John's way when something affects him.'

'Is it?' Kate stared at Liz in astonishment. She had seen John cool and composed, sarcastic and sardonic, quiet and withdrawn, in fact he was rarely the same twice running, but she had never seen this impassioned side to his character that his mother spoke of. 'But why would John objecting to my having the party affect Louise anyway?'

Liz stared at her for a full thirty seconds before she spoke, and then her voice was guarded when she said, 'Louise is very possessive, unnaturally so, I would say. Perhaps she didn't like John's interest in your welfare.'

'You mean? . . .' Kate gazed back, her mouth half open in a little gape of surprise. 'But that's ridiculous, she doesn't think John . . . That I . . . Oh, Liz.'

'I told you, the girl is slightly unbalanced,' Liz said briskly in a matter-of-fact voice that stated the conversation was finished. 'I really can't see John continuing the relationship much longer, Kate, although that is strictly between us. She's a solicitor in the firm where he works, so it makes things a little difficult, but he's had a somewhat hunted expression on his face the last few times he's called in to see us, and that's not my John. He seems to be rather attractive where the opposite sex is concerned I'm afraid, and the poor boy is quite unaware of it. I don't know . . .'

She was about to go on when her gaze focused on something over Kate's left shoulder and as Kate turned she saw Hank standing in the doorway, his face slightly truculent, although his expression changed the moment he became aware of their eyes on him. 'Everything all right, sugar? John said you're a little upset.'

'It's nothing, I'm fine now.' She couldn't endure any more of his acting without screaming the truth about their marriage to the world, and something of what she was feeling must have shown in her face, because he made no attempt to approach any further.

It was as they were waving their guests goodbye a few minutes later, Paul in Hank's arms and Joy snuggled deep into Kate's chest, thumb in mouth, that the tumult of emotions Kate had been experiencing all day opened her mouth. 'I can't, I just can't go on like this any longer, Hank.' As the tail-lights of John's car disappeared from view, she turned to face him, but he wasn't looking at her, his eyes still fixed on the empty drive. 'Do you hear me?'

'What?'

'We have to talk about everything, about us.' She hadn't intended to say it, it was the worst possible timing, with all the uncertainty surrounding Rosie's condition, but something about this whole day had troubled her far more than she could express or even understand and suddenly she wanted things out in the open, washed clean.

'Us?' For a moment his face was blank and then he seemed to come back from a distant place as his eyes focused on hers. 'Why? What's the matter?'

'Oh, stop it, Hank! There's no one here now, you don't have to pretend.' As Joy stirred in her arms she forced her voice into a more moderate pitch. 'We have to get things straight.'

He stared at her, his face stiffening, and then, to her

surprise, brushed past her and walked into the house without saying a word.

'Hank?' She grabbed at his arm as she caught up with him in the hall and then gasped as he jerked himself free of her hold so roughly that he almost caused her to drop Joy.

'What, exactly, do you want to get straight, Kate?' he asked tightly as both children, sensing the atmosphere, began to whimper softly. And as she stared back at him, Paul's little face crumpling as he began to wail loudly, there arose in her such a feeling of hatred, such a wild loathing that it completely obliterated the last lingering shreds of tenderness she had harboured deep inside for this man who was her husband. It was frightening in its intensity and she held his gaze for one more loaded moment, her eyes blazing, before she turned for the stairs.

'I'm putting Joy to bed, I'll see to Paul in a minute.'

She was shaking from head to foot as she stood by Joy's cot, the child still in her arms, but part of her was urging that inner self that shrunk from confrontation to follow the matter through, *now*, *today*. Was she going mad? The thought didn't have the power to frighten her like it would have done just a few days ago. She might be, yes, she might be. She placed Joy gently in the cot and then, as the child began to whimper again, knelt by the wooden bars and stroked the baby's face quietly, her eyes wandering round the room.

The bedroom furniture, the numerous cuddly toys and books she had bought so hastily the day before, they were all solid and normal and real, but how could everything appear so ordinary when her mind felt as though it was going to burst? Hank didn't love her, he had never loved her. The churning in her stomach made her feel as though she was going to be sick and, with a quick glance at Joy, who had turned on her side with her eyes closed, she rose and left the room, hesitating on the landing before walking along to Paul's room.

'I'll see to him.' Hank had been standing by the window

with his son in his arms but now he handed Paul to her without a word.

It was some thirty minutes later before she joined Hank downstairs. Paul had needed feeding and changing for the night, and all that time her stomach had been turning over as though she was on a fairground ride, so when she walked into the sitting room and found him comfortably stretched out on the sofa with the cats, a glass of beer to hand and eyes fixed on the television set, the yell that rose from her throat was beyond her control.

'Turn it off! *Turn it off!*'

He swore, loudly and violently, as he jumped visibly into the air from his prone position, his face holding such an expression of outrage as he rose to face her that she would have found it funny in any other circumstances. 'Are you crazy, woman? Are you? You could have given me a heart attack.'

'Yes, I'm crazy, stark-staring, clear-round-the-bend crazy. I would have to have been to have married you, wouldn't I!'

'And don't shout –'

'Why shouldn't I? Why shouldn't I shout if I want to? This is my house as much as yours, I'm your wife, *your wife!* Do you know what that means? Do you? And it wasn't me who was in so much of a rush to get married either, you were the one who couldn't wait, and, though you might regret it now, *I am your wife, Hank.*'

'I know what you are, Kate.'

'"I know what you are, Kate."' Her mimicry was vicious. 'I wish I could say the same for you!'

'And what does that mean?' If she had been half-way rational she would have wondered at the sudden bleaching of his skin, but such was her rage as the misery and hurt and humiliation of months poured out she could barely see him.

'You're having an affair, aren't you? There's someone else. And don't bother to lie. I know I'm stupid but I'm not that stupid. Why I've tried to fool myself this long I don't know. No, I do, I do know, I wanted our marriage to work. Isn't that funny? You can have a good laugh with her about that, can't you.'

'You're mad.'

'You've already said that. Can you deny it then? Can you stand there and tell me to my face that you aren't having an affair with someone? I've done everything I can to try and make you happy –'

'Like alienating my family?' His voice had risen. 'Oh sure, sure.'

'Oh no, not your family again! Shouldn't you substitute mother for family? If she was in this country I'd think it was her you sneaked away at nights to see.'

'I don't sneak away to see anybody.'

'Oh – yes – you – do.' Her voice was low now, soft even, but each word was weighted with the burning humiliation she had suffered for months past, and the enmity in her face was new to him.

He stared at her as his mind raced. She didn't know, it was clear she didn't know, she was stabbing around in the dark, but he hadn't thought she'd react in this way. This wasn't the cool, ladylike girl he had married, in fact this was a whole new ball game. He made the mistake of saying so.

'You cheeky –' She further convinced him that the worm had indeed turned by the use of a word that was anything but genteel as she questioned his legitimacy. 'Well you might not like me objecting to your . . . your what, Hank? What shall we call her? Your other woman? Your lady-friend? Or shall we get really vulgar and refer to her as what she is? Your bit on the side, your tart –'

'You're hysterical.' His voice was cold now, icy, but this new Kate didn't wilt before him as he had expected.

'Possibly.' She glared at him, her cheeks fiery. 'But I'd say it's way overdue, wouldn't you?'

'What's got into you tonight?' He stared at her, his

amazement only half feigned. 'Accusing me of goodness knows what –'

'Goodness has got nothing to do with it –'

'Is it Rosie? Your concern about her? I can understand that.' As he made to reach out to her, his expression changing to one of conciliation, she leapt back from him with a savage gesture of repudiation. What had got into her? She didn't know, but she did know she could have done with it months ago. She stared at him now, her breath coming in short panting gasps and her chest heaving. How could she have let him treat her as he had done for the last . . . oh, since they were married, before even, maybe? What she had put down to respect during her courting days had been something altogether different, something . . . ugly, dark. And to think she had been grateful to him! She bit on her lip, hard, as self-contempt swept through her. She had thought he was being so restrained, so noble in curbing his natural inclinations when all the time he had been getting his pleasure elsewhere with someone who obviously suited him far better. Was she married? Was that why he couldn't make an honest woman out of her? *But why had he married her?*

She didn't realize she had spoken the last thought out loud until he replied, 'Because I wanted to, you know that. I love you, Kate.'

'You don't know the meaning of the word.'

Didn't he? In those early days of agony he had forced his thoughts away from his beloved, knowing if he allowed himself to dwell on the rejection, the sense of indescribable loss, he would send himself insane. They said time healed. They were wrong.

'Kate, you've got this all out of proportion . . .'

As the phone began to ring he paused, reaching for the receiver as she continued to glare at him. He spoke the number, dropping his eyes from her ferocious face, and then listened quietly without speaking for a minute or two. 'I see.' He didn't raise his head as he finished the call. 'I understand what you are saying and we'll certainly discuss the implications before we visit tomorrow. Yeah, it sure is a difficult situation.' *This was it.* If he handled this right he could still keep hold of the reins, prevent everything from blowing up in his face. But he had to choose his words carefully, make her see how it was. 'Goodbye, matron.' After replacing the receiver he waited for some moments before looking at Kate, and then he let her ask the question, his eyes expressionless although his mind was racing as to what to say next.

'Rosie?' The name was a whisper.

'She's conscious and in a stable condition.' As his wife stared at him he paused, and then said, his face grim, 'but she is ill, very ill.'

'How ill?'

'Nothing that can't be improved with time, but we're talking about months, maybe a year or two, before she's fit enough to look after herself properly, let alone a young child.' His eyes were boring into hers, his voice heavy. 'I presume you want to keep your niece here for the moment?'

'Of course I do.' She was quiet now, sensing what was about to come.

'And later? The matron is talking about months of physiotherapy on Rosie's legs which will be taxing both physically and mentally on top of everything else she's endured, not ideal with an active child around. Of course the authorities could perhaps find them a place in some kind of sheltered accommodation, it's an added complication that their housing was tied to William's job . . .'

There was a sickening sensation deep in her bowels now as the knowledge of what he was really saying made itself known. If she wanted Joy, and later Rosie, to have a place of refuge with them until her sister was fully recovered then things continued as they were. Did he know she had been about to ask for a divorce? Yes, of course he knew, she told herself bitterly. But he wanted to keep the façade in place, he had always wanted it, for some dark reason of his own.

As she looked into the face before her she knew she had never known him, that the Hank of her courting days had been a figment of her imagination, but that was almost unimportant now beside the decision she had to make. She could possibly have worked out the finances for just her and Paul, taking into consideration the legacy Albert had left her which was still intact in the building society, but with two other mouths to feed and the sort of care Rosie would need in the early days? No, it was a straight choice.

She could walk away from this marriage with her son and what was left of her self-respect, or she could provide her daughter, and her sister, with the love and security they needed and turn a blind eye to Hank's liaison with person or persons unknown. There was no contest.

CHAPTER FOURTEEN

It was the sixth of September 1981, the official date of Joy's third birthday, and the excited little girl had woken Kate early to a Sunday morning that was clear and bright, the blue sky swept clean of even the smallest cloud.

'I'm a big girl now, aren't I, Mummy Kate?' Joy said gleefully as she clambered on to Kate's bed, Paul's fat little legs having a little more difficulty as he followed the object of his adoration a few moments later. 'I'm a whole three years old – one, two, three,' she counted on her fingers for Paul's benefit, who eyed her silently, thumb in mouth, as he nodded solemnly. She could have said she was thirty as far as he was concerned and he would have agreed with her, everything Joy did was perfect in his eyes.

'Five o'clock she had me awake this morning.' Rosie gave Kate a perfunctory nod from the doorway before continuing, 'Come along, Joy, that's enough of that. Let Aunty Kate wake up in peace.' Rosie always referred to her sister as Aunty Kate when speaking to her small daughter, in spite of the fact that Joy insisted on the 'Mummy Kate' she had adopted within days of coming to live in the house twenty-one months before. Kate had tried to dissuade her at first, thinking, quite rightly, that Rosie would object, but as both women were to discover, Joy had a very definite mind of her own and a will of iron that was often disconcerting in one so young.

'Do I have to?' Joy gazed up at Kate now, big blue eyes beseeching, but although there was nothing more Kate would have liked than to have both her children snuggle up to her for a morning cuddle, she knew how her closeness with Joy was affecting her sister these days.

'Do what Mummy says, sweetheart, the sooner we're all dressed and ready for breakfast the sooner you can have your presents, can't you.' It worked like a charm and within moments Kate was alone again as Joy bounded off the bed, dragging Paul with her, and disappeared through the doorway in a whirl of blonde curls and frilly pink nightie, Rosie following.

Three years old . . . Kate lay back against the pillows as she gazed after the children, Rosie's voice filtering through from the bedroom she and Joy shared a minute or so later at a pitch that informed Kate they were engaging in one of their numerous battles of wills. She couldn't believe three years had elapsed since her daughter's birth, or that Albert had been gone nearly as long. Albert. There wasn't a day that went by that she didn't remember the old man with love and gratitude, he was the only man she had ever known who had loved her for exactly what she was, warts, pimples and all . . .

Her eyes narrowed as Rosie's voice rose a few decibels, Paul scuttling back into the bedroom a moment later and climbing in with her, clearly having decided to leave the scene of conflict. Why did Rosie do it? Didn't she have any understanding of the tenacious, mercurial little being she called her daughter? Joy could be handled fairly easily with persuasion and reason but the head-on battles Rosie engaged in resulted in tears and misery for them both.

'Me good boy.' Paul took her head in his small chubby hands as he knelt by her side, guiding her gaze away from the open door and down to his serious little face. 'Me wear my play clothes, Mummy.'

So that was what it was all about, Kate thought, as she smiled down at her son, her amiable grave little son who always wanted to please, unlike his volatile half-sister. Joy had wanted to wear her new party clothes Rosie had laid out on a chair the night before in readiness for the festivities later that afternoon. 'I told her what would happen,' Kate murmured to herself as Paul snuggled into her side. The frothy lace and satin dress with its billowing petticoats and pretty puffed sleeves was any little girl's dream, but when Kate had suggested leaving it in the wardrobe until it was time for the party, Rosie had brushed her aside, her face setting in the way it did so often lately.

'What the hell is going on now, damn it?' She heard Hank's growl as he left the bedroom next to hers a moment before his bulk filled the aperture, his face sullen. 'Hasn't she got any control over that kid? It sounds like the Brixton riots in there.'

'Hardly.'

'Hardly? Well either you've got trouble with your ears or you've become conditioned to the noise. Hey, hi there, little buddy . . .' As he caught sight of Paul, Hank's whole persona underwent a complete transformation, and as their son scrambled on all fours to the foot of the bed where he was whisked high into the air, Kate found herself marvelling, for the hundredth time, at the utter devotion in Hank's face as he looked at the tiny miniature of himself he had had a hand in creating. That he loved his son, adored him, she had no doubt, but it hadn't stopped him continuing that . . . other life. She had asked him once, a few months back, after a particularly trying day with Rosie which had reduced her to an all-time low ebb, whether he had, or would think of having, a child with anyone else. It was a thought that had haunted her more than once as she imagined herself shopping, or perhaps at the park, even at home, and suddenly being confronted with the reality of his secret life.

'What?' He had stared at her, his hand frozen half way to the fridge where he had been reaching for a beer, and then he had straightened, slowly, and his voice had been quiet when he said, 'Oh, Kate, Kate . . .' She couldn't, even now, describe the tone of his voice but there had been something, a sadness that was beyond words, that had made her heart thud with an intensity that actually hurt. 'Is that what you've been thinking?' She couldn't speak or even nod her head, and they had stared at each other for what seemed like an age before he had turned away, shaking his head slowly. 'You are my wife, Kate, and Paul is my *only* child. There is no question of anything like you suggest ever happening.'

The incident had upset her for days, the more so because it had broken through the barrier she had erected against him, the barrier that enabled her to live her life with some measure of enjoyment, gaining pleasure from her children, her garden. When she hated him she could cope, she could shut him out of her thoughts and her daily routine to the point where it was almost a surprise, some nights, when she heard his key in the lock.

His coldness, his bitterness against her for what he saw as the alienation of his mother and the American side of his family, the blame he spewed out over her head now and again when he had too much to drink, the humiliations, the endless pretence in front of everyone else, even Rosie, which was perhaps the worst thing of all, all that she could struggle through and handle, albeit badly at times. But just for a moment, in the kitchen, she had seen something else and it had wrenched her heart for what might have been. It hadn't lasted, the sensation of pain and regret, he had committed some act of cruelty and the feeling had been burnt clean away, but even now she didn't like to dwell on how his face had looked for those few minutes some months ago.

'So what are the plans for madam's birthday?' His tone was deliberately goading as he placed Paul back on the bed, but for once she didn't rise to the bait, her voice quiet as she said, 'A party, this afternoon. I told you a couple of weeks ago.'

'Oh yeah, I remember, half the kids from nursery and family too? The big attorney favouring us with his presence, then?'

'John said he might pop along, if that's what you mean.'

'That's real good of him,' he drawled mockingly.

'There's no need to be like that. He's very fond of Paul and Joy, you know he is, and they adore him.'

'How would I know? He always makes sure I'm not around if he calls by, or haven't you noticed?' He laughed, but there was no humour in the sound, and she looked at him quickly, unsure of what he was suggesting.

'That's ridiculous, you're here more often than not.' But he wasn't and she knew it. Not that there was anything in the least clandestine about John's occasional visits to their home. He came if he was in the area, that was all. Her heart raced and then thudded painfully and she spoke sharply to herself, none of that, none of that. John tolerated her presence because she was Hank's wife, he made that painfully clear in that cool, controlled manner of his.

He might laugh and joke with Rosie, and he played the most crazy games with the children at times, but with her there was always a stiffness, a formality, that made her suspect her earlier feeling that he didn't like her was the right one. *And that was fine*. It was. Just fine. She forced herself to adopt a casual air now as she said, 'Anyway, you'll be here this afternoon won't you? Liz and John are coming over with the children and there are quite a few mothers staying for the party, the ones who live some distance away.'

'Wonderful.' He raised his eyebrows sarcastically. 'I'd hate to miss out on such a fun deal.' His gaze lowered to Paul, who was sitting cross-legged on the bed gazing up at him, grey eyes wide. 'What ya think, little buddy? You want Daddy to come to Joy's party?'

'Yes, yes, yes!' Paul bounced up and down with each word and Hank laughed, his face softening. 'Then I'll be there. Now I think it's time you left Mommy to get dressed, don't you? Let's go downstairs and find something to eat, huh?'

How much longer could she go on like this? The thought jumped in before she could apply the tactics she usually used, the tactics she had been using for the last twenty-one months to keep it at bay. She had learnt, in those first days and weeks, when she had worn herself to a frazzle coping with the demands of two healthy and energetic babies under the age of eighteen months, besides daily visits to the hospital to give Rosie all the reassurance and support her sister so desperately needed, to shut her mind to the demands of self.

It hadn't been a noble act, a sacrifice in any sense, just an awareness that unless she dealt purely with what she could see and hear and touch without delving any further into her consciousness, there was no way she was going to get through. If she allowed just a tiny grain of the hurt and humiliation and utter sense of self-abasement to filter through the steel door in her head, she was lost, weak, useless.

'And you aren't.' She spoke out loud now into the quiet bedroom, shutting her eyes tightly for one moment before opening them wide and climbing out of bed. She was as good as the next woman, as attractive as anyone else, *she was*. She walked through to the en-suite and stood for long minutes under a warm shower as she struggled to bring her emotion under control. Her daughter had been born three years ago yesterday and even the date of her birth was a lie. She loved her, she loved her more than life, she couldn't believe what had possessed her to give her away to someone else, but she had. She had. She took a long shuddering breath, salty tears mingling with the flow of water. Whatever it took, whatever she had to put up with, she'd do it, gladly, for Joy's sake.

The children were already busy spooning cereal into their mouths when she walked into the kitchen ten minutes later, seated at the large, scrubbed wooden table in the part of the L-shaped room designated as a breakfast area. The sunlight streaming through the open window haloed their blond heads in a brilliance that was breathtaking, and as they both turned towards her, she breathed in the moment, savouring it to the full. Of such things happiness was made.

'Look, look, they're all mine, Mummy says they're all mine.' Joy pointed to the stack of presents piled on the pine dresser opposite. 'Aren't I a lucky girl, Mummy Kate?'

'Terribly lucky.'

'But I said Paul can have something, 'cos he's only little, isn't he.'

'I only little.' Paul was happy to confirm his minor status in view of the reward.

'That's very kind of you, Joy.' Kate turned to Rosie who had just shuffled over from the sink, her right leg dragging a little. 'Isn't it, Mummy.'

'Yes.' Rosie glanced across at her daughter as she plumped into the cushioned seat with a little sigh. 'Very kind, darling.' As the two exchanged a smile the moment was bitter-sweet for Kate. The constant friction between Rosie and Joy worried her, and it was getting worse as the child grew older, but then Joy was a handful, she knew that. And Hank didn't like her . . . She frowned at the thought but it was true. Almost from the moment Joy had entered the house Hank had taken a dislike to the little girl.

At first her guilt had sent her into a frenzied state of panic as she had worried, day and night, that he suspected the truth. But it wasn't that, she knew that now. He didn't have the faintest idea Joy was her daughter. He just . . . disliked her. Joy was too determined, too forceful and strong-minded for Hank, and her husband, being the sort of man he was, never missed an opportunity to find fault with the small child. It was as though he had to remind Kate, constantly, of his magnanimity at the time of the accident and his continuing munificence in allowing his home to be invaded by her sister and child when he found the infant in question more than a little disagreeable. And she knew why he behaved like that. Oh yes, she knew.

Her eyes narrowed, more to do with her thoughts than

the shaft of sunshine lighting her face. He would need to justify his actions, wouldn't he, if half of what she suspected was true.

Oh, but she didn't *know* he was seeing someone else, it could be perfectly innocent . . . She raised her head sharply as though to repudiate the ridiculousness of the idea. Why hadn't she done something about it before now? There were ways and means, she knew that, and she also knew it wasn't merely Rosie and Joy who stopped her pursuing that aching desire to know the truth. No, it was her cowardice too. If she didn't know for sure, if it didn't rise up and smack her in the face, then perhaps it would go away. As Albert would have said, at times she wondered if she was threepence short of a shilling . . .

As though her thoughts had conjured up the last tangible links with the old man, Murphy and Tripe came sauntering in the open kitchen door from their early morning sojourn in the garden, tails erect as they surveyed their saucers for milk.

'Oh, hang on a minute, you two.' Kate smiled as she reached for the milk jug and tipped some milk into each saucer. 'There you are, satisfied now?'

'Those cats are too bossy for their own good.' Rosie wasn't smiling as she uttered her little soliloquy and Kate knew it was directed at her. Rosie didn't like Murphy or his brother, a feeling which the cats fully reciprocated. The children, on the other hand, treated the two felines as playmates, dressing them up on some occasions and carrying them about as though they were dolls, manhandling which the cats endured with perfect aplomb. To Kate's knowledge Joy and Paul had never even been scratched, which spoke volumes about the placidness of the two animals.

Kate turned to Rosie now, intending to point out the cat's attributes, but the words died on her lips as she caught the look on her sister's face before Rosie swiftly bent her head. It wasn't the first time she had sensed the hidden animosity that had grown, week by week, over the last few months, but she had never had such visible proof of her sister's hostility before. 'Rosie?' She sat back in her seat slowly. 'Is something wrong?'

'Wrong?' Rosie stretched her neck a little as she raised her head, her eyes blank as they met Kate's. 'What do you mean, wrong?'

'I don't know.' Kate shrugged slightly. 'You don't seem yourself, you haven't for weeks.'

'You're imagining things.' But her smile was tight. 'I'm perfectly all right, Kate.'

'Are you sure –'

'I've told you, haven't I?' Her voice was too sharp, too cutting, and she saw the shock of it register in Kate's eyes at the same moment as she cautioned herself to go steady. 'Really, I'm fine.' She swallowed, forcing back the bitterness that was tart on her tongue. 'Now, shall we let a certain little birthday miss open her presents, or shall we make her wait until tea-time, Aunty Kate?'

'Now! Now!' Joy jumped off her seat and ran across to the dresser, gathering the parcels in her little arms before returning to the table, and as Paul caught her excitement he clapped his hands frenziedly, sending a mug of milk spinning to the floor. In the ensuing pandemonium the incident was lost, but both women thought about it later as they prepared for the party, Kate with puzzlement and Rosie with burning resentment. Why had things turned out like this, *why*? It wasn't fair, it just wasn't fair. She watched from the kitchen window as Kate bent down to listen to something Joy was telling her, their fair heads close together, and bitterness rose up like bile in her throat, choking her.

Twelve months she had been in that hospital, *twelve long months*, and after the operations on her legs and pelvis had come the torment of learning to walk again, of coping with the reality of her damaged body. It was all very well for the doctors and nurses to tell her she wasn't trying hard enough, that she had to do more or face the inevitable consequences, but they didn't *know*, no one did. William had understood her, he had known she wasn't strong, that she had to be looked after. The tears of self-pity, ever ready to fall, stung her eyes, blurring the figures in the garden.

And Kate? Kate had everything. Look at today . . . She rubbed her eyes angrily, staring out through the window at the scene in the garden. A large trestle table with benches either side had been placed in the centre of the lawn, with balloons and gaily coloured streamers tied on the surrounding trees and bushes, creating a brightly coloured wonderland. The party would be a huge success, everything Kate did was a huge success. She ground her teeth, turning from the window and hobbling across the room to gaze down at Joy's birthday cake, an elaborate affair in pink and white.

A beautiful house like this, a husband who loved her, her own child, so why did she have to take Joy too? Rosie clenched her fists together as the urge to take the cake and smash it on to the floor rose hot and fierce. She ignored the little voice in her head that reminded her Kate had asked her first if she would like to make Joy's cake, and that she had replied she was too tired, too ill, to make the effort. No one knew how she felt, no one. Her mother had understood she had to be pampered, that she was delicate, and William had too, but they had both left her. It wasn't fair, nothing was fair, she wasn't able to cope with a high-spirited energetic child like Joy without help, but why did Kate have to get on so well with her? She knew Joy loved Kate more than her, she knew it.

'Well, that's the main bit done.' As Kate entered the kitchen, both children following her like excited little puppies, Rosie forced a smile. 'Phew, it's hot out there, but I shouldn't complain, it'll make it much easier to have all the mess in the garden.'

'Can we play hide-and-seek, Mummy Kate, can we?'

'Joy, Kate is your aunty, you know that, and I think a big

girl of three should talk properly, don't you? You don't want everyone to think you're a baby surely?' Rosie asked coldly. Her hands itched to smack the small girl into obedience, to subjugate that stubborn will, but she knew that wouldn't work. For the hundredth time she asked herself what on earth the parents had been like to produce such a wilful, headstrong child.

'I'm not a baby,' Joy flashed back instantly.

'I know that, dear, so now you're getting so grown-up I think you should call Aunty Kate by her proper name, like Paul calls me Aunty Rosie? You're a big boy too, aren't you, Paul?' Rosie smiled as she played her trump card, 'and a clever boy.'

Joy's head moved slightly, but her voice was hesitant when she said, 'I'm clever.'

'Yes, you're clever, Joy.' Now they were facing each other, hostility in their eyes, and Kate wanted to shout out for her sister to stop this . . . baiting. That was what it was like, she thought bewilderedly, the baiting of a small animal to confuse and overpower it so a stronger will could triumph. But this was a three-year-old child and her sister was an adult, it wasn't right . . .

'I want to call Mummy Kate, Mummy Kate.' Joy's voice was disconcertingly grim for one so young. 'And if anyone says I'm a baby, I'll bash them.'

'Joy!'

'So there.'

'*Joy* –'

'Don't, don't, Rosie.' Kate's face was chalk-white at the enormity of the confrontation that had suddenly sprung up from nowhere. She knew, and her sister knew, that something was being discussed that went far beyond the outward shell of a name. Joy had made her choice, a choice that Rosie had forced upon her, and having made it so vehemently it couldn't be ignored. She didn't want Rosie and Joy to leave this house – the possibility of such a happening sent a violent throb of sickness through her body – but neither could she see her sister staying now, and she owed it to her to make the leaving as easy as possible. 'Mummy knows you're not a baby, Joy.' She turned to the small girl, whose round face was red with rage. 'But she was worried other people might not understand, that was all. Mummy loves you, she doesn't want anyone to upset you by saying something unkind. All right?'

Joy gave a jerk to her head as she eyed the one person in her life whose word was law. She knew, somehow, that Mummy Kate didn't believe what she was saying, and she also knew that the same feeling she sensed in Uncle Hank when he looked at her sometimes with his eyes all narrowed and his mouth straight, was in her mother. But Mummy Kate . . . Mummy Kate loved her. She rushed at her now, burying her face in Kate's stomach and clasping her legs tightly.

'Come on now, come on.' The lump in Kate's throat couldn't be allowed to dissolve into tears and so her voice was abrupt as she said, 'Say sorry to Mummy and we'll all forget it, there's still lots of work to be done before your guests arrive.'

'We'll all forget it.' The echo of her words mocked Kate as they finished the preparations for the party, Rosie tight-lipped and silent and the children subdued. She would have to speak about this to Rosie, get everything out into the open, unless Rosie spoke to her first, of course. But it couldn't be allowed to continue, it wasn't fair on Joy. And Rosie would want to leave, taking Joy with her. She shut her eyes for a moment against the pain. Well, it would mean Hank's hold over her was finished, she thought bitterly, and if that happened she had made up her mind what she would do. Oh, she had, she most certainly had.

Hank had just arrived back from his normal Sunday lunchtime at the pub when Liz and James and their children arrived just after half past two, and from that point on the atmosphere seemed to lift as more young guests and their mothers arrived. The party was in full swing later in the afternoon when Kate spotted John's tall, lean figure emerging from the French doors into the garden, and although she despised herself for the abrupt thud her heart gave, she couldn't deny the excitement that flooded her at the same time, or the way everything was suddenly brighter, more clearly defined.

You're stupid, you're so so stupid, Kate, she told herself sharply, turning her back on the house and busying herself with stacking some dirty plates. John didn't even like her, she knew that, he couldn't have made it plainer, so why did she feel this attraction for him that didn't seem to die, however much she tried to scourge it from her? It was humiliating, shameful, she was a married woman when all was said and done with responsibilities and commitments, how could she have a schoolgirl crush on her husband's cousin who was four years younger than her and seemed to have a different girlfriend every other month? She would die, shrivel away to nothing, if he ever suspected it for a moment, it would be the final degradation in a life that seemed to be made up of nothing else.

'Mummy Kate! Mummy Kate! Look what Uncle John bought me!' Joy plummeted towards her, her face alight as she held a beautifully dressed baby doll high above her head, and Kate forced a smile to her face, kneeling down to give due homage to the present.

'An' me, an' me. Uncle John give me 'fing too, Mummy.' Paul was a few steps behind Joy, carrying his own gift of a bright red racing car with huge black wheels.

'They're lovely presents, lovely, have you both said thank you?' Kate asked carefully, painfully aware that John had followed the children over to her side. And then, as she raised her head, 'You shouldn't have bought Paul something too, John, there was no need for that.'

'I thought he might be feeling a bit left out,' John said easily as he stood looking down at the three of them. 'He's only a baby, it's difficult for him to understand why he isn't getting any presents.'

'Well, it's very good of you to think of him,' Kate said stiffly. 'I . . . I'm grateful.'

'No need.' He smiled at her and she allowed her mouth to relax a little before turning to the tray on the table.

'If you'll excuse me . . .'

'I'll carry that.' He had reached across and taken the tray out of her hands before she could object. 'Where do you want it, in the kitchen?'

'Please.' There was nothing for it but to trot along at his side as he walked across the garden and down to the far end of the house, turning the corner which led to the L-shaped part of the kitchen and through the open door, where he placed the heavy tray on the kitchen table.

Joy and Paul had followed them, still holding their presents, and now Paul tugged at John's trouser legs and, having got his attention said, 'Me like my car, Uncle John, and me got that too.' He pointed a fat little finger at the dresser where the present Joy had donated to him, a gaily knitted clown that was nearly as big as the small boy, was sitting. 'Joy give me it.'

'Did she?' John smiled down at both children, his voice tender. 'That was good of her, she must like you an awful lot.'

'She do.' Paul nodded solemnly, his fair curls bouncing. 'Don't you, Joy?'

'Yep.' Joy was basking in the sensation of approval. 'I like *everyone*.' She flung her arms wide to emphasize the point, twirling round on her heels as she did so, with such a comical look on her face that they were all laughing a moment later as Hank walked through the door, but although the others continued chuckling, Kate's smile was cut off as though with a knife at the sight of her husband.

'What's this then? Another party indoors?' The words were jocular but Hank's face was straight, his gaze swinging first to Kate, then to John, and lastly to the two children, who, sensing something they didn't quite understand, had become quiet.

'No.' Kate brought Hank's eyes to hers as she answered him, her voice low and cool. 'John carried the tray in for me and the children wanted to show me the presents he bought them, that's all.' And as the children's gazes moved to her in troubled perplexity, she added, 'You go and play now, leave your new toys in here. It won't be long and everyone will have to go home.'

'So . . . how are things, John?' There had been a long pause before Hank spoke and there was an even longer one before John replied, 'I can't complain, and you?'

'Fine, just fine. Has she been looking after you? Do you want a drink – a beer, a cup of tea?'

'John's only just got here,' Kate said hastily and although Hank nodded easily, his voice casual as he said, 'Oh yeah? Well the rest of us big kids are sitting up at the far end, there's beer and some sandwiches left, if you're interested,' she knew he had noticed the second of John's arrival and then followed them purposely into the house.

'Do you want some help with the dishes?' John had inclined his head at Hank but it was to Kate he spoke now, his gaze on her flushed face as she stood watching the two men.

'No, no, I shall do all these later, Rosie will help.' She had to restrain herself from physically pushing both men towards the door as she sensed that . . . something, that undefinable something that filled the sunlit kitchen with a sickly, thick atmosphere, causing her throat to tighten and her heart to pound.

She leant against the sink for some moments after the two had left and then on impulse walked across to the small, square mirror in the corner of the room and peered at her reflection. She didn't look twenty-eight, people were telling her that all the time . . . She stared at her flushed face for one more moment before shaking her head slowly at her own foolishness. What did it matter what she looked like? She felt old, ancient, inside. Old and ugly and unwanted.

All through her lonely childhood she had comforted herself with dreams of her own Prince Charming and then she had grown up, and Hank had arrived . . .

Did she love him? John's eyes were narrowed as he watched Hank lift his son high into the air and whirl him over his head. And did Hank love her? Paul was undeniable proof of their physical relationship, but he knew enough now to know that that meant nothing. Sex could be a mere sating of certain annoying biological needs that surfaced as regular as clockwork. He, of all people, knew that. But love . . . love was something different, separate, and he also knew that to his cost.

He sensed all was not right between them but he couldn't trust his own emotions where Kate was concerned, and especially in view of what he knew about Hank . . . *Damn it.* He bit down on the jealousy that surfaced, red hot, if he let it.

He had known, the moment he had seen her walk through the door that Sunday lunchtime three and a half years ago, that she was the one for him. The knowledge had hit him in the guts, like a live thing, and from that second he had never been free of her and never would be. Not that he wanted to be . . . He lay back in the deck-chair and shut his eyes, aiming to shut out the banal conversation that ebbed and flowed about him. He hated these sort of affairs, no one could ever accuse him of being a social animal . . .

'John, darling, you're looking thinner. Are you eating enough?' As Liz sank gracefully on to the grass beside his deck-chair, he opened dutiful eyes and smiled at his mother. He'd been lucky to have a childhood, parents, like he had. He'd known it before that night, four and a half years ago, but it had been brought home to him with sickening force then.

'I eat like a horse, dear.' He grinned at her and she smiled back, still beautiful at forty-seven. 'The sad fact is

I've inherited your build rather than Dad's, whereas poor Susan . . .' They both looked to where Susan, broad-shouldered and muscular, with legs on her that would grace any athelete, was playing an enthusiastic game of hokey-cokey with the little ones. 'Still, I'm tall and she's small, so all is not lost.'

'Oh, John . . .' Liz pushed at him with her hand as she laughed but then she noticed his gaze was elsewhere and watched as Kate came into view, Paul and Joy leaving their game immediately to run to her side. 'They do so adore her, don't they.'

'What?' As John turned back to her she looked at him levelly, her eyes sad.

'It's no use, darling.'

He had known she sensed something, she was closer to him than anyone else after all, but still her words shocked him. It made the unthinkable real, solidified all the desperate sleepless nights and days of harsh talking to himself and laid it bare. But he didn't try to pretend, merely shaking his head slowly as his eyes moved to his hands clasped together in a tight fist. 'I know.'

'They're married –'

'I know.' He had never used such a tone with her and raised his eyes quickly, putting out a hand to grasp hers. 'Really, I do know.'

'Oh, John . . .' They sat together then, in the warm afternoon, watching the children as they played . . .

Chapter Fifteen

'What's wrong with your mam this morning?' Paul asked.

'Don't say, "mam", you know they don't like it and there's enough trouble in this house without you adding to it.'

'All right, all right. You know I don't say it in front of them anyway but it's so damn difficult to speak one way with all the lads at school and another at home.'

'And don't swear either.' Joy ignored the muttered curse Paul gave at this point and continued, 'Mum's sulking because I'm going to Jane's barbecue tonight instead of staying in with her. It's not her birthday till tomorrow anyway, why she has to make such a fuss about everything is beyond me. It's not as though she even bothers to talk to me if I'm around, all she does is sit in that chair and eat chocolates and read those romances she gets delivered by the dozen.'

'She's lonely and she must get bored I guess.'

'Oh, come on, Paul.' Joy's voice was scathing. 'If she got up off her backside and actually *did* something for a change instead of leaving everything to Aunt Kate she wouldn't be bored, would she? Your mum falls over backwards to please her, you know she does, and she never gets any thanks, not from her and not from your father either. I've often thought it should be my mum and your father that's married, they're both so selfish and yet if anyone comes you'd think they were all sweetness and light. I don't know how your mother stands it at times, I don't really.'

'She's got us.'

'And that's supposed to be a life, is it? I heard her saying to Susan she'd like to get back into her career when we're at college, perhaps as a GP or something. Has she told you that?'

'She wouldn't tell me anything she didn't tell you first, now, would she.' There was no animosity in Paul's voice, just a plain statement of fact. He had never felt jealous of the special closeness between his cousin and his mother, he loved them both too much for that, and he knew, however caustic Joy's manner might be at times, that she loved him more than anyone else in the world. He smiled at her now and she immediately smiled back, the action softening the aggressiveness in her sky-blue eyes and tilting the edges of her mouth upwards.

'I wish we were a normal family, Paul.'

He didn't reply to this, he knew precisely what she meant. He couldn't pinpoint the time he had first worked out who was related to whom and how in their house; perhaps it had been about five years ago when he was seven and at the stage of asking endless questions, but from that time onwards a few of the things that had puzzled him were clearer. The way his mother looked after his aunt for one thing. His mother had told him she felt guilty his aunt had been hurt and his uncle killed when they were travelling to Glasgow at her invitation, and that they all had to be sympathetic of Aunt Rosie's variable mood swings. And she was grateful to his father for taking Joy and Aunt Rosie in, he could appreciate that. But the way his father was, he didn't understand that . . . He rolled over on to his stomach in the warm green grass dotted with daisies and pretended to study his French as he trundled everything around in his mind, Joy engrossed in her own homework now at his side.

His parents might act as though everything was all right, but you couldn't live in the same house without sensing the truth. He loved them both, he did, although he felt guilty about loving his father sometimes, especially when he was horrible to Joy. But then again, she did rub him up the wrong way pretty often and she didn't even seem to care . . . He glanced at her now, slanting his eyes in her direction to see her nibbling the end of her pen, her brow creased with a frown of concentration.

'You'll get blue lips.'

'What?'

'Take your pen out of your mouth.' He indicated the offending object as he spoke and she obeyed automatically, her eyes still on her work.

He wished his father could see Joy as *he* did, he'd love her then. But perhaps he wouldn't . . . His father didn't love his mother after all, in fact he didn't even seem to like most people. But he loved him, his son, he'd always known that. His forehead wrinkled with his thoughts. And he agreed with Joy, although he could never bring himself to voice it out loud, he didn't know how his mother put up with his father's treatment of her. It wasn't what he said or did, more what he didn't say or do . . .

His thoughts were getting too complicated and Paul rolled over again with a little sigh of exasperation. Oh blow them, blow them all, he had to master this French or old Dickens would go mad on Monday morning. But thank goodness he'd got Joy, how many times a day did he think that and he knew she felt the same. He glanced at her again and this time her eyes were waiting for him.

'You're not concentrating, Paul.' But she grinned as she said it, her love encompassing him as always.

It surprised him when he heard the lads at school telling of the rows they had with their brothers and sisters, he and Joy had never been like that. He couldn't imagine falling out with her, making her cry, she was like his other half, the female side of himself. He couldn't visualize a life in which she wasn't the main cog. His thoughts prompted him to speak now and he sat up, raking his shock of dark blond hair from his forehead as he said, 'wouldn't it be awful if we were ever separated?'

'Us? Separated?' He had her full attention now as she peered up at him. 'Who would separate us then?'

'Oh, I don't know.' He shrugged, feeling slightly foolish for having spoken. 'When we're older, going to college, university and that? We'll meet other people, perhaps be in different parts of the country.'

'Not if we don't want to be.' Joy sat up now, her blonde hair the exact shade of his. 'I'm only ten months older than you, I can wait a year and we can go somewhere together.'

'I suppose so.' He shrugged again. 'But people'd think we were daft.'

'I don't care what people think, do you?' He shook his head and she smiled at him. 'That's all right then. I don't ever want to be separated from you, Paul. Anyway, we don't have to be, do we?' Her smile widened. 'Cousins can marry, even first cousins like us, so it's no problem, is it.'

'Marry?' He stared at her, his mouth falling into a gape before he shut it with a little snap.

'Yes, marry.'

'But you're only thirteen –'

'I don't mean tomorrow!' She laughed then, the sound echoing round the quiet garden, but it was a moment before he joined in, his mind absorbing her words.

Marry. Yes, they could marry. He felt a little stir of excitement and then, as Joy brought his attention to his French, bent his head again as he put his mind to his work.

He was such a baby at times. Joy's face was tender as she continued looking at him. And yet in other things he seemed years older than lads of his age, some of them were so silly, childish. Look at that Dave Collins for example, he acted like a kid of five or six most of the time and he'd had the cheek to ask her out! Her mouth settled into a small smile of satisfaction as she recalled how she'd put the unfortunate master Collins in his place.

As if she'd go out with him, as if she'd go out with anyone other than Paul. She'd known since, oh, forever, that they would marry one day. He belonged to her, he was hers, the bond that joined them was unbreakable. She nodded to herself. It was. And Paul was beginning to think along those lines now, it always took lads a bit longer to wake up to things. Her face was indulgent. Especially shy, reserved lads like Paul. But she wouldn't have him any different, oh no, she wouldn't change a thing about him, except, perhaps, his father.

She frowned a little now as she contemplated her uncle. He was so cold, touchy, why on earth did Aunt Kate put up with him? She was so pretty, she didn't look anything like her age. In fact her own mother could have been Aunt Kate's older sister, none of her friends could believe it was the other way round. Why did she love Paul's mother and not her own? The thought narrowed her eyes although it wasn't new to her. There were times when she couldn't stand being in the same room as her mother and it was getting worse lately. How Aunt Kate stood her all day she'd never know . . .

CHAPTER SIXTEEN

Kate was thinking along exactly the same lines as her daughter as she stood at the kitchen sink, listening to Rosie pour out her daily tale of woe.

'No one knows what I suffer, no one . . .' Rosie took a big bite of her bacon sandwich as she finished speaking, her third in as many minutes. There was a blessed silence for a few seconds and then, 'And I said to that doctor at the hospital, you want to be thankful you haven't got arthritis, because it's no joke. Him criticizing my weight, damn cheek.'

'Rosie, they are just concerned about your health, that's all. If you lost a little weight it would help your knees tremendously. I'm sure he didn't mean to be insulting.'

'Oh, are you?' There was a hostile pause and Rosie's voice was tight as she said, 'I've got arthritis as a result of the accident, you know that. My bones were damaged so badly they never really recovered. Just because I don't make a fuss . . .'

Oh give me strength! Kate gripped the cup she was washing so hard the handle snapped clean off. At sixteen stone Rosie was at least six stones overweight, her figure a round little balloon and her pretty features lost in a podgy plump face that was pallid and sallow. She moved from her bed to the dining table and sofa, never took any exercise and firmly resisted all efforts Kate made to get her to leave the house, even for a brief sojourn in the garden. She wouldn't learn to drive, although Kate had offered to pay for lessons. She wouldn't attempt any housework or gardening, however light. But the worst thing, the very worst thing – Kate shut her eyes tight as the monotone started again – was the constant endless round of complaints against everyone and everything.

'I'm going to change the beds.' Kate cut into the flow knowing she would scream if she remained in the kitchen one second longer. 'You can finish this washing up if you like.'

'What? Oh, right. In a minute.'

The dishes would be waiting for her when she got back, Kate thought grimly as she left the room and walked upstairs. As always.

She went into her own bedroom first, standing at the open window and breathing in the mild summer air scented with roses from the trellis fixed to the wall of the house. She could see the children sitting on the smooth expanse of lawn, their books spread out about them, and smiled to see the two blond heads close together as always. 'Siamese twins . . .'

She sighed suddenly as her gaze focused on Paul, she wished they were closer, that their relationship was more like Liz's with her sons. Both John and Adam were so fond of their mother – not that Paul wasn't fond of her, she corrected herself quickly. She knew he was. He loved her, as she loved him. It was just that . . . Oh, she didn't know what it was exactly. Perhaps a combination of several things; the fact that his features were so like Hank's, that he was so quiet, sensitive and reserved in his manner, that she could never work out what he was thinking, how he felt . . . Whatever, she had found it easier to communicate with Joy through the years and she had let her closeness to her son slip. She knew she had. But she didn't know how to put it right. At least they did converse though, unlike Rosie and Joy . . .

She turned away from the window and began to strip her bed, her hands moving rapidly as she removed the week-old covers and replaced them with freshly laundered sheets and pillowcases. She had really thought all those years ago, after Joy's third birthday party when she had felt it necessary to speak to her sister and find out where they all stood, that the relationship between Joy and Rosie would improve. Rosie had been adamant that she wanted to stay with Kate, as adamant as she had been about the fact that Kate had misunderstood everything. No, she wasn't jealous that Joy got on with her aunty so well, of course not, how could Kate think such a thing? They were one big happy family, weren't they? and she was so happy to be with Kate and Hank. Poor William would have been so relieved to know his wife and daughter were in such good hands . . . On and on she had gone, reiterating points two and three times, until Kate's mind had been – not put at rest exactly – but quietened. And Rosie's determination to stay had settled her own future as securely as if someone had slid the bolt and turned the key locking her in.

She owed her sister, she owed her daughter, and her son? Yes, she owed it to Paul too to make his life as happy as it could be. The only person she didn't owe anything to was the man who had put her through hell, yes hell, for years. Her lips drew away from her teeth in something resembling a snarl as she thought of her husband. She hadn't believed, in her early years, that she was capable of hate. She had had reason to hate her mother, even her stepfather at times, but she hadn't. No, she hadn't. She paused now, her hand smoothing the coverlet as she let herself sink down on to the bed. But she hated Hank. Loathed and detested him with a fierceness that frightened her if she let herself think about it. But that's how it was.

Her eyes moved to the wall which connected their two rooms and she forced herself to move off the bed and gather the dirty linen into her arms from the floor, turning her thoughts aside by sheer willpower. She would change Rosie and Joy's beds next, then Paul's. Hank did his own, a practice that had sprung up by unspoken mutual consent when the children were still small. She hadn't set foot in his room for, oh, what, eight years now? He could have anything in there for all she knew, a harem . . . She smiled bitterly. And she wouldn't care if he had. Their private war had raged so long nothing he said or did would surprise her any more.

She had long since recognized that the obsession he had with his mother, and Miriam with her son, had hate and not love at its root. She also perceived that to a greater or lesser extent marriage had been his means of breaking free from that strange domination, a fact he would never admit to himself, because to do so would involve acknowledging that the hatred and resentment he had loaded on to her shoulders belonged to the woman who had given birth to him.

When he had taken a wife he had known, subconsciously or consciously, that Miriam wouldn't tolerate it and he had used the union first as a catalyst for the break and then as a whipping boy for the inevitable guilt and torment that followed. And she had tried to console him, laid herself open to rejection after rejection, humiliations . . . How could she have been so *stupid*?

'Don't think about it.' She literally ground her teeth together as she marched into her sister's room. It didn't matter, none of it mattered, the only important things were sitting together in the garden and when she thought of them she knew she had plenty to be thankful for. Against all the odds her daughter had been given back to her but as with everything in life there had been a price to pay. Well, she wouldn't whine about the payment, Joy was worth it.

And the need, the longing, that kept her awake night after night, tossing and turning in the chaste comfort of her bed? She actually flapped her hand at her thoughts, making a sound deep in her throat against the voice in her head. She wouldn't think about that, him, either because, as sure as eggs were eggs, he wouldn't be thinking about her.

As though to prove her wrong, when the phone rang a moment later the voice at the other end was John's. 'Kate? Is that you?'

'Yes. Hallo, John.' She hoped the weakness that had gripped her throat and churned her stomach wasn't reflected in her voice. It was ridiculous, *she* was ridiculous. A mature woman of thirty-eight and she still went to pieces every time she heard his voice or caught sight of him. Not that he came around much these days, busy influential lawyers with the world at their fingertips didn't waste time on housewives and children. Oh, that was unfair. She bit down hard on her lip and blinked her eyes as he began to speak. He needn't call by at all, need he? Then she'd have something to moan about. And she hadn't had to deal with him getting married yet, although no doubt that would happen sometime.

'Kate?' She suddenly realized he had been speaking for some moments and she hadn't heard a word.

'I'm sorry, John, there was a distraction . . .' She didn't elaborate the lie. 'What were you saying?'

'I asked if my mother has spoken to you recently, about Matthew Ratcliffe?'

'Matthew Ratcliffe?' Who on earth was Matthew Ratcliffe? 'I'm sorry, John, I don't know what you mean.'

'She hasn't then.' There was a brief pause. 'And Hank hasn't mentioned Ratcliffe's at all?'

'No, not that I remember.' Hank, talk to her of his own accord? That would be the day. 'Is something wrong?'

'You could say that.' As the silence lengthened she was just about to speak herself when his voice came all of a rush, sounding most un-John like. 'I really shouldn't be speaking to you about this but I'm going to. It's worrying Dad to death and what worries Dad worries Mum, you know how they are.'

'Yes, I know how they are,' she said quietly.

'The thing is, Kate, Matthew Ratcliffe is an old friend of Dad's, probably his oldest, they were at school together and so on, and Dad thinks quite a lot of the old fella. Matthew started his manufacturing business back in 1958, built up from nothing by the sweat of his brow touch, and he's done quite well.'

'Oh, that Ratcliffe's.' She knew who he meant now, or the location of the factory at least. The business occupied a small unit on a little industrial estate on the outskirts of Glasgow, and she remembered seeing the Ratcliffe vans, with their distinctive red and black logo 'Ratcliffe's for Quality Clothing' round and about. 'Yes, I know who you mean now. Well, what's wrong?'

'Hank.'

'Hank?'

'He's putting the squeeze on, Kate, not to put too fine a point on it. Old man Ratcliffe has been sailing pretty near the wind at times, with the recession and all, and he's made a couple of unwise business moves. You know that little clash in the Commons the other day when Kinnock attacked Major on the high interest rates being charged by banks to some businesses? Well, it looks like Dad's old friend's concern is one of them. He's been crippled by the bank and now Hank is putting him through the wringer, won't wait for payment, that sort of thing.'

'Can he do that?' she asked softly.

'It's legal, if that's what you mean.'

'But your father –'

'Dad doesn't agree with Hank's business methods, he never has. It's been a sore point between them for years, but you know what my father is like, Kate. It's got to the point where he does what he's told to avoid more confrontation. Weren't you aware of that?' His tone suggested she might be.

'Why should I be?' She stared at the phone as she held it slightly away from her ear, her face frowning with her surprise. 'Hank never discusses business at home, John.' Hank never discusses *anything* at home. 'I knew he was doing well of course –'

'Often on the backs of people like Ratcliffe.'

'I see.' She didn't know what to say, she was dumbfounded. Firstly by John's revelations about Hank's ruthlessness and secondly at the state of play between the two partners. She had wondered why they saw so little of Liz and James as a couple the last few years, Liz restricting her visits to coffee mornings and such like when the women discussed nothing more radical than their children, the state of the education system and matters relating to family and friends.

'I'm not getting at you, Kate, don't think that.' There was an urgent note in John's voice now that told Kate he meant what he said. 'But Dad stepped into the firing line for once, he really does think a lot of the old man, and he and Hank had a blazing row that is still going on some two weeks later.'

'But if your father doesn't agree with pressurizing Mr Ratcliffe . . .'

'It isn't as simple as that, believe me. If it was I wouldn't be bothering you now. I'm breaking all the family rules by taking work problems out of the workplace as it is.'

'You want me to talk to Hank? Is that it?' she asked with a sinking heart, knowing how futile such a course of action would be if she could bring herself to approach him in the first place.

'Would you?' His voice held none of the eagerness it should have, rather a flat dullness that surprised her again. 'I was speaking to Dad yesterday and this thing is really getting to him, the fact that he discussed it with me at length proves that. I really don't know what else to suggest.'

'You don't . . . you don't think it would be better coming from you?'

It was a stupid question and his voice reflected his recognition of the fact. 'No, not really, Kate,' he said dryly.

'You two have never got on, have you?' The words were out before she could stop them and, although she wanted to say, 'But that's none of my business,' she didn't. She waited.

There was a long silence, so long she wondered if she had been cut off at one point, before he said, 'We *were* friends once, when we were children, but we found as we grew up we wanted different things.'

'And that stopped you being friends?'

'Yes. Yes, it did, Kate.'

'Oh.' She swallowed deeply. He clearly wasn't going to say any more on the subject. 'I'll do what I can about Mr Ratcliffe, but I think you should know that it won't do any good. Hank . . . Hank doesn't take much notice of me . . . regarding business.' Or anything else for that matter.

'Well, don't worry about it, I shouldn't have mentioned it in the first place. Don't make things awkward between you and Hank, will you?'

'No. No, I won't do that, John.' She wanted the call to finish now. 'Goodbye.'

'Goodbye, Kate.' His voice was deep and soft and she shivered at its power over her as she replaced the receiver, standing on the wide, light-filled landing for some minutes as she remained staring at the small table that held the phone and a notepad. So Hank had estranged James and probably Liz? She felt the anger begin to bubble inside her. And things must be bad, really bad, for John to speak to her about it all. The pity of it was, he credited her with a lot more influence than she had. Influence? She almost laughed out loud. Hank would be more inclined to go the opposite way to anything she suggested, that was for sure. But she would have to speak to him, she had given John her word and besides, she couldn't let him behave like this without at least making her feelings plain. But he wouldn't like it . . .

It was almost mid-day when Hank came downstairs. She had contemplated knocking on his bedroom door, it was difficult to have a private discussion at the best of times in this house, but had decided against it. There was a distinct possibility their conversation was going to get heated and, knowing Hank as she did, he would be more inclined to keep his voice and temper under control if there was a chance of Rosie or one of the children overhearing him. The façade still had to be preserved, at all costs. Her lip curled at the thought. But he didn't fool the children, she knew that. Rosie, maybe. Her sister was so wrapped up in herself she only saw what she wanted to see, but Paul and Joy . . . They were her own flesh and blood after all.

She knew he would come into the kitchen first, it was his normal routine on a Saturday to make himself a sandwich at lunchtime before he went to the pub, and then he would disappear for the afternoon and evening unless he had arranged to take Paul to a football match. So now, as he sauntered through the doorway, she raised her head from a pile of mending and said quietly, 'I need to have a word with you, Hank, in private.' As he glanced round she added, 'the children have popped round a friend's and Rosie is in the sitting room.'

He continued walking across the room, pausing to lean against the stanchion of the door which led into the garden and was open before turning and saying, 'Well?' The word was arrogant, his whole stance was arrogant, but she forced herself not to rise to the subtle provocation he had become a master at. When she did, he always endeavoured to turn the tables, to become the innocent one, nonplussed by her wrath and injured by her attitude.

'I had a telephone call this morning regarding a certain business matter you are dealing with.'

'And you want to give me a message?' There was a slight sneer to the question and again she knew it was intended to irritate.

'No. Not exactly.' She paused for a moment and then continued along the lines she had rehearsed all morning. 'The matter in question concerns Ratcliffe's, the clothing manufacturer. I understand he owes you some money?'

'Oh, you do, do you?' His eyes narrowed and he straightened from the lounging position he had first adopted. 'And how, exactly, do you understand that?'

'That doesn't matter –'

'Don't play dumb, Kate. Who have you been talking to?'

'I have no intention of telling you that. Let's just say it isn't anyone directly connected with the matter.' She had made up her mind, straight after the call from John, that she wasn't going to mention his cousin's name to Hank. It wouldn't do any good and it might make things considerably more difficult. 'But they were concerned, about Matthew Ratcliffe. It appears you are pushing him pretty hard.'

'And?'

'Well, that's it.' She stared at him warily as she slowly rose to her feet, leaning her buttocks against the hard wood of the kitchen table as she faced him. 'He's an old friend of James's and –'

'Ah, I get it. So it was dear old James who's been giving you the sob story?'

'I told you it wasn't anyone directly involved and that's the truth. But this person is worried about Mr Ratcliffe, he's struggling at the moment –'

'Exactly.' His eyes narrowed still more until they were just dark slits in the tanned skin of his face. 'Which is the best time to apply a little pressure, he'll be all the more eager to fulfil his obligations if he doesn't think we're an easy touch.'

'And you think that's the right tack to take?'

'I don't have to explain myself to you, Kate.'

'I know that, I'm just your wife, aren't I.'

'Now look –'

'No, you look!' She glared at him now before cautioning herself to go steady. Losing her temper would do no good at all. 'The man is James's oldest friend,' she said quietly, 'doesn't that count for anything?'

'There are no buddies in business.' His face, like his voice, was grim. 'Winning is the name of the game and that means doing what needs to be done. Damn it all, I'm merely asking him to pay up what he owes. We've supplied him with one hell of a lot of cloth which the guy was only too happy to take. Now it's reckoning time.'

'But if he needs time to pay?' she asked carefully.

'Tough.'

'What does James say about it all?'

'You mean you don't know?' he asked mockingly. 'My, my . . .' She remained quiet, staring at him and he raised his eyebrows derisively. 'James is happy to give him more time, I'm not, end of story. Ratcliffe's business is folding anyway, the signs have been there for months.'

'Does your company need Ratcliffe's money so badly? Right now, I mean.'

'That has nothing to do with it.'

'I would have thought that had everything to do with it.'

'Then that explains why you stay home and play house and I earn our living, doesn't it.'

'You . . . you . . .'

'Look, before you get carried away after your cosy little phone call let's not forget who benefits from all this, shall we? You are the wife of a prosperous businessman, respected, with a purse full of charge cards –'

'I never use them.'

'That's up to you, isn't it. You don't want for anything, *anything*, and neither does Paul, or that sister of yours and her kid. They go to good schools, have their own allowance, clothes –'

'Every father gives his family what he can –'

'But Rosie and her brat aren't my family, are they, Kate. They are yours.'

'Something you never let me forget for a minute,' she said bitterly. She had been conscious of a phone ringing a few seconds before and now her sister's voice came from the sitting room in a shrill treble, the words indistinct.

'I think you're wanted.' Hank's voice was controlled and unpleasant and as she still continued to face him, he added, 'Come on, jump to. Don't let the earth mother image slip at this late date.'

There were words in her mind, base profanities that she wanted to scream and shout at him, but instead she moved away from the support of the table, her eyes still fixed on his as she fought to control the blind anger.

'Kate?' Rosie appeared in the doorway of the sitting room as she walked into the hall. 'John's on the phone, he said it's urgent.'

'John?' She was conscious of Hank in the doorway of the kitchen as she picked up the hall extension. 'What is it?'

'Have you spoken to Hank yet? About Ratcliffe?' If she hadn't known it was John she wouldn't have recognized his voice. As it was, it sent a chill down her spine.

'Yes, just now.'

'You needn't have bothered, the problem's solved. The old man threw himself under a train late last night, Dad's just rung me. He and Mum are in a terrible state.'

'*John.*' She couldn't form any words other than his name. 'John . . .'

'He left a note, I dread to think what's in it. If there's any blame attached to Dad it'll kill him, Kate, I know it.'

'What is it?' Hank was talking at the side of her but she stared at him with enormous eyes, her face chalk white.

'Is that Hank?' There was a quality to John's voice she had never heard before and never wanted to hear again. 'Put him on, I want to talk to him.'

'No, John.' Her knuckles were gleaming through her skin, she was clutching the phone so tightly. 'Please, not now –'

'Put him on, Kate.'

'Give me that.' Hank took the decision out of her hands by wrenching the phone from her grasp before she could stop him, speaking into the receiver as she stumbled across the hall and sank down on the first tread of the stairs.

Matthew Ratcliffe had killed himself? And it was clear that, rightly or wrongly, John held his cousin to blame for the old man's death and the resulting distress to James. Oh, she hoped Hank wouldn't lose his temper, things were bad enough already without that.

Hank didn't lose his temper. He listened, without saying a word, as John cut him to pieces and even when the phone was slammed down at the other end he didn't react for a full thirty seconds.

'Hank?' Kate stood up as she spoke, moving to his side and touching his arm tentatively. The look on his face was frightening her. 'Hank, what did he say?'

He remained quiet, staring at her. There was a terrible sensation rushing through his body, an agony that couldn't be worse if he had been disembowelled, but his face was still frozen in the stunned disbelief he had felt when John first began to speak.

'Hank?'

'Leave me alone.'

'Hank, please –'

'Kate . . .' He took a deep breath as the feeling that he was shrinking, becoming smaller and smaller as he slowly diminished into that person he knew he really was, took over. 'I'm going out.'

'You can't, not like this.'

He looked at her and the genuine concern for him that he read in her face was the final twist to the knife. He had treated her like dirt for years, used her, humiliated her, and she could still dredge up the milk of human kindness when it was needed. But he hadn't meant it to be this way, he had thought – he *had* thought he could make it work. He had, for a short time.

When he walked past her she almost reached out to pull him back, but the chastening she had suffered at his hands for years was too ingrained for her to risk further humiliation and so she let him go, watching him as he opened the front door and stepped outside, quietly closing it after him.

He stood just outside the front door for some moments as the sick churning in his stomach communicated itself to his bowels. He hadn't caused that old man's death, he hadn't. He shut his eyes against the light as John's voice drummed in his head. The things John had said to him . . . How could he have spoken to him like that? They had been like brothers once, before – His eyes opened as his mind slammed to a full stop, refusing to venture into 'before'.

Would any of them have thanked him if he'd been weak and soft with the business? Would they? Like hell they would. He'd forced himself, year after year, to carve out a reputation that would be respected if not liked, he'd needed to, the way James pussy-footed about. That company had been on its last legs when he'd stepped in. If he hadn't been tough, ruthless, shown them all that he was a man who took no prisoners, where would James be now? Finished, done for. The recession would have eaten him alive. And the private schooling for Susan and Adam would have gone, along with the entertaining Liz enjoyed so much, the expensive holidays abroad, the golf club, all the trappings of middle-class wealth . . .

And he'd shown her too, hadn't he? She would have made sure reports filtered back across the Atlantic, 'motherly' enquiries via Liz or James. He found himself glancing over his shoulder as he walked to his car, like he had done in the early days when he had felt his mother's presence breathing, pulsating round about him, willing him to fail. But he hadn't failed. He had proved he was a man. *He was a man*. He had succeeded. So why couldn't he get his mother out of his blood, his head, his bones? Every time he was alone, when he slept, she fastened back on him like a great leech, sucking at his mind, reducing him to nothing until he was filled with the fear she had always induced.

No, he mustn't think like that. As he slid into the driver's seat the fear began to choke him. She was his mother, she had given him life and she loved him. The discipline, the beatings, the . . . other things, had been for his own good. She had been his teacher, that's what she'd always said. Mother knows best . . . He opened the car door quickly as he began to retch, his stomach disgorging his supper of the night before as he heaved and shook. He musn't think of those things, she had told him he didn't understand, that he had to trust her. They were secret, private, family business. *Damn it*, get control. And gradually he pushed them back in their box, closed the lid and turned the key in the lock.

He wiped his mouth with his hanky as his eyes cleared, shut the car door, started the engine and drove carefully out of the drive, his movements restrained and precise.

He wouldn't think of Ratcliffe either, or the old man's eyes at that last meeting, reaching out to him, imploring. Like the eyes of that puppy he'd found and brought home one day when he was about Paul's age. He didn't allow himself to dwell on what his mother had tried to do to the puppy, just the fact that it had been one of the rare occasions that his father had stepped in in answer to his screams, transporting the little animal to a friend of his where, as far as he knew, it had lived to a ripe old age.

But Ratcliffe wasn't a small defenceless mongrel – he bit back on the terrifying remorse that was shrivelling his insides and searing his brain – the old man should never have let himself get into that position. He'd brought his failure on himself, that's what he'd done. But the eyes kept escaping from their particular box, staring at him, begging him for help, and when he pulled into a lay-by, his body racked by great shuddering sobs that tore through his guts and the very core of him, he knew his mother had won after all.

Part Three

A Time to Love and a Time to Hate

Chapter Seventeen

She was going to have to make some decisions.

Kate stared out over the quiet garden shimmering in the last of the afternoon sun from her seat on the patio wall. Sixteen. She couldn't believe Joy was sixteen, but last weekend they had celebrated her birthday, her first step into independence. Not that her daughter had ever been anything else but independent . . . She smiled to herself but her face straightened almost immediately, lines of strain about her eyes.

The last three years had been the worst . . . What had happened to Hank when old Mr Ratcliffe had died? He had shown no remorse, no regret, but he had been a devil to live with from that point on, making the misery of the years before seem light in comparison. And yet when the cats had gone within a week of each other the following winter he had been devastated . . .

'Oh . . .' She spoke out loud into the dying day, closing her eyes and lifting her face to the sun. Who cared what made that monster tick? She didn't. If he could be obliterated from her life so she never had to see him, think of him again, she would be content. But that wasn't going to happen, so she was back to the fact that it was down to her to make some decisions.

At the very least she was going to have to work again, in spite of the emotional blackmail Rosie had used unrelentingly for the last couple of years to keep her with her all day. But she had to escape, she knew that. Sometimes she felt her mind was so precariously balanced that it would only take one little push to send her over the edge, and it wasn't only Hank who had reduced her to a walking zombie. Notwithstanding the way Rosie clung to her, demanding attention like a child, she had the strangest feeling her sister hated her as much as Hank did at times. Thank God – and she did, every day – for Joy and Paul. What would she do without them . . .

As though her thoughts had conjured them up she heard the sound of their voices now, her eyes snapping open as she glanced at her watch. Half-past five? She hadn't realized it was so late.

'Out here.' She answered their call and the next moment they bounded out through the open French doors, their faces bright as they saw her.

Joy immediately launched into a tale of woe about a maths test, shaking her heavy fall of long blonde hair free from its band as she did so, but Paul was quiet, his eyes on his mother's face, and when he could get a word in edgeways he leant forward. 'Are you all right?'

'Me?' Kate smiled at him. 'Of course, dear.'

'You don't look it,' he said with the blunt honesty of youth. 'You need to get out more. Why don't you have a day in town soon, tomorrow even? Do some shopping.'

'Oh, Paul . . .' Kate's smile was tender as she looked at her son. It would be Paul who sensed she was low, even though she was closer to Joy.

'Yes, why don't you, Aunt Kate?' Joy approved as she scrutinized Kate's face. 'It'd drive me mad to be stuck in with mum all day, you need a break sometimes.'

'*Joy.*' Kate shushed her often embarrassingly outspoken daughter, before glancing at the house. 'She'll hear you.'

'She's dead to the world in front of the television,' Joy shrugged offhandedly, 'as usual. I mean it, Aunt Kate, you ought to have a day to yourself sometimes. Mum isn't as bad as she makes out, you know. It's the same old story, the more you do the more she'll let you. Go into Glasgow tomorrow, treat yourself to lunch and catch a film in the afternoon. Paul and I can see to dinner when we get home from school, can't we, Paul?'

'You can.' Paul grinned as she pushed at him with her

hand. 'I don't agree with this new man era, a woman's place is in the home. Isn't that right, Mum?'

'It's a good job I know you're joking.' Joy turned back to Kate with a little flounce but she was smiling. 'That's settled then, you have a day out on the town and we'll have dinner waiting when you get back. Can we have a lift to the disco in the evening, Aunt Kate?'

'Of course.'

'Brill. Right, Paul, come and do your homework. I want to watch *Top of the Pops* later, Take That are probably going to be on.'

'Wonderful . . .' Paul's voice was scathing.

'Come on.'

Kate's troubled expression didn't clear as the two went into the house. They were very close, perhaps too close, she thought worriedly. She wished they would make more friends of their own age, go out separately more often. Paul was going to be lost when Joy went to university in a couple of years' time. She didn't worry about her daughter, with Joy's dominant, outgoing personality she would soon find a niche anywhere, but Paul . . . Paul was different, sensitive. Still, it was hardly surprising the two clung together like they did having been brought up in this house, was it? She frowned to herself as she rose and stretched in the warm air. She had tried to make their childhoods as normal as possible, protect them from the rows and dark atmosphere, but between Rosie and Hank she hadn't had a chance. Children were so intuitive.

She was still thinking along the same lines the next day as she sat on the top of the bus looking out of the window; she rarely took her car when she went into Glasgow these days, finding car-parking a chore.

Hank had barely been able to stand when he had arrived home the night before, how he hadn't been breathalysed she would never know, and he had stunk of some cheap scent. He had timed his return for when the rest of the household would be in bed, as he always did, but Paul had been complaining of an upset stomach and they had been downstairs when his father had lurched in the door. She winced as she remembered the look on Paul's face before he had turned without a word and walked out of the room, crossing the hall and climbing the stairs without looking back.

Hank had watched his son go, the expression on his face much the same as a boxer who has received the knock-out blow without going down, and his voice had been slurred when, swaying from side to side, he had stumbled across to stand just in front of her before saying, 'You did . . . you did that on pur . . . purpose, didn't you. Kept him down here –'

'Don't be so stupid.' She had glared at him before walking across and shutting the living-room door. 'And keep your voice down, you don't want to make matters worse.'

'Wor . . . worse?' He had tried to gesture with his hands but the movement caused him to fall spreadeagled across one of the chairs, his leg catching a pile of magazines on the coffee table next to it and sending them spinning to the floor.

'Yes, worse.' She came to stand in front of him, keeping her eyes blank as she stared down into his blotched face, his mouth hanging open in a slack gape. 'Hank . . .' She raised her hands only to let them fall helplessly at her side. 'Can't you stop the drinking? For Paul's sake if not your own?'

'Wha . . . what?'

'Don't you realize he's at an impressionable age? You're his father, he looks up to you. What sort of standard do you think you're setting for him to see you like this?'

'I'm all right.' He tried to sit up but had merely slumped further into the chair.

'You are not all right, you're dead drunk.' She bent towards him, her voice low and her eyes willing his to make contact. 'Do you hear me, Hank? You're stinking drunk and in more ways than one.'

'Wha . . . what does that mean?'

'I can smell her, whoever you've been with.' Her lip had curled in spite of her efforts to keep her face blank. 'You reek of a brothel –'

'No, no . . .' He had struggled into a sitting position then, shaking his big head from side to side as though to clear it from the effects of the alcohol. 'I haven't bee . . . been to a whorehouse, nev . . . never been in one of them.'

'Well, she's got a whore's taste in perfume.'

The conversation had got heated then and she had finished it, thinking of Paul listening upstairs, by walking out of the room and leaving him to sleep it off in the chair. But there had been something about that smell . . . She sniffed now, as she watched the streets flashing past, something she couldn't quite place. Had she smelt it before? Was that it? But if so, on whom?

She was so lost in trying to remember she almost missed her stop and consequently catapulted off the bus with more haste than aplomb, straight into the arms of a tall, brown-haired man who was walking by.

'I'm sorry –' Her voice was cut off as she raised her head to stare straight into John's amazed countenance.

'Kate? What on earth are you doing on the streets of Glasgow at ten o'clock on a Friday morning?' He didn't let go of her as he moved back a foot or so, his hands holding her elbows as he stared down into her flushed face, her hair tousled by the force of their contact. 'Although I'm not complaining, this is the nicest thing that's happened to me all week.'

'I . . .' The content of his words rather than the surprise of their meeting strangled her reply before it was uttered.

'Are you meeting someone? Is that it?'

She took a deep breath and managed to answer in a fairly coherent voice, 'No. No, I'm here to do some shopping, that's all.'

'Without any of your menagerie?'

'I wanted to be on my own.'

'Oh, I see.'

He let his hands drop from her arms and she said quickly, without thinking, 'Oh, I didn't mean you. I meant . . .' Her voice trailed away.

'I know what you meant.' He was smiling at her now and she wished, she really wished he wouldn't, because it had the effect of making her want to burst into tears, and more to combat that sensation than anything else she turned sharply away without returning the smile, smoothing her dress with nervous hands.

'Well, goodbye, John . . .'

'Can I buy you a coffee?'

'A coffee?' She glanced up to see his eyes tight on her face. 'I . . . No, it's all right. You must be very busy.'

'I'm not busy.' He ignored the mountain of files that were sitting on his desk at that very moment, along with the appointment with a very influential client at half-past ten. 'And I'd love a coffee. We don't see much of you these days.'

We? Was that the royal we or did he mean Liz and James too? she thought weakly. Whatever, it was true. Since the affair of Matthew Ratcliffe and the ensuing aftermath of bad feeling between James and Hank, relations between the two families had been strained. Or perhaps 'we' meant John and his girlfriend; what was her name, Liza, or Lena, or something? He had had so many she couldn't remember but they never seemed to last longer than a few months.

'John . . .' She swallowed deeply, intending to make an excuse but she never got the chance. He leant forward, tucked her arm in his and began to walk down the street and out of sheer surprise her footsteps matched his. 'John –'

'I haven't done this since I was at school.' He cut off her protest as he looked down at her, his face straight but his eyes slightly crinkled as though he was going to smile any moment.

'What?'

'Played hookey.' And now he pulled a face at her that was most un-lawyerlike. 'Dreadful, isn't it.'

She didn't know what to say and so she said the thing that had been on her mind for the last few moments. 'How's your girlfriend?'

'Lora? Oh, she's a friend now, without the girl in front.'

'Oh, I'm sorry.'

'Don't be. She's going out with a very good friend of mine who wants the same things as she does, so it's all ended very amicably.'

'And you don't mind?'

'Mind? I introduced them. I didn't think it was fair . . .' He paused, rubbing his fingers across his chin.

'What?'

'Well, at the risk of sounding conceited, I didn't think it was fair to let her believe there was anything permanent with me. She was, is, a very nice girl, she deserves better than that.'

'Yes, I see.' The relief she felt was crazy, absurd. One day he *would* meet the love of his life and they *would* marry, she knew that, and perhaps it would be better if it happened soon, because every time he met someone else she felt sick for days – what was she talking about? – weeks, months, more like, right up until the time what had just happened with Lora occurred, as it inevitably did. But one day it wouldn't. And she would have to be glad for him.

'Anyway, how are you?' They had reached an elegant little coffee shop that looked both exclusive and expensive, and as John opened the door and stood aside for her to precede him, she forced herself to answer in a natural fashion, 'Fine, just fine.'

Fine, just fine. As a pretty uniformed waitress ushered them to a small table for two in a little alcove, she berated herself for the banality. But how could she say, 'I'm at the end of my tether, John. I've lived for years with a man who can't bear to touch me, even look at me without any clothes on, who is cruel . . . Oh, not physically, no, his cruelty is a thousand times worse than any physical violence. I'm nurse, housemaid and companion to my sister, because I've effectively ruined her life, and the weight of the guilt I've carried for years about my daughter is so heavy I don't think I can bear it another day. But the worst thing right now, with you sitting so close to me and looking so . . . wonderful, is that I love you. I've always loved you. I always will. And some day soon you are going to meet someone special, but I shan't come to the wedding. I hope you can understand why.'

'So . . . you're fine?' As the waitress bustled away with their order he leant slightly across the table, but his face was unsmiling and the question was more in the nature of a query than a social pleasantry.

'I . . . Yes, of course. I just needed a break, you know how it is.' She smiled quickly but his face didn't alter. 'Rosie is a bit demanding at times, it's understandable of course, and the children are at that age where they regard parents as taxi-drivers.'

'And Hank?' His voice was flat.

'Hank's well, he's quite well.'

'I wasn't enquiring as to his physical welfare.' His face was very tense, she noticed that, but then his next words took all her attention. 'I was asking how he is with you. I shouldn't, I know that, but I am. I thought in the beginning, when you first married, that everything was all right but now I don't. Or perhaps I didn't think it was all right, but being British, and having been brought up to be very proper' – his face was bitter – 'I did the right thing and accepted you didn't want to talk about it. *Is* there anything to talk about, Kate?' he asked urgently.

She knew she was going to cry, that there wasn't anything she could do to stop it, and she knew she couldn't, she must not . . . She kept her face rigid, staring at him with hunted eyes as her thought process slammed to a halt.

'Don't . . . don't look at me like that.' His hands reached out to grasp one of hers, unwinding the fingers that were pressed into her palm as he spoke, and he felt his touch register in the jerk her body made before she brought it under control. 'You don't need to be afraid of me, Kate, I promise you that. I just want to help.'

She lowered her head as the tears began to seep from her eyes, horrified that she was making a spectacle of herself and with John, *John* of all people. He was trying to be kind, probably because he disliked Hank he had sensed a little of how things were, but she was going to embarrass him horribly by weeping like this and she couldn't confide in him, not him. He was the last person on earth . . .

'Oh, my darling, don't cry. I didn't want to make you cry.' She could hear his voice, soft and low and tender, but his face was a blur and she couldn't believe he was really saying what she was hearing. She had finally cracked, flipped, whatever. This was probably how a mental breakdown first started, hallucinations, projecting one's own longing to the exclusion of the real world. But in a coffee shop of all places, at just after ten on a Friday morning?

'Kate? Here . . .' He had moved his chair to the side of her, his body effectively blocking her from anyone's sight and the alcove enclosing them in their own space, and now as he passed her a large white handkerchief she held it to her face, but such was her distress that it was soon sodden. 'Darling, come on. I can't bear to see you cry, my love . . .'

She heard the waitress come and go, obviously realizing she had picked a bad moment, but it was another full minute before she could control herself enough to raise her head and make some attempt to apologize. She didn't allude to what she thought she had heard because her rational mind told her it was impossible until he smiled, with a dark self-derision and said, 'It's no use pretending you haven't heard what I've said, Kate. It's too late. It's very kind, considering I've made a complete fool of myself, but I've told you now and I'm not sorry. I love you. Not that I expect anything from you –' He raised his hand as she went to speak. 'I don't even know how things are between you and Hank for sure, but you might as well know now that I've loved you from the moment I first set eyes on you, I think even before, in my dreams. This is probably the last thing you want to hear right now . . .' He paused, looking into her stunned eyes as he shrugged slowly. 'But there it is. I'm sorry.'

'But . . .' She stared at him vacantly, her mind and body numb. 'You've never liked me, and you've had lots of girlfriends . . .'

'Ah yes, the girlfriends.' He moved his head slowly. 'I didn't sleep with them all, if that's what you're thinking, but I can't pretend I've been celibate either. But more than sex I needed company, companionship . . . Oh hell!' He rubbed a hand tightly across his mouth, almost glaring at her. 'I'm not explaining this right, but I suppose . . . I suppose I was hoping I might meet the one who would allow me to forget you. I'm sorry, that's not very gallant, but it's true. I'm a normal man, Kate, I want children, a family, a hearth to come home to. I don't really want to be single, damn it, but . . . I am, I will be.'

'Oh, John . . .'

'Don't look at me like that, Kate, don't be sorry for me, damn it –'

'I'm not.'

'This is not some sort of line, you know, I don't want your sympathy –'

'*John.*' Her tone of voice was not in keeping with the softness of her face. 'Don't you see? Don't you?'

'See . . . see what?'

She watched him wet his lips and she stared straight into his face as she spoke the words she had never imagined herself saying, 'I love you too.'

'You can't.' But his hand shot out and gripped hers. 'You can't.'

'I can.' She was half laughing now but she knew in another moment she would cry again and so she said, 'The waitress has come and gone three times now, do you think you ought to call her over?'

'Damn the waitress.'

'John –'

'Come on, we're getting out of here, I want to talk to you.' He threw a ten pound note on the table as he stood up, pulling back her chair and taking her arm.

'But the coffee . . .'

'I can't talk to you in here.'

Once in the street she found herself almost flying along beside him, his hand still gripping her arm. 'There's a little park just along here, I eat my lunch there most days.'

She couldn't reply, it was taking all her breath to keep upright, and her heart was thudding so hard with a mixture of fright and excitement and sheer joy that she felt faint by the time he deposited her on a wooden bench in the tiny, deserted square of fenced lawn surrounded by trees and bushes.

'Kate . . .' He took her face in his hands which were trembling. 'Oh, Kate.'

The kiss was gentle, wondering, before it deepened and then she was pressed against him, his heart thudding against hers, as they sat together in the scented warmth of the little park for some minutes without speaking. She didn't allow herself to think in those few moments, they were too precious, she just breathed them in.

But they couldn't last and when he turned to look down at her, a wealth of love in his eyes, she knew she had to tell him. About Joy, Richard Wellington, the part Rosie and William had played so innocently and which had ended so badly. And Hank. She had to tell him about Hank. She felt her stomach heave in protest at the thought. John thought she was just an ordinary wife and mother, a respectable woman, perhaps he had even placed her on something of a pedestal? And this . . . this can of worms that was her life. How could she tell him?

'What is it?' His face had straightened at the look in her eyes.

'John, we have to talk. There are things I have to tell you.'

'Same here –'

'No.' She cut into his eager enthusiasm. 'I don't mean . . . They are difficult, painful. You . . . you might not still want me when I've finished.'

'Don't be ridiculous.' He pulled her into him again and she leant against him for one moment, gathering strength for what she had to do.

'Will you just listen? Without saying anything, I mean, until I've finished?'

'Kate –'

'And however you feel, I'll understand, I want you to know that. I don't expect you to condone what happened at the beginning but it wasn't my fault –' She stopped abruptly. This was not the way. She had to tell it calmly and without making excuses, either for herself or anyone else. Present him with the facts, as though this was a case he was dealing with, and let that lawyer brain sort it out from there. And she would start at the real beginning, with her childhood and the lack of love there, and work through. But oh . . . if she lost him now what would she do? She forced the panic back and began to speak.

'Oh Kate, my love, my love . . .'

She hadn't looked at him as she had related her story, her voice quiet and composed but trembling now and again at some particularly painful memory, and now as she raised her head and met his eyes she knew it was going to be all right. And with the knowledge came the wonder that she was loved, her, Kate Ross, and the little girl inside her that still cried for a mother's love was finally laid to rest in a small Glasgow park on a warm September day.

They had lunch later, at a quiet little restaurant tucked away in a back-street where the food was nevertheless superb, talking and laughing and talking some more. And all the time, and through the afternoon that followed as they wandered through the sunlit city streets, calling in at an art gallery and later a little tea room, John tried to find the words to tell her. He knew he had to, she had laid bare her soul for him, but to bring such ugliness into this one perfect day touched on the unthinkable. And she hadn't mentioned Hank again, after the telling of it all. It was as though she, too, had conspired to shut him out of the bubble they were in.

But she would have to know, that fact was inescapable, if only because the enlightenment would take some of the weight off her shoulders, show her that the catalyst for disaster was only precipitated a little by Joy's conception. Why hadn't he followed through on his impulse that first day he had met her and told her the truth? Because he had chickened out, he thought disgustedly, but no, to be fair, it wasn't just that. Kate had seemed so happy, so in love with her big American, and he had thought that maybe, just maybe, it was going to work out. And she had hidden the real state of her marriage so completely through the years . . . Damn it, when he thought of how she had suffered he would like to take him apart, slowly, inch by filthy inch.

'John?' She touched his arm gently. 'I'm going to have to go.' They were back in the little park again, sitting on the same bench, but now the evening shadows stretching across the tiny square of green had banished the warmth of the day.

'Not yet.' He pulled her into him, the movement almost violent. 'We must talk, decide what we're going to do. You are going to leave him, aren't you? The children will understand, you've said yourself they both have a pretty good idea how things are, and they aren't babies, Kate, they're young adults.'

'I know, but Joy is starting her A levels soon and Paul –'

'Will understand. They *will*, Kate. They'll understand. And they can live with us, Rosie too, I don't care. But I don't want you with him.'

She stared at him, the enormity of what they were discussing making her heart thud. Separation, divorce . . . But how often during the last miserable sixteen years had she thought of leaving him, dreamt of it, longed for it? And now she had John. She didn't have to consider a small flat somewhere with Rosie once the children had left. *She had John.* And he would have them all.

'All right.' She spoke so softly that for a moment he didn't realize what she had just said and then he lifted her wholesale from the bench, whisking her round and round in his arms until they were both dizzy.

'Oh Kate, Kate. I'll make you happy, no woman will ever have been so happy, I promise you.'

'I'm happy now.' And for the first time in her life she was.

'You can have anything you want, live anywhere you want –'

'John . . .' She touched his lips with the tip of her finger, her eyes tender. 'I only want you.' But even as she said it she knew it wasn't true. She loved him. He was the only man she had ever really loved, could love, but . . . he wasn't enough. She wanted her children even more. There was something deep inside her, something primitive and fierce and overridingly strong that had never cut their umbilical cords and probably never would. She read of women leaving their husbands and she could understand that, oh, she could certainly understand that, but when they left their children too . . . But it wasn't a choice. She wasn't having to make a choice, was she. John was going to take care of them all.

'Kate, about Hank –'

'John, I really do have to go.' She glanced at her watch, panic thudding in her chest. 'I'm so late already.'

'I'll drive you, and we can talk on the way.'

'No, please.' She put out a hand and touched his mouth to soften her refusal. 'I'll meet you tomorrow, we can talk then but I don't want them to see us together yet. Please, John.'

'I can get you home quicker than the bus.' But he smiled as he spoke, lifting a lock of her blonde hair in which there was no sign of grey and letting it fall back into place.

'I know, but just for today?' She stared lovingly back into his face. 'And I'll meet you here tomorrow afternoon, about two?'

'Kate, I don't want you to go.' He held her tightly as he spoke, his tone low and urgent. 'Don't ask me to explain, I can't, but I feel something's going to happen. Let me come back with you, we'll face them all together.'

'John . . .' She couldn't say it was all happening too fast, that she needed time to think, to absorb the immensity of the step she was taking, because he would think she wasn't sure about him and it wasn't that. She had never been more sure about anything in her life. But she had to go back and make the break with her old life by herself, in her own way. 'Please, give me a day or two. We'll tell them in a few days, I promise.'

'They'll seem like a lifetime.' He moved her slightly from him to look down into her face. 'It's not as though we've just met or started an affair . . . You've been part of me for so long, so many years. I feel . . . I feel as if I can't wait another day, another hour, and yet before we bumped into each other this morning I had the whole of my life to get through. Oh, I'm not making sense.'

'You are, you are.' She stood on tiptoe now to reach up to his lips, his height, his smell, the sheer masculinity of him thrilling and strange. She had been married fifteen years, borne two children and yet she felt like a virgin meeting a man for the first time. Oh, what was she thinking, she asked herself with a touch of bitterness. There had been memories cauterized on her soul that no virgin could have. All those wasted years . . . Her voice had a sad note as she said, 'If only we'd met first, how different things would have been.'

Yes, they'd have been different. For a moment he let the savage regret have free rein before consciously blanketing its destructive force. It had to start from today, it all had to start from today and the only way was forward. He said as much now, his voice not quite steady. 'We've the rest of our lives, my love, and I don't know about you, but I intend to live a long, long time.' He smiled but it was a moment before she smiled back. 'Kate . . .' He searched for the words he needed to convince her he understood. 'You've been through much worse than me, I know that. It must have been hell on earth and how you've survived without becoming all twisted up –'

'I am.' Her voice was shaky now. 'Believe me, John, sometimes I am.'

'But the real Kate is still there,' he said softly. 'The Kate I met that first Sunday lunchtime who was the most perfect thing I'd ever seen. We can work everything out as long as we're together. You believe that, don't you?'

'I want to, I do, but people are going to talk, you know that, don't you? And you being a lawyer –'

'Kate, this is 1994, it'll be a seven-day wonder, if that. And do you really care what people think? The only ones who matter will understand, you know they will.'

'I know.' She relaxed against him for a moment before jerking away as a clock chimed the hour. 'I've got to go, John. I'm late for dinner already and I promised the children I'd drive them to the school disco.'

'All right, all right.' He kept his arm round her waist as he walked her to the bus stop and she didn't try to dissuade him, even though the streets were still full of folk hurrying home. She felt light-headed, dizzy with happiness as they stood together in the few minutes before the bus came, and when it arrived and he kissed her, whispering,

'Things *will* be different from now on, I promise,' she almost floated up the steps and into a seat near the window where she waved at him until the bus turned a corner and he was lost from view.

John stood staring down the busy thoroughfare long after Kate had gone, the sense of disquiet that had attacked him earlier returning tenfold. He should have gone with her, insisted they confronted the whole household tonight and faced the resultant pandemonium together. He wasn't a man given to fancies – huh, that was the understatement of the year, he thought wryly – more than a decade of dealing with the twists and turns of human nature had taught him to put his trust in plain, unvarnished fact, but nevertheless the feeling of impending doom was so strong he could taste it.

But she wasn't going to do anything, say anything, tonight. He shook his head at his own panic. Nothing had altered, not really, the situation was just the same as it had been for the last fifteen or sixteen years, it was only he and Kate that knew different. And he would tell her everything when they met tomorrow, put her fully in the picture, painful though that might be. Might be? It damn well would be. He ran his hand over his face and began to walk in the general direction of his office, his mind focusing on his work as the lawyer took precedence.

It was going to take something short of a miracle to explain why he hadn't rung in today, they must have been running round like chickens with their heads cut off. He winced as he remembered his work schedule. Well, he'd come clean with Alan, his partner, and the rest of them could think what they liked. But Kate was right, certain people would have a field day when the news got out, he could name one or two right off that would just love to turn the knife. *Well, let them.* He stopped dead in the middle of the pavement as the knowledge that he didn't care hit him and with it the feeling he'd been keeping in check all day, that made him want to jump and shout and turn cartwheels like a lad of eight or nine, intensified.

All that mattered was Kate. She was the only important thing in his life, the rest was dross. But he wished he'd gone with her, damn it all, he did.

CHAPTER EIGHTEEN

'Oh, Paul, for goodness sake, she's fine.' Joy tried to keep the impatience out of her voice and failed. 'She's probably had a wonderful day of freedom and forgot the time, that's all, she'll be here any minute. Do go and get changed.'

'It's seven o'clock.'

'I know what *time* it is, that's why I want you to get changed. Look . . .' She turned from the kitchen sink and waved a plastic-gloved hand in the direction of the hall. 'There's the front door, I bet that's her.'

Joy sighed with relief as she heard Kate's voice answer Paul's a moment later. Perhaps he'd go and have a bath and get ready now, they were going to be late as it was. If it had been a football match he'd have been ready hours ago.

'I'm sorry I'm late, darling.' As Kate popped her head round the kitchen door Joy turned and smiled. 'Has everything been all right?'

'Fine.' Joy nodded as she turned back to the dishes. 'Mum's eaten along with us and she's watching TV now. She's a bit grumpy . . .' She shrugged as she tipped the last of the washing-up water away. 'But that's nothing unusual, is it.'

'*Joy*.' But Kate was smiling. 'You go and get ready for the disco then.'

'I've already had a bath and washed my hair, I've only got to change now but I suppose we'll be waiting ages for Paul. He doesn't want to come anyway.'

'Doesn't he?' Kate detected a note of irritation in her daughter's voice and something else she couldn't quite place. 'Why not?'

'Oh, I don't know.' Joy shrugged again, before walking across to the kitchen table and perching on the edge of it as Kate walked fully into the room. 'He says he can't dance, and some of the kids get on his nerves.' She shook her head before adding, 'But he doesn't make much of an effort, Aunt Kate.'

'No, I don't suppose he does.' Kate's voice was sympathetic but for the first time in years her mind wasn't fully on her family as she glanced round the familiar surroundings. In a few days, perhaps even tomorrow or the next day, she was going to drop a bombshell that would send shock waves into all their lives and nothing would ever be the same again. But did she want it to be the same? Her eyes narrowed as she looked out of the window to where the two cats were buried under an old apple tree. Heaven forbid. She couldn't have carried on another year, and then another, she just couldn't have. Something would have had to have given and it would probably have been her sanity.

In the last three years since the Ratcliffe affair there had been times she had been frightened, really frightened, of her husband. The darkness in him, this deep, ominous something that she had sensed almost from the beginning, was aggravated, not soothed, by his heavy drinking bouts. She had taken to locking her bedroom door at night, not because she feared an assault of a sexual nature – her lip curled at the absurdity – but because there had been murder in his eyes once or twice when he had ranted and raved at her in an incoherent drunken rage.

'I'll go up then.' Joy's voice was slightly peeved as she levered herself off the table but Kate didn't notice, and Joy waited a few moments, her eyes on Kate's back, before leaving the room in something of a flounce. She continued to frown to herself as she walked up the stairs and into the bedroom she shared with Rosie, another bone of contention in her life.

She couldn't wait until she was eighteen and able to go to university, she thought irritably as she pulled her new skimpy top savagely off its hanger and flung it down on her bed. She didn't know anyone else, *anyone*, who had to share a bedroom with their mother. Not that she would have minded if her mum had been like Aunt Kate, they might even have had a laugh if she had been. But no, she was stuck with a fat, crabby old woman who did nothing but moan when she was awake and snore when she was asleep, and she was sick of it, sick to death. She sat down heavily on the bed as a wave of guilt washed over her. Oh, she was mean, she knew she was, but she was so *fed up* . . .

She let herself relax back on to the quilt, bringing her legs up off the floor as she rolled over on to her side. Why didn't Paul *say* something, she asked herself desperately, anything, just to let her know how he felt? Oh, she hated him, she did. No she didn't, she loved him . . . She bit on to her clenched fist as she tried to bring her emotions under control.

This last year he had changed so much and she didn't mind that, not really, except that he'd stopped talking to her like he used to. And she knew she was partly to blame for that, she could almost pinpoint the day he had begun to withdraw: Geoffrey Ranger's barbecue. Oh, how could he think she was interested in a twerp like Geoffrey Ranger anyway? Just because she'd had a couple of glasses of cider and acted a bit stupid, everyone else knew it was just in fun. And she hadn't actually kissed Geoffrey anyway . . .

But perhaps she was imagining things? She sat up suddenly, brushing her long hair out of her eyes. They still had a laugh together, didn't they, and he never talked about any of the girls at school, not in . . . that way. Oh, she knew he still felt the same, deep inside she knew, the way he looked at her sometimes, especially when he thought she wasn't looking . . . He *had* to feel the same. She ground her teeth together as her eyes narrowed. He had to, she'd die if he didn't.

She moved impatiently now, jerking her legs over the side of the bed and stripping off her blouse and skirt before pulling on the new black jeans she had bought the day before, to team up with the long-sleeved, skin-tight black top that ended two or three inches above her waist. She contemplated her reflection in the mirror, lifting her hair high on top of her head before letting it drop to hang loosely about her face and shoulders. Should she have it up? It showed her earrings off better and they had cost a fortune in themselves but Paul liked long hair. Most of the lads did. She left it down.

By the time she was ready she had worked herself up into a state of agitation that showed in the brightness of her eyes and flushed cheeks. She couldn't stand another disco that ended with Paul sitting in a corner with the other lads who never danced, and her trying to pretend she was having a wonderful time being belle of the ball. All the other boys wanted to dance with her, even the ones who were supposed to be going out with someone else more often than not, so why didn't Paul?

And she was sick of pretending everything was all right between them when she knew it was only surface-level, but how could she ask him, straight out, if he still loved her? She'd tried to hint at it often enough the last few months, give him openings, but to actually *ask* him? What if he said no, or worse still, tried to make some excuse because he felt sorry for her? She knew Paul's soft heart, she'd spent most of her life trying to protect him because of it, hadn't she? But if he didn't love her any more? . . . She stared into the mirror with huge eyes. She'd die, she would, she'd die. She would never love anyone else but him.

Paul was downstairs waiting when she walked into the sitting room a few minutes later and the look in his eyes, for just an instant before he brought his lids down, gave her hope. He did love her, he did, she told herself emphatically as her heart thudded and raced. She knew he did. He just had to be . . . prodded into declaring it, that was all. She'd tell him tonight, somehow, that her flirting and acting around didn't mean anything, that it was all for him, to get him to tell her how he felt. The more he closed in on himself the more stupid she was and it had to stop, it would stop.

'All ready?' Kate smiled as she put down the book she was pretending to read and reached for her car keys, glancing at her sister who was sitting across the room apparently lost in the television. 'Rosie? Do you fancy coming for the ride?' she asked pleasantly as she stood up.

'What?' Rosie dragged her eyes away from the quiz show with obvious effort and spared them all a fleeting glance before shaking her head. 'No, you go. My knees are hurting.' It was the same excuse she made every time she was asked to move from the chair but it didn't rankle to-night, or irritate, Kate thought to herself as she ushered the children out to the car. In fact, she had felt a quick stab of pity for her sister as she had turned her fat, bloated face towards them all, along with a rush of determination that she would continue to care for her for as long as Rosie needed her.

Joy was quiet on the drive to the school hall but Kate, lost in her own thoughts, didn't notice. Paul did, and it was on the tip of his tongue to say, 'What's the matter with you, then? Geoffrey found someone else?' but he bit back on the searing jealousy, knowing he would only make a fool of himself if he let it out.

He knew the way his cousin affected the male population, oh yes, he knew all right. The number of lads, from the sixth-formers down, who asked him about her love life . . . And each time, with each gormless grinning moron, he had to pretend he didn't care, shrug, and tell them to approach her themselves if they were interested. *If they were interested?* He could see her now in his mind's eye as she sat beside him, although he was looking out of the window. Skin like thick cream, eyes of a brilliant sapphire blue and her hair . . . Oh, shut up, shut up. He almost swore out loud as his mind groaned. He shouldn't have come tonight, he didn't want to, but he couldn't stay away either. It was like some exquisite torture watching her flaunt herself in front of them all, Geoffrey and the others turning inside out in their endeavours to impress, but it'd be worse if he stayed at home and didn't know what was going on. He'd tried that once and nearly driven himself up the wall.

Did he love her? He shut his eyes as he continued to keep his head turned to the window. Well, whatever the emotion was he didn't want to feel it again for anyone else. It was too painful. Perhaps if he'd been a different type, able to laugh about it with her, joke against himself, get it out into the open, things would be better. Oh, that was stupid, it wouldn't make any difference, would it, except to add humiliation to the way he felt on top of everything else! If only they could go back two or three years to how they used to be, before she noticed Geoffrey Ranger and the others. He knew she hadn't meant it, of course she hadn't meant it, but she'd even talked about marrying him then . . .

'Here we are then, have a good time you two. You want me to pick you up at half-ten as usual?' Kate asked brightly as she drew up in the car-park, which was full of parents dropping children off.

'Please, Mum.'

'Thanks for the lift, Aunt Kate.'

They walked into the school hall together but as the music blasted their ear-drums, courtesy of the hired DJ, one of Joy's friends grabbed her and Paul slipped away to join the group of lads sitting in the corner swigging coke.

'Usual load of dogs here tonight.' Ronnie Blackett, who fancied himself as something of a tough nut, leant back in his chair as he took a long swallow of his drink. 'Here, Paul, try a can.'

'No thanks –'

'Go on, you'll like it.' Ronnie gave a long, slow wink that was supposed to be discreet. 'It's good stuff.'

'Come on then.' Paul took the can, throwing his head

back and then choking slightly as hard liquor hit the back of his throat. 'Hell . . . What you got in there, Ronnie, meths?'

'Pinched a bottle of my dad's whisky on the way out.' Ronnie looked inordinately pleased with himself. 'Good, eh?'

'Wonderful,' Paul said sarcastically as he took in his friend's flushed face and slightly unsteady voice. 'Just what we all want, to be suspended.'

'That's what I told him.' Brian Hemming, another of the group, nodded at Paul. 'Beer is one thing but whisky is just asking for trouble.'

'Where's the bottle?' Paul asked flatly and then, as he followed Ronnie's eyes downwards, he saw the plastic carrier bag under the table. 'Right, we're getting rid of this, now.'

'You can't, it's nearly full. I've only had half a can out of it.' But although Ronnie was protesting, they could all see his heart wasn't really in it.

'I'm taking it outside to that clump of bushes at the end of the drive, okay? You can pick it up as you go.' Paul stared hard at Ronnie who held his glance for a moment or two before shrugging with assumed nonchalance.

'You'd better wait a minute or two, Paul.' Brian Hemming flicked his head in the general direction of the stage as the music stopped. 'Old Cartwright is going to make his usual announcements. Wait till the music's back on and the lights are down.'

But once the disco was resumed they were joined almost immediately by a group of girls from their year who had a reputation for being both mouthy and wild. 'What you all sitting here for, then?' Amy Armstrong, a tall willow-thin girl, whose micro mini-skirt barely covered her backside, slanted her eyes invitingly at Paul. 'Don't you know what your legs are for?'

'We're just going to get rid –' Ronnie's voice was cut off with a yelp as Paul's boot hit his shin. 'Ow, you gone mad, Paul –'

'Shut up.' Paul levelled one long look at his friend, who subsided in his seat muttering and rubbing his leg.

'Well?' Amy's sharp, heavily-made up eyes moved from Ronnie's face to Paul's. 'You going to dance, or are you going to sit here like a bunch of old men all night?'

'We're going to sit here like a bunch of old men all night,' Paul said drily, but he smiled at the pert little face looking down at him. He knew Amy fancied him, not that he would touch her with a barge-pole, he thought quickly, but you had to admire her for sheer nerve.

'Right, we'll sit with you then.' Amy signalled at the others who were giggling behind her to get chairs and the next moment the girls had joined them.

Great, just great. Paul hid his dismay behind a bland face. If any of this lot caught a smell of what was in that carrier-bag, he'd never get it outside. He'd seen Amy and a few of her mates down in the town once or twice on a Saturday night, dressed to the nines and looking about twenty and invariably half sloshed. Oh, Ronnie was a fool. He glanced across at him but Ronnie studiously avoided his gaze. He'd get them all suspended at this rate, because one thing was for sure, if Cartwright found out alcohol, especially spirits, had been brought on to school premises, he'd throw the book at them.

'Lousy DJ, isn't he.' Amy leant forward, crossing her endless legs anchored down with heavy Doc Martens. 'You want to come down Kelly's on a Saturday night, now they really do know about music, don't they, Sandi?' She half turned to one of the girls at her side. Kelly's was a night-club in the middle of Glasgow credited to do more trade in drugs than anything else. 'Sandi's uncle owns the place, so we always get in free. We could get you in, if you want.'

'What, tomorrow?' Ronnie asked eagerly.

'Sure.' Amy answered him but with her eyes on Paul. 'Just be down there about ten, no problem.'

*

What was Paul doing, sitting with that Amy Armstrong, Joy asked herself from her vantage point on the stage at the end of the room, as she handed the perspiring DJ a drink one of the teachers had sent over. He must know what she was like, *everyone* did, there was even talk she'd had an abortion last year when she had that time off with 'stomach trouble'. Look at her! Her heart was pounding so hard it was making her ears ring and buzz as she walked back to her friends. Amy was all over him and he was loving every minute of it.

Jane Scott, her best friend, said much the same thing as Joy sat down. 'Paul's going to find he's bitten off more than he can chew if he's not careful.' She flicked her head in the direction of the group across the room. 'Have you seen them?'

'What?' Joy pretended a nonchalance she was far from feeling. 'Oh, Amy you mean? Well I'm sure Paul can look after himself.'

'With her? You must be joking. She's a real tart.'

'Perhaps he likes tarts.'

'Yeh.' Jane giggled now. 'Perhaps he does.' She gazed across the room for a moment as Joy deliberately faced the other way. 'He's really good-looking, your cousin, isn't he. He hasn't half changed in the last few months. He's so tall –'

'Are we going to dance then?' Joy included the rest of the girls as she spoke, cutting across Jane's chatter with a cool voice. 'It's so boring if we don't.'

The moment they stepped on to the floor Geoffrey and his cronies, who had been standing leaning against the wall watching them for some time, joined them. 'Do you mind?' Geoffrey smiled, his eyes all over her as each lad singled out a girl.

'It's a free world.'

'You look really smashing tonight.'

'Thanks.' She mellowed her abruptness with a smile but she wished he'd go away. Apart from anything else he was blocking her view of Paul. What was she going to do? Stupid question, she told herself bitterly. What could she do? He was a free agent after all and if he fancied Amy . . .? Oh, she hated him. She really really hated him. And Amy wasn't even pretty, with her thin, scrawny legs and big nose. How could he do this to her? How could he? Through a break in the dancers she saw Amy push against Paul's chest with her shoulder in answer to something he had said, and the physical contact made her nerves jump as though she'd been hit with a bolt of electricity.

Well if that was the sort of girl he wanted he could have her, see if she cared. She forced back the acrid jealousy but it was screaming there at the back of her head as she continued to dance, her eyes dry but the tears seeping from every pore. He needn't think she was just waiting for him to deign to notice her, no way. She could get anyone she wanted, look at Geoffrey, she'd lost count of the number of times he'd asked her out. And at least he didn't try and get off with another girl under her very nose. The thought brought a surge of gratefulness that caused her to smile more warmly at the youth in front of her than she had ever done before. Her smile registered in his startled expression and then he edged a little closer, making them more of a couple than one of the group.

The next hour was one of subtle torment for both Paul and Joy. He had known the exact moment that Geoffrey joined her on the dance-floor, that was one of the strange things about this feeling he had for her. He could always identify her whereabouts without having to turn his head and look in her direction, and it was the same whether they were in a room with one or one hundred other folk. It amazed him sometimes but it was a fact. It would have amazed him still further if he had known that Joy felt exactly the same, that the bond that bound them together, the strong mental, as well as emotional, tie was on a par with an extra sense and one that was stronger than the accepted faculties of sight and smell.

When Amy and the other girls got up to dance after an hour or so of provocative banter, Paul took the opportunity to remove the offending carrier bag, while Brian and a couple of the other lads walked Ronnie, who was suffering from the equivalent of six double whiskies, round the outside of the building a few times. Paul didn't glance at Joy as he left but he knew she was wrapped round Geoffrey like a second skin, and the urge to punch the other boy's face into a pulp was strong.

He was breathing hard as he walked down the drive and, after depositing the whisky under a convenient bush, he stood for several minutes in the quiet of the warm September night, the sounds of the disco pounding slightly in the distance. He didn't need this. Damn it all, he should have followed his instincts and stayed well away. And Ronnie acting like a prize prat! He had seen his father stoned out of his skull enough to know that the only way along that particular road led downwards.

What did she see in him anyway? He couldn't keep his mind off the thing that was tearing him apart, not with his guts twisted so tight it was a physical pain. Couldn't she see what Ranger was really like? He had a job to string two sentences together most of the time, unless he was expounding on his favourite topics of football and his sexual prowess. The latter thought brought his teeth tight together as his hands clenched into fists at his side. If he tried anything with her he'd kill him, so help him he would. The possibility of Geoffrey making a move, which was not unknown on these occasions, sent him hurrying back along the drive but once in the hall he could see no sign of Joy and, more worrying, no sign of Geoffrey either.

She hadn't gone outside with him? She couldn't be that stupid, he thought savagely. She had been.

When Joy had seen Paul and his group leave the hall, Paul not even glancing in her direction, the raging jealousy and frustration had been replaced by a sick emptiness that brought hot tears stinging at the backs of her eyes. She didn't know where he was going and she didn't care, all she did know was that he cared so little about her he hadn't even checked to see where she was or who she was with. She felt bereft, the gnawing background anxiety that had grown and grown over the last few months as she had sensed their relationship deteriorate, suddenly swamping her.

Her face must have betrayed her, because she was aware of Geoffrey's keen glance a moment before he turned to follow the direction in which she had been looking. 'Anything wrong?'

'No, nothing.' She forced herself to smile brightly. She would die, just die, if he guessed the truth. It wouldn't have mattered if she had been rejected by someone else but she couldn't stand anyone knowing about Paul.

'Sure?'

'Yes, of course. I . . . I'm just a bit warm, I think I'll sit down for a while.'

'Come outside for a minute, there's a bit of a breeze out there.' He smiled at her, his face guileless. 'I could do with some fresh air myself, it gets claustrophobic in here after a while, doesn't it. This hall isn't really big enough but I suppose it's better than nothing.' He continued to talk as he put a casual arm round her waist and encouraged her towards the door, turning to wink and nod at his friends behind her back before leaving the hall. 'Now that's better, isn't it?'

As the cooler night air met their faces Joy took a couple of deep breaths before nodding a reply. She felt hot and sticky but it wasn't that which was making her head ache and her heart thud. It was disappointment, searing disappointment and bitter hurt and a hundred other emotions besides, all mixed up together into a self-destructive cocktail that made her smile brittle and her voice reckless as she said, 'Shall we walk for a bit?' She'd show him! If he didn't want her there were others who did.

There was a certain strut to Geoffrey's walk as they left

the brightly lit exterior of the hall and moved towards the empty, dark playground, around the perimeter of which were dotted several wooden benches with the black expanse of the bike sheds beyond. His mind was fixed on these convenient shelters, so it was with a stab of disillusionment that he heard her say, 'Let's sit here, my legs are aching.'

'Here?' He glanced round the shadowed playground as Joy sank down on one of the benches. 'Oh, all right.'

She didn't like the feel of his mouth as he kissed her, it was too wet, too sloppy, and she could hardly breathe he was pressing her so close, but she didn't actually object until as one hand moved over her right breast his other one began to fiddle with the belt of her jeans. 'What are you doing? Stop that!' She slapped at the hand on her breast as she jerked away, her voice indignant.

'Oh come on, Joy.'

'What do you mean, come on? I'm not like that, you know I'm not. If you want to paw someone about go and get Amy Armstrong or one of her crew.'

'I don't want Amy Armstrong,' he said thickly, 'I want you, you know I do. I've wanted you for ages.'

'Well keep your hands to yourself, we're not even going out.'

'Come out with me, then, I've asked you often enough. Don't you fancy me, is that it?'

No she didn't, she didn't fancy him at all, but she couldn't very well say so, could she? Joy stared at him in the dim moonlight. 'It's not that,' she said stiffly, 'I just don't want to go out with anyone at the moment.'

'Why? You're not frigid are you?'

'*Geoffrey.*'

'Sorry, sorry.' He held up his hands. 'Out of order, but you get me like that, Joy. Come on, give us a little kiss at least then, that's not too much to ask, is it?'

'Not if you keep your hands to yourself, no.'

'I promise.' But as his arms went about her and his

mouth covered hers she was tense and apprehensive, everything in her wanting to go back to the bright lights. She didn't notice Brian and the others pass a few feet away as they led the now sullen Ronnie back to the hall, but as Geoffrey's hands again resumed their assault on her body she tried to push him away, her protests becoming more frantic as he didn't respond.

'Get off, Geoff, I mean it –'

'Shut up.' She had jerked her mouth from his but now he forced himself on her again, his breathing rapid as his fingers moved under her bra.

Her slap across his face instantly followed by a hard push in his chest that sent him sprawling over the side of the bench on to his back caught him completely by surprise, but one of his hands caught her shoulder as he fell causing her to lose her balance and half slide, half fall off the wooden seat on to the rough concrete with a thud that made her cry out.

As he reached for her again they both froze at the sound of running footsteps, and she had never been more glad to see Paul in her life as he materialized out of the shadows, his face black with rage. 'You take your dirty hands off her, Ranger.'

'What?' Geoffrey struggled to his feet, one hand holding his cheek. 'What are you talking about? She just hit me –'

'That's nothing to what I'll do if you don't beat it.'

'Oh yes, you and whose army?'

'I can take you, Ranger, with one hand behind my back.'

'Huh . . .' But Geoffrey's voice was blustering. 'I'd like to see you try.'

'How about now?'

'Paul, don't.' She hung on to his arm as he moved a step forward. 'Let him go, he didn't do anything.'

'Why did you hit him then?'

'Because she's a stinking little tease, that's why.' The

string of obscenities that followed brought Paul springing forward but he was hampered by Joy clinging to him, and merely caught Geoffrey a glancing blow across his shoulder. Nevertheless, it was enough to convince the older boy Paul meant business, and he backed away as Joy continued to hold on to Paul, keeping his eyes on his adversary's face. 'Look, I didn't do anything, she'll tell you.' As his feet touched the edge of the path that led out of the playground he obviously felt safer. 'Not that she didn't ask for it, mind.' He had anticipated Paul's lunge and was already running with the swiftness of a greyhound as the growl of rage followed him.

'Let go of me!' Paul nearly jerked Joy's arm out of her socket but still she wouldn't release her grip on him.

'Let him go, Paul, he's not worth it,' she sobbed frantically.

'And you? What the hell do you think you were doing to come down here with him anyway?' Paul glared down at her with such ferocity that her fingers dropped from his arm of their own accord. 'You must have known what he wanted, what he would expect?'

'I didn't, not . . . not that, at least.' She flung her hand towards the bench. 'I thought . . . I don't know what I thought.'

'You didn't think!' She had thought she knew Paul inside out, better than herself even, because the thoughts she had been having of late had surprised her when she had time to consider them, but this enraged maniacal being was a stranger, and a terrifying stranger at that. 'You were so busy flirting with him, weren't you, getting them all hot under the collar –'

'*Them?*' She stared at him, her face white. 'We were talking about Geoffrey.'

'I'm not blind, Joy, or stupid and neither are you. You know how the lads feel about you –'

'And what about you?' The shock that had had her in its grip evaporated in blazing-hot anger at the unfairness of his accusations. 'Don't you preach at me, Paul Ross, not when you've been with that Amy Armstrong!'

'Don't be so ridiculous –'

'I'm not! I'm not being ridiculous.' She stamped her foot in her rage and then, at his caustic 'And you can pack that in too', suddenly flew at him, hitting out at his head and chest as he tried to hold her off him and then subsiding in a shuddering heap at his feet as her legs and temper ran out.

'Joy, come on, don't cry . . .' He sat down beside her on the rough surface and put his arm round her, drawing her head on to his shoulder. 'He's not worth it.'

'*I'm not crying about Geoffrey Ranger*,' she bawled with a touch of her old spirit. 'I couldn't care less about him.'

'Couldn't you?' He didn't make the comment that sprang immediately to mind, namely, she could have fooled him from the way she had been acting all night, but settled her more securely into his side as his stomach muscles clenched at her closeness. She smelt of baby shampoo and Geoffrey Ranger's after-shave, and it was the latter that stopped him from making a complete fool of himself and following through on the burning desire to kiss her. 'What then?'

'Oh, Paul . . .' She was going to tell him, she thought as a fresh bout of weeping assailed her. She didn't care about making herself appear silly or cheap, she just couldn't carry on like this any more. At least if he knew it would make the problem his as much as hers and at the very least he would avoid inviting Amy Armstrong, or anyone else, to the house. That, she acknowledged, would be the final straw. 'It's you.'

'Me?' he asked in surprise. 'Oh, don't be daft, Joy. You can't blame me for objecting to you coming down here with him. Him, of all people. You ought to hear how he talks about girls when he's with the lads, boasts about how he's got on and all that. You're my cousin and I don't want –'

'I don't want to be just your cousin,' she interrupted in a very small voice, 'and that's what the problem is. I want . . . Oh, I don't have to spell it out, do I? You must know what I mean.'

He had become very still as she spoke, his body tensing, and when he made no reply she felt the humiliation begin to shrivel her up inside. But she had had to tell him. She answered the section of her mind that was shouting at her with a snarl. She had had to and that was all there was to it. But she couldn't admit right at this moment that at the bottom of her, deep deep in the core of her being, she had thought he felt the same.

'Joy –'

'Don't. Don't say it, don't say you're sorry for me –'

'*Joy!*' His voice was a bellow now as she tugged herself free and then he had caught her to him, taking her face between his large hands as he looked straight into her eyes. 'Do you mean it?'

'Of course I mean it.' There was a ray of hope lighting the blackness at the look on his face. 'I've . . . I've always felt the same, you know that, you must know it.'

'Must I?' He gave a little 'huh' of a laugh, his voice shaky. 'Oh, Joy . . .'

It was a full hour before they left the playground, explanations and loving complete, and by then cars were lining up in the car-park and down the drive as children streamed out of the hall. 'Paul?' Joy caught his arm as she saw Kate's car in the distance. 'Are we going to tell them? Tonight I mean?'

'You don't want to wait?' He couldn't explain the niggle of unease that had sprung to life when he saw his mother's car.

'Why? What's the point?'

'You know what they'll say, we're too young to know what we're on about, we've got our school-work and then university.'

'I don't care what they say, do you?' She faced him now,

her stance militant. 'And I don't care about A levels and university either. Well, I do . . .' She gestured with her hand, flapping the air. 'But none of that is a problem. I can wait a year till you're ready for university and then we can go up together, we could even get married before we go.'

'Joy –'

'Well, we could, couldn't we?'

'Yes, we could.' He smiled at her now, his voice low as he gently took her by the shoulders and pressed her against him for a moment. 'But do me a favour, tell them when they're all together.'

'Oh, Paul, I wanted to tell Aunt Kate tonight, you know how pleased she'll be. She's always been more of a mother to me than my own mum, and I can't wait to see the look on her face. Do we have to wait until tomorrow?' Joy didn't say why she expected to have to wait until the next day, Hank's absences from the family home and the drunken bouts that had got progressively worse over the last three years were something they never discussed, by mutual consent. She knew his father's behaviour distressed Paul, which she could understand, and she also accepted her cousin still had some feeling for her uncle, which she couldn't understand, thoroughly disliking him herself.

'I want to tell them all together.' He couldn't have offered an explanation as to why if she had asked him, but it was something to do with the fact that Aunt Rosie was Joy's mother and she would sense without being told if his mother knew first. He could understand why Joy loved his own mother so much but there were times when he felt desperately sorry for the woman who was his aunt, but to put such feelings into actual words would have seemed like a betrayal to all three of them somehow.

'All right.' Joy pulled a face at him but she wasn't really miffed, how could she be when everything had turned out so fantastically, she asked herself happily. And she knew she'd have an ally in her Aunt Kate. Her uncle might not like it, she was well aware he liked her as little as she liked him, and her own mother? She had never liked the fact that she got on so well with Aunt Kate, the rows they used to have about it when she was younger . . . But her aunt would be over the moon. She smiled to herself as they walked towards the car. Over the moon.

CHAPTER NINETEEN

'I . . . I don't believe it.' But even as she spoke Kate knew she wasn't questioning the truth of Paul's words, the way Joy was hanging on to his arm and the look on her face was proof enough. She glanced at her husband who was leaning against the mantelpiece, one elbow resting on its wooden surface and his demeanour showing the consequences of the excesses of the previous night, and then Rosie, who was sitting at her side. Both their faces reflected the same stunned amazement that was probably on hers, but not the sick terror that had sprung into her throat like a live thing. Oh please, God, no. Not this, never this. In all her wildest dreams . . .

'What on earth do you mean, you've fallen in love?' Rosie's voice was harsh as she glared at the pair standing in front of them. 'You're children, you're still at school –'

'We might still be studying but we're not children.' Joy entered the conversation now, her face lengthening at her mother's attitude. 'You started going out with Dad when you were sixteen.'

'He was a good deal older than me.'

'And that makes it all right?' Joy's voice was tight and scornful and Rosie's face flamed as she continued, 'I'd have thought it was better to fall in love with someone of your own age, not someone from another decade.'

'*Joy*.' Paul pulled her closer into him as he stopped her saying any more, and the gesture cut through Kate like a knife. They did, they really did love each other. Oh, God, help me. Tell me what to do.

'I know it's a shock,' Paul said quietly, his eyes leaving his aunt's face and moving first to Kate's and then to Hank's. 'But we are serious, please believe that. And it's not something that's happened overnight, we've always loved each other.'

'But as family, like brothers and sisters.' Rosie could feel the sickening realization of what it would mean sweeping over her and it was this that made her voice panic-stricken. Kate, as Joy's mother-in-law? Her sister would take her place in Joy's affections absolutely then, she knew it. It was bad enough now, but she had always comforted herself with the thought that when Joy left to go to university, and later, when she married and had children, the closeness between her daughter and her sister would of necessity become less and her role in Joy's life as mother and grandma would increase. But this? She couldn't bear this.

'That's only the way you've seen us.' All attempt at conciliation had flown out of the window as far as Joy was concerned. 'Just because you've got the wrong idea you can't blame us.'

'All right, all right, that's enough.' Hank levered himself off the mantelpiece. 'Let's all calm down. You say you love each other? Well, fine, no harm in that but you'll find in a year or two, maybe less, that you'll both have changed.' He kept his face bland, unconcerned. That little harpy marry his son? He'd rather see them both dead first. 'In spite of what you might say and think now you *are* both young' – he forced a smile to his face – 'certainly from where I'm standing, and feelings change, it's a fact of life.'

'I shan't change my mind, Dad.'

'You might.' The smile was wearing thin. 'So all I'm saying is take it nice and easy. Do your A levels, both of you, get good university places and then see how things are. That's not too much to ask, is it?'

'We're getting engaged when Paul's sixteen.'

'Now that's just plain crazy.' He shouted at Joy now, his shoulders hunching, before bringing his temper under control. *The little bitch.* He never had been able to stand the sight of Rosie's kid since she had first come into this house and how right he had been! She was the power behind the throne in this little lot, make no mistake, but if she thought he was going to let her trap his son she'd soon find out she'd bitten off more than she could chew. Her, for a daughter-in-law? He'd rather walk through coals of fire and drag Paul with him. 'I won't allow it.'

'Why?' Joy asked tightly.

'Why?' He stared at her and she knew exactly what he was thinking, and she also knew he wouldn't voice it. 'I've said, haven't I? You're too young.'

'Dad, sixteen isn't young. You've got no idea how things are these days.' Paul's voice was quiet, restrained.

'I don't care about all that.' Hank glanced at Kate but she was still standing with her hand clutching her throat and looking as though she had been poleaxed. 'You're my son, not one of the nameless millions. What goes on in other families doesn't concern me but I'm not having you do something you'll regret for the rest of your life. Heck, Paul, I'm only asking you to give it time. That's not too much to ask at your age, is it?'

'Dad, at my *age* most lads have already slept with a couple of girls, it's not like it was in your day. There's a boy in my class who's going to be a father at the beginning of next year and he probably isn't the only one, the way some of them carry on –'

'You . . .' It was the convulsive jerk Kate made, rather than her strangled whisper, which cut off Paul's voice and caused them all to look at her. 'You haven't . . . slept together?'

'No, of course we haven't.'

'But I don't see anything wrong in sleeping together once you've made a commitment,' Joy put in calmly, 'as long as you take precautions, that is.'

'*Joy!*' Rosie seemed to lift up off the sofa with her horror.

'I don't, Mum, not if you're in love. I wouldn't sleep around but if you love each other and you're engaged what's the point in waiting?' She stared at them all defiantly. 'It's a perfectly normal thing to do, isn't it, like eating and sleeping.'

'It's nothing like eating and sleeping, you silly little –'

'*Hank!*'

'Well I've never heard such garbage.' He had rounded on Kate as she spoke his name. 'Sixteen and she thinks she knows it all. And this is your fault, I blame you for this. You've been too lenient with her, you and that sister of yours, and this is the result.'

'Don't you blame me!' Rosie sprang to her feet in spite of her considerable bulk. 'What say have I had in her upbringing, I'd like to know? The only one she's ever listened to is Kate and you know it.'

'And a fine job she's done.' The words were spat out, contempt in every syllable, and even Rosie was silenced by the hostility they revealed.

'There's nothing wrong with Joy.' For the first time Kate could see Hank in more than Paul's outward appearance as her son moved a pace forward, his young face black with rage and his eyes narrowed. 'And we will get married, as soon as we can, whatever you say, do you hear me? I love her and she loves me and that's all that matters.'

'You can't marry Joy, Paul.' Paul had been speaking to his father but it was Kate who replied, and there was a quality to her voice that caused all eyes to turn to her white face. And for some strange reason at this moment it was William that Kate was thinking of, his face so vivid on the screen of her mind that it was as though he was in the room with them. He had sensed the truth all those years ago and he had told her, in his own way, that they needed to keep distance between the two families. Had he known this was going to happen? Had some sort of revelation of the disaster that was going to come upon her? On them all?

'Aunt Kate?' Joy's hand had been tight across her mouth but she reached out now, her eyes swimming with tears. 'I thought . . . I thought you at least would be pleased. I thought you loved me.'

'I do.' Kate looked at the young face in front of her and she was consumed with the pain of what she had to do to her daughter. She was going to break her heart, she knew that. The shock of finding out Rosie wasn't her mother would be bad enough, and discovering Kate had been lying to her, to them all, but when she learnt of her real relationship to Paul – what would she do? Kate felt the knife turn in her heart. Paul might get over it, in spite of his sensitivity he had a way of looking at things with a calm logic and strength that often surprised her, but Joy? Joy was all emotion and passionate fervour, fire against Paul's cool deep waters. She would burn herself up. 'Believe me, Joy, I do.' Did she have to tell her, did she? 'Won't you trust me when I say it's impossible and leave it at that?'

'I can't.'

'You must.'

And now it was the little girl who had horrified them all with her wild tantrums who stared back at her, anger and not tears turning her eyes bright and her mouth hard. 'Well I won't.' Joy's gaze swept round them all. 'Do you hear me, I won't. I won't let you spoil what Paul and I have, whatever you say. We are going to be married, we'll run away somewhere if we have to, won't we?' She didn't wait for Paul to respond before continuing, 'And like Paul said, this isn't something that's just happened, we've always known we'd end up together one day. We can be married before we go up to university and do our studying together, our getting married doesn't mean we don't want to carry on with our education.'

'That wouldn't work, you'd distract each other or a baby would come along –'

'Mother!' Joy's voice held the mocking disdain of the young. 'Babies don't just come along. We wouldn't have a family until we were ready. I shall go on the pill.'

A family? Oh, God, I've got to tell them, haven't I, give

me the strength . . . Kate gulped but it was as if her vocal cords had been cut and the words just wouldn't come.

'You've got it all worked out, haven't you.' Hank glared at Joy, grinding his teeth together for a moment before continuing, 'You think you've stitched the lot of us up, is that it? *Fait accompli?* Well there's a long time to go until Paul is sixteen –'

'Stop picking on Joy, Dad. I'm the one you should be shouting at.'

'You?' Hank's lips came back from his teeth in a sneer and he swore softly as he shook his head. 'You haven't got a clue, have you, not a clue. She's manipulated you, boy, can't you see it? She's been doing it ever since you came out of diapers. You think you thought of this, is that it? Is it?'

'Don't, Hank.' As Hank took a step towards his son, Kate came between them, her hands pushing against his shoulders. It didn't occur to either of them that it was the first physical contact they had had in years. 'Leave them alone.'

'Leave them alone? Are you crazy, woman?' His hand swiped her arms away so suddenly she was forced to relinquish her grip, taking a step backwards to steady herself. 'You want our son to ruin his life before it begins?'

'He won't –'

'Too right he won't, I'll make sure of that.' The words were spoken with such menace, such cold malevolence, that it chilled the blood of those listening, bringing Rosie to Joy's side as Paul moved slightly in front of them both.

'You don't have to make sure of it, they can't marry.' Kate's head was bowed now, her thick hair falling about her face and hiding her expression from him, her back to the other three.

'"Can't"? What are you on about, "can't"?' he ground out angrily.

'They . . . they aren't cousins' – She heard Rosie's 'No, Kate' but didn't pause – 'they are brother and sister.'

'What?' It was clear Hank hadn't taken it in. 'Don't talk garbage, woman.'

'Joy is my child, my first child.' Her voice carried the flat dullness of truth along with an unmistakable thread of bitterness. 'I . . . She's my daughter, Paul's half-sister.'

The silence was absolute as a stillness descended on the room, time holding its breath for an endless moment before she raised her eyes to Hank's face.

'I couldn't give her up, not completely. Rosie didn't know, she thought the baby was a nurse's at the hospital –'

'You . . .!' He shook her violently, her head bobbing on her shoulders like a rag doll's, but as he raised his fist to punch her in the face Paul was there, hanging on to his father's arm as he shouted, 'No, no, Dad, stop it. Let go of her.'

'*I'll kill you!*' Saliva was spurting from his mouth as he shouted, but now Paul had both Hank's arms from behind and was clinging on to his father with all his might, his feet leaving the floor as Hank turned and twisted, trying to throw him off.

'Dad, please! Please, Dad, you mustn't. Leave her! Get away, Mum.'

But Kate didn't move beyond turning her head and looking towards Joy and Rosie a few feet away. Her sister's fist was pushed in her mouth, her teeth biting on the bent fingers as she remained frozen to the spot, but it was Joy who drew her eyes, the look on her face causing Kate a pain that was physical.

'Is it true?' Joy's lips were bloodless.

'Yes.'

'You're . . . you're my mother?' The horror and revulsion in her voice hit Kate straight between the eyes. She had thought she had suffered before, known anguish, desperation, but the feeling that was upon her now was incomparable to anything she had endured previously.

'I . . . yes. I am but . . . let me explain –'

'And my father? It's not . . .' Joy's eyes moved to Hank

who had become quieter now, knowing the only way he could pluck Paul from his back would be to fling him aside in a way that would undoubtedly hurt him.

'No.' Her voice was a croak and she gulped, swallowing some spittle before she said, 'No, not him.'

'Who then?'

'Someone . . . He's not important. I haven't seen him since . . . He doesn't know about you.'

'How could you?' As Kate made to move towards her Joy jerked away so violently she sent Rosie stumbling to one side. 'Don't you come near me, don't you touch me. *Paul?*' The last was an agonized moan. 'You don't believe them, do you? She's making it up.'

'Joy . . .' Paul dropped his hands from his father now, moving from behind Hank's broad figure but remaining at his side as he stared at the girl he had always thought of as his cousin, his stricken expression speaking for itself.

'It won't make any difference, will it? You can't let it make any difference?' Joy was gabbling now, her words on top of each other as she fixed Paul's eyes with her own. 'I don't care what she says, I don't believe her. You're not . . . We can still be married, we can go away –'

'Joy, stop it.'

'I won't let it be true, Paul. You're mine, you've always been mine. You know, you said it, we belong together –'

'*Joy.*'

'No, I won't listen.' She swung back to Kate now, the look on her face terrifying for one so young. 'I hate you! I hate you!' And then she was gone, flying from the room in a storm of weeping.

'I'd better go after her.' Paul spoke as though to himself but his eyes were on his mother and Kate nodded, gesturing quickly at the door Joy had banged behind her.

'Yes, go on, Paul. See to her,' she said urgently.

'You'll be all right?'

'Yes, I'll be all right.' Just go to her, talk to her, comfort her. Oh, God, oh, God, why? Is this retribution? Then why punish Joy when she's innocent? Oh, she couldn't bear it. What had she done? *Joy*.

The door had hardly closed again before Rosie rose from the chair she had collapsed into when Joy had banged against her, and the envy and frustrated rage of years was in her voice when she said, her voice a low hiss, 'How could you? How could you be so wicked?' She should have known, she should have known. The words were like a constant record drumming through her mind since the realization that she had been duped, made a fool of – and what a fool, she thought bitterly – had burst on her consciousness like a blinding light. And Kate had told them all so quietly, so matter-of-factly even. This thought added more venom to her voice. 'Aren't you ashamed of what you've done? You've ruined all our lives. When I think of all the years you've kept quiet.'

Kate's head had been bowed but now she raised it and her face was awash with tears. 'Try to understand, Rosie, please. I didn't mean anyone to get hurt, I was never going to say –'

'But you'd still have kept hold of her, wouldn't you? You've never let me be a mother to her and now I know why.'

'That's not true.' Kate held out her hands like a penitent seeking absolution. 'I've just tried to do my best for everyone.'

'For yourself, more like.' Rosie flashed a glance at Hank but he was still standing exactly as Paul had left him, his eyes fixed on Kate's face and the look on his face chilling. Well, serve her right if he gave her a good hiding, Rosie thought bitterly, if anyone deserved it Kate did. Her sister had had everything through the years and she had had nothing, it wasn't *fair*. A husband, this home, Paul, and Joy was hers too. Oh, she'd like to smash her face in herself, she would. Joy, her daughter. *Her daughter*.

'Did you know?' Rosie spoke directly to Hank now, her voice harsh. 'That she'd had a child, I mean?'

It was as though he hadn't heard her for a moment and then he moved his head very slowly, staring at her silently until she swallowed hard, gesturing with her hand. 'Did he know?' she asked Kate now as Hank's eyes returned to his wife.

'Yes.'

'And he was still prepared to marry you?' Rosie's tone suggested she should be down on her bended knees thanking God for such a man.

'If I had it adopted.'

'And instead you came to us with that cock-and-bull story, pretended that you cared about me –'

'The only person my dear wife cares about is herself, haven't you learnt that yet, Rosie? But you're going to regret the day you were born –'

'You think I don't already?' He hadn't expected her to react like this, she could see it in his eyes, but Rosie's inference that Hank was whiter than white added to his dismissal of the years and years she had spent caring for them all, being general drudge and dogsbody, had snapped something that had been taut for a long time. 'I've regretted it from the day we were married! *Married!*' She gave a snarl of a laugh. 'There should be a different word to describe what we've lived as all these years because it doesn't resemble any marriage I've ever heard of.'

'*Shut up.*'

'Why? Why should I shut up? It's about time Rosie knew, isn't it? About time they all knew. You've never been a husband to me, not in any sense. *Twice!*' She flung herself round to face Rosie now, her eyes blazing. 'In all the time we've been married we've made love – no, I won't describe the sort of mating you forced on me as that – in all that time he's taken me twice, Rosie, and on both occasions he had to be drunk before he could bear to touch me.'

'I don't believe it.' Rosie's mouth was agape, her eyes shooting between their faces.

'Oh, it's true all right,' Kate said bitterly. 'Right from our honeymoon he's come home smelling of other women's perfume, stinking of it, reeking of it –'

'I said, shut up.'

'*The hell I will!*' She was screaming now. She wanted to hurt him, bring this façade of respectability he seemed to value so highly crashing about his head, see him shrivel and die like she had done when Joy had looked at her. Oh, Joy. She was cut to the heart for her, to find out like this. 'You try it.' As Hank raised his hand to strike her she spat the words at him, her face contorted beyond recognition. 'You just try it and I'll scream the truth from the rooftops, do you hear me? I'll lay you so low in this town you'll never recover from it. And believe me, Hank, once I start shouting people will come forward. You think your lady friends can't be found? Think again. I'll get all the dirt, I promise you, and there are plenty of your business colleagues that are good family men and they won't like it, so consider that before you hit me, because that's the one thing I won't stand.'

'Kate?' Rosie's voice was little more than a whisper but Kate was concentrating on Hank, who was glaring at her with maniacal rage.

'You . . . you . . .'

'Yes, what am I, Hank? Stupid, gullible, your patsy? I won't even argue with you about that. But you!' She took a deep gulp of air. 'You're something else. You've used me, blackmailed me, abused me – oh, not physically, I'll give you that, but what you've done through the years was far worse than that. You destroyed my confidence in myself as a woman, made me feel less than dirt under your feet, unlovable, unwanted. And then you wonder why I wanted my children around me? They were the only things that made life worth living.'

'You don't believe this garbage, Rosie?' Hank turned to his sister-in-law who was riveted to the spot. 'You see what she's trying to do, how she's trying to twist it all round? I've been a good husband, I've provided well –'

'Provided well?' Kate cut in bitterly.

'Yes, provided well.' He glared at her, his eyes two pieces of jet-black coal in his red face. 'It's all lies, you know damn well it is. You've done the dirty on all of us and now you're trying to put the blame on me. Well, it won't work. Rosie has lived here long enough to know we were all right before this tonight.'

'All right? We were never all right.'

'Then why did you stay?'

'You know why. You would have thrown Rosie and Joy out on to the streets if I hadn't.'

'Oh, come on.' His lips drew back from his teeth in a contemptuous smile. 'You don't expect your sister to buy that, do you? I've never minded them being here any more than I've been a bad husband to you. You've been caught out, that's the top and bottom of it, and you can't take it.'

'Rosie?' Kate breathed in deeply, trying to control the pain and fury that made her want to leap on Hank and tear his face apart. 'Do you believe him or me?'

'You don't think she is going to trust the word of someone who palmed their kid off on her, do you, and then engineered to take it back again.' He was walking towards the door now, still talking. 'You're a liar, Kate, everything you've said tonight is a lie, and you've told the biggest one of all to Rosie. I don't know how you got her and William to buy it in the first place, but no doubt there was some subtle arm-twisting there.'

He turned as he opened the door, staring at her for one long moment as his hatred snaked between them. 'All those years of lying to her, to us all.' He allowed his eyes to fall momentarily on Rosie's white face as though he was speaking for her too. 'Couldn't you have trusted your sister, Kate? Thought enough of her to tell her the truth from the beginning?'

She knew what he was trying to do but the sense of

disbelief and amazement that he could still attempt to keep up the façade of family man and husband amid all the devastation, that he could still care about his precious reputation, made her dumb.

'I just hope that Rosie and Joy can rebuild the relationship that you've done your best to destroy,' he continued softly, 'not just today but since they first came here. As far as I'm concerned, Joy is still Rosie's daughter and I'll do all I can to help.' He turned to Rosie again. 'You have my word on that. Anything you need, financially or whatever, don't hesitate. We can find you and Joy somewhere to live, I'll take care of all that side.'

'And you . . .' His eyes were unblinking on Kate's face. 'You owe it to Rosie to keep this . . . revelation between the five of us, it needn't go any further than these four walls.'

'That's all you care about, isn't it?' Her voice held a note of incredulity.

'I care about Paul,' he countered grimly. 'And you've done enough without making him a public laughing stock. There's no need for anyone to know, it's better that way.'

'Better? . . .' She was still staring at him, telling herself she should have expected this, anticipated his reaction, when he shut the door.

'I'm going to find Joy.'

'Rosie?' As her sister made to leave Kate caught at her arm only to be pushed aside. 'Please, please, Rosie, we have to talk.'

'I don't want to hear any more.' Rosie drew herself up and away from Kate as though she was something unclean, her fat face screwed up with disgust. 'I trusted you, Kate. Even though you tried to take Joy away from me for years I kept reminding myself that without you I wouldn't have her in the first place, that I owed you so much, that you had been thinking of only me at the beginning. But it wasn't like that, not a bit of it. You wanted it all, didn't you? Hank, your position as his wife, Paul, Joy.'

'Rosie, listen –'

'Don't "Rosie" me. I can see through you now, I know what you're really like. Mum was right all along, wasn't she. She could see you were bad and that's why you never got on. And to try to blame it all on Hank . . . Oh, you're cunning, Kate, you're a sly one.'

'It's not like that. I know you're hurt –'

'Don't pretend you care, not now, and don't think you can talk Joy round either. You might Paul, he's always worshipped the ground you walk on' – the words were acidic with bitterness – 'but Joy is a different kettle of fish. You've lost her now, and I shall make sure it stays that way.' And so saying, she marched out of the room, bitter indignation and self-righteous wrath in every step.

As the door shut behind her sister's quivering bulk, Kate sank into the chair, her head moving slowly from side to side as she struggled to take in the enormity of what had occurred. She had lost them all, Joy, Paul, Rosie . . . There was nothing left, nothing. And in that moment of blackness even John's love was consumed in the grief she felt over her children. They were part of her, as essential to her as living and breathing, and she had let them down, destroyed their lives.

She swayed backwards and forwards with her eyes shut as a hundred splintered images tore at her mind, and then dropped her face into her hands, her shoulders heaving as her anguish burst forth in a long moan that sounded as though it came from a dying animal.

CHAPTER TWENTY

'Mum? Come on, Mum. It's all right, everything will be all right.' She became aware of Paul kneeling at her side a moment before she felt his arms go round her, and she slumped against him, her silent weeping of the last few minutes becoming a wail. 'Come on, come on. You'll make yourself ill.'

How long they sat there Kate didn't know, but along with the feelings of anguish and remorse concerning her daughter was added a deep guilt about her son, this son she had always kept slightly at arm's length. And he had known. She knew he had sensed how she felt. But he was the very image of Hank to look at, more so in the last eighteen months since puberty as he had grown and filled out, towering over her by a good few inches even at fifteen and with his quiet, introspective nature and cool logical way of looking at things she had never felt able to get close to him. But no, she had to be honest here . . . She raised her head now, her face awash with tears, and touched his cheek with her hand. She hadn't tried over hard because Joy had always been there to talk to. 'I'm so sorry, Paul . . .'

'I know, I know, Mum, but why didn't you –' He stopped abruptly and swung his head downwards. 'Oh, it doesn't matter now.'

'Why didn't I tell you?'

He nodded as he looked at her again, and then answered his question himself. 'But it wasn't as easy as that, was it.'

'No, no it wasn't.' She wet her lips before asking, 'Joy? Where . . . where is she?'

'With Aunt Rosie in the garden.'

'She hates me,' Kate said dully.

'Oh, Mum . . .' He pulled her against him again, his

voice shaky. 'She doesn't, not really, it's just the shock.'

'It was a shock to you too.'

'Not so bad though.'

'Perhaps not, but it still means you can't . . . love her in that way. Oh, I've made such a mess of things, Paul. I thought I was doing everything for the best but all I've done is ruin your lives –'

'That's not true.' He hugged her fiercely for a moment before leaning back and looking into her face. 'It isn't, Mum. Ever since I can remember you've looked after us all, Aunt Rosie, Dad, me, Joy, and who's ever been there for you? You've only stayed with Dad for our sakes, haven't you?'

'Was it so obvious?'

'Only to Joy and me, we . . . sensed something. I love him, I can't help it –'

'Of course you love him, he's your father, and whatever else he does love you.'

'But there's something wrong with him, isn't there? He's all right with me but you, and Joy too, it's like he's a different person. And he's always left you alone at nights, and his drinking . . .'

'Oh, Paul.' His understanding had the dual effect of comforting whilst pouring coals of fire on her head.

'Mum?' His voice was quiet. 'Joy wants to go and stay with Jane Scott for a few days –'

'No! Oh, no, don't let her do that, Paul. I have to talk to her, make her understand how things were, why I did what I did.'

'It would be better to let her go.' He put his hand out and took hers, his flesh warm whereas hers was chilled. 'She . . . she doesn't want to see you for now and you know what she's like when she makes her mind up about something. She'll come round, in time, but it won't help if you make her stay here. Jane Scott is always wanting her to go over there, being an only child in that great big house I suppose she gets lonely and her parents love Joy.'

'But I'm scared she won't come back.'

'Oh, Mum . . .' How could he answer that, he asked himself. There was a side to Joy he had always shut his eyes to, whether consciously or unconsciously he wasn't sure, but today it had confronted him bang in the face and he had had to acknowledge that threaded through his love for his cousin – his cousin? but he couldn't think of her as his sister yet – was something approaching fear. It wasn't her tenacity, although that was formidable in itself, but rather an innate selfishness, a will to have her own way come hell or high water, that made her frighteningly strong. He loved her, oh, he felt his guts burn with the force of his love, he probably always would, but if his future had been joined to hers in the way they had planned she would have pushed and pulled him, moulded him, into the pattern she had determined was best for their lives.

He thought again how she had ranted and raved in the garden before Rosie had joined them, her rage making her vitriolic, and then, as now, part of him had wondered where the softness was. She never seemed to doubt herself, not right down deep inside where all the personal demons were hidden. Even with him, in the midst of their loving last night, she had told him she knew it would turn out all right, it had had to, she had wanted it that way.

Stop it, you're being unfair. He was, he was being unfair. Joy loved him, she had always loved him, as he had her. This had thrown him off course, that's what it was. Made him imagine things he would never think normally. Nevertheless, suddenly he couldn't bring himself to reassure his mother that Joy would be prepared to hear her side of the story, not and mean it. In fact, he had a strange presentiment that when Joy walked out of this house, and she would, he sensed now, with or without Kate's agreement, she would wipe the dust from her heels and not look back.

'When . . . when does she want to go?'

'Now, today. She has asked me to call her a taxi and go

to Jane's with her, add weight to the story that she's had a row with Aunt Rosie and walked out. Jane knows they don't get on. She . . . she wants me to stay there with her until tonight but I don't think that's a good idea. I'll come straight back.' He didn't add that Joy's intensity that he stay with her had unnerved him a little, or that the way she had flung herself at him in the garden, demanding that they go through with their plans regardless had first shocked him and then – yes, he had to admit it to himself – repulsed him.

'We can't, Joy.' He had held her at arm's length, looking into her tear-stained face, although she hadn't been crying then. 'You know we can't, not now.'

'*Why?*' Her eyes had blazed at him as she had spoken. 'They haven't got any proof, I've seen my birth certificate and –'

'But whether there is any proof or not doesn't matter,' he'd said softly, his mind still stunned by it all. 'You know it's true, you do, don't you?'

'I don't care.' She didn't answer his question. 'I don't care, do you hear? All I want is you, I don't care about anyone else.'

But he didn't feel like that. The guilt that washed over his head was like a solid sheet pressing him down. Perhaps he ought to but he didn't.

'Paul?' His eyes focused on his mother as Kate spoke. 'Do you think it's for the best, that she gets away for a time? You know her better than anyone. I want . . . I want just to be able to talk to her, to at least explain how things happened and why I acted as I did. I don't expect her to forgive me but . . .' Her voice trailed away. 'I love her, I do love her, Paul and I want a chance to tell her.'

'I think she knows you love her, Mum.' But that wouldn't be enough, not for Joy, he thought with a certainty that made him shiver. It was funny, but he'd always had this feeling he was older than his mother, why was that? And never so strongly as now. Perhaps it was because she didn't seem to have the self-protective shell that everyone else did, her vulnerability was there to see, exposed, naked. He was sure that was what his father had sensed when he had first met her, and being something of a bully he'd taken full advantage of it. But he didn't know that, not for sure, did he, he upbraided himself quickly.

But he did know it was better for Joy to go. If she repeated half the things to his mother that she had spat out with such fury and loathing in the garden, his mother wouldn't survive it. She loved too much, that was the trouble, and she seemed to have a childlike naïvety where she loved that blinded her to the shortcomings of the beloved. She gave too much and expected too little . . . Oh, stop it, stop trying to work everything out now, he told himself impatiently. Just deal with what you can see and touch, the analysing can come later.

It was an hour later when Kate heard the taxi come and the sound of running feet down the stairs and in the hall. She had gone twice to Joy's bedroom door, knowing Rosie and Paul were helping her pack, but each time her daughter had refused to see her and she had returned to the sitting room to sit out her penance, her head aching and her heart sick.

When, a few moments later, Rosie's heavy footsteps reentered the hall, paused, and then continued up the stairs she knew Joy had gone, and with her departure came a desolation that was unbearable. She had left without saying a word, without offering any hope of reconciliation but she couldn't blame her . . . Oh, what Joy must be suffering, her baby, her poor, poor baby. The anguish became so fierce that she felt sick, sick and frightened of what she might be tempted to do, and as her hand went to the telephone it was more a gesture of self-preservation than a wish to be comforted.

John answered immediately, almost as though he had been waiting for her call. 'John? Oh, John, John . . .' She couldn't say anything other than his name for some good few seconds.

'What's happened?' His voice was sharp with anxiety. 'Kate, what is it, dear? Talk to me, tell me.'

'I . . . I can't, I can't.'

'Is it Hank? He's found out about us? He hasn't hurt you? Look, I'm coming over –'

'No.' Her voice was a gasp through the tears that had begun to flow the moment she had heard him. 'No, it isn't that. It's . . . it's Joy. Oh, John.'

'Joy? There's something the matter with Joy? What is it, an accident?'

'She . . . she knows.'

'Knows?' Joy had found out about them? But how the hell could she? There hadn't been anything to find out until yesterday and then they had merely looked like two people enjoying each other's company for an afternoon. Had she been watching them? He cast his mind back but then Kate's next words narrowed his eyes and stiffened his body.

'She knows about me, that I'm . . . I'm her mother.'

Oh no, no, not now. He found he was shouting in his mind. All the years, all the empty long years when they had been like two ships passing incessantly in the night and now they finally reach the same harbour and then this? Well, he wouldn't let anyone keep them apart now, not Joy, not Hank, none of them. Whatever complications this caused they'd handle them together. 'How did she find out?' he asked quietly.

'I told her, I had to tell her. Her and Paul . . . they've fallen in love –'

'*What?*'

'They thought it was all right, that they were cousins. Oh, John,' her sobs were choking her now, 'what am I going to do?'

'Sit tight, I'm coming over.'

'No, you can't. Please, John, I've only just told them all and Joy has gone –'

'Where's Hank?'

'What?'

'Hank, where is he?'

'In his room, I think. Rosie is upstairs too, but Paul's taken Joy to her friends . . . Oh, I can't bear it, John, I can't. I've ruined her life and she's my daughter.'

'She's young, Kate, she'll get over it.'

'She won't, you don't know Joy like I do.' Didn't he? Perhaps not, John thought grimly, but he knew enough to comprehend that Joy should have been Hank's child, not Paul. Thankfully Paul had nothing of Hank in him, but the older Joy had got, the less he had liked her, and he had always wondered why Kate was so devoted to the girl. Until yesterday, that was.

'Kate, you've been mother and father to her for years in a way Rosie never has, never wanted to be. Oh, Rosie liked to grumble that Joy thought too much of you, liked to make you feel guilty, but when did she ever get off her backside and do anything about it? Never, that's when. It was Rosie that came first and second in Rosie's book and you know it. You were the one who was there to listen, putting the kid's worries before your own. You were the one who provided emotional support, ran them about, danced at their beck and call. Damn it, Kate, you've carried the whole family for years.'

'But that doesn't make what I've done right.'

'No, no perhaps it doesn't but whatever you did, you did out of love. Misguided maybe, but love all the same. Darling, listen to me . . .' He paused, searching for the right words. 'I love you, you know I love you more than life and we'll sort this out together, you're not alone. Do you hear me, Kate? You're not alone, you'll never be alone again. And Joy will come round when she's had time to think, to remember all you've done for her.'

'John' – her voice was tragic – 'I don't want her to be grateful.'

'I know you don't, darling, I know you don't.'

'If you could have seen the way she looked at me –'

'That was shock, Kate, that's all. She's an intelligent girl, when she hears the full facts she'll understand, even if she doesn't approve.' Would she? He doubted it. There was something in Joy, something hard and unyielding that came to the fore if she felt she was crossed. He had seen it since she was a toddler and it had grown, not diminished, with age. If she hadn't loved Paul, if Kate had sat her down years ago and quietly explained the circumstances of her birth and her subsequent decisions, there might have been a chance she would have understood. But now? Never. 'How has Hank taken it?' he asked carefully when Kate didn't speak.

'He . . . he was angry, furious, but Paul wouldn't let him hurt me. And then he said things to Rosie, twisted everything round.'

'That's his forte.'

'I'm going to have to talk to him.'

'Kate, you don't know Hank like I do.' The irony of his words after fifteen years of marriage didn't occur to either of them. 'It won't do any good talking to him now. Wait until we face him together and then you can say it all. Now, promise me,' his voice became urgent, 'promise me you'll do that.'

'John –'

'Promise me.'

'I promise. Look, I'm going to have to get some aspirin, my head is pounding. I'll call you later.'

'All right, now don't worry, darling.' But he knew, even as he replaced the receiver, that he wasn't going to wait for her phone call. He was going over there because he felt in his bones that whatever was happening to them all wasn't finished yet.

*

Kate had just reached the top of the stairs, intending to go into the bathroom for the aspirin which were in the wall cabinet, when the door to Rosie's bedroom was flung open and her sister advanced on to the landing. And advanced was the right word. Her body bent slightly forwards and her neck stretched, Rosie covered the distance between them with slow, measured steps that held a dark hostility more formidable than any verbal aggression. 'You've been seeing John! On top of everything else' – Rosie took a deep breath as her teeth clenched and held for a moment – 'you've been having an affair.'

'I haven't.' Kate found she had backed against the wall and for a second she thought Rosie was going to spring at her as her sister's voice rose to a bellow.

'I heard you! I heard you on the phone, so don't lie, you . . . you . . .' She seemed unable to continue, her face turning turkey-red and the veins on her forehead standing out in stark contrast to her skin.

'I haven't had an affair, we've never –'

'I heard him call you darling, ask you to wait until you could tell Hank together,' Rosie cried savagely. 'John! John of all people! He's his cousin.' She gestured violently at Hank's door. 'What is it with you that you have to keep everything in the family?'

'Rosie, please.'

And then, as Hank's door creaked slowly open, both women froze as he stood framed in the doorway, his face white and his head jerking slightly as though a wire holding it in position had become loose.

This was the end, he was going to kill her. Kate stood perfectly still as she stared at him, some odd segment of her mind churning on. All his other women, the way he had treated her for years, all that would count for nothing against learning about Joy and now this. He would kill her, and Rosie wouldn't lift a finger to help her. She was going to die . . .

'What is she saying?' He made no movement whatsoever other than his hand flapping towards Rosie as he kept his gaze fixed on Kate's face.

'I was listening on the extension, I heard –'

'Shut up.' He cut off Rosie's gabble without raising his voice, but such was the quality of his low-pitched tone that Kate felt the fear twist her bowels, turning them to water, as she continued to stare into his face.

'She heard me talking to John.' She was shaking, the tremors visible, but there was nothing she could do about it. 'I rang him to tell him what had happened this morning.'

He had shut his eyes momentarily at the sound of his cousin's name but now his gaze transfixed her again as he said, 'And?'

'And . . .' She despised herself but the fear was paralysing her.

'You love him?'

She nodded, swallowing deeply before saying, 'But we haven't been having an affair like she said. I . . . We met yesterday by accident in the town and he asked me to have a coffee. I've . . . I've loved him for years,' now it was Kate who shut her eyes, 'but I didn't know he loved me.'

'He said that? He said he loved you?'

'Yes. We started talking over coffee. I was upset and then he told me, but we didn't . . . I haven't . . .' Oh, God, help me. Help me to explain, to tell it as it is. Make him believe me.

'So until yesterday neither of you knew how the other felt?'

'You don't believe her, do you?' Rosie's voice was harsh with bitter resentment. 'A story like that –'

'*Shut up.*' The movement that Hank made with his body combined with the look on his face sent Rosie backing to her room, her hand to her mouth.

'I didn't know. He . . . he didn't know. I wouldn't have an affair. I know I shouldn't have lied about Joy but I couldn't do anything else, I couldn't let her go, Hank.'

'She's gone now.'

'I know.' She wanted to let her body slump to the floor but kept it straight and still by sheer will-power. 'But I wouldn't have an affair,' she repeated dully. 'I was going to tell you, today or tomorrow some time, and then this happened.'

'You were going to leave me?' She nodded and after a long pause he said, 'And then what? Does he want you to live with him, is that it?'

'Until . . . until I get a divorce.'

'And then?'

'He wants us to get married.'

'Married? John?' The disparagement was bitter but curiously without weight. 'After the number of girlfriends he's had you seriously think he would marry you?'

'Yes.' For the first time since they had started speaking her voice was firm. 'I know he will. He loves me.'

And now the silence stretched on and on, a shaft of sunlight slanting across the landing from the tall, narrow window at the side of Kate's head, picking out tiny dancing particles of dust in its beam.

When Hank moved she steeled herself for what was to come but he passed her without another word or even a glance, walking with slow, measured steps down the stairs and disappearing into the sitting room. Her hand went to her throat as she heard the cocktail cabinet open and the chink of glass against glass, but other than that she made no movement at all and neither did Rosie, who was standing just inside her bedroom doorway. And a few moments later Hank passed her again, a bottle of whisky in one hand and a heavy, crystal-cut tumbler in the other and walked into his room without looking at either of them, shutting the door quietly behind him.

The two women stared at each other, Rosie's tongue wetting her lower lip as though she was going to speak, but then she seemed to think better of it and slammed the door shut by kicking out viciously with her foot, the bang reverberating on the air for long seconds.

Kate blinked her eyes and then rubbed at them dazedly as though waking from sleep, glancing round the wide, sunlit landing as though she had never seen it before, her thoughts, unbeknown to her, following the same pattern John's had. *Fifteen years.* Fifteen years of misery and sacrifice and gruelling routine, and then in just twenty-four hours her world had shattered in a hundred directions. How had it happened? She shook her head in despair. And why? She had thought, yesterday afternoon with John, that at long last things were going to work out. A quiet divorce, Hank had never loved her anyway so there would be no deep emotion involved, and she had determined she would take all the blame, allow him to cite John as the other party so that his precious reputation remained intact. John hadn't liked that but he had agreed to it, for her. And now, now everything was in tatters and it was all her fault.

She moved to the top stair, sinking down on the carpeted steps as her mind sought to make sense of it all. But she had known really, known but never admitted it to herself, that each year had been like a powder keg just waiting for a spark to ignite it, causing the safe world she had made for her children to explode. And now, now the worst had happened but she had never allowed for Joy and Paul falling in love. She moaned softly to herself at the horror of it. Never, never in her wildest dreams had the possibility of that happening occurred to her. They were brother and sister, they had been brought up like brother and sister . . . hadn't they? She had thought so, but the old saying, there's none so blind as them that won't see, had certainly come home to roost in her case.

It was over half an hour later when John knocked on the door and he had driven like a maniac to get there in that time, his eyes constantly watching the mirror for flashing blue lights. And as he waited on the doorstep in the warm

September sunshine he shivered, the feeling of doom that had swept over him the evening before stronger and more virulent.

His relief, as Kate opened the door, caused his shoulders to slump for a moment and then, as he looked into her face, he pulled her into his arms, still without speaking, shutting the door behind him before leading her through into the sitting room. 'It's all right, it's all right.' She had begun to cry again at the sight of him and now he led her to the sofa, sitting down beside her with his arm round her shoulders as she buried her head in his chest. 'Kate, it might feel like the end of the world but it's not, I promise you it's not.'

'Hank . . . Hank knows.'

'Hank knows?' He lifted her chin with one hand to look into her face. 'About us you mean?'

She nodded. 'Rosie was listening when I phoned you earlier, there's an extension upstairs. She started shouting and carrying on and Hank heard.'

'I'm sorry it happened like that but –' he shrugged slowly, 'I would have told him myself today anyway, especially in view of what's happened. I don't want you staying here, Kate. My flat has two bedrooms, you and Rosie can have one and Paul can have a put-u-up in my room –'

'She wouldn't come, I don't even know if Paul would.'

'Nevertheless, you're not staying here.' How could he explain the feeling that had gripped him? Likely she would think he was mad, but he'd dealt with too many tragedies in his work not to know that human beings were capable of almost anything when the ground started slipping away under their feet. And the ground had certainly slipped with this family, it had turned into a positive landslide. Whatever it took, she was leaving here with him today, he wasn't going to lose her now. Even the thought sent hot panic surging through his body, churning his innards, and, closing his eyes, he pulled her into him, holding her against his heart as he sent up a swift, urgent prayer, the first one in years.

When he opened his eyes again Hank was standing just inside the room silently watching them, and the two men stared at each other for some moments before Hank turned and left as noiselessly as he had come.

CHAPTER TWENTY-ONE

It was four o'clock in the afternoon of the same day and Paul had been back half an hour, and was now adding the weight of his agreement to John's insistence that Kate should leave the house.

'Mum, please.' He leant forward from his chair facing Kate and John who were sitting on the sofa, not touching now but close. 'If Dad's been drinking all afternoon . . .'

'Oh, Paul, I'm sorry. I'm so sorry.'

'Don't . . . don't keep saying that.' He had been relieved when he had returned to find his uncle John looking after his mother, he had worried about her the whole time he was at Jane's, but Joy had made the swift escape he had envisaged impossible. But when John had explained how they felt about each other . . . it had shocked him, he had to admit it, knocked him for six, and yet was it so unexpected? He looked at Kate now as she sat, head bowed, in front of him.

He didn't know the ins and outs of it all with his parents but he did know that his mother had had an awful time of it with his father, how she'd stood it this long he didn't know.

He said as much now, reaching out and taking her hand as he spoke to her bent head. 'I know you've been unhappy for years, Mum, however much you've tried to hide it from us, so I do . . . I do understand. It's just that with Joy and everything . . .'

'I know, I know.' She raised her head, her eyes pleading with him, and swallowed hard before she said, 'I just don't want to lose you too.'

'You won't.' But he felt sorry for his father, he couldn't help it, and this was reflected in his voice when he turned to John. 'But I think Mum's right, about staying in a hotel.

It'll make things easier.' He didn't add, than if she stays with you, but the unspoken words hung in the air as John nodded slowly.

'I just want her out of here, Paul. If a hotel is what she wants, that's fine by me.' It wasn't, but considering how reasonable the lad had been about all this he owed him that much at least, John thought as he looked at Hank's son. Strange, but he had never thought of Paul as Hank's son in spite of their similarity in build and looks. Right from the time the lad could toddle he had known he was different to his father, and he'd never been more relieved about anything in his life. 'But you agree it's safer all round, while emotions are running high?'

'Yes.' Just go if you're going to go, will you? All the talking in the world won't alter anything now and I understand, I do understand, but I just want to be able to cry and I can't do that with you sitting there. But he wouldn't be able to do it when they'd gone either, not with his father in the state he undoubtedly was, and there was his Aunt Rosie too. Oh hell, his Aunt Rosie . . . He didn't allow his thoughts to touch on Joy or he knew he wouldn't be able to prevent the tears from falling.

'I've told you, I'm not leaving without you, Paul.'

'Mum –'

'I mean it.'

'I can't go today, Mum, not till I know he's going to be all right,' he said flatly.

'Then I'm staying too.'

'Kate!'

'John, please try to understand.' She twisted to face him and in spite of her tear-stained face and swollen eyes she had never been so beautiful to him. 'I can't leave Paul here by himself, I just can't.'

'I'm fifteen years old, Mum –'

John raised his hand, cutting off Paul's voice as he said, very gently, 'He won't be alone, Kate. Rosie is here.'

She made no answer to this but such was her expression

that John sighed deeply, glancing at Paul before inclining his head in defeat. 'Well, if you won't, you won't, but I'm not prepared to leave you here so it looks as though we've reached stalemate. I'll have to sleep on the sofa.'

'Don't be so silly.'

'I'm not being silly, Kate, and if you were thinking rationally you'd know it.'

'But now Hank knows, you can't stay in the house, not all three of us together.' She couldn't have sounded more shocked if he had suggested the three of them sleeping in the same bed, John thought ruefully, but her innocence alarmed rather than amused him.

He didn't know what Hank was capable of, but from the little Kate had confided in him yesterday it was clear that other side of him had been fed through the years, and it would have had to be done secretly and no doubt unsavourily at times. Who knew who he had mixed with or what depths he had sunk to? No, he couldn't risk leaving Kate here unless he stayed too, and he was going to have to tell her how things were. He owed her that. She had taken all the blame on her shoulders and a good proportion of it was down to Hank in his book. Just how much more she could take today though was questionable, and then there was Paul . . . Hell, what a mess.

'I'm going to get a drink.' Paul stood up abruptly. 'Do you want one?' His gaze included both of them.

'Put the kettle on and I'll make some tea –'

'I can do it.' He could see his voice was too brusque by the look in his mother's eyes and softened it as he added, 'I'll go and see if Aunt Rosie wants one, shall I?'

'Thank you, Paul.' The gratitude in Kate's voice was all out of proportion to his offer but all three of them knew she wasn't thanking him about the tea.

Once they were alone, John took Kate's hand in his but made no attempt to kiss her or pull her close. He could sense her nerves were at breaking point, and would have suggested she go upstairs and lie down but for the fact that would mean Hank was just a few feet away. Damn it, this was ridiculous, she would *have* to leave here with him tonight, he thought angrily. And if she wouldn't leave without Paul he'd have to drag the lad out by force if necessary.

He was opening his mouth to say exactly that when the sound of urgent footsteps thudding down the stairs brought them both to their feet, but although John was halfway across the room when Paul burst in Kate was still standing by the sofa, her hand pressed tightly across her mouth.

'Dad's gone!'

'What?'

John's voice was harsh but Paul utterly ignored him as he said again to Kate, 'Dad's gone. I just thought I'd check on him after I'd asked Aunt Rosie about the tea, I thought he'd be sleeping' – in a drunken stupor, but he didn't say that out loud – 'but he isn't there, and there's a note for you.'

'Where?' Kate glanced at his empty hands.

'I . . . It's in his room.'

'Why didn't you bring it?' She was moving across the room as she spoke and had already reached the doorway when his voice, young and very childlike, turned her round. 'I didn't know what to do.'

'Oh, Paul.' She hugged him fiercely and then spun round to run upstairs as he added, 'The car's gone and he's been drinking.'

Rosie was standing in the doorway to her bedroom, the portable TV that Kate had bought her a few years before blaring away in the room behind her, and she watched without speaking as Kate hurried into Hank's room closely followed by John and Paul. The large window was open to the warmth of the September evening, the lightly patterned curtains billowing gently in the slight breeze and in the distance Kate could hear the sound of an electric lawnmower whirring away, the faint smell of newly-cut grass drifting in on the air. Ever after that scent was intrinsically linked in Kate's mind with what followed.

She saw the envelope with her name on it immediately, it was propped on top of the ornate dressing table directly facing the door, but she moved across to the small table by the bed first, reaching out for the whisky bottle that was quite empty. 'He's drunk the whole bottle, John. And if he's driving . . .'

'Read the letter. He might have gone to a friend's and you can ring and check if he's got there all right.'

She stared at them both, her gaze shifting for a moment to Rosie who had appeared in the doorway, her lips pursed and her fat face expressing condemnation. She didn't speak but everything in her sister's stance stated that Rosie knew whom she held to blame for the present state of affairs.

Perhaps Rosie was right, Kate thought as she walked across to the dressing table and picked up the envelope, which was sealed. If she had tried harder in the early days, *made* Hank love her, maybe they wouldn't all be standing here now? But how did you force an emotion that should come naturally? She had loved him, in the beginning she *had* loved him, but she had known within days of their marriage that he had never really loved her. And when she thought of the times she had tried to entice him, coax him into some show of affection, only for it to end in humiliation and self disgust . . .

'Open it, Mum.' Paul had moved to her side, putting his arm round her as she stood with the envelope in her hand, and as Rosie sighed a loud, significant sigh behind them, he turned to fix his aunt with a glare that brought her mouth shut with a little snap. 'Do you want me to do it?'

'No, I'd better read it first.' She didn't say that, having suffered the devious twists and turns of Hank's mind for years, she was frightened, panic-stricken, at what the letter might contain. She loved John, she had never thought to love any man after those first few years with Hank, but she did love him with a passion that was all the more fierce for having been kept in check so long. But her children . . . She felt she was going to be sick as her ears began to ring. Her children were everything, her life-blood, and it was only Paul's support that was enabling her to hope that Joy would come round. If she lost Paul too, if Hank had used the written word to destroy her in her son's eyes, then she would die. She might continue to exist in the shell of her body but she would be dead, finished. Paul had been so good about all this, so good, he would never know what it had meant to her.

'Mum?'

'All right.' She ripped the end of the envelope, pulling the single folded sheet from inside with a shaking hand, and as she straightened the paper she saw lines and lines of words but was quite unable to focus on the letters. Sinking down on to the straight-backed chair to one side of the dressing table she took a deep breath and began to read, her eyes scanning the lines with growing disbelief.

'Quick! Hold her, Paul. She's going to faint.' She heard John's voice from a great distance, but as she slumped forwards into her son's arms, Paul having dropped to his knees to catch her, the light had changed into a roaring darkness filled with the sound of rushing water and her own incoherent cry that echoed in her ears as she went into oblivion.

'Kate? Kate, love? Open your eyes, come on.'

'Mum, oh, Mum.'

'I've got some smelling salts in one of my old handbags somewhere. I'll go and find them, shall I?'

She could hear their voices, each one concerned in its own way, but they didn't mean anything through the thick, heavy blackness that was holding down her limbs and making any movement impossible. But she didn't want to fight it, no, she didn't, because something was telling her that what had to be faced on the other side of this darkness was unbearable.

When something unspeakable was held under her nose she coughed and twisted away from it, becoming aware for the first time that she was lying on the floor cradled in someone's arms. 'Mum?' Paul half raised her torso against the wall of his chest as John knelt down in front of her, taking one limp hand in his as she opened her eyes.

'She'll be fine in a few minutes, Paul. Just give her time.'

'John?' She stared at him, her eyes dilated. 'He said . . . He said –'

'I know, I've just read it. I was going to tell you myself.'

'It's not true, it can't be true. I would have known.'

'Oh, Kate.' She was echoing the words he had heard spoken in his office a hundred times for a hundred different reasons by a hundred different people. It wasn't the moment to tell her that she wouldn't have known, that whatever the problem it was often the nearest and dearest that had no idea what was going on in the lives of their family and friends.

'You knew? All these years you knew and you didn't say anything?' she said slowly as his previous words registered on her mind.

'I hoped it wasn't true, people change, and neither of you ever let on how things really were.'

'What is it?' Rosie broke into the conversation now, her voice militant, but Paul didn't say a word as he sat still supporting his mother. 'What's he supposed to have done?' The tone indicated that as far as Rosie was concerned nothing Hank was guilty of could justify Kate's treatment of her husband.

'Here, you'd better read it.' As John went to pass Rosie the letter he was holding scrunched up in his hand, Kate jerked in protest, her fingers reaching out.

'Kate.' John's hand stilled in mid-motion but his voice was firm. 'They've got to read it, both of them.'

'No, not Paul!'

'You can't keep it from him, Kate, not after this. This is Hank's way of telling him too, don't you see? Kate, don't you see?' he persisted when she didn't answer.

She made a little assenting movement with her head, but the tears were streaming down her face as John lifted her up before passing the letter to Rosie, who now took it as though it was going to bite her as Paul moved to peer over his aunt's shoulder.

Kate sank down on the bed as they began to read, her brain repeating the gist of each paragraph as she shut her eyes tightly, unable to look at Paul's face.

Kate,

This is my last act of cowardice in sixteen years which have been full of them, but I can't tell you the truth face to face, although I have wanted to from our wedding night when I realized it wasn't going to work.

I should never have married you, Kate, but we both knew that from day one, didn't we. What you didn't know was why I betrayed and hurt you, tortured you for so long. There are no excuses I can offer for what I've done to you, none at all. All I can offer is an explanation for the years of torment you've endured. It wasn't you, I want you to know that. All those times you tried to make it work? It made me feel more guilty and the only way I could live with myself was to hate you, blame you for things that were done to me by another woman, a woman I think must be insane.

My childhood – it was hell on earth, Kate. And even when I became a man and tried to escape, I couldn't. I was pulled back, sucked up, devoured.

You always thought I loved my mother, didn't you, but I hate her, although that is too weak a word for the feeling inside me. But she's part of me, she's in my head –

Here the writing had veered sharply before continuing,

I'm homosexual, Kate. I don't use the word 'gay', because there is nothing of that emotion in the way I feel. The last fifteen years I've slept with countless men, hundreds, but I've only ever wanted one. I love John, I've always loved him, but I made the mistake of letting him know, but then he'll have told you all about it.

His disgust and horror made me think I could go straight and that's why when I met you I acted like I did. I thought I could prove to him it was all a mistake, get back on our old footing as friends if I was a married man, respectable. But I hadn't counted on the physical side – I can't do without it and it gets worse, not better.

I did want it to work – I needed to prove to her I could make it on my own, and after Paul was born – he's the one good thing in my life, Kate. I love him, I love him like any father loves his child, I promise you that. There's never been – the other side. Nothing of that, not in my feeling for Paul.

I could say a lot more but you don't want to hear it and I don't want to say it.

Forgive me, Kate. Oh, that's stupid, you can't forgive me and I can't forgive myself. We both know if I hadn't seen John with you – known that the façade was well and truly blown – I wouldn't be writing this now. I still want him you see.

I'm all alone, Kate. I've always been alone but never like this.

Goodbye.

Hank.

No, no, no, no . . . There was a thickness in Paul's head but through it the one word was repeating itself over and over. His father couldn't be, he couldn't be. He'd had him, hadn't he? He'd physically impregnated his mother and he was the visible result. He couldn't be one of . . . them. He didn't act like a nancy or talk like one of them, you could always tell. Always. Look at Peter Fowles at school, everyone steered clear of him, especially in the showers. You could tell, you could always tell. *You could tell!*

'Paul?' He became aware John had taken him by the arms and was staring into his face. 'This makes no difference, do you hear me, not to you. Your father's been the same for fifteen years, ever since you were born, before, and just because you now know about it you aren't any different. You're the same person, do you hear me?'

'I . . .' He couldn't speak, the fear spiralling through his body and out the top of his head in a terrifying silent scream. In this moment he wasn't thinking of his mother or Joy or John, just of himself and the man who had sired him. He had his genes, oh, God, help me . . . I've got his genes. 'I've got his genes.' His voice was a whisper but John heard it.

'Yes, and your mother's, and your grandparents' and their grandparents'. You love Joy, don't you? Don't you?' John had never dreamt he would be reminding the boy of all he'd lost today of all days.

'Yes.'

'And you would have married her. Because you want her, physically you want her. You aren't like your father, Paul. If you were, you'd face it and get on with your life, but you aren't. You aren't. *Look at me.*'

Paul's eyes had flickered downwards but now they snapped up to John again.

'You're the one thing in his life he's proud of, the one thing that he loves unselfishly. He knew you'd see this letter and yet he still wrote it, he trusted you enough to think you would understand. I'm not excusing what he's done, how he's treated your mother through the years, but he's always been there for you, hasn't he? *Hasn't he?*'

'I . . . Yes.'

'That's what you concentrate on for as long as it takes.'

'You . . . you don't like him, you've never liked him.'

'That's got nothing to do with it, Paul. Life is never black and white, it's all shades of grey, and if anyone tells you any different they're lying. You've had a number of shocks today, any one of which would be enough to throw you off balance, but that's the way it is in life. You can't always control what happens to you, especially when other people are involved, but what you can do is face things, learn from them and go on from there. If you don't, the only way is down, and it's not a good place to be. Take it from someone who's been there.'

'I . . . I can't believe it.'

'Neither can your mother.'

Paul glanced to where Kate sat staring at him, her face as white as a sheet and her eyes full of the same pain and shock and rejection that were ripping him apart, and as she opened her arms he went to her, falling on his knees as she pressed his head close to her chest, muttering words of endearment and love against his hair. He wanted to cry, he'd been wanting to cry all day ever since he found out about Joy, but now he found he couldn't find a release from the agony with tears, his eyes remaining perfectly dry. He had lost his father. Whatever his Uncle John said he knew from this point on he had lost the father he had always known, and with the knowledge came a bitter sense of betrayal and rage. In the space of twenty-four hours his whole world had been turned upside down and by the people who were supposed to love him the most.

The thought brought him jerkily out of Kate's arms as he rose to his feet, running a shaking hand across his face as he said, 'I want to be by myself for a while.'

'Paul –'

'Let him be, Kate.'

As Paul walked out of the room John's hand on her shoulder restrained Kate from following him. 'But I have to talk to him –'

'All that can be said has been said. Leave it for now. He needs some time to sort things out for himself.' He had seen the anger in Paul's face as he had left and he didn't want any of that to spill out over Kate. You couldn't blame the boy, he must be feeling like a punch-bag, John thought soberly, but knowing Paul as he did he had no doubt that he would bring that unusual depth of understanding into play and get himself on some sort of even keel, fragile though it might be.

No, he wasn't so much worried about Paul as Hank, and he admitted to a thread of surprise in his thoughts that this could be so. If anyone had asked him yesterday, he would have said the world would be a better place without Hank Ross in it, but now . . . Now his emotions weren't so clearly defined. As he had said to Paul, there were all shades of grey, and from the tone of that letter Hank had had a hell of a life before he had left America. They'd always suspected it, of course, at home, it had been one of the reasons his mother had encouraged Hank to stay with them fairly frequently. But it looked as though things had been worse than they'd thought. Certainly it wasn't the clear case of possessive mother love his parents had conjectured, but something altogether more . . . sinister.

And he hadn't liked the 'goodbye' at the end of the note. It had sounded final, ominously final. And the sense of impending doom was stronger. 'Do you think I ought to go and look for him?' He didn't need to say to whom he was referring.

'I don't know. He could be anywhere, couldn't he?' Kate asked nervously.

'What about the golf club?' Rosie entered the conversation for the first time in minutes, her voice subdued. 'He often plays a few holes on a Saturday afternoon if he isn't taking Paul to a football match. You could phone there.'

They did phone there, and several other places besides, but to no avail, and now it was getting dark, a thick, warm dusk blanketing the air and bringing a hush to the surrounding gardens. John had looked in on Paul a few minutes before and found him fast asleep on his bed, his young face showing the evidence of a bout of weeping, which John took to be a good sign. He hadn't liked the dry-eyed bitterness he had glimpsed in the lad's face as Paul had left the room earlier.

'John, you don't think . . . he'd do anything silly?' Rosie asked softly as she wheeled in a tea trolley holding a plate of sandwiches and another of small cakes besides the requisite tea. It was the first time in years Kate could remember her preparing food, but she was too heartsore and exhausted to eat anything, although she sipped at the hot, sweet tea Rosie handed her, knowing the night was far from over.

'I don't know.' There was no mellowing in either John's face or voice as he glanced at Kate's sister, and Rosie flushed slightly as she passed him his tea and sandwiches.

She wasn't proud of her part in all this, Rosie thought tightly as she sucked in her cheeks and narrowed her eyes, but how had she known what was going on? And no one could blame her for being upset about Joy, now could they, no one? When all was said and done she had right on her side there. Kate should have told her about that and confided in her about the real state of affairs between her and Hank, she was her sister after all. They'd lived in the same house for over fourteen years, and not a word had passed Kate's mouth about Hank's goings-on. No, Kate should have said, she should, she shouldn't have played it so close to her chest. Nevertheless, the accusing little voice in her head that had sprung into life since reading the letter wouldn't be denied, and Rosie found herself in the unusual and uncomfortable position of feeling distinctly at odds with herself.

She had taken from Kate for years, taken without even considering how her sister was feeling, accepting all the care and attention as her due. 'Blood's thicker than water.' How often had she quoted her mother's favourite saying in her mind as a panacea against any outward show of gratefulness on her part? Kate was her sister, she had reasoned, she was only doing what any other sister would have done in the circumstances, what she herself would have done if their positions had been reversed. But she wouldn't have. She made herself face the fact. No, she wouldn't. She was too selfish to devote her life to others in the way Kate did. Blood might be thicker than water but the thickness could vary, and in Kate it ran like treacle. That was why she hadn't been able to relinquish all links with Joy. There was an intensity, almost a sacrificial quality to Kate's love that was more than a little unnerving, although she had to say she herself had benefited from that same intensity.

But Hank, where on earth was he? He shouldn't be able to walk, the amount he had imbibed, let alone drive. She knew he could knock it back a bit, but a bottle of whisky in the space of a couple of hours? Still, perhaps he was used to that sort of hard drinking, she didn't know, did she? In fact, she was beginning to think she didn't know anything about anyone, least of all herself. Oh, they'd all be mad before this lot was finished . . . She sighed, finding the normal solace of food didn't hold the appeal it usually did. *Where on earth was he?*

CHAPTER TWENTY-TWO

Hank didn't know where he was himself at that precise moment of time. He had driven aimlessly for a while on leaving the house, passing Old Kilpatrick and turning right across the toll bridge where the fact that he was far from sober was brought forcibly home as he sprinkled the car floor with change from his pocket.

The car was almost driving itself as he turned in the general direction of the coast, leaving Elderslie and Newton of Beltrees behind him as he made for Kilbirnie, although without any conscious decision on his part. He just knew he had to get away, far away, before he ended it. He couldn't risk any chance of Paul or Kate finding him, he had put them through enough already. No, a detached breaking of the news by a trained police officer would be easier to handle.

'I'm sorry, Mrs Ross, but I have to inform you that there has been an accident.' He pictured the tall, sympathetic officer with the young policewoman in tow, kind but not too kind. 'I'm afraid your husband's car seems to have gone off the road, and he didn't survive the crash.' He'd seen it a hundred times on the box, variations on a theme.

But what if he wasn't killed, perhaps only badly injured or maimed? What then? He felt himself break out into a cold sweat at the same time as the car mounted the grass verge before swerving violently back on to the road. He had to get control, this had to be done right, he thought as he struggled to keep the car between the edge of the road and the white lines. Perhaps he ought to stop a while, take stock of what happened next? Yes, that's what he'd do.

He turned off at the next side road into the hills, driving for a short distance before pulling off the road and partly into a field, cutting the engine and almost immediately falling into a deep, dreamless sleep, his head resting on his folded arms as he leant over the steering wheel.

How long he slept he didn't know, but he awoke to darkness and the realization he had no idea where he was or how he had got there. 'Damn it . . .' He leant back against the seat, stretching cramped limbs before getting out of the car and glancing around him. The night air was cool and fresh, its tang reminiscent of nights spent camping in Scottish hills with John and James, and the recollection of those happier days caused his stomach muscles to contract in protest. The times he had spent with James and his family through the wilderness that had been his childhood and youth had stood out as tranquil green places in a desert land, but now he forced the memories from him, leaning back against the car as he took great gulps of air to try and clear his aching head. Hell, he was thirsty . . .

He could hear the trickle of water close by and walked further into the field, stumbling along in shadows made grotesque by the moonlight. He found the narrow little stream by falling in it, the water covering his shoes and reaching halfway to his calves, and, crouching down, he cupped his hands, taking long deep mouthfuls of the icy flow before splashing his face and neck several times.

His head was still swimming . . . He lurched backwards to sit on the small bank, his feet still in the water. Still, it was hardly surprising, was it, a bottle of whisky on an empty stomach was pushing it even for him. He closed his eyes, the reality he had been keeping at bay breaking through the alcohol-induced stupor.

He didn't know where he was but he could remember why he was here, he thought grimly. Kate and John. *Kate and John*. It had to be the ultimate irony in a life that had been full of them but strangely, even now, he couldn't summon up the rage and bitter pain that had carried him through the last seventeen or so years since John's rejection of his advances. He still felt the overwhelming sadness and hopelessness that had covered him when he had seen them together. Until then, until that very moment, even after all Rosie had said and Kate had confirmed, he hadn't thought John loved her. But he did. He groaned aloud in the silence. It had been in his face, his body, the very angle of the way he had curved her into him. Damn it! Damn him! Damn them all! But the curses were hollow and without substance.

He rose slowly, walking back to the car as the picture of Kate as he had first seen her flickered into his mind. Kate, blonde and beautiful and composed as she had dealt with the injured child he had brought into Casualty, sparing him the odd shy smile as he had tried to sweet-talk her.

Kate on their wedding day . . . and the wedding night. Hell, the wedding night, that was when he should have finished it. He had known then he couldn't make love to her, not sober. But he hadn't wanted to lose her, part of it *had been* that he hadn't wanted to lose her. Through their courtship, when she had revealed her unhappy childhood and her insecurities, he had felt closer to her than any other human being he had ever known, even John. He had thought it might, it just might work . . .

He reached the car, wrenching open the door and falling into the seat as his head swirled. Damn, but he felt bad, he was seeing two of everything.

It took him several tries before he managed to insert the key in the ignition but once that was accomplished he started the car with no problem, backing out of the field and over the grass verge to the road far too fast.

What he should have done was let her keep that first baby when she told him about it, offered to provide for her until the kid was old enough to be left and she could work again. He'd known that was the way then, known it in his heart but hadn't accepted it in his head. He had wanted to be respectable, a married man, show John he was normal. *Normal!* He gave a bark of a laugh that grated round the car. What was normal anyway? Hell, the things he'd seen and done, yes done, in the last fifteen years – he shook his head to clear it of the images seared there.

And his mother – he'd fought to show her he was successful and in control. He'd known he was sacrificing Kate on the altar of his ego-trip and still he had kept on. If he could have brought himself to tell Kate, back there in the days before Joy's birth, she would have been there for him, he knew that now. He would have kept his self-respect, such as it was, and they would have been friends. He might even have met someone . . .

No, no, he wouldn't have met anyone. He shook his head savagely against the thought. There had only ever been John, would only ever be John. He was like Kate in that way, it was another thing he had recognized about her in the early days but not given sufficient credence to, that she loved single-mindedly, wholeheartedly. Perhaps it was something to do with the fact that they had both been starved of love or even affection as children? He should have known she wouldn't give up her child, the ties of blood could be as tenacious as they were hurtful, he of all people knew that. He drove the car faster, his teeth clenched against the pain.

Joy, her daughter . . . He narrowed his eyes at the dark road in front of him. He couldn't see anything of Kate in that little bitch – his mother, oh yeah, now he could see his mother in Joy. That's why he'd always loathed the kid, probably. The only good thing that had come out of all this was that Paul was out of her clutches with no way back. Paul . . .

He didn't allow his thoughts to dwell on his son, the pain becoming too intense to bear. But his son had loved him. Yeah, he'd loved him. He'd take that with him to wherever he was going. He'd always been afraid of the great dark spectre of death, petrified, waking in the night sometimes with his heart pounding and his hands clammy, but now the thought of remaining in this world frightened him more. The torments of his body, the debasement of those street-corner liaisons and loveless acts of carnality – he groaned, the sound a long, low moan of despair – he wanted an end to it, to the cravings that were fulfilled in sick self-disgust, the pretence, the deception.

If John had wanted him, if he'd been honest with Kate at the start, if he'd had the courage to admit what he was; 'if, if, if . . .' The word was still on his lips as he rounded the corner on the wrong side of the road, tyres squealing, and met the lorry straight in front of him. He saw the lorry-driver's mouth open in a silent scream at the same moment as he spun the steering wheel, causing the car to leap across the road out of the lorry's path and straight down the slope beyond the grass verge towards the dry stone wall at the bottom of the incline. If it hadn't been for the narrow ditch at the bottom of the descent the car might well have smashed through the one layer of stone and into the field beyond, but as it was the nearside front wheel hit the gully with the sound of tearing metal, the engine screaming as the car somersaulted crazily in the air before crashing down into the wall in a fury of flying stone and metal. There was a moment of deep silence, then a creaking and groaning as the car settled on its roof in a mangled heap, the three tyres still left on the mutilated body spinning wildly before the quiet of the night took over, blanketing the startled baaing of sheep and the sound of the lorry-driver's running footsteps in the distance.

CHAPTER TWENTY-THREE

'Mrs Ross? I'm sorry, but I have to inform you there has been an accident.' The middle-aged police officer *was* tall, he was also kind and sympathetic, which worked against him in situations like this when the need to distance oneself from the misery was strong.

'Hank?' Kate stood flanked in the open doorway to the house, Paul just behind her on one side and John on the other, and her voice was a protest against what she now accepted had been inevitable since reading the note. 'He's . . .'

'Badly injured, I'm afraid, Mrs Ross.' The officer inclined his head to the policewoman behind him. 'I think it would perhaps be better if we discussed this indoors?'

'Oh, yes of course, I'm sorry.' Kate stepped back so abruptly the heel of her shoe ground into John's foot and he caught her arm, as she would have tottered, turning her round as he said, 'Please, come in. The sitting room is just through here.'

Now what exactly was the set-up here? The policeman's eyes narrowed as he followed Kate and John into the sitting room, Paul and the young policewoman making up the rear. If he wasn't much mistaken there was more to all this lot than met the eye. He'd seen too many eternal triangles not to recognize one when he saw it, besides which it wasn't the normal practice for people to be up and dressed at nearly two in the morning as though they had been expecting a call. And the lad, surely he should have been in bed?

'What's happened?' Kate turned round in the middle of the room, her face white. 'You mentioned an accident?'

'I'm afraid your husband's car was involved in an accident just before twelve this evening,' the police officer said stoically. 'Perhaps it would be better if you sat down, Mrs Ross. I take it this is your son? You'd like him to stay?'

'Paul?' Paul answered his mother's unspoken question with a nod of his head, and Kate turned back to the policeman as she said, 'We . . . we've been expecting something. My husband left here this afternoon and he wasn't well.'

'No?' The world-weary eyes flickered towards John, and Kate flushed as she sat down in an easy chair, indicating for the policeman to do the same.

'This is a friend of mine, my husband's cousin. He's . . . he's been waiting with me.'

'I see.' He didn't, but he could guess plenty. 'Well, from all accounts it would appear your husband was making for Kilbirnie when he took a corner too fast on the wrong side of the road. He had to swerve to avoid a lorry coming in the opposite direction and he lost control of the car.'

'And . . . and you say he's badly hurt?'

'I'm afraid so. There are severe internal injuries, so I understand, besides broken bones, but he's in theatre now.'

'Can I see him?'

'Of course, my colleague and I came to take you to the hospital, in fact, but I understand from the surgeon in charge that it will be some time before he's out of theatre.'

'I don't care, I'll come now.'

'Mrs Ross?' He paused, adjusting his collar for a moment before continuing, 'It would seem he had been drinking before the accident. Do you know anything about that?'

'I . . .' Kate stared at the face in front of her as her mind spun. What should she say? How much should she reveal? She couldn't tell them the truth, not the whole truth, so what –

'My cousin was a little upset when he left the house late this afternoon.' John's voice was cool, in lawyer mode. 'His marriage to Mrs Ross has been in name only for a good many years, by mutual consent I might add, but it was somewhat of a shock to him when we announced that we intended to get married once Mrs Ross was free to do so. He probably had a couple of drinks to get used to the idea, enough to lower his reactions –'

'More than a couple, Mr . . .?'

'Ross, John Ross. I'm a partner in a firm of solicitors, Biggins and Hill. Perhaps you know them?'

'Indeed I do, Mr Ross. Now you come to mention it I think I know your face from the courts.'

'Possibly.' John forced a polite smile of acknowledgement. 'I'd like to accompany Mrs Ross to the hospital, if that's all right?'

'Of course.'

'Mum? Can I come?' Paul was standing by John just behind Kate's chair and now she twisted round to look into her son's face, her eyes apprehensive.

'Do you think that's a good idea, dear? If he's badly hurt . . .'

'I want to.' He moved one lip over another before adding, 'I need to.'

'All right.' She turned back to the police officer but had to swallow deeply to relieve the lump in her throat before she could say, 'my sister is asleep upstairs, she lives with me. I need to explain . . .'

'Of course, would you like WPC Wilson to come with you?'

'No.' She softened the refusal with a nod at the young girl. 'Thank you, but no. I'll go and tell her and then we'll leave. Is it Crompton General?'

'Yes, you know it?'

'I used to work there,' she said quietly, 'I'm a doctor . . . I was a doctor.'

'Oh, right.' There would be no hiding the facts from her once they got there, then, the policeman thought grimly. How the poor devil had survived the crash he'd never know, he should have been dead ten times over. Still, you saw some funny things in this job, not funny ha ha either.

He always wondered if it was worth operating on hopeless cases like this one, it didn't seem right somehow, trying to prolong the pain and suffering. Still, they didn't look at it like that, did they, these doctors? He was glad he didn't have to make the sort of decisions they did at any rate. This job was hard enough, but theirs . . . And he supposed they had the odd miracle case that proved all the diagnoses wrong, that'd be enough to make you try for the next one.

Kate felt strange as she walked up the stairs, numb. She supposed she should be feeling a whole host of emotions at this moment but she couldn't, she couldn't, and it frightened her if she thought about it. What was she turning into, that she couldn't feel something at a time like this? He was still her husband for goodness' sake, no matter what had happened in the past, and after she had read his letter this afternoon she had certainly felt something, she would never have believed the scurry of emotions that had swept her up and sent her half mad in the process.

She had thought she hated him, for years she had thought she wanted him out of her life. No . . . she *had* hated him. She stopped on the landing, her hand on the knob of Rosie's door. She had, but she didn't now. Something had changed when she had read that note. Perhaps she should hate him more in view of what she knew, but she didn't, couldn't. She wrinkled her brow as she tried to make sense of her reasoning but it was difficult with her emotions in deep freeze.

And at this moment he was lying on the operating table . . . She had seen the results of bad car crashes, she didn't need to be told the ins and outs to visualize his injuries, so why didn't she *feel* something – sorrow, compassion, rage, concern? Why this odd unnatural calm?

That policeman had known, he had sensed how she felt and disapproved of it. The thought didn't have the power to bother her at all. She didn't care what he thought, she didn't care what anyone thought except Paul, and perhaps John. But definitely Paul. He mustn't have another grievance to weigh in the balance against her. The thought brought a shaft of pain, hot and fierce, and then it disappeared as quickly as it had come as the quietness came on her again. What was her son thinking? About her, John, his father? She had wanted to ask him earlier, when he had come downstairs just before midnight looking so ill her heart had wept, but she hadn't had the courage in view of what she might hear.

She was glad she felt this numb detachment if she was honest. She lowered her head as she stared at the door knob. She was. How she had felt earlier . . . she couldn't have survived for long feeling like that. The anguish she felt over Joy then couldn't have been worse if she had been told her daughter was dead. It was the way Joy had looked at her, she had never seen such blazing contempt and rejection and hatred, yes hatred, in another human being's face, and she had thought she'd seen the lot with Hank.

Oh, she had to stop thinking, it was getting her nowhere and they were waiting for her downstairs.

Rosie was fast asleep in her bed and snoring slightly as Kate spoke gently from just inside the room. 'Rosie? Rosie, wake up.' There was no response whatsoever, so she moved carefully to the side of the bed and shook her sister lightly, but it was some seconds before Rosie opened bleary eyes.

'Kate? What's the matter?' And then she came fully awake and sat up as quickly as her bulk would allow. 'Is Hank back?'

'No, he's not back.' Rosie always slept with the bedside lamp on and the half-light was kind to her, mellowing the bloated features and bringing the ghost of her baby sister into view, causing Kate to kneel by the bed before she spoke again. 'I've got some bad news, there's been an accident.'

'Oh no.' Rosie's hand went to her mouth as she pulled

the flowered coverlet over the mound of her stomach in an instinctive self-protecting gesture. 'What . . . what's happened?'

'The police are downstairs, they say he was driving too fast and went off the road,' Kate said softly. 'He's being operated on now but he's badly injured. We're going to the hospital, Paul and . . . and John and me.'

'You think John ought to go?' Rosie couldn't prevent the thread of condemnation sounding through. 'It's him that's caused all this, after all.'

'It isn't, Rosie, and you know it.' Kate stared hard at her sister as she spoke. 'You read the letter, you know how it was. Perhaps Hank couldn't help the way he felt about John but that didn't mean John had to like it, does it? How would you feel if you had been him? If someone you had grown up with, trusted, loved like a brother, suddenly tried to get you into bed? He was worried about Adam too, how Hank would look on him as he got bigger. He probably had no reason for concern but he felt it was his duty to protect Adam and I don't blame him. I'm sorry, but I don't. I can understand that you're angry with me, you have every right to be. I should have told you about Joy –'

'Yes, you should.'

'I know.' Kate stood up slowly. 'But I didn't. And now you hate me, Joy hates me, and Paul . . . I don't know what Paul feels. Anyway, I'm going to the hospital, I thought I should tell you.'

'Can I come?'

'Yes, if you want to.'

'I do. Do you think I ought to let Joy know?'

'Not at two in the morning. Anyway, they didn't exactly get on, did they.'

'No.'

They looked at each other for a moment more before Kate turned and walked to the door, pausing as Rosie said, 'Kate?'

'Yes?'

'I . . . oh, it doesn't matter.'

Kate hesitated for one more infinitesimal moment and then continued out of the room, shutting the door quietly behind her.

The drive to the hospital was conducted in total silence apart from the crackle of the police radio now and again as disembodied voices pursued conversations in which Kate had no interest. She and Rosie were sitting in the back of the car with Paul between them, his hands between his knees and his face white, John following in his own car close behind.

This couldn't be happening, it had the nightmarish quality of a dream, Kate thought as they drove into the heavily built-up confines of the city, strangely deserted and eerily quiet in the dark of the early hours. But once they drew up outside the massive plate glass doors of the reception area at Crompton General, things became more normal, more familiar.

They all stood waiting while the police officer spoke to the man on the reception desk, John joining them within a few seconds and squeezing Kate's hand in one comforting gesture before moving slightly apart from her. She knew it was in consideration of Paul's feelings and she wouldn't have had it any other way, but still she missed the support of his arm as they followed the policeman towards the intensive care unit where Hank had now been placed.

She was unutterably thankful to see a familiar face when the sister in charge of the unit met them in the small waiting room. 'Kate.' Mary Bletchley took both of Kate's hands in hers. 'I wondered if it was you when I saw the name Ross. Dr Michael is with him now, he'll be out shortly.'

'How is he, Mary?' Kate asked quietly.

'I'm not sure.' She was lying and they both knew it.

Once the police officers had left and the others had

settled down in the big easy chairs with the pot of tea one of the orderlies had brought in, Mary spoke to them all for a few minutes, her voice bright, before taking Kate's arm and leading her away. Dr Michael was still at Hank's bedside, talking to the nurse assigned to care for the still unconscious patient. Kate had prepared herself for how he would look, she had seen human beings who resembled raw lumps of meat in her time on intensive care, but there was none of the horror she had expected, apart from the inevitable wires and drips radiating from every orifice.

'Dr Michael?' Sister Bletchley spoke to the small, thick-set doctor who straightened from his stance over Hank's bed, his face unsmiling as he glanced at the two women.

'Yes?'

'This is Mrs Ross, the patient's wife.'

'I see.' He stared at his colleague coldly as he said, 'I wasn't aware you were bringing family in until we had finished our procedure.'

'Mrs Ross is a doctor herself, Dr Michael, she used to work here before her marriage.'

'Did she.' His tone clearly said he wasn't in the least interested in what she used to do. 'How do you do, Mrs Ross?'

'Hallo, Doctor.' As they shook hands their eyes met for a moment and she recognized in his the soul-destroying exhaustion she had felt more than once in the job, and it softened the stiffness out of her face and relaxed her muscles, allowing her to say in a more natural voice, 'Thank you for all you've done so far,' and mean it.

He looked at her for a second more and then he seemed to deflate as he said, 'I'm sorry, Mrs Ross, it's been a long thirty-six hours and I haven't slept for what seems like years. How much have you been told?'

'Nothing, not really. Just the police . . .'

'Come with me.' He took her arm as he spoke, adding, 'He won't come round for . . . some time.'

If at all, Kate thought weakly. The brief hesitation had said it all.

She sat quietly in the little anteroom as Dr Michael talked her through Hank's injuries, his voice gentle and his face sympathetic as he gave her what virtually amounted to an immediate death sentence.

She had suspected, when they had arrived to find him in intensive care rather than in surgery, that the internal injuries were inoperable but still she couldn't seem to *feel* anything.

'How . . . how long?'

Dr Michael didn't need to ask to what she was referring and he didn't beat about the bush as he said, 'An hour, a day, who knows? I'm sorry, Mrs Ross, I wish it was better news but it's a miracle he survived the crash with such a massive amount of internal bleeding. He . . . he certainly is a fighter.'

A fighter? She looked into the doctor's face but she wasn't really seeing him as her brain chewed at the words. A fighter . . . She hadn't really considered that Hank was a fighting man, not in the warrior sense of the word, but perhaps she had done him an injustice? His childhood, his youth, this feeling he had for John – her mind found it difficult to accept the word love even now – and the stress of leading a double life for years, *years*, without the comfort of being close to another human being, he had needed to be a fighter to get through all that, hadn't he?

'I'm all alone, Kate. I've always been alone, but never like this.' The last words of the letter were suddenly stark and clear in her head, cutting into the ice round her heart, and she felt weak, slightly faint, and had an overwhelming desire to cry for the little boy who had never known a mother's unconditional love, never known warmth and security, never *belonged*. 'How could she do that, how could she ruin his life, hurt him, like that?'

'I'm sorry?' Dr Michael bent towards her as she whispered out loud.

'I . . . it's all right. Can I sit with him?'

'You do realize it's likely he won't regain consciousness?'

'Yes, yes I know, but I want to be there.'

'I understand.'

No you don't, you can't possibly, Kate thought as she retraced her steps to Hank's bedside, accepting the chair and then the cup of tea the little nurse brought her with a grateful smile.

His face was hardly marked by the accident, just a faint smudge of a bruise on one white cheek, all the injuries had been in the chest cavity which had crumpled when the steering wheel had knifed up into his body, and his legs which had virtually been smashed to smithereens.

She continued to sit there as it grew light, John and Paul coming in for a few moments mid-morning and Rosie joining her for ten minutes after lunch, but she didn't want anyone with her, she wanted it to be just her and Hank. The feeling inside her was fierce and all-consuming, and it was worse even than when Joy had left and she had thought her world had come to an end. Now, when there was no hope, no possibility of telling him, she understood the man lying there so still in the hospital bed better than she had ever understood anyone.

She wanted to tell him that he wasn't alone, that her life had been bound up with his even before they knew each other in the misery they had suffered as children, and those same childhoods had shaped their adult psyche in such a way that they had been destined to misunderstand each other in their desperation for love. She had had no confidence to reach out to him and try to get into his mind, because she had been taught to think of herself as unlovable, unworthy, his rejection of her had come as no real surprise but almost expected.

Would it have made any difference if they had been honest with each other after that disaster of a wedding night? If she had told him about Joy, how she couldn't give her child up, because it would have been like giving tacit approval to everything her mother had done to her through the years? Perhaps if he had confided in her he still would never have been able to have a physical relationship with a woman, not after the torment of his childhood when the woman in his life had displayed such cruelty, but at least they would have been friends. She would have liked to think he had at least one friend.

'Are you all right, Mrs Ross?' The day nurse popped her head round the screen with yet another in an endless series of cups of tea. 'Why don't you go home for a while, get some rest? We'd call you if there was any change.'

'No, I'll stay, thank you.' She forced a smile as she accepted the tea and then she was alone again. This was the only thing, the last thing, she could do for him. He wouldn't die alone, even if he didn't know it.

Please, please wake up. She stared into the still face, the eyelashes dark against the white of his skin in which all vestige of colour had fled. Please, God, please make him wake up. Make him wake up long enough for me to tell him that I care, that I forgive him, that I'm as much to blame as he is. Please . . .

John had taken Paul and Rosie home in the early afternoon so that they could rest before returning to the hospital in the evening, and Rosie had whispered that she would call Joy, explain how things were, but now that all seemed strangely unimportant, the world outside the little unit unreal and insubstantial.

It was late afternoon when the doctor in her noticed a change in him, an indication that he was coming out of the comatose state he had been in since she had arrived. She didn't call the nurse, although she had promised she would do exactly that if such an unlikely thing happened as him regaining consciousness. She had asked for screens to be put round the bed, which again was not usual in the unit where all the occupants were easily seen and monitered, but in deference to her medical expertise they had acceded to her wishes. That, and the fact they knew there was no hope. So now, as his eyelids began to flicker and his breathing changed, she leant forward, carefully adjusting the wires and drips as she bent over him.

'Hank? Hank, wake up. It's me, Kate. Wake up, dear. Open your eyes.' She kept up a steady monologue for long minutes, willing him to respond, and then suddenly his eyes were open and he was staring up at her. 'Hank? Hank, darling. Do you know me? It's Kate.' There was no reaction, and she was just thinking he was still in the coma when he gave a deep sigh, his hand raising an inch or two from the starched white coverlet before dropping limply to his side, but his eyes were beseeching now, talking to her.

'What is it, dear?'

He moved his hand again and she realized he was gesturing at the drips in his nose and mouth.

'You want me to take those out?'

He inclined his head, very slightly, and again his eyes pleaded with her. She shouldn't, she knew she shouldn't, but she didn't care. As she carefully removed them he sighed again, his eyes opaque with a mixture of morphine and the pain the drug couldn't quite dispel.

'Is that better?'

'Kate?' His voice was whisper-soft, a breath of nothing, and she leant even closer as she stroked his forehead. 'Why?'

Why? He was asking her why he was here? 'You've had an accident, Hank, a bad accident. Your car –'

'Why? After . . . all . . . all I've done?'

And then she understood, and with the understanding the tears flowed and she fought to control them and her voice as she said, 'I'm here because I want to be, Hank. Because I love you.' And she did, she loved the hurt, abused child that was looking out from his eyes, the little boy who had never had a chance at life.

'No . . .' He shook his head slightly and then winced in pain. 'John. You and John.'

She took his hand as she continued to stroke his forehead, and now she didn't try to stop the tears. 'I love John but in a different way. You and me, we've been together so long, Hank, and I'm sorry too. If I'd told you about Joy, that I couldn't give her up, perhaps things would have been different. I'm as much to blame as you, I am.'

'No . . .' As a tear seeped out of his eyes he shut them for a moment, before opening them to stare up into her face again. 'Me, all me.'

'No, it wasn't all you. Oh, Hank . . .' She rubbed her wet face with the back of her hand as her other one continued to hold his tight. 'We've been so foolish. If you'd only told me, I might have been able to help, we could have been friends.'

'Yes.' He nodded slowly. 'Friends.'

'But you aren't alone, do you hear me, Hank.' She could see the mantle of death moving over his face, she had seen it too many times in the past not to recognize it now. 'Hank? Do you hear me? I'm with you, I love you, you aren't alone, my darling. Paul loves you, he's been waiting all night and day to see you.'

'Paul?' The shadow receded for a moment as the eyes became more alert. 'Don't . . . let . . . him see . . . me like this.'

'No, all right, dear, but he loves you. He wanted you to know that he loves you.'

'Kate?'

'Yes, dear.'

'I'm sorry. Sorry . . . Kate.'

'I know, I know. I'm sorry too, I am.' As the sobs racked her body she wiped her face again before bending down and touching his blue lips with her own. 'Oh, Hank.'

'Want . . . want you to be happy. John . . .'

'Yes, I know.' She kissed him again, her tears dripping on his face as she bent over him.

'Not alone, Kate . . .'

'No, you're not, you're not alone, darling.'

'You're here.'

'Yes, I'm staying here, with you.'

And then he had gone, not with a long rasping breath or struggling for air as she had seen so often in the past, but with a quiet expelling of breath as he smiled up at her, a smile so trusting and childlike that it broke her heart.

'Oh, oh no, no . . .' She laid her head on his chest as she wept, the pain pressing up through her ribs and into her throat until she felt consumed by grief. She wanted to hold him, cuddle him, make things right. It was such a waste, to have lived such a life and died like this. She couldn't bear it, she couldn't . . .

How long she stayed like that, her head on his still chest and her hand still tightly holding his, she didn't know, but when Dr Michael touched her gently on the shoulder she raised swollen eyes to his, her face puffy and tear-stained.

'He's dead.'

'I know, my dear, I know. It was inevitable.'

'He came round, just before he died.'

'Did he?' He had noticed that the drips were gone from her husband's face but had assumed she had removed them after he had died, to look at him as she wanted to remember him.

'He was able to talk a little.'

'So he knew you were with him?'

'Yes.' And the first little tinge of peace stole into her heart. 'Yes, he knew I was with him.'

'That's good.' As the doctor raised her slowly to her feet he gave her a large white handkerchief from his pocket. 'It doesn't often happen like that.'

'No . . . but it was important.' She wasn't making much sense except to herself.

'And now you must go home and get some rest, there is nothing more you can do here and your family have just arrived. They are waiting for you outside.'

'Are they?'

'Your son? Would he like to come and see his father before you leave?'

'Hank didn't want him to, with all the . . .' She gestured at the paraphernalia round the bed.

'I'll get rid of that, Mrs Ross, while you break the news, and then if he wants to come in for a moment or two, he can. How about that?'

'You're very kind.'

As she walked out of the unit into the hushed sterile corridor beyond and then through the door of the waiting room, the silly thought hit her that she had arrived in darkness and was leaving in darkness. Someone had drawn the striped green and white curtains in the waiting room and her eyes went to them before she turned to the others, her gaze resting briefly on John and Rosie with a quiet message in its depths, before she looked at Paul.

'He's gone, Paul.'

As his face crumpled she held out her arms and he flew into them as though he was five instead of fifteen, hugging her tight as he cried his grief into her shoulder. She let him cry for a few minutes before speaking softly into his hair. 'He came round, before he died.'

'Did he?' He moved back slightly to stare into her face. 'Did he say anything?'

'Oh yes.' She smiled a wobbly smile. 'We . . . we talked about you, he was so proud of you, Paul, and I told him you loved him.'

'Were . . . were you two all right, before . . .'

'Yes, oh yes.' She took a deep breath before saying, 'I told him I loved him, and I did in a way, Paul.' She saw John stiffen out of the corner of her eye but continued, 'I've done a lot of thinking the last twenty-four hours and one thing I'm sure of now, your father and I were both to blame.'

'Kate –'

'No, John.' She raised her hand at his exclamation. 'I mean it, there were mistakes on both sides.' She turned back to Paul as she said, 'He understood, your father understood and he knew we were all right, you know?' Paul nodded, his lower lip trembling. 'Do you want to see him? He hasn't got all the wires and things there now, it just looks as though he's asleep. It might be better to remember him like that than how he was earlier, but it's up to you.'

'Will you come with me?'

'Of course.'

It was nearly half an hour later, as they were walking out to the car-park, that Rosie caught at her arm bringing them both to a halt. 'Kate?' Rosie's eyes were fixed on her face.

'Yes?'

Kate stared back at her sister and then was amazed when, Rosie's face crumpling in much the same way Paul's had done, she was suddenly hugged tight in a way she couldn't remember Rosie ever hugging anyone before. 'What you said in there, in the hospital, well I know I'm to blame too, about Joy I mean.'

'Oh, Rosie . . .'

'No, listen, Kate. I don't want to lose you, I don't. I love you, and I know I haven't been much help through the years.'

That must be the understatement of the year, John thought wryly, as he and Paul waited to the side of the two women.

'Joy, well Joy is my daughter but she's never really been mine, do you know what I mean? Even before we came to live with you, I didn't know how to handle her, those tantrums, she used to frighten me. And . . . and then when she loved you better than me, I was jealous. I thought you'd got everything, you see, and I'd got nothing.'

'I know, I know.' She was so tired, so exhausted she could hardly take in what Rosie was saying, the effort of staying on her feet was taking all the strength she had.

'I didn't know about Hank, you didn't *say*. If I'd known . . . But you're my sister, Kate, you're the only real family I've got and I don't want us to fall out.'

'We won't, we haven't.'

'Blood's thicker than water, isn't it?'

'Yes, yes of course it is.'

'Oh, Kate.'

And as Rosie hugged her tight again, John smiling at her over Rosie's head, Kate saw the ghost of a smile touch Paul's mouth for the first time in twenty-four hours, and knew everything was going to be all right with her son. But Joy? She couldn't think of Joy now, not when she was so exhausted physically and mentally. But she'd go and see her, talk to her soon. Yes, that's what she'd do.

CHAPTER TWENTY-FOUR

They had been in the new house two weeks and already John, Paul and Rosie were settled and happy. Kate looked at them now, from her vantage point at the bedroom window as the three of them flung armfuls of winter debris into the massive bonfire that was crackling red in the bright March sunlight, and then her gaze moved to the shiny new gold band on the third finger of her left hand. Mrs John Ross . . . She had no regrets about that, none at all, in spite of the furore it had caused in certain quarters: 'Her husband dead just barely six months and she's up and married his cousin.' Oh, she'd heard them, the gossips, and it hadn't stopped there. Most people had put two and two together and made ten, as people will.

She glanced out of the window again, over the rolling fields that ran from the stone wall of the garden and on to the swell of the Kilsyth Hills in the distance. She had wanted to get right away from Dumbarton and all the memories the surrounding district held, and when this cottage-style house on the other side of Glasgow had appeared on the market, they had fallen in love with it at once, all of them. Oh, John was good. He hadn't once moaned about taking Paul and Rosie on too, not even when Rosie was being at her most difficult, although she did try now. But like John said, she was very trying at times . . . Still, the weight she'd lost and the new interest she'd taken in her appearance had made all the difference to her ailments.

And Paul was happy . . . She found herself smiling as she watched her son roll about in a pile of leaves, the collie pup John had bought him just after Hank's death jumping all over him as it barked loudly, nipping at his hands and legs as he squealed in mock fear. John always seemed to know just what he wanted, needed, he was intuitive in that way, never encroaching on the memories he had of Hank or trying to be a father to him, but taking the role of an older brother in a way that had been entirely natural.

John. Her eyes feasted on him now and, almost as though he felt the power of her gaze, he turned from the leaves to look towards the house, waving madly as he caught sight of her at the window. She waved back, her eyes full of love and slightly misty with the force of her emotion. She was lucky, oh she was, to be loved the way he loved her. And the way Liz and James had been so thrilled about her becoming their new daughter-in-law . . . It could have been difficult, she wouldn't have blamed them if they had been a bit hesitant in the circumstances, but Liz had cried and laughed and hugged her until it hurt when they had broken the news, saying Kate had always felt like a daughter and now she would be one in reality. Yes, she was lucky. She had John, her son, her sister and Liz and James, she had to count her blessings, she *must.*

But then her eyes turned to the photo on the bed that she had been gazing at before the sound of the others' laughter in the garden had attracted her attention. She didn't look at it now if John was present, she knew it both upset him and made him angry since that last time he had picked Rosie up from the house where Joy was staying. She didn't know what had been said, Rosie would say nothing beyond John and Joy had had a few words, but it must have been bad. And about her. Joy, oh, Joy . . . The bright-eyed laughing girl in the photograph was gone according to Rosie, changed beyond all recognition.

'Hair's cut to an inch all over,' Rosie had sniffed some time ago after one of her visits. 'Looks like a loo brush to me. And her make-up, if she plastered it on with a trowel it couldn't be thicker.'

'She's just experimenting.'

'Experimenting?' Rosie had stared at Kate in disgust. 'She looks like a tart, Kate, and that crowd she's got mixed up with . . . I didn't mind when she was staying with Jane, her family are so nice, but since she's left and gone in that flat, she's gone to the dogs.'

'It's my fault.'

'It is *not* your fault.' Rosie had been unusually militant. 'Did you tell her to leave school, throw it all in when the world would have been her oyster? Oxford, that teacher said. She could easily have gone to Oxford if she'd continued getting the grades she'd been doing, they'd got such high hopes of her getting all A's and B's with her A levels after the results of her GCSE's. But no, madam decides to leave and go on the dole and hang about with that bunch of losers. I wouldn't be surprised what they're mixed up in, Kate, I really wouldn't.'

'She's doing all this to get at me.'

'Then she's more stupid than I gave her credit for. You've phoned, stood on the doorstep, not just once but time after time, written letters . . . It wouldn't hurt her to see you once and just talk about things. I'm glad John put his foot down in the end, you were making yourself ill hanging about trying to see her. You've got to wait for her to come to you now.'

'She won't.'

'Then it's her loss.'

Kate put the photograph down as her tears blinded her. Joy, think of me. Think of me, Joy, don't shut me out.

She thought of the letter she had sent the week before. She hadn't told John, she knew he would forbid it after the last time she had tried and the letter had been returned in an envelope addressed to her. She had been so thrilled when she saw Joy's handwriting on the envelope and then when she had opened it and all the tiny pieces of her letter had showered over the floor . . . Paul had had to physically restrain John from leaving the house that very minute.

But she couldn't stop trying, she couldn't. Everything she had done she had done for her daughter and the pain of her continued loss was like a cancer eating away at her soul. Yes, she had Paul, Paul and John and Rosie. Thank you, God, for them, she prayed quickly as she felt a stab of fear at her ungratefulness. And John wanted children and she wasn't too old to try for a baby, she owed him his own child at least, but nothing would replace Joy.

Still, the letter hadn't come straight back this time, surely that meant there was a chance? Perhaps in time, and she didn't care how long, she didn't, God, really, perhaps in time Joy would forgive her? As Rosie was prone to say these days, blood was thicker than water after all.

Down in the garden John threw the envelope he had retrieved from the mail that morning into the fire after checking that Kate was no longer at the window first. The tiny pieces of paper that had been enclosed in the envelope scattered into the heart of the fire, flaring brightly for one moment before they blackened and turned to ashes . . .